The Last Days of Rabbit Hayes

Anna McPartlin

TRANSWORLD IRELAND

TRANSWORLD IRELAND
an imprint of The Random House Group Limited
20 Vauxhall Bridge Road, London SW1V 2SA
www.transworldbooks.co.uk

First published in 2014 by Transworld Ireland,
a division of Transworld Publishers

A CIP catalogue record for this book
is available from the British Library.

ISBN 9781848271937

Addresses for Random House Group Ltd companies outside the UK
can be found at: www.randomhouse.co.uk
The Random House Group Ltd Reg. No. 954009

The Random House Group Limited supports the Forest Stewardship Council® (FSC®),
the leading international forest-certification organisation. Our books carrying the FSC
label are printed on FSC®-certified paper. FSC is the only forest-certification scheme
supported by the leading environmental organisations, including Greenpeace. Our
paper procurement policy can be found at www.randomhouse.co.uk/environment

Typeset in 11½/15pt Sabon by
Kestrel Data, Exeter, Devon.
Printed and bound in Great Britain by
CPI Group (UK) Ltd, Croydon, CR0 4YY.

2 4 6 8 10 9 7 5 3 1

Dear readers,

This book was inspired by my funny and courageous mother, a brilliant band, their tragic loss, supportive and loving families and enduring friendships.

It's dedicated to my mother- and father-in-law, Terry and Don McPartlin, for their love, support, kindness, warmth and wisdom. And it's written in memory of a rock star and two loving mothers.

I hope you enjoy reading it as much as I did writing it.

Warmest wishes,

Anna McPartlin. X

Rabbit Hayes's Blog

1 September 2009

DEFCON 1

Today I was diagnosed with breast cancer. I should be terrified but instead I'm strangely elated. Of course I'm not happy about having cancer, or my breast being lopped off, but it's reminded me how good I've got it. I love my life. I love my family, my friends, my work and, most especially, my little girl. Life is hard for everyone but I am one of the lucky ones. I will overcome.

I am bypassing fear, anger and sadness in favour of putting all my energy into this fight. I will take every recommended treatment. I will eat right. I will read, listen and learn everything I can on the subject. I will do what it takes. I will overcome.

I am mother to a strong, funny, sweet and beautiful child. My job is to be there for my daughter. I will watch over her as she grows. I'll help her through those awkward teen years. I'll be there for every scrape and tussle. I'll help her with her homework, support her dreams. If she marries, I'll walk her down the aisle. If she has children, I'll babysit. I won't let her down. I will fight, fight, fight, and then I'll fight, fight, fight some more.

I am a Hayes woman, and I am promising, with every ounce of love and strength in me, that I will overcome.

DAY ONE

Chapter One

Rabbit

Outside, pop music played, a child squealed with delight and a bearded man holding a 'Walk with Jesus' placard danced a jig. The leather seat felt warm against Rabbit's skin. The car rolled forward, forming part of a slow and steady stream of traffic snaking through the city. *It's a nice day*, Rabbit thought, then slipped into a doze.

Molly, Rabbit's mother, looked from the road to her daughter, taking one hand off the steering-wheel to adjust the blanket covering the thin, frail body. Then she stroked the closely shaved head.

'It's going to be OK, Rabbit,' she whispered. 'Ma's going to fix it.' It was a bright April day and forty-year-old Mia 'Rabbit' Hayes, beloved daughter of Molly and Jack, sister of Grace and Davey, mother of twelve-year-old Juliet, best friend to Marjorie Shaw and the one true love of Johnny Faye's life, was on her way to a hospice to die.

When she'd reached their destination, Molly came to a slow stop. She turned off the engine, pulled up the handbrake, then sat for a moment or two, focusing on the door that led to the unwanted and unknown. Rabbit was still sleeping and Molly didn't want to wake her because as soon as she did their terrible short future would become the present. She thought about driving on but there was nowhere to go. She was stuck. 'Fuck,' she whispered, and gripped the steering-wheel. 'Fucking fuck sticks, screwing, shitting, frigging, fucker fuckness. Oh, fuck.' It was clear that Molly's heart was already smashed to pieces but the fragments were scattering with every 'fuck' that tripped off her tongue.

'You want to drive on?' Rabbit asked, but when her mother looked her way, her eyes were still closed.

'Nah, just wanted to curse for a while,' Molly said.

'Good job.'

'Ta.'

'I particularly liked "fuck sticks" and "fucker fuckness".'

'They just came to me,' Molly answered.

'Keepers,' Rabbit said.

'You think so?' Molly pretended to ponder while placing her hand back on her daughter's head and stroking it again.

Rabbit opened her eyes slowly. 'You're obsessed with my head.'

'Soft,' Molly mumbled.

'Go on, then, give it another rub for luck.' Rabbit turned to the double doors. *So this is it*, she thought.

Molly rubbed her daughter's head once more, then Rabbit removed her hand and held it. They stared at their interlocking fingers. Rabbit's hands looked older than her mother's. Her skin was flaky and paper thin, riddled with raised and broken veins, and her once beautiful long fingers were so thin they seemed almost gnarled. Her mother's were plump, soft and, with perfectly painted short nails, pampered.

'No time like the present,' Rabbit said.

'I'll get a wheelchair.'

'You will not.'

'No way.'

'Ma.'

'No way.'

'Ma, I'm walking in.'

'Rabbit Hayes, you have a broken bleedin' leg. You are not walking in.'

'I have a stick and I have you and I am walking in.'

Molly sighed heavily. 'Right, bloody right. If you fall down, I swear to God I'll—'

'Kill me?' Rabbit grinned.

'Not funny.'

'Kinda funny?'

'Fuck-all funny,' Molly said, and Rabbit laughed a little. Her mother's curses upset many, but not her. She found them entertaining, familiar and comforting. Ma was kind, generous, fun, playful, wise, strong and formidable. She'd take a bullet to protect an innocent, and nobody, not the tallest, strongest or bravest, messed with Molly Hayes. She didn't suffer fools gladly and she didn't give a toss about pleasing people. You either liked Molly Hayes or you fucked off. Molly got out of the car, and when she'd pulled the walking-stick out of the back seat, she opened the passenger door and helped her daughter to her feet. Rabbit faced down the double doors before, between her stick and her mother, she walked slowly and steadily into the reception area. *If I walk in, I could walk out. Just maybe . . .* she thought.

Inside they took in the lush carpets, dark wood, pretty Tiffany lamps, soft furnishings and the shelf filled with books and magazines.

'Nice,' Molly said.

'More like a hotel than a hospital,' Rabbit added.

'Yeah.' Molly nodded. *Stay calm, Molly.*

'Doesn't even smell like a hospital.'

'Thank Christ for that,' Molly said.

'Yeah,' Rabbit agreed. 'I'm not going to miss that.'

They walked slowly towards a short-haired blonde woman, with a toothy Tom Cruise smile. 'You must be Mia Hayes,' she said.

'People call me Rabbit.'

The smile grew and the blonde woman nodded. 'I like it,' she said. 'I'm Fiona. I'm going to show you to your room and then I'll call one of the nurses to settle you in.'

'Thanks, Fiona.'

'A pleasure, Rabbit.'

Molly remained silent. She was doing her best to keep it together. *It's OK, Molls. Don't cry, no more tears, just pretend the way they're pretending that all is well. Come on, ya mad auld one, just suck it up for Rabbit. It's going to be OK. We'll find a way. Do it for your girl.*

The room was bright and comfortable, furnished with a pristine bed, a soft sofa and a reclining chair. The large window looked out onto a lush garden. Fiona helped settle Rabbit on the bed and, in a bid to escape the moment, Molly pretended to investigate the en-suite. She closed the door behind her and took a few deep breaths. She cursed herself for insisting on transferring Rabbit from the hospital to the hospice. Jack hadn't spoken since he'd received the news of Rabbit's impending demise. He needed to steel himself. He didn't have the stomach for it yet, and Rabbit didn't need to be minding anyone but herself. Grace had wanted to help but Molly was adamant. 'No fuss, she just needs to convalesce,' she'd said, lying out loud to herself and to anyone who would listen. *Stupid old woman*, she thought. *They should be here.*

'Are you all right, Ma?' Rabbit said, from behind the door.

'I'm grand, love. Jaysus, the bath is as big as Nana Mulvey's old galley kitchen. Do you remember that?' she asked, hearing her voice shake and hoping that Rabbit was too tired to notice.

'She's gone a long time, Ma,' Rabbit said.

'Yeah,' Molly agreed, 'and she spent more time in ours than we did in hers.'

'It's a good bath, though?' Rabbit asked. Molly knew that her daughter was aware of her struggle, which gave her the kick she needed to pull herself together.

'It sure is,' she said, emerging. 'You could drown in it.'

'I'll keep that in mind if things get too bad.' Rabbit laughed.

Rabbit had long ago accepted that Ma was the kind of person who, given the opportunity, would say the wrong thing at the wrong time, every time. There were countless examples of this, but one of Rabbit's favourites had happened many years ago: an old neighbour with a prosthetic hand had asked Molly how she was coping with her mother's death. Molly had replied, 'I'm not going to lie to ya, Jean, it's like losing me right arm.'

Once Rabbit was settled, Fiona left them to it. Rabbit had travelled in her nightwear and dressing-gown even though she'd originally planned to wear day clothes. Molly had brought an expensive pair of wide-legged jersey trousers and a cotton V-necked jumper from Rabbit's house to the hospital, but by the time she'd seen the consultant, received her meds from the pharmacy and been formally discharged, Rabbit had been too tired to change. 'I'm just bed-hopping anyway, Ma,' she'd said.

'It makes more sense to stay as you are,' Molly agreed, but it didn't make sense to her. None of it did. She wanted to scream and shout and rage at the world. She wanted to do some damage, overturn a car, set a church on fire and unleash hell. *If I was just five per cent crazier*, she thought. Molly Hayes was not in her right mind.

The previous day, an oncologist had sat Molly and her husband Jack down in a small yellow room that smelt of anti-bacterial soap. When they were settled in their seats, he had destroyed them with one sentence. 'We're looking at short weeks rather than long months.' The room fell into complete and total silence. Molly stared at the man's face and waited for the punch-line that never came. Jack remained motionless. It was as though life had just left him and he was slowly turning to stone. She didn't argue. The only two words she uttered were 'Thank you', when the oncologist booked Rabbit's place in the hospice. She felt the weight of Jack's stare. It was as though she was disappearing right in front of his eyes and he was wondering how he would navigate the new reality without his wife. *Give me time to think, old man.* They had no questions – at least, none that the man sitting opposite could answer.

The silence had allowed Molly to do some thinking of her own. It was time to retreat: she needed to arm herself with more information, and she had to come up with a plan, start a new conversation. She was not about to give up, no way. Rabbit Hayes might be dying but she was not going to die because Molly was going to find a way to save her. She wouldn't talk about it, just do it. In the meantime, she'd play the game. The clock was against them: Rabbit was slipping away. No time for talking.

Staying quiet was unusual for Molly, who liked to talk and battle things out even when she was full sure she wouldn't receive a conclusion or an answer. In the early days after Rabbit's diagnosis, she had often taken herself down to the church to abuse God. Prepared for no answers, she'd asked a lot of questions, shaking her fist at the altar and once even giving the finger to a statue of the Baby Jesus.

'Where's your deals now, God?' she had screamed, in her empty local church, one day a year before, when Rabbit's cancer had returned in her right breast and had metastasized into her liver. 'You want the second breast? Take it, you greedy bastard, but don't you dare take my girl. Do you hear me, ya—'

'Ah, there you are, Molly.' Father Frank had appeared out of thin air and pushed himself into the seat beside her. He rubbed his bad knee and put his hand to his grey hair, then knelt and leaned on the pew. She remained seated. He looked forward, saying nothing.

'Not now,' she'd said.

'I heard.'

'And . . .'

'You're angry, and you wanted to give the Baby Jesus the finger.' He shook his head.

'How did you know that?' Molly asked, surprised and a little unnerved.

'Sister Veronica was polishing the tabernacle.'

'I didn't see her.'

'She's like a ninja, that one.' Now he rubbed his head. She wondered if he was getting a migraine – he suffered a lot with it. 'Molly,' he said, in a more serious tone, 'I understand.'

'No, you don't, Frank.'

'My mother died of cancer.'

'Your mother was ninety-two.'

'Love is love, Molly.'

'No, it isn't, and if you lived a life with love in it as opposed to simply preaching it, you'd understand that. You've never been a husband or father so, God love you, Frank, of all the people to try to comfort me, you really haven't a clue.'

'If that's the way you feel, Molly.'

'It is, and I'm sorry for it.' She got up, leaving Father Frank dumbstruck. She hadn't darkened the church door since. But Molly still prayed; she still believed.

Still, this emergency needed something more rational than prayer. She'd been researching Rabbit's condition for four years. She'd looked at all the studies, the new drugs, the various trials, and knew more about genetic mapping than a second-year laboratory student. *There's something we haven't thought about, something we're missing. It's on the tip of me tongue. I just need to concentrate, work out the problem. It's going to be OK.*

'What are you thinking about?' Rabbit asked.

'What I'll make for your daddy's tea.' Molly settled on the recliner.

'Just bring home a curry,' Rabbit suggested.

'He's getting a belly,' Molly said.

'Jaysus, Ma, he's seventy-seven! Give him a break!'

'I suppose I could give him a chicken curry with egg fried rice, and make him do four laps of the green afterwards.'

'Or you could just let him be.'

'Right, we'll settle on two laps.'

As she spoke, a dark-haired nurse, with a suspect tan and a nice neat bun, entered the room carrying a chart. 'Hiya, Rabbit, I'm Michelle. I just wanted to see if you were settling in and if we could go through your meds, once and once only. Then I promise I'll leave you to it.'

'No problem.'

'Great. So far so good?' she asked.

'Well, I'm still alive so that's a bonus.'

'People usually make it past the door,' Michelle said, and grinned.

'I like her,' Rabbit said to her ma.

'She's got a bit of shite to her, all right,' Molly said.

'And I take it having a bit of shite is a good thing?' Michelle asked.

'In our house it is,' Rabbit said.

'As the fuddy-duddy aristocrat said to his Jewish tailor, "Good-oh."' Michelle sat on the sofa. Rabbit and her mother caught each other's eye and smiled. *Clearly a nutter.*

'Any questions?'

'No.'

'Sure?'

'Yeah.'

'Well, I'll be here if you need me. Can we talk meds?'

'I'm on a Fentanyl patch, OxyNorm liquid, Lyrica and Valium.'

'Any laxatives?'

'Oh, yes! How could I forget?'

Michelle nodded towards Rabbit's leg. 'How's the wound post-surgery?'

'Fine. No sign of infection.'

'Good. So, the fracture was your first sign it had spread to the bones?'

'They were monitoring high calcium levels the week before.'

'How's your pain level now?'

'It's fine.'

'Keep me posted.'

'Will do.'

Michelle looked at her watch. 'Hungry?'

'No.'

'Well, we've got bacon and spuds on the menu in an hour.'

'Sounds repulsive.'

'Bite your tongue. We've got the best chefs this side of the Liffey here,' Michelle said, with mock disgust, then smiled. 'You need anything – a back rub, a foot massage, a manicure, physio for that leg of yours – ring your bell.'

'Thanks.'

'You're welcome.' She opened a window and left Molly to attend to her daughter's bedclothes.

When Molly had finished, she went back to the recliner, sat down and watched as Rabbit's eyes flitted between open and closed. 'Davey's on his way home, love. He'll drop in later if you're well enough,' she said.

'That's nice.' Rabbit was asleep almost before the words were out of her mouth.

Johnny

The past and Johnny often waited for Rabbit in sleep. That afternoon, in her dream, he was sixteen, tall, beautiful, his soft curly brown hair resting on his shoulders. She was her younger self, and twelve-year-old Rabbit was a very different-looking girl from the paper-thin ghost that lay in the hospice bed. She was tall for her age but so thin her mother worried that the large space between her legs would affect her gait. 'Walk in front of me, Rabbit,' she'd say, and then to her friend Pauline, 'Do you see what I'm sayin', Pauline? A toddler could jog through that gap.'

'Ah, not to worry, Molly. She'll fill in,' Pauline said, and she was right. Rabbit did fill in, but not for another three years, despite everything Molly cooked, baked and roasted in duck fat to add weight to her youngest child. Back then, Molly's mantra was a simple one.

'Rabbit, eat more. Grace, eat less. Davey, stop picking at your nose.'

Grace would complain and talk about unfairness, but Molly wasn't interested. 'You're big-boned like your ma. Big bones equal small servings, so if you want to be your best self, live with it.'

Grace would continue to complain, but Rabbit didn't feel sorry for her because, back then, when Rabbit was still so gawky, Grace was a real beauty. She had hips, breasts and luscious lips. She was a proper brunette with emerald-green eyes and, aged eighteen, Grace was a woman while Rabbit was still a child. Rabbit would often stare at Grace and wish, *If only I could lose me eye-patch, fill out a bit, darken me hair and plump up me lips. If only I could look like me sister.*

The eye-patch was gone by the time she'd hit ten but Rabbit, although beautiful in her own right, would never look like her sister. Her poor eyesight didn't help: the dark brown horn-rimmed spectacles dwarfed her tiny face. They were heavy and slipped down the bridge of her nose, so she spent a good deal of her time pushing them up. Sometimes, when she was thinking hard about something, she placed a finger on them, holding them tight against her face and scrunching her nose. Johnny was the first to call Mia 'Rabbit'. She insisted on wearing her long mousy brown hair in two high bunches at either side of her head. To him, those bunches looked like rabbit's ears and, with her glasses, she reminded him of Bugs Bunny in disguise.

Unwittingly, Johnny Faye was a trendsetter. If he decided patches were cool, within days everyone for miles wore patches. If he liked coats worn open and down to the ankles, or short silver jackets or woolly hats with diamonds, they became trendy without so much as a peep from the lads. It was simple. Johnny was cool so anything Johnny did, said or wore was cool. And when he coined the name Rabbit and Mia Hayes happily answered to it, everyone had followed suit within a week, including her own parents.

In Rabbit's dream, Grace was dressed to the nines in a tight black dress, heels and big red lips. She was going out with a man she'd met at the disco and it was exciting to watch her get ready. Rabbit liked to sit in her room as she applied her makeup in the mirror. Grace didn't mind, so long as Rabbit didn't talk. Grace would turn the tape deck on her dressing-table up high and sing along to Bruce Springsteen's 'The River', then Lloyd Cole and the Commotions' 'Brand New Friend'. She'd play them on repeat and, instead of wasting her own time holding down the rewind button, she'd make Rabbit do it.

'Stop. Play. No. Rewind. OK, stop. No, rewind. Too far – go forward,' she said, as she painted her eyelids. Happily Rabbit obeyed, pressing the buttons while her big sister transformed herself from beautiful to exquisite before her very eyes. Afterwards Rabbit followed Grace down the stairs and into the kitchen to where her brother Davey was eating his dinner with his earphones on. Davey always liked to eat alone. He'd wait until everyone else was done, then Ma would heat up his plate, he'd put on his earphones and shovel the food down his neck in the time it took to play two songs. Grace said goodbye to Ma and shouted the same to Da in the back room, watching the news. She didn't bother saying a word to Davey because he wouldn't have answered anyway.

Davey was sixteen, tall and skinny, like Rabbit. He had long, mousy brown hair, which hung past his shoulders. Despite incessant slagging from the lads, he insisted on wearing denim on denim. He sat chewing and rapping his knife on the table in time to the music playing in his ears.

Molly called after Grace, 'Ask him for tea on Sunday.'

'No way, Ma!'

'I want to meet him.'

21

'Not yet.' Grace grabbed her coat.

Molly appeared with pink rubber gloves on. 'Don't make me track him down.'

'Jesus, Ma, will you let me live?' Grace opened the front door and sashayed down the path towards the little iron gate.

Molly sighed and headed back into the kitchen, but Rabbit followed Grace outside to where Johnny was sitting on the wall, playing guitar and waiting for her brother to finish his dinner. Grace said, 'Hi,' and he smiled at her, but, unlike the other boys', his eyes didn't follow her down the road. Instead he focused on Rabbit and patted the wall. 'Rabbit,' he said, and she sat down beside him.

'Johnny.'

'You look sad.'

'I'm not.'

'You are.'

'Not.'

'What's up?'

'Nothing.'

'Tell me.'

Rabbit's eyes started to fill with big fat stupid tears and she couldn't work out why. She really hadn't known she was sad until Johnny had said it, and it was all a bit of a shock.

'Spit it out,' he added.

'I wish I looked like Grace,' Rabbit whispered, embarrassed.

'No, you don't.'

'I do.'

'Don't.'

'Do.' Rabbit felt a little sulky but then Johnny grinned at her, and when he grinned the skin around his big brown eyes wrinkled slightly. It made her feel warm inside and out. Her cheeks flushed a little and her tummy flipped.

'When you're Grace's age, you'll be the most beautiful girl in Dublin, Rabbit Hayes,' he said. 'There'll be nobody else quite like you.'

'Liar,' Rabbit said, biting her lip to curtail a spreading wide gummy smile.

'Truth,' he said.

She couldn't think of anything to say so she punched him playfully on the arm, then pushed her spectacles onto the bridge of her nose and held them there while he played his guitar and sang a funny sweet song to her.

Jay, Francie and Louis arrived as Davey came out of the house. Jay and Francie, twins, were Johnny's next-door neighbours, the heart and soul of his band. Jay played bass and Francie played guitar. It was Jay who had fought for Davey to be drummer after his audition hadn't gone as planned: he was battling severe stomach cramps and shat himself halfway through the second song. Jay was blond, Francie was dark, and they were both handsome, with short hair, square jaws and a big build. They were also talkers: if they hadn't chosen music, they could have been a pair of comedians in the morning – at least, that was what Rabbit's ma always said. Louis was smaller and more serious. He played keyboards and fancied himself as the band leader, although nobody really listened to him even when he threatened to quit, which he did at least once a week. Once Rabbit had watched him lose it in the garage.

'We could really have something here if yous would all stop mucking around,' he'd shouted.

'Stop crying, Free Fatty,' Jay had said. Louis wasn't fat, just short and blocky. Francie had observed that he looked like a thin guy who'd eaten a fat one. Since then, much to his annoyance, the lads had insisted on calling him Free Fatty. It was harsh, but not as harsh as Davey's nickname. Back then, Davey was so thin his hooked nose looked too big for his face. After his audition, when he was walking out of the door with a load in his pants and four fellas crying tears of laughter, Jay called after him, 'Here, Big Bird, come back when you're cleaned out.'

'Big Bird? He looks like a dead fucking bird,' Francie said, and the twins had called him DB ever since.

Davey didn't like Rabbit hanging out with the band, so he was quick to tell her to get lost. The lads liked to sit on the wall, chatting, catching up and watching the girls go by before they went into Davey's garage to practise for a few hours. Davey's parents were really supportive of the band. His da was a big music fan and his ma was a fan of anything that didn't include her son washing dishes for a living. Davey got himself thrown out of school when he was thirteen by punching a geography teacher in the face when he'd tried to drop a hand down his pants during a detention. At the time Davey wouldn't say what had driven him to such an extreme, and word passed around the local schools that his attack had been unprovoked. When no local school would take him in, he had discovered his passion for music. Davey's first set of drums was a phone book he practised on morning, noon and night, and from the start it was obvious he was gifted. For his fourteenth birthday his da arrived home with a beautiful red drum kit and Davey was so happy he burst into tears. When he played that evening, his parents agreed that, whatever it took, they'd get him to where he wanted to go.

When he joined the band, Davey's parents could see that they had something – good songs, good musicianship, good work ethic – but, more than that, they had Johnny Faye. If ever a star was born, it was Johnny. He was the real deal. Davey's da spotted his potential the first time he watched their acoustic set in the local hall one Sunday afternoon. That night they cleaned out the garage, put in heaters, then lined it with egg boxes and heavy draping to soundproof it. Two weeks later, Davey became Kitchen Sink's new drummer; his family's garage became their official rehearsal room, Molly and Jack Hayes their biggest supporters.

From the start Rabbit loved being in the garage with her coat and gloves on, watching the lads play and listening to Johnny singing. She'd sit quietly in the corner for hours, so quietly that, hidden behind draping, amps and an upturned sofa, they'd often forget she was there. Sometimes she read a book, others she'd just lie on the floor and listen to them play, banter and laugh. Rabbit could listen to Johnny sing all day. He had such a cool, clear, sweet, sorrowful voice, and despite her brother's many attempts to get rid of her, Johnny always stood up for her.

'Let's take it from the bridge. One, two, three . . .'

Rabbit loved it when her brother counted in before hitting the drum. She loved the bass and guitars kicking in, then Johnny's voice, giving her goose-bumps and making her spine tingle.

Rabbit spent half her childhood in that garage, listening to her brother and his band rehearse and dream. They were going to make it. After all, one of the lads from U2 had grown up down the road and they were filling stadiums in the USA. It was a sign and, like the lads often said, soon Kitchen Sink would make U2 look like a bunch of bleedin' amateurs. And Rabbit had been there from the beginning, lying on her duffel coat on the cold hard floor while Johnny Faye sang just for her.

Now the past was so real it sometimes felt more real than the present. It might have been the opiates or perhaps it was because Rabbit was so tired when she was awake that her mind only became energized in sleep. And when she was awake she had to face the truth of her situation. Two weeks ago she had been living with cancer; now they were telling her she was dying and would leave behind her twelve-year-old daughter. *Nah . . . I'm just tired. I need a few days to rest and I'll feel better. I'm not leaving Juliet. No way. Not happening.* She couldn't face it. She couldn't talk about it. She couldn't accept it. Instead of forcing herself awake and into the present, she remained in the past, listening to Johnny Faye sing his heart out.

Davey

Davey hadn't slept for more than four hours straight in at least twenty years. That meant it was easy to talk to the family on the phone or Skype, no matter what time zone he was in. He had been playing poker on the tour bus when his mother had called four years ago to tell him his sister had breast cancer. He came home just after her mastectomy when she was hopeful that it had all gone. After chemo and radiation it *was* gone, but only until the second call had come three years later. He was just about to go on stage when his ma had told him tearfully that it was back in the other breast and in her liver. He'd flown home immediately. Things were bleaker, but Rabbit Hayes was nothing if not a fighter. She would get better, and if she didn't, the medication would help her manage the cancer. That time, he'd stayed for three weeks, until Rabbit had demanded he go back to work.

'I'm not going anywhere,' she'd promised. Besides, he couldn't let his drum tech step in for ever. 'What if they realize he's better than you?' she asked, and laughed.

'Funny,' he said.

'Go back to your bus,' she told him, and they hugged. Even though she pretended not to cry, his shoulder was damp when they parted.

That third call, four months back, had taken his breath away. It was in her lungs but there was still hope. She'd see him at Christmas. He wasn't to worry. She had years in her yet. The last call had come when he was lying in bed in a hotel room in Boston. He was just about to hop into the shower when he saw his ma's name appear on his vibrating phone. He considered not answering, but then he remembered . . . Rabbit.

'Hey, Ma,' he said, but she was silent. 'Ma?'

She couldn't speak. All he could hear was her muffled sobs and he knew. He remained sitting on his bed in silence, listening to his mother cry. He didn't move one inch. He didn't say one word.

'It's in her bones,' Molly said eventually. 'She fell in the kitchen – Juliet found her. It's really bad, son.'

'I'm on my way, Ma.'

Then his mother had said the most frightening word he'd ever heard: 'Hurry.'

For ten years Davey had been drumming for a successful female country singer. He divided his time between Nashville, New York and a tour bus. Casey was a Grammy-winning artist and the mother of two boys. When she was recording he lived in Nashville; when she was on tour, he was on tour; when she took some time off he headed to his place in New York. Davey often worked with other bands if they were stuck for a drummer and Casey was on sabbatical, but she always came first, even if he'd never imagined he'd end up playing country music. 'Life has a funny way of rolling out.' That was what Casey had said to him when she'd seen her old friend looking wistful. They were halfway through a gruelling tour and venues weren't selling out like they used to, so she had a very heavy promotional schedule on top of performing most nights. She was mentally and physically exhausted and the last thing she needed was her drummer leaving her in the lurch.

When he'd knocked on her door and called her name, she'd told him to come in. He found her lying on the sofa in her room with a cold cloth covering her eyes. 'Another headache?' he said.

'Yip.'

'You need to get that checked.'

'There's nothing wrong with me. Hell, it would be a damn miracle if I didn't have a permanent headache.' She lifted the cold cloth from her eyes. 'What?' she said, sitting up.

'It's Rabbit.' He burst into tears. 'Oh, God. I'm sorry.' He was ashamed of the tears but still he cried.

'Oh, Davey, I am so, so sorry.' She stood up and put her arms around him.

'They say she's dying, Casey.'

Casey soothed him while her PA booked him onto the next flight home.

'Don't you worry about a thing. Stay as long as you need to. We'll be here waiting when you get back,' she said, and he was grateful: he'd been in the business long enough to know that, no matter how talented a player you were, if you weren't a songwriter you were easily replaced. But Davey often underestimated himself and his role in Casey's life.

They had met when he worked in a New York music bar. She was a singer-songwriter, while he was bar-tending and looking for a band to play with. She was petite and pretty, and when she sang, even though it was raw, he knew she had something. They made polite conversation a few times and nothing more until one night a guy came on to her at the bar. She politely declined. He pushed anyway. She said no. He asked her if she was a lesbian and she told him she was. He called her something vile and Davey stepped in, warning him to stay away.

'What are you going to do about it?'

'You don't want to know.'

Later he was putting out the trash when he heard a scream. Casey was fighting off the same guy – he'd waited for her outside. Davey knocked him out with one blow. At the time Casey was living in her car but that night Davey moved her into his apartment. She got the bed, he took the floor, and they had been working together ever since, through a lot of rough times. At one point when a second record company had dropped her, he was the one band member who stayed with her. He gave her that thumping sound. 'I am the C to your DB,' she often said. To her he was irreplaceable and they were their own kind of family.

She had walked him to the limo that would take him to the airport. 'I'm with you,' she'd said. 'You know I'm with you.'

'I do.' They'd hugged it out.

'Don't make me miss you for too long, ya hear?' she said.

He had sat quietly on the plane, didn't stir out of his seat or engage with fellow passengers; he didn't sleep or eat or watch a movie, just thought about his sister and that funny, sweet, precocious little girl of hers. *What about Juliet?* Davey had missed much of his niece's short life but even as a toddler she had never failed to recognize him. Her excitement on seeing him always made him feel special. Rabbit kept his photo on the wall and spoke about him often, but it had been clear early on that Juliet and Davey had a strong connection. He dreaded seeing her. *Poor Juliet.*

When the plane landed, as he had only carry-on luggage he walked straight through Customs to where Grace was waiting. Her eyes filled when she saw him and they held each other tightly for a long time.

'The car's this way,' she said eventually.

'Where's Juliet?' he asked.

'She's at ours at the moment but Ma wants her with Rabbit when . . .' She didn't finish the sentence.

'How are the boys?' he asked.

'Ryan's such a lunatic, we'll be lucky if he doesn't burn the house down. Bernard needs three grands' worth of orthodontistry if he ever wants to eat anything chewier than porridge. Stephen's failing his first year in college and Jeffrey is clinically obese.'

'Wow.'

'Yeah.'

'You need money?'

'No, thank you. The diet we've put Jeffrey on is saving us a fortune.' She smiled at her brother and he laughed a little, but then they remembered Rabbit was dying and their smiles faded. They were silent until they were nearly home.

'How long?' he asked.

She shook her head as though she couldn't believe what she was saying. 'Weeks.'

'But . . .'

'She was fine,' Grace said. 'The palliative chemo was going great but then she fell over last week and her bone snapped and . . .'

'Does she know?'

'She knows, but has it really sunk in? They told us last night and moved her into the hospice today.'

'And Ma?'

'Ma is Ma. She's barely left Rabbit's side. She's not sleeping, eating or drinking but she's insisting everyone else does. She's in fighting form. She's Ma.'

'And Da?'

'Not talking.'

'And you, Grace?'

'I don't know, Davey.' She was clearly struggling not to cry.

When they got home, Davey saw his da standing at the window. Grace used her key so Jack Hayes remained where he was, only turning to face Davey when he entered the room.

'Da.'

'Son.'

They nodded at one another.

'Have you had your tea?' Grace asked.

'I had a biscuit,' her father said.

'I'll put something together.'

'No, it's all right. I'll wait for your mammy.'

'She could be late.'

'I'll wait anyway.'

'OK.'

Jack gazed at his son. 'You look well,' he said.

'I'm grand.'

'Good. Would you like some tea?'

'Lovely.'

'All right.' He walked towards the kitchen, his children following. He insisted on making the tea himself so Grace and Davey sat together at the table, watching him. He had aged ten years in two days. He was pale and seemed suddenly ancient, even slightly doddery. Until now, seventy-seven-year-old Jack had looked young for his age. He was never much of a drinker, had no time for smoking and had enjoyed sport of all types well into his early sixties. In later years he'd taken to bowls and had become captain of the team. The man muttering to himself 'Where will I find milk?' looked nothing like their father. He was a shadow of himself.

Nobody spoke until he finally placed the tea on the table. He sat with his children but focused on his mug.

'How's America?' Jack asked, after what seemed like an eternity of quiet.

'She's good,' Davey said.

'And Casey?'

'She's fine.'

'That last one was a great album. I play it in the car all the time.'

'Thanks, Da.'

'And her lovely wife Mabel?'

'She's great and so are the kids. It's all good.'

'And that other stuff in New York, how's it going?'

'I did some studio work for an up-and-coming act, a soul singer. He's got the talent and the songs, now it's just publicity and luck.'

'You'll go on the road with him?'

'Only if it doesn't clash with Casey.'

'Oh.'

'Yeah.'

'What's the weather like?'

'I've come from Boston. It's raining there.'

'It was snowing here last week. Snow in April, never thought I'd see that. Feels like the end of the world.' He pushed his chair back and stood up. 'I'm going for a lie-down. It's good to have you home, Davey.'

'Thanks, Da.'

After Jack had left the room, Davey lifted his mug. 'The end of the world, huh?'

'Yeah,' Grace said, and they finished their tea in silence.

Molly

Molly was in the canteen when she bumped into Rabbit's consultant oncologist. Mr Dunne, a short, fit, bald man in his forties, was queuing with a middle-aged woman, who had frizzy black hair, the kind you'd see on a rocker in the eighties. She was wearing a dense wool dress, thick tights with rosebuds on them, a cardigan that matched the tights, with the same rosebuds, and the kind of clunky shoes you'd only see in documentaries about psychiatric patients in the last century.

'Molly, I've just arrived. How's Rabbit?' Mr Dunne grabbed an orange.

'Sleeping mostly.'

'I'm so sorry I wasn't there yesterday to talk to you myself.'

'Your friend did a fine job,' Molly said.

'I'm so very sorry, Molly,' he said, and she could tell he meant it, even though he dealt with death every day.

She tried to smile. 'Thank you, but all is not lost.'

He looked from Molly to his friend and back to Molly. Clearly he was unsure as to whether or not she realized how grave Rabbit's condition was.

Molly registered his unease. 'She's here today, isn't she?' she said, and he seemed to relax.

'I'll be in to see her in about an hour if you're still around?'

'Where else would I be?'

'Nowhere but here,' said the woman with the clunky shoes.

'This is Rita Brown. She's a medical social worker,' Mr Dunne said.

'Nice to meet you, Molly. I'm here for you and your family if you need me,' Rita said.

'Thanks,' Molly said, and moved away. She'd decided against a mug of tea: her stomach was playing up. She looked around for the toilets. *Quick, quick, quick, Molly, don't have an accident. That's all you bloody need, Arctic winds and no knickers.*

She made it to the Ladies, then spent some time washing her

hands under piping-hot water. The soap was a luxury brand, which smelt delicious on her hands, not the antibacterial cleanser that hospitals supplied. She looked at herself in the mirror. Molly had always been plump but her weight had served her well in old age until now. Her skin had always been soft and flawless but it was dull now and her eyes were dark holes in her head, surrounded by firm creases. At seventy-two, she asked herself, *When did I get so old?* Her hair had been grey for many years and she usually added a little silver blonde to it, but since Rabbit's fall and her subsequent diagnosis, Molly had had little time for anything or anyone else. Now the roots looked bad and Rabbit kept reminding her that she needed her hair done – but how could she spend a few hours at a hairdresser's when her youngest child needed her most?

She didn't notice Rita come in as she examined her hair and tried to work out whether or not a hat would be appropriate indoor wear.

'I can have a hairdresser come to the room for you,' Rita said, making Molly jump.

'No, no, it's fine.'

'Nothing's fine, Molly,' Rita said.

'No, it's not.'

'So I'll arrange for a hairdresser to come to the room. It will be tomorrow, if that's OK? She can do something for Rabbit too.'

'Rabbit's head is shaved. Her hair never grew back properly.'

'She'll give her a head massage.'

'She might be too tired.'

'We'll see how she is tomorrow.'

'OK, thanks,' Molly said, and began to leave.

'Molly,' Rita said, and Molly turned back. 'I'm here if you want to talk.'

'I'll keep that in mind.' She left the room.

Rabbit was still sleeping when she got back, but Davey and Grace were there.

'Hiya, Ma,' Davey said.

'Hiya, son.' She walked up to him and held him close, exhaling loudly as she rubbed the back of his neck. 'Still can't get used to the short hair.'

'It's been ten years, Ma.'

'It seems like yesterday.' She looked from him to Rabbit asleep in the bed. 'She'll be awake soon.'

'Da's coming in tomorrow.' Grace said.

Molly nodded. 'He's not able. He keeps crying in her face. If she told him to fuck off once yesterday, she told him to fuck off a hundred times.'

Davey laughed a little. 'Only in this family,' he said.

They sat down, Grace and Davey on the sofa, Molly in the recliner chair. 'Did your da eat?'

'He's waiting for you,' Grace said.

'I'll pick up a curry. Speaking of which, how's Jeffrey?'

'Starving.'

'He reminds me of you, Grace. When you were five you used to eat dirt – I was worried you were simple for a while. Thank God it was just greed.'

'Thanks, Ma, I feel so much better about things now,' Grace said. 'If you want I can make something for Da instead.'

'I'm not sure he'll have the stomach for anything,' Davey said. 'He looks shook, Ma.'

'And the rest of us don't?' She stared at his tired pale face. 'We're all shadows, son. How could we not be?' Her dark eyes filled but the tears dared not fall.

Rabbit woke when Michelle was changing her Fentanyl patch. 'There you are,' she said, as Rabbit's eyes slowly opened. 'Your sister and brother are here.'

Grace and Davey stood up and met her gaze with smiles painted on their faces. Davey even waved at her, like a contestant on a quiz show.

'Jaysus, I'm so bad my siblings have turned into two big goons,' Rabbit whispered.

'At least I didn't wave,' Grace said.

'Fuck off, Grace,' Davey said, in as playful a tone as he could muster.

'Welcome home, Davey,' Rabbit said.

'Don't want to be here,' he admitted.

'You and me both.'

'How's your pain?' Michelle asked.

'A seven.'

'The fresh patch should kick in soon. If it doesn't, you call me.' She looked at her watch. 'I'll be leaving in half an hour, but before I go I'll introduce you to Jacinta. You'll like her – she fancies herself as a singer, so, if you want a laugh, get her to sing "Delilah".'

'She's that bad?' Rabbit asked.

'She makes that chicken-stuffer on *The X Factor* look like Justin Timberlake,' Michelle said, 'but she's good at the day job and she's a great old egg.' She winked. 'Jacinta'll look after you. Now, how's the bowels?'

'Whistling "Dixie".'

'I'll take that to mean they're grand. I'll leave you to it.' Michelle walked out.

'She's nice,' Rabbit said.

'And pretty,' Grace said. Davey's eyes were following Michelle's arse out of the door.

'Slow down. You're only here five minutes,' Rabbit said.

'Don't be making enemies of Rabbit's nurses or I'll murder you,' Molly said.

Rabbit laughed. 'Yeah, there'll be two of us in the hole.' Everyone stopped dead. It was a classic tumbleweed moment. 'Too much?' she asked.

'Too much,' Grace replied.

'Hey, Davey,' Rabbit changed the subject, 'I've been back in time.'

'Oh, yeah?'

'Yeah. Back to our wall, back to the garage. I could see you beating the drum, the boys kicking it on guitar, bass, piano, and Johnny singing. I swear I stayed there until you'd all re-hearsed every song twice.'

'You always did.' He took her withered hand in his.

'Lying on the cold floor, daydreaming to your music – those were some of the best times I've ever had.'

'That's not at all depressing,' he joked.

'It was lovely, actually,' she said.

It was then that Grace brought up Juliet. The subject was delicate and Molly dreaded Rabbit's reaction.

'Tomorrow,' Rabbit said. 'Bring her tomorrow.'

'But what should I tell her?' Grace was unable to hide the tremor in her voice.

'Tell her that her ma loves her.'

'But . . .'

'Grace, please.'

'She's asking.'

'I don't care what they say. I'm not giving up.' Rabbit's eyes were suddenly drowning, and tears flowed as though a dam had burst inside her.

Suddenly she was choking, and Molly was on to it, lifting her up, rubbing her back and soothing her. 'There, there, my girl, no more tears. We'll fight and fight and fight.' She stroked and kissed Rabbit's head, and when the choking had passed, she laid her down and stroked her cheek until Rabbit's tears slowly stopped. 'Go to sleep now, love,' she said, and Rabbit's eyes closed. She let out a sigh and was asleep as suddenly as she had woken.

Grace and Davey were horrified. Although Grace was forty-six and her brother forty-four, they were reduced to helpless children standing at the end of their little sister's bed, unsure what to say or do and desperately willing their mammy to make everything all right.

Grace

'Lenny?' she shouted to her husband when she arrived at home with ten bags of shopping.

Nine-year-old Jeffrey appeared in the sitting-room door. 'He's across the road looking at Paddy Noonan's new car – well, it's not new, it's a 2008, but it's new to Noonan.' He took a bag from her, leaving her with the other nine. He looked into the bag. 'It's all green in here,' he said sadly.

'Get used to green because, until you've dropped two stone, it's all you're going to be eating and playing on.' She walked through the hall and into the kitchen.

'Harsh,' he mumbled.

'Where are your brothers?'

'Stephen's still in college. Ryan's in Deco's and Bernard is upstairs playing Nintendo.'

'Jesus Christ! Ryan is supposed to come home straight after school.'

'He told me da he'd a school project to do with Deco.'

'Lying little toerag,' she muttered.

Jeffrey sat opposite her at the counter while she put away the shopping. 'That's what I said but Da's a sucker.'

'Stop watching me,' Grace snapped.

'Wha'?'

'You're following the food, Jeffrey, and I'm telling you, I'll have every morsel accounted for. If one morsel goes missing, I'll chase you with a hammer.'

'Jaysus, Ma, there's something wrong with you.' He got down from his stool.

'Where's Juliet?' she asked.

'Where she always is.'

'Is she OK?'

'Don't know. She won't talk to me.'

'OK. Well, get your tracksuit on. We're going for a run before dinner.'

'Wha'?' Jeffrey was evidently appalled.

'You heard me.'

'I'm not running anywhere with you.'

'Oh yes you are.'

'I'll be laughed out of it if the lads see us.'

'Well, they'll be the ones who are sorry when you lose all the weight and all the girls want you.'

'Girls are disgusting.'

'They're disgusting when you're nine, but by the time you're thirteen, they'll be one of the few things you think about.'

'Not if I'm gay.'

'Well, son, if you're gay, trust me when I say the body is everything.'

'You're so mean!' he shouted.

'Get up those stairs and get your tracksuit on.' She went into the sitting room and sank down beside Juliet on the sofa. The TV was on in the background but Juliet wasn't watching it. Instead she was buried in a book, which she closed.

Twelve-year-old Juliet looked a lot like her mother had at that age. She had long mousy hair, although hers was layered and had a bounce to it. She was stick-thin and had a pretty little face – no spectacles, but she scrunched up her nose as her mother did when she was thinking. 'Did you see her?' she asked.

'Yeah, she's all settled.'

'When can I see her?'

'Tomorrow.'

'Why not tonight?'

'She's tired.'

'She's always tired.'

'I know, but tomorrow, OK?'

'When is she coming home?'

'I don't know,' Grace lied.

'I can take care of her,' Juliet said.

'Of course you can.'

'I know what to do.'

'I know you do, darling.'

'So she should be home with me. She doesn't need a conva-lescent home.'

That lie had tripped off Grace's tongue the night before, when she was completely at a loss as to what to say to the child whose mother had just been told she was dying.

'Let's see what happens tomorrow,' Grace said.

Juliet nodded. 'I just want to go home.'

Grace said nothing, just flicked Juliet's hair off her face and talked about what she was planning for dinner. Juliet listened politely, waiting to return to her book.

Grace left the room in time to see Jeffrey come down the stairs in a tracksuit that was two sizes too small. 'Jeffrey.'

'Wha'?'

'Is that a joke?'

'It's the only tracksuit I have.'

'Put your jeans back on.'

Delighted, he clapped his hands. 'Deadly.'

'You're running in them.'

'Ah, for God's sake, Ma.'

Grace had just changed into her tracksuit when Lenny came into the bedroom. 'Taking Jeff for a run?' he asked.

'I did this to him so it's up to me to fix it,' she said.

'You didn't.'

'I'm greedy, always was, always will be. Me ma saw that and she wouldn't let me eat whatever I wanted, so I learned self-discipline. I knew Jeff was like me. I knew he found it hard to say no, but instead of saying it for him, I let our youngest eat himself to the brink of death. What the hell is wrong with me?'

'You're exaggerating.'

'Pre-diabetes, Len,' she said. 'He's nine and at risk of type two diabetes, just like his granda, not to mention heart disease, kidney failure and blindness, and it's my fault.'

He put his arms round her. 'It'll work out.'

'Not everything does,' she said.

Lenny understood why his wife had taken the news of her son's health check so badly. She had been scared of losing Rabbit for so long, and now it was happening.

'How's Rabbit?' he asked.

'She's bad, Len.'

He kissed his wife's forehead. 'All right, my love,' he said. 'We'll do our best by her.'

'And then what?'

'And then we'll say goodbye.'

Grace cried quietly into her husband's shoulder for a long five minutes.

Chapter Two

Johnny

Twelve-year-old Rabbit Hayes was hidden behind the heavy old fabric and the egg boxes lining the garage wall when Johnny found her. He didn't pull back the curtain, just sat down on the floor cross-legged, as though they were on two opposite sides of a confession box.

'Hi,' he said.

She was quiet for a moment or two, trying to stifle her sobs. 'Hi,' she said, once the sobbing had ceased.

'What's up?' he asked.

'Nothing.'

'There's something,' he said. 'You don't cry for nothing.'

She fixed her spectacles on her face and held them there.

'I can hear you thinking,' he said.

'You can't.'

'Can, so stop thinking and start talking.'

Rabbit exhaled loudly behind the old curtain. 'Two boys are always calling me names. Today they took me glasses and said if I don't bring them money tomorrow after school they're going to break them.'

Johnny was annoyed by Rabbit's revelation. 'What did they call you?' he asked, maintaining an even tone.

'Don't want to say.'

'Have they hurt you?'

'They pushed me into a wall, but I'm OK.'

'How long has this been going on?'

'A while.'

'Who are they?'

'Better not to say.'

Johnny unclenched his fist, then pulled back the curtain to re-veal his young friend in her school uniform, two scraped knees raised to her chin as she held her spectacles to her tear-stained face. 'I need you to tell me,' he said.

'Why?'

'Because me and the boys are going to sort it.'

'I can't.'

'Rabbit, we're either going to frighten the shite out of two boys in your school or every last one of them, so spit it out.'

For a moment she looked as if she was going to cry again but then she didn't. Instead she smiled a big, wide smile. 'Frighten the shite out of them?' she said. He nodded. 'Can I watch?' she asked. He nodded again. 'Nice one,' she said.

He helped her up, and as they walked along the little corridor that led to the kitchen, he pressed her to his hip. 'You're my family, Rabbit. Don't forget that.'

The next day Rabbit stood with Johnny at the meeting spot by the clump of big trees two minutes from the school. Francie and Jay waited too. They practised hitting golf balls. Francie used a putter, while Jay messed around with a wood. The two twelve-year-old boys arrived. Chris was the big one, but not as big as either of the two sixteen-year-olds with the golf clubs, and Eugene was the short stubby one with large fists. They noticed the two lads before they saw Rabbit leaning against the wall with Johnny. He had his arms crossed, and when they met his eye, he raised an eyebrow, winked and looked towards the lads, giving them the nod. They responded with a sniff. Then, before the two boys knew it, they were being approached by two lunatics swinging golf clubs.

Francie kicked the legs from under Chris and knocked him to the ground. Then he sat on him and held the golf club to his throat. Jay backed Eugene into a tree, shoved a golf ball into his mouth and practised swinging while the kid held his hands up and started crying.

Rabbit watched, terrified and thrilled. 'They're not really going to hurt them?' she said urgently.

'Nah,' Johnny said. 'They'll be happy when at least one pisses himself.'

They didn't have to wait long. Eugene was the first to go and, as urine darkened the leg of his red tracksuit bottoms, Johnny took a Polaroid camera out of his bag. 'Say cheese.' He took a photo of the boy, with a golf ball in his mouth, who'd just messed himself. The kid on the ground was crying so hard he had mud tracks on his face. Johnny snapped him too. The lads held the two boys where they were while Johnny waited for the Polaroid photos to process. When they were ready, he peeled them. 'The miracle of the modern age, boys.' He showed them the photographic evidence of their humiliation. Francie and Jay allowed them to stand up. Johnny called Rabbit over from the wall and she walked to him cautiously, still scared and exhilarated, her heart beating in her ears. Johnny handed her the photographs and she shoved them into her schoolbag.

He turned to the boys, his friends holding them by the backs of their collars. 'See her?' He pointed to Rabbit, and both boys nodded vigorously. 'From now on, your job is to protect her. Anyone lays a finger on her, or says anything that upsets her, you need to sort them out or the penalty is you both lose your little dicks, understand?'

'Yous can't do that,' Chris said, in a voice full of tears. Eugene, with the ball still stuck in his mouth, nodded again, to show he agreed with his friend.

'Yeah, we can,' Francie said.

'And we will,' Jay agreed.

'Yous'll go to prison.'

'Five years for GBH, cut in half immediately because the prisons are too full, then halved again for good behaviour.'

'And when it suits us, we're real charmers,' Jay said.

'So that's just over a year. I could do that standing on me head,' Francie said.

'There's a course in prison I'd love to take a look at,' Jay said.

Johnny smiled. 'A year in a cell with me own TV is nothing, but a lifetime without a dick, well, that's a long time, kids.'

The two boys burst into tears again.

'Right,' Chris said. 'We'll do it.'

Eugene agreed enthusiastically.

'Good,' Johnny said.

'Great.' Francie patted Chris on the shoulder while Jay pushed Eugene forward.

'You can take that ball out of your mouth now,' Johnny said to Eugene, and he tried, but it seemed really wedged in there. 'Help him,' Johnny ordered Chris.

'How?'

'Stick your fingers in.' Jay offered the basic solution.

'Ah, wha'?' Chris said.

'Just do it,' Francie said.

'Ah, Jaysus, lads . . .'

'Don't be a bleedin' baby,' Jay told him.

'Right, right.' Chris stuck his dirty fingers into his friend's mouth. 'It's really tight in there.'

'Just pull it from behind,' Francie said.

'But watch his teeth,' Rabbit warned, walking up behind Johnny.

'Ha hotch me meat,' Eugene tried.

'Wha'?' Chris asked Eugene.

'He said, "Yeah, watch me teeth,"' Rabbit said.

'Just open up a tiny bit more, Euge, will ya?' Chris made a gagging sound. 'Oh, I can feel his tongue.'

'Right, I'm bored, let's go.' Francie slung his golf club across his shoulders and hung his arms over it.

Johnny pointed at the two boys. 'Don't forget now, watch out for our girl or . . .' He made a snipping gesture with his fingers.

Chris stopped digging in Eugene's mouth long enough to agree. Johnny smiled at Rabbit, and she fell into line between him and Jay, with Francie at the end, talking about his yearning for a battered sausage. When the boys had branched off to stop at the local chipper, Johnny walked Rabbit to her wall, where they sat for a few minutes to watch two dogs chasing each other on the green.

'Why didn't you bring Louis and Davey?' Rabbit asked.

'Louis doesn't have the stomach for it, and Davey . . . Well, if we'd told your brother he would have cut off their little dicks right away.' He laughed.

'Really?' Rabbit asked, scrunching her nose. At twelve she wasn't sure her brother liked her enough not to throw her under a bus if she was in his way, never mind stand up for her.

'Everyone loves you, Rabbit,' Johnny said. 'How could they not?'

Rabbit blushed and he flicked her bunches, got off the wall and walked up to the side door. By then the band had their own keys to the garage. He unlocked it and turned to her. 'See you on the other side, Rabbit,' he said, and was gone.

Rabbit

Rabbit woke in pain and, for a moment, she had no idea where she was. All she could process was an agony so intense she had to call out. It was when the nurse came running in that she remembered. *Oh, no, I'm dying.* Jacinta was a country woman, five foot nothing with a friendly face, a large chest and tiny hands. She checked Rabbit's file, quickly managed the breakthrough pain, then waited until Rabbit's fists unclenched and she was breathing more regularly.

'Better?' she asked.

'Better,' Rabbit said.

'Good stuff. I'm Jacinta, by the way.'

'The singer.'

'Ah, you heard.'

'"Delilah",' Rabbit said, and curled in her cracked bottom lip.

Jacinta took a swab lolly out of her pocket, unwrapped it and handed it to her. 'Try it.'

Rabbit sucked it and rubbed it on her lips. 'Thanks,' she said. 'So "Delilah".'

Jacinta checked her watch, then sat in the recliner and stifled a yawn. 'Well, now, truth be told, "Forever In Blue Jeans" is my favourite but "Delilah" is the crowd-pleaser,' she chuckled a little to herself, 'but while I'm being honest I don't get half enough acclaim for my "Wonderwall".' She was joking: she knew she was bad but she didn't care and Rabbit liked that about her.

'I knew a singer once,' Rabbit said.

'Oh, yeah? Any good?'

'He was amazing,' Rabbit said. 'He could have been the biggest star on the planet at one point.'

'What happened?'

'He let me go,' Rabbit said.

'I'm sorry,' Jacinta said, and clearly meant it.

'Me too,' Rabbit said, eyes closing.

Davey

Davey was the first to leave the hospital. He found it too difficult to stay. He didn't know what to do or say and it was easier to walk away. It was still early enough in the evening to meet up with the lads. Francie was working late, but Jay was around for a pint, if he was willing to make his way across the city. He picked up a cab outside the hospital and called him en route. Jay was subdued on the phone. He'd heard about Rabbit's diagnosis, even though he'd moved to the mountains.

'Me ma met Pauline in the shops,' he said, by way of explanation. 'I'm sick for you, man. In fact, I'm sick for us all.'

'I know.'

'It'll be good to see you, though.' Jay hung up. It had been six months since Davey had been home and Jay had been on holiday with the family in Spain then so they'd missed one another. Davey realized it had been two years since they'd met.

The taxi driver was quiet: he was listening to Talk Radio. The presenter was attempting to get a politician to answer a straight question, with little success. Every now and then, the driver would mumble to the radio: 'Oh, it's all right for you, you shower of bastards.' Or 'Where's my petrol allowance? You sons of bitches.' And 'You can shove your property tax up your bleedin' hole.'

Davey didn't engage with him. Instead he watched Dublin City pass him by. It was dusk and the pavements were filled with people in suits walking to their buses, cars and trains. Some were talking on their phones, some listening to their iPods, others walking in twos, chatting and laughing. One guy was singing to himself as he walked past the taxi, which was stuck at traffic lights. It was just a normal April evening in Dublin. *Life goes on*, Davey thought. *I've always hated that poxy saying.*

Jay was waiting for him in the pub. As soon as they spotted each other he stood up and greeted Davey with a bear hug, then ruffled his hair as they pulled apart.

'Looking good, DB.'

'Back at ya,' Davey said. They sat on stools and Jay ordered two pints without asking Davey what he wanted. They clinked glasses and took a sup before either spoke again.

'How's she holding up?' Jay asked.

'You know Rabbit. She's hanging in there.'

'Sucks, man,' Jay said.

'That's life.'

'So I'm changing the subject,' Jay said. 'How's life in the fast lane? Tell me something good because I've just spent the day engineering sound for a cartoon that consists of beeps and whistles.'

'It's the same old same old.'

'That's not good. I want something good.'

'I live on a fucking bus.'

'Still not good.'

'I'm boring.'

'Don't make me punch you.'

Davey took out his phone and pulled up a photo of a young blonde American beauty. 'I've been seeing her, on and off.'

'Oh, wow! What age is she?'

'Twenty-five.'

'A model?'

'Aspiring actress.'

'Who would have thought it? DB's such a stud.'

'Not me,' Davey said.

'Not any of us, the bleedin' state of you. You like her?'

'She's nice but . . .' Davey shook his head '. . . she's not—'

'Marjorie?'

'Don't start.'

'She's separated now. It's been official for ages.'

'Not interested.'

'Bollocks.'

'How's your missus?'

'Closed the door to her business three months ago.'

'Poor Lorraine.'

'She's one of many. She's trying to sell off stock online. If it works, maybe she'll continue in cyberspace. We'll see.'

'The kids?'

'Den moved to Canada last year. He's working in Nova Scotia. He likes it. Justine is doing her Leaving Cert in a couple of months.'

'I feel old.'

'You are old – too old for that girl.'

'I know, I know.'

'Marjorie's renting an apartment in town now.'

'Jay . . .'

'Right, right, I'll leave it at that.'

Francie arrived just before last pints. He lifted Davey up in the air and shook him. 'It's great to see ya, DB. I'm heading in to see your sister tomorrow, so let's just enjoy our catch-up tonight.'

'Sounds good to me,' Davey said.

'Nice one.' Francie slapped him on the back. 'Now show us the photo of the beaut you're molesting.'

'How did you know?'

Jay raised his phone in the air. 'It's called an iPhone,' he wiggled his fingers, 'and these are called fingers, Columbo.'

The lads chatted for another hour in the pub and then they stopped for chips, just like the old days. In the queue Francie's in-depth description of his vasectomy brought tears to Davey's eyes.

'Me plums actually looked like plums.'

'Fucked-up plums,' Jay chimed in.

'Talk about *The Color Purple*! Where's my bleedin' Oscar?'

'I've never seen anything like it,' Jay said. 'Put me right off.'

'You saw them?' Davey asked.

'He kept shoving them in me face.' Jay was clearly still disturbed by the vivid memory.

'You know what they say – it helps to share,' Francie quipped.

Davey could listen to the boys banter for hours. It was good fun but, then again, being with the boys was among the best fun Davey Hayes had ever had. For a few short years, when they were a band full of hope and promise, he had laughed and loved more than he had in the many that had followed. He had a good life. He had fulfilled his dreams. He'd made a lot of money. He had great friends. On paper he was a success, but coming home never failed to remind him of the life he had given up. *Would I be happier here? Would I be married to a woman I loved and who loved me? Would I be a father? Or am I destined to live life with a hole in me?* He looked at his two old friends, sitting side by side, eating chips, all elbows and hand gestures, at a table a little too small for them. Despite the inconceivably tragic circumstances of his trip, his current state of shock and the heart-breaking pain that every minute delivered him closer to, for a short time that evening Davey Hayes was reminded of what it felt like to be happy.

Jack

Jack had been there when his youngest daughter was born. Hers was the only birth he'd ever witnessed and it wasn't by choice. In seventies Ireland it was unusual for a man to be present in the room. It just wasn't done. Women had babies and men waited in the pub with friends, a pint or two and cigars at the ready. During Grace's birth Jack had attended a local football match, enjoyed a slap-up meal with the lads and then two scoops in the local. At ten minutes past ten, the barman had answered the phone and announced to the entire pub that Jack Hayes was the proud father of a little girl, seven pounds seven ounces. The whole place had celebrated, and he was bought so many drinks that Nicky Morrissey, the local barber, had had to carry him home.

Grace's birth had been a good one for Jack. Davey's hadn't been so good: he'd given them a little scare right at the end of Molly's pregnancy so she had spent the last two weeks in the hospital leaving Grace to run circles around Jack.

By then his own parents were dead; Molly's father had died when she was still a child, and her mother was bananas so could not be trusted with a two-year-old. Jack was all Grace had in her mother's absence and he couldn't cope with that wilful child. He spent the day Molly went into labour running the legs off the child so she'd pass out after her dinner. They fought over fish fingers: Grace threw a tantrum and fell asleep five minutes after he'd locked her in her room, threatening through the closed door to run away and leave her there. The midwife rang the house with the news of his son, six pounds four ounces.

He thanked her, collapsed in front of *The Saint* and was asleep before the first ad break.

But Rabbit was different. She was in such a rush to come into the world that Molly insisted Jack drive through red lights. 'If it's safe to do it, do it!' she screamed.

'Are you mad, woman?'

'The baby is coming, Jack.'

'Ah, now, hold on a minute, Molly, would ya? I'm not having that.'

'Oh, fine, why don't I just cross my legs, then?'

'Do you think that would work?' He experienced fleeting hope.

'Don't make me hurt you,' Molly said, then yelled at him to pull over.

'Oh, Mother of God, hold it, Molly, hold it!' he shouted, as he pulled into the forecourt of a Ford garage just off the Drumcondra road. It was nearly lunchtime and the garage was empty, save for one salesman and a wide-eyed kid, who was cleaning the cars until Jack's Escort careered past him, knocking over his bucket and threatening his toes. The salesman, a Vincent Delaney, ran from the office to be met by Molly's nether regions and Jack yelling, 'I can see the head!' Vincent promptly fainted. He only came round when Jack had Rabbit in his arms and Molly had covered herself with a coat. She instructed Vincent to call a fucking ambulance. Jack loved all his children equally, but he'd have been lying if he'd said that bringing his youngest into the world wasn't the best day of his life.

When she was first diagnosed with breast cancer, he read all there was to read on the subject and was content that she would be all right, which she was, until the next breast had to go. That was all right, too – Rabbit could live without breasts – but they'd found it in her liver too and he worried, because Google told him to, but the doctors were positive they could still beat it, until they'd found it in her lungs. That was when they began talking about living with cancer and controlling the disease, but they still had hope. Millions of people were living with cancer, they were told. It's not ideal but it's life, and Rabbit is such a trouper. Then Rabbit had fallen in her kitchen and her bone had snapped, and poor Juliet had found her in terrible distress. Within an hour of her admittance, they knew it was in her bones and that was the beginning of the end. Jack's daughter had broken her leg and now he was losing her. As long as she was in the acute hospital, surely there were things they could do, but in transferring her to a hospice, they had given up on her.

It had been like receiving a blow to the head. Jack couldn't think straight because to do so would be to think the unthinkable. *We're losing her. She's leaving us. It's over . . .* And that was simply impossible. *No way, not my girl. I won't have it. I WILL NOT HAVE IT.* After his initial shocked silence, he had returned to the hospital and fought any doctor or nurse who made themselves available to speak to him. He'd begged them to keep her and treat her, experimentally, if necessary. 'You can put cow bones in if you think it will help.' He'd just wanted them to go on as they had for four years, but they wanted to stop and Molly was letting them. He had married a warrior. Molly had fought on the streets for the right to work after marriage; she had talked a man off a ledge while volunteering in the local mental hospital; she had even chased a mugger down the road and beaten him to the ground with a bag of oranges. He couldn't understand why the woman wouldn't fight for her own child. *We have to fight for our girl, Molly. We have to fix her. We can't let her down. It's our job, for God's sake.*

Jack had not spoken to his wife since she had watched Rabbit sign the hospice forms, not that Molly had noticed: she was too busy driving Rabbit to her death. When she'd returned home that night, she'd brought a curry, and instead of talking about Rabbit, she'd babbled on about him needing to walk it off. *But what's the plan? When are we going to pick up the fight?* She had sat in the chair and promptly fallen asleep. He'd binned the curry and headed up the stairs. He'd lain in bed alone in the dark, burning eyes focused on the ceiling, his brain so full of rage it ached. *Why are you allowing this to happen, Molly? Who the hell are you? Where is my wife? I can't fight for her without you, Molls. Please, please, help me.*

Juliet

It was just before midnight when Juliet heard the front door open and close quietly. She turned down the TV so that it was barely audible, hoping that Stephen would make his way to his room without checking on her; but then she heard the click of the sitting-room door opening and he tiptoed in. She'd been sitting up and it was too late to pretend she wasn't awake.

'Hey,' he said.

'Hey,' she responded.

'The benefits of sleeping in a sitting room.' He was referring to the TV.

'Suppose.' The sofa was converted into a pull-out bed and she was covered with a mound of blankets.

Stephen sat in an armchair in a corner of the room. 'Can't sleep?'

'No.'

'It's hard to be away from home.'

'Yeah,' she agreed.

'I'm sorry about your ma. I wish there was something I could do.'

'Thanks, but it's only a broken leg. She's battled worse,' Juliet said.

Stephen nodded, then changed the subject. 'You hungry?'

'It's late.'

'I've just spent the last twelve hours studying in an attempt to make up for the fact that I've spent the year drinking beer and chasing after a girl called Susan instead of attending classes. I'm tired and pissed off with myself, the world and stupid Susan, who wouldn't know a good thing if it bit her on the nose. When I'm tired and pissed off, I like to eat.'

Juliet grinned. Stephen was cool and she was tired and pissed off too. She was tired because she always found it hard to sleep when her mother was in hospital, and she was pissed off because she couldn't understand why Grace had insisted she sleep on the sofa, surrounded by mental-case boys, rather than allow her to stay in Nan's spare bedroom in peace. Also, she hadn't eaten anything except a nut bar all day, despite Grace's cajoling. 'Yeah, I'm hungry.'

'Follow me.' He got up and left the room.

She put on her slippers and dressing-gown, then followed him into the kitchen, where he began frying sausages and boiling the kettle.

'Nothing quite beats a sausage sandwich at midnight,' he said, as she sat up at the counter.

'Do you have ketchup?' she asked.

'Of course! What do you take us for?'

'Why did you want to do engineering?' she asked.

'I got a Meccano set when I was ten and I was obsessed. It's all I've ever wanted since then.'

'So why did you spend the year drinking beer and chasing Susan?'

'I'm an idiot.'

She laughed a little.

'How about you? Do you know what you want to do?'

'Science.'

'Are you going to build rockets or work on an alternative to water?'

'I'm going to help find the cure for cancer,' she said, which seemed to stop him in his tracks.

For a moment it looked like Stephen wanted to cry. Instead he pulled out some bread and buttered four slices. He scooped the sausages out of the pan and laid them on two of the slices, squirted them with ketchup and covered them with the remaining slices, cut the sandwiches in half, plated them and handed Juliet hers. Then he took a huge bite of his own and said, 'Yum.'

Encouraged, she took a bite. 'That's really good,' she said. 'If engineering doesn't work out you could be a chef in a greasy spoon or buy a hotdog stand.'

'Ha-ha. It *will* work out if I have to beg, borrow or steal.'

'Or study,' she said.

'Or study.'

'OK.' She hadn't thought about her mother in more than sixty seconds. She had smiled, enjoyed a sandwich and even giggled once. For the first time in days, Juliet Hayes was living in the moment.

'You know you're my favourite cousin.'

'I'm your only cousin,' she reminded him.

'On that note, do you think Uncle Davey's a homo?'

'Definitely not.'

'Why so sure?' he asked.

'Because I caught him in bed with me ma's best friend, Marjorie, when I was ten.'

'No!'

'They said they were playing leapfrog.'

Stephen nearly choked on his sandwich with laughter and Juliet joined in. *Oh, Ma, I'm so sorry. I hope you're OK. I miss you. I love you. Come home to me.*

DAY TWO

Chapter Three

Molly

MOLLY WOKE IN THE chair. She was stiff and cold and still unsure if it was night or day when she heard Davey banging around in the kitchen. She got up, stretched and stamped her foot – the leg was dead – waited for the pins, needles and numbness to pass, then went towards the noise. Davey was boiling the kettle when she entered the kitchen. 'What time is it?' she asked.

'Around nine.'

'You should have woken me. I should be with Rabbit.'

'You should be in bed,' Davey said. 'Sit down, Ma, and I'll make you some breakfast.' She did as she was told. She was exhausted, drained and shaken to her core.

'Where's your da?' she asked.

'He's been in his room practically since I arrived.'

'He's not able for all of this,' she mumbled.

'None of us are.'

'He just needs some time to get his head together. We all come at things differently.'

Davey handed her a mug of tea, then some toast and a knife. 'Butter it, eat it.'

She looked up and smiled at him. 'I will. Thank you, son.'

He sat opposite her at the table. 'How are you coping, Ma?' he asked.

'I'm not sure. I keep thinking about what we could have missed. Maybe there is a miracle out there for us yet.'

'We've chased enough miracles, Ma,' Davey said sadly. 'It only leads to disappointment and suffering.'

'Rabbit's still here,' Molly whispered. 'There's still hope if she's here.' She wiped a stray tear that had escaped from the stockpile inside her, then bit into her toast. Each mouthful seemed to take every ounce of her strength to chew and swallow, but she continued to eat as though it was a challenge she refused to fail.

'We all need our strength now,' she said, getting up and lifting her plate.

Davey took it from her. 'Go and get washed, Ma. I'll take care of everything else.'

'You're a good man. You always were so kind, a fucking eejit but kind. I'm so proud of you, Davey.' She left the room and walked up the stairs, holding the banister for support. Her legs felt tired and twisted.

The light was streaming into her bedroom from the window that looked out onto the green. Jack was lying still, with his back to her. She could tell he was awake because he wasn't snoring and was far too stiff to be relaxed. He didn't speak and she didn't have anything to say. Instead she moved towards the light and focused on the green, watching a boy and girl play chase with an Irish Wolfhound that was bigger than both of them.

She had watched her kids and her grandchildren play on the green from that window so many times over the years, but the boy, girl and dog reminded her particularly of one summer's evening when Davey and his little sister Rabbit were lying on one of her old blankets, wearing sunglasses and staring into the sun.

'It makes you feel spacey, Ma,' Rabbit had said, when Molly

had gone across the road to see what her children were doing.

'I can see black spots,' Davey said, moving his hands through the air.

The sun was still high and Molly wasn't sure that staring at it was good for their eyes, especially as Rabbit already had eye problems.

'I don't like it. You could do yourself damage,' Molly said.

'Lie down beside me, Ma, and see for yourself,' Rabbit said.

Molly had always been a reasonable sort of woman. She was never one of those mothers who ordered their kids to do or stop doing something 'because I say so'.

Molly accepted her daughter's invitation. Her kids moved over and she lay down on the ground beside them with her sunglasses on.

Her face felt warm and she immediately blinked a few times, but then she settled on the light. It felt nice but slightly strained.

'It takes a while to feel spacey,' Rabbit said.

'How long? I've got the tea on.'

'About five minutes,' Davey said.

'Ah, here, I don't have five minutes and my eyes keep closing. I don't like it.'

'Just give it a minute, Ma,' Rabbit said.

Lying on the warm ground felt good, so she stayed for a minute longer to please her youngest, but also because she was now a little too lazy to stand up. Then the strangest thing happened. Molly Hayes felt herself floating in the air and she was heading for the blue sky above. The sensation was so real that she grabbed the blanket and gripped it tight. Her heart raced and she sat up.

'Christ on a bike!' she shouted, and her kids sat up too.

'Wha'?' Davey said.

'Are you all right, Ma? You look like you've seen a ghost,' Rabbit said.

'I think I almost was one!' Molly said, alarmed, as she scrambled to her feet.

'Wha'?' Davey asked again, clearly confused by his mother's reaction.

'Did either of you feel like yous were leaving your body?' she asked them.

Rabbit and Davey looked at each other, then at her. They shook their heads and said no.

'Right, good! Get up – get up! Never do that again.'

As she walked across the road, she heard Rabbit say to her brother, 'I think me ma is losing it.' And she'd wondered if her youngest was right.

She laughed at the memory. Maybe she *had* momentarily lost it, or maybe she was just tired or overwhelmed, or she'd taken too many headache tablets. She wondered what she'd have seen or imagined if she'd stared into the sun that day. It made her shudder. The warmth of the memory was gone and it had left her feeling cold.

When she turned from the window, her husband was sitting up in bed. 'You should come to the hospice today,' she said to him.

'To do what?' he asked. 'Just to get a front-row seat? Maybe we should sell tickets.' Jack was not often sarcastic and it didn't suit him.

'I'm going to be with our daughter who needs us,' Molly said evenly.

'That's right,' he said, 'she needs us, and what are we doing? We're doing nothing. That's what we're doing.'

'What do you want from me, Jack?'

'I want you to fight, the way you always fight.'

'I am fighting.'

'No, you've given up. The minute you drove her into that place you gave up on her.'

'How dare you?'

'We didn't even discuss it.' He was shouting now. His face was red and his fists were balled.

'What is there to talk about?' Molly roared back.

'Rabbit, our little girl, is dying and we're supposed to protect her, Molly. Why aren't we doing everything we can to save her?'

Molly was rooted to the spot. Her heart was aching, her stomach turning and her brain somersaulting. She needed to sit: her legs threatened to give way. She moved towards the chair. Her face must have paled so considerably that her husband, despite his anger, jumped out of bed, pulled out the dressing-table stool and settled her on it. She put her face into her hands and considered what he had said as he waited for her response. *Fight for her, Molly, for God's sake. If you can't do it, no one can.*

Molly looked up into his eyes and spoke quietly but firmly. 'If you ever accuse me of giving up on one of my kids again, I'll take a carving knife to you.' She stood up and grabbed her dressing-gown.

'Molly!' Jack shouted after her. 'Please!' His voice was breaking. 'I'm begging you! Get her out of that death house, Molly.'

'Fuck you.' Molly walked onto the landing, biting back tears of anger and frustration. *How dare you, Jack Hayes? How could you?*

Davey was at the top of the stairs. 'He didn't mean it, Ma.'

'He did.'

'Please, he's just—'

'Blaming me.'

'It's not like that.'

'It's exactly like that,' she said. 'He's a coward, snivelling in her face, avoiding the responsibility, leaving it all up to me, then judging how I handle it. How fucking dare he?' She went into the bathroom and slammed the door. Then she opened it, came out onto the landing and screamed as loudly as she could: 'I have not given up, Jack Hayes. I will never give up, do you hear me?'

She turned back into the bathroom, closed the door and cried till she couldn't cry any more.

Rabbit

Rabbit hated bed baths.

'Oh, please run me a bath,' she begged Michelle.

'Are you sure?' Michelle asked, her gloved hands resting on her hips.

'I'd like to float for a while,' Rabbit said.

'OK, but I'm staying with you.'

'Fine.'

'Good.'

'You can tell me your troubles,' Rabbit said.

'I don't have any troubles.' Michelle laughed. 'I'm the luckiest woman in the world.'

'Everyone has troubles,' Rabbit said. 'Give me something.'

'Let me think about it.'

'You have till the bath is drawn.'

'You're bossy, aren't you?' Michelle said.

'You have no idea,' Rabbit replied, with a smile.

She was lying in a bath of bubbles with a facecloth placed on her bony chest and her eyes closed. The water was so high it touched her chin.

'Don't slip now,' Michelle said, dropping the lid onto the toilet and sitting on it.

'Tell me your story,' Rabbit said.

'I asked my boyfriend of five years to marry me and he said no.'

Rabbit opened her eyes. 'And?'

'And he told me he had met someone else.'

'And?'

'We're still living together in separate rooms.'

'Why?'

'Because we bought a house that's worth half of what we paid for it, and even if we rented it out it wouldn't cover a quarter of the mortgage.'

'And the girl?'

'She shares his room a few times a week.'

'Jesus, that's terrible. It's not stage-four-cancer terrible, but it sucks big-time.'

'Thanks, I appreciate the sympathy,' Michelle said.

'Are you seeing anyone?' Rabbit asked.

'I slept with an old boyfriend a week after we split up, but it was terrible . . . not stage-four-cancer terrible, but it sucked big-time.' Michelle mimicked Rabbit, making Rabbit giggle.

'Do you like anyone?' Rabbit asked.

'Nope, you?'

'Mr Dunne's not bad,' Rabbit said.

'Wow! That's an image I really don't care for.'

'Well, it's not like I get out much,' Rabbit said, by way of explanation. 'Besides, he's nice, good bedside manner. He's been with me since this all started.'

They were quiet for a while, both comfortable in silence; neither felt the need to fill empty space with meaningless words. After about ten minutes, Rabbit opened her eyes again and raised herself slightly. 'I'm not planning on dying.'

'I know,' Michelle said.

'I'm determined to get out of here.'

'OK.'

'You don't think I can,' Rabbit said.

'I meet the most extraordinary people every day, Rabbit, men, women and children who survive days, weeks, months and years against all the odds. I won't count you out.'

'Thank you.' Rabbit closed her eyes and slipped down into the bath again. 'It's lovely in here,' she said. 'I could stay like this for ever.'

When Rabbit found it difficult to hold her head up and was sleepy, threatening to slip under the water, Michelle lifted her out, wrapped her in warm towels and wheeled her into her bedroom. She dressed her in clean, soft, fragrant pyjamas and helped her into bed. Once she'd given Rabbit her pain meds, she tucked her in.

'Ma will be here soon,' Rabbit said.

'What about your dad?' Michelle asked.

'I think he's afraid to come here.'

'I understand that,' Michelle said, but Rabbit didn't respond. 'And Juliet.'

'Who's that?'

'She's my little girl.'

'What age is she?'

'Twelve.'

'And her dad?'

'A fling I had with an Australian guy who doesn't even know she's alive.'

'You're a dark horse,' Michelle said.

'I tried to track him down on Facebook once, but he's either dead or living in a cave. That's why it's so important I don't leave her, not yet.'

Rabbit's eyes were closing and she was fighting hard to stay awake to make her point. 'I'm staying right here. You're not getting your room back any time soon.' She was so tired her words were slurring a little.

'I'll hold you to that,' Michelle said. 'Now get some sleep. You'll need your strength when your family arrives.'

Rabbit was asleep before Michelle made it to the door of the room.

Later she woke to find a hairdresser, a tall girl called Lena, from Russia, putting highlights in Molly's hair. Michelle propped her up so that she could watch. Davey read the newspaper out loud and grumbled that the only article Molly and Rabbit were interested in was about a heartbroken novelist whose husband had left her for her sister.

'You couldn't make it up,' Molly said, and the Russian agreed.

'They should be shot,' she declared. 'Two bullets, one for each of them.'

'I read two of her novels,' Rabbit said. 'She's good.'

'Well, at least she got another book out of it,' Molly said.

'Bestseller,' Lena said.

'Every cloud,' Rabbit said.

It was nice, Davey reading the newspaper and grumbling, Molly getting her hair done, the hairdresser telling them about her holiday in Spain. It felt normal for a while, as if things could actually go back to the way they once were. Rabbit would recover and leave. She'd go back to work and raising Juliet. *It can still work out.*

Molly looked much better with her hair done. Lena even inspired her to put on some makeup, telling her that darker eyes and a nude lip would suit her best. Molly applied it in the mirror while Lena massaged Rabbit's head and Davey moved on to articles about the economy.

'OK, what do we want? "Government hopeful of bank deal" or "Policy of extend and pretend can't go on indefinitely" or "Tacit admission that austerity isn't working"?'

'I still don't know what a promissory note is,' Rabbit admitted.

'IMF, ESM, promissory notes, austerity all mean two things: the death of Irish democracy and the middle classes,' Molly said, 'and those fuckers in government are too stupid, too frightened or too corrupt to do anything about it. We need to bring back hanging.'

'Jaysus, Ma, don't hold back,' Davey said, and Rabbit and Lena laughed.

Grace arrived with Juliet in her school uniform just after five o'clock. She was hassled and Juliet was anxious.

'You look good, Ma,' Juliet said. Her voice was a little shaky but she kept a smile firmly plastered across her face.

Rabbit hugged her daughter for a long time. She kissed the top of Juliet's head and whispered three words in her daughter's ear. Grace remained silent during their exchange. When Juliet finally let go, Rabbit turned to Grace. She needed to lighten the mood before somebody cried. 'Go on, bitch about the traffic. You know you want to.'

Grace dutifully obliged. 'Over an hour to drop Jeffrey off to the clinic for bloods. We could have walked there quicker, and don't talk to me about crossing the river to this place.'

Juliet laughed. 'Grace called a man in a BMW a wonky-nosed wanker.' She pushed herself back on the chair and swung her feet.

Rabbit smiled at her daughter. 'A wonky-nosed wanker, huh?'

Juliet nodded and pushed her nose to the side. 'It was like this.'

Rabbit chuckled. It was lovely to see Juliet acting her age.

Grace held her hands up. 'I'm a bad person.'

'How is Jeffrey?' Rabbit asked.

'He's fine. We've caught it in time.'

'Good,' Rabbit said, and everyone in the room silently wished the same could be said for her.

'How's the diet going?' Rabbit asked, with an inward smile, because she knew her nephew would be having none of it.

'He's threatening to run away.'

'Not to worry, he won't get far,' Molly said, and Davey laughed.

'Not funny,' Grace said. 'Bloody Ryan keeps calling him Fat Chops and I swear to God if Stephen tells one more fat joke I'm going to scream.'

'He's lost three pounds already,' Juliet told Rabbit.

'That's great.'

'Yeah,' Juliet said. 'How are you feeling, Ma?'

'Great,' Rabbit lied.

'When are you coming home?'

'I don't know yet, Bunny.'

When Juliet was born, her grandfather, Jack, had announced that Rabbit had a bunny, and although the name hadn't stuck, it had become a term of endearment. Juliet grabbed a chair and dragged it as close to the bedside as she could. She sat down and took the moisturizer from her mother's locker, opened it and began to smooth it onto Rabbit's right hand.

'Because *I* can take care of you. I know your meds and we can turn the dining room into a bedroom if you can't go up the stairs.'

'You always take care of me,' Rabbit said, brushing the hair out of Juliet's face with her free hand.

'So let's go home,' Juliet said.

'You have school.'

'I can take a week off, or I can get up extra early to do what's needed, and we can ask Mrs Bird to drop in when I'm not there. I can leave a list of your meds and stay in touch with both of you by phone. Jane Regan lost her job two weeks ago so she's home all day too.'

'You've thought of everything,' Rabbit said.

'So?'

'So let's see how I am next week,' Rabbit said.

Juliet looked as though she was going to burst into tears but she feigned a smile and nodded.

'OK,' she said, then squeezed out some more moisturizer and massaged her mother's other hand. Everyone else in the room was silent. The weight of Rabbit's lies lay heavily on every shoulder . . . but maybe she was right, maybe she'd be OK, despite everything Mr Dunne had said. After all, he was a consultant, not God.

When Rabbit's pork chop was served, Juliet cut it up small. 'Just try a little bit with some spud, Ma.'

Rabbit obeyed, but it was all she could do to swallow three spoonfuls. 'Lovely,' she said, and Juliet seemed pleased.

'Would you like the ice-cream?' she asked, taking the lid off the pot. Rabbit shook her head: she'd had enough. Juliet held it up. 'Who wants ice-cream?'

Grace and Davey's hands went up. Juliet looked at her mother. 'The power,' she said, and Rabbit grinned.

'Go on, give it to Grace,' Davey said.

'Yeah, come on, I'm living on greens with Jeffrey.'

The others laughed. 'Ha-ha,' Grace said, grabbing the ice-cream and spoon. 'Oh, yeah, that hits the spot.'

Juliet looked at her mother to share in the fun, but Rabbit had drifted away.

Davey nodded at Molly. 'Let's see what's on the box, Ma.' Molly turned on the TV and Juliet watched an old episode of *Friends*, holding her mammy's hand.

Johnny

It was the night of Kitchen Sink's first TV appearance. All the lads were getting ready at Davey's after a quick rehearsal. Francie and Jay's uncle Terry was to pick them up in his bread van, which doubled as the band's tour bus. Grace was going with her da and even though her ma wouldn't be found dead dancing around some TV studio, she was as nervous and excited as anyone else. The show was Ireland's answer to *Top of the Pops* and it was a big deal to be asked on. That night Kitchen Sink would share the stage with stars from the UK and the USA. Francie and Jay were so excited they kept punching each other and getting into scraps. Davey kept running to the toilet until Molly was forced to medicate him.

'Now I won't have a shite for a week,' he grumbled.

'Better than having one on stage.'

Louis needed help with his braces. 'I think they're broken, Mrs H.'

'They're not. Just calm down and stop dancing about,' Molly said.

Grace was necking vodka and orange with her friend Emily, both dressed to the nines but still preening each other every five minutes.

Johnny was quiet, sitting in a corner, dressed like a rock star and ready to play. Rabbit was beside him, strumming his guitar.

'Don't do that, Rabbit,' Jack said. 'We don't want it going out of tune.'

'It's all right, Mr H,' Johnny said. 'Rabbit knows what she's doing.'

Rabbit wasn't allowed to go because she was too young. She'd moaned about it most of the day to her best friend, Marjorie.

'When's Uncle Terry arriving?' Johnny asked.

'In about half an hour,' Francie answered.

'Grand. So we have time for some tea,' Jay said.

'Good man, put on the kettle,' Molly said.

'I don't feel much like tea. How about we go for a walk, Rabbit?' Johnny suggested, and Rabbit nodded enthusiastically.

'It's freezing out there,' Molly said.

'Just need to clear me head, Mrs H,' Johnny said.

'Well, put on coats and, Rabbit, gloves, hat and a scarf. I don't need you coming down with something this week.'

Rabbit and Johnny left together, Rabbit looking like the Michelin Man, but even with Jack's big old heavy funeral coat on over his ripped jeans, loose shirt and purple velvet jacket, with a tea-cosy hat, Johnny still looked like a rock star.

They walked around the corner and his silence made Rabbit nervous. She wanted him to talk or maybe he wanted her to talk but she didn't know what to say. *Say something cool. Say something cool. Say something cool.*

'What?' He'd read her mind.

'Nothing.'

'You're pissed off you're not coming tonight,' he said.

'Oh, yeah. I am.'

He grinned. He grabbed her hand walking across the road, letting it go as soon as they hit the other side.

They walked up the steps of the church and Rabbit followed Johnny inside. It was empty and dark, save for a few red candles glowing in the corner.

'It's weird in here,' Rabbit whispered.

'But kinda cool, don't you think?'

'No,' she said, and he smiled at her.

'You are the only person aside from my own family who dis-agrees with me.'

'Really?'

'Really.'

'Everyone disagrees with me,' Rabbit said.

They sat down side by side.

'What are we doing here?' Rabbit wondered.

'I always come here before a show.'

'Why?'

'It's where I find peace.'

'Oh.'

'What about you, Rabbit, where do you find peace?'

'I've never really looked for it,' she said.

He lit a candle, knelt and prayed. Rabbit sat and waited while he mumbled to himself and drew crosses on his chest with his right hand. She felt awkward, embarrassed even, and she wasn't sure why, but she really wanted to get out of the place. As she descended the steps, she braced herself for him to hold her hand to cross the road. When he took it, she looked up at him and grinned widely. 'You'll be amazing tonight,' she said.

'We'll see.'

'I don't have to see,' she said. 'Ma said you were born for this and my ma knows things.'

'Yeah, she does.'

They turned the corner and saw the lads piling the gear into the back of Uncle Terry's van. Johnny arrived just in time for Francie to point out that he was a lazy wanker, always arriving just after all the work was done.

'That's singers for ya,' Jay said. 'Pox bottles the lot of them.'

Johnny didn't care. He just jumped into the back of the van and the lads bundled in after him. Uncle Terry climbed into the front seat. Davey was last in, running out of the house shouting, 'I'm coming, I'm coming!' Johnny beat the side of the van with his hand as Jack shut the doors and Uncle Terry took off down the road.

Grace and Emily were already in Jack's car, giggling and talking excitedly. Jack looked at his youngest daughter. 'Your day will come, Rabbit, and way sooner than you think.'

'Not sooner,' she said. 'Sooner would be yesterday.'

'We'll have a party on the night it's shown on the telly,' Jack promised.

'Yeah?' Rabbit jumped up and down. 'Can Marjorie come?'

'Of course she can.'

'Thanks, Da.'

'Who loves ya?' Jack said.

'Me da does,' she replied, and hugged him. *And I love Johnny Faye.*

Jack

Jack arrived alone. He met Fiona in Reception and she pointed him in his daughter's direction, although she did mention politely that Rabbit already had a lot of people with her.

Michelle was passing at the time. 'Jack Hayes?'

'Yes.'

'Good to see you. I'm Michelle. Why don't you follow me?' she said, then turned to Fiona. 'I'll take it from here.' Fiona nodded and Jack went with Michelle down the hallway.

'She's doing well. She'll be happy to see you.'

Jack remained silent. Michelle opened the door, revealing Rabbit, Juliet, Grace, Davey and Molly.

'Hi, Da,' Rabbit said, smiling.

He could see that she was anxious he might cry in front of Juliet so the 'hi' sounded extra-buoyant and her eyes pleaded with him to stay strong. He read his daughter's mind and body language. *I'm not going to cry, Rabbit. I promise. I'll be stronger for you. I won't let you down. Not today.* 'Hi, your-self,' he said, matching her tone.

'Grace, Davey, Molly, could I see you for a minute?' Michelle said, and suddenly they were gone, leaving Rabbit with her dad and her daughter.

Jack sat on the sofa and picked up Davey's newspaper. 'Depressing,' he said. 'If it's not about the shite we're in, it's about that bloody politician's death. I've seen more programming about that woman in the past two days than I saw through her entire time in government. Hated her back then but in the end . . .' He trailed off, realizing he'd stumbled on a difficult topic.

'Who was she?' Juliet asked.

'She was a very important figure when we were growing up,' Rabbit said.

'It was all doom and gloom back then,' Jack said.

'Kinda like now,' Juliet said.

'Exactly, Bunny,' Jack agreed.

'Ma.'

'Yes, love?'

'When you're better, let's go away,' Juliet said.

Jack's eyes widened and bulged.

'Where do you want to go?' Rabbit asked.

'Let's go to Clare.'

'Back to that little cottage by the sea, the one we went to when you were eight?' Rabbit said.

'We could go when I finish school in June,' Juliet said.

'You spent all day every day in the sea. I had eye strain from watching the water.' Rabbit chuckled. 'What was the name of that boy you played with?'

'Bob.'

'Poor Bob followed Juliet wherever she went,' Rabbit explained to Jack. 'He loved her.'

'Ma!' Juliet said, feigning embarrassment, then breaking into a smile. 'He spent that whole summer standing in the water with his teeth chattering and asking can we go in yet.'

'He was sweet,' Rabbit said.

'He's a really good golfer now,' Juliet said.

'How do you know?'

'Facebook.'

'Oh. That's nice.'

'So? Can we go back?' Juliet asked.

'We'll see.' Rabbit took her daughter's hand, squeezed it, then put it to her lips and kissed it.

Jack stood and made an excuse about needing water. His body and mind were colluding: tears were brewing and threatening to spill. He wasn't sure if he was strong enough to will them away. He knew if he cried in front of his daughter his wife would find out and kick him. He couldn't stay. He had to go. He needed to do something. *Oh, Rabbit, if only* . . . 'Anybody want anything?' he asked.

Juliet looked into her mother's eyes and brushed her eyebrows with a finger.

'It will be no time before school ends,' Juliet said, 'and then we'll be free to do what we want.'

Rabbit nodded. Jack saw that she was fighting the urge to sleep.

'It's OK, Ma,' Juliet said. 'Go back to sleep – it's getting late anyway.'

Rabbit's eyes rolled back and she was gone before Juliet said, 'I love you.'

Jack practically ran out of the room. He felt awful about making an excuse to leave his granddaughter alone with her mother. She didn't seem to mind, though. Of everyone bar Molly, she was the most comfortable around Rabbit. He walked down the hospice corridor and, instead of finding Davey, Molly and Grace, he turned right into the prayer room. Molly was still so angry with him and he with her, and the kids were going through enough without their parents picking at one another. He knew it was unreasonable to blame Molly for Rabbit's condition, but he couldn't help himself. He relied on her to sort things out – he always had. They'd had a silent pact since the day they married. He'd provide for them and she'd protect them. She was a shit-kicker, his missus, and it was one of the things he loved and honoured most about her. He could be a gentleman because his wife was no lady and it had worked for them for more than forty years; but now, when he needed her to take them over the top, she was laying down her arms. *Why, Molly, why?* Jack was angry with her for conceding defeat, with himself for being weak and, worse, with Rabbit for threatening to leave them.

Jack had boxed as a young man but he hadn't hit anyone in forty-one years and never outside a ring. He wanted to box something or someone. He wanted to kick, punch and pummel, and he wanted to be kicked, punched and pummelled. He yearned for black eyes and swollen lips, cracked ribs and burst knuckles. That kind of pain he could tolerate, but not the gnawing heartache that manifested as a constant, dull, crushing pain, which threatened to take his breath away but never quite did. *This must be what it feels like to drown.*

He looked around the room, at the blue, yellow and red stained glass, at the painting of Jesus on the cross, at the table, covered with a white linen cloth, that served as the altar and at the heavy iron cross that stood on it. The room was painted cream and the lights were set to dim. He was sitting on one of twenty wooden chairs. He'd been to many prayer rooms in his day, mostly with Johnny. It was impossible to sit there without being transported back in time.

The room he remembered best was bigger and filled with statues. Johnny liked to call them by name and he'd talk to them as though they were old friends; sometimes when he was angry he treated them more like enemies. Johnny once told the statue of Padre Pio to go fuck himself, and Jack still blushed at the boy's suggestion for the Virgin Mary. Now he couldn't enter a prayer room or pass a church without thinking of Johnny. *God is good, Jack*, he'd said time and time again. *The poor deluded bastard*, Jack often thought, but he kept his reservations to himself. He had often listened to that boy talk about God and the next life, but he wasn't sure if he'd believed in God even back then, and he was definitely sure he didn't believe in God now. *Rabbit was right*. The kid was always suspicious of the religion she was born into. When she was five, she'd told her teacher that she didn't like the God in the Old Testament because He was really mean, and the New Testament was horrible because it made her cry. Why would a father send his son to earth to be killed in such a disgusting way? How does that save anyone? she'd ask, stumping her teacher. When she was a teenager she'd bought a red clay Buddha in a charity shop, and when her mother asked her why she wanted it, she told her she preferred to look at a fat god laughing rather than a skinny one dying. Rabbit never needed to believe in any god to marvel at the world, to feel joy, hope, love and contentment. Rabbit lived in the moment. She didn't know what came next, nor did she care. It was likely that death meant a full stop and that didn't scare her. In fact, when she thought about it, the notion of eternity was far more worrying.

'I get bored if I have to spend longer than an hour at the hairdresser's,' she'd said to him once. 'No way could I do eternity – even the word gives me chills, Da.'

For Rabbit, a full stop was her reward. Jack wondered if she still felt the same. He wondered if she would find God in these her darkest hours. Would she pray for a Heaven? She had lied to her daughter: Rabbit was a lot of things but she was never a liar. Much like her mammy, she'd shoot from the hip, tell it like it was, no matter how much trouble it got her into. It was probably what made her a good journalist, but she also had a habit of alienating those who preferred a pleasant lie to an uncomfortable truth. He was scared she couldn't accept what was happening, or maybe she just didn't know. If she was still in the acute hospital surely there would be some hope, but here, in a hospice, well, people only came to these places to die. *Molly should have fought the consultant. People listen to Molly. They do what she tells them to do. It's all so wrong. And Rabbit, my little Rabbit, hasn't she suffered enough in this lifetime?* Although the logical, rational Jack didn't believe in God, his indoctrination over the course of his life, and most especially during his early years, meant that he often found himself talking to the God he didn't believe existed. *How could you? Why would you do this to her? I don't want to believe in a God like you. I'd rather she's right and there is no afterlife than an eternity spent honouring a psychopath like you.*

'There! I said it,' he shouted to the painting on the wall. 'If you do exist I hate you.'

'I doubt you're alone there,' a woman said. She was sitting two rows behind him.

Jack turned and blushed. 'I'm so sorry. I thought I was alone.'

'You were lost in thought so I didn't want to bother you.' She got up and walked over to him, sat down beside him and put out her hand. 'I'm Rita Brown, the medical social worker assigned to Rabbit and her family. I saw you coming from her room.'

'Jack Hayes, Rabbit's father.'

'Would you like to talk, Jack?' she asked.

'There's nothing to say.'

'That's not true.'

He looked at the woman and shook his head. 'I'm lost.'

'And Molly?'

'She's given up on our girl . . .'

'But you haven't?'

'. . . and Molly never gives up on anything.' His eyes stung.

'Have you talked?'

'She threatened to stab me this morning. Does that count?'

'Your daughter is looking for you,' Molly's voice said.

Rita and Jack turned to her. Her face of thunder suggested she'd heard at least part of their conversation.

'Please come in and sit down for a moment,' Rita said.

'No.'

'Molly, please, I'm sorry,' Jack said.

'No, you're not. You think I've brought her here to die.'

'Haven't you?' He got to his feet.

She walked up to him. 'Of course not, you old fool. I'm buying us some time.'

'For what?' He was battling tears.

'For science, for medicine, for a miracle, but in the meantime she's in pain, Jack, and they can manage it much better here.'

'Our Rabbit is dying, Molls,' Jack said. His jaw trembled and his eyes leaked.

'I won't let her,' Molly said, and her tears flowed freely. They walked into each other's arms and held on tight.

'I'm so sorry, love,' he said.

'I know you are, ya big bollocks.'

When they parted, Rita was gone. 'She's like a panther, that one,' Molly said, grabbing her husband's hand. 'Now, let's put a brave face on and tonight we'll go back online.'

He nodded and sighed. *It's going to be OK.*

Chapter Four

Molly

THE TABLE WAS COVERED with all of Rabbit's copied files, charts, X-rays and scans. Molly made tea while Jack scoured the internet for some good news. An hour and two chicken salads later, he found a new site, which offered trials that seemed to include stage-four patients.

'Let's do it,' Molly said. She spread all of Rabbit's details in front of her and grabbed a notebook and pen.

Jack clicked on the button that read 'Match to Trials' in line with the statement 'I have metastatic (stage IV) disease. I have cancer that has spread from my breast to other parts of my body.'

Jack rubbed his hands together. 'And we're in, Molls, we're in. Do we have the pathology report and treatment history?'

'What do you take me for?'

He grinned at her.

'OK, OK, I've read the conditions, click, I'm resident in Europe, click, pressing start . . . Here we go. OK, "About me".'

Molly looked over his shoulder at the questions. Before he'd even finished reading 'date of birth', she was rattling off the answers.

'Twelfth of September 1972, female, "no" for genetic testing and "no" for currently on a clinical trial.'

Jack keyed in the answers. 'OK. "My current health".'

'Key in the last option,' Molly said.

He read it. 'Ah, no, Molls, the second last one. "I require a large amount of assistance and frequent medical care."'

'Jack, we've got to be realistic.'

'She's not completely disabled and she's only confined to a bed because we put her in that place.'

'She can't do anything for herself, and if she wasn't confined to a hospice bed, it would be another bed.'

'Completely disabled? We've seen completely disabled and it's not our girl.'

'Click "completely disabled".'

'No.'

'Jack.'

'They won't take her, Molly.'

'They won't take her if we lie to them, love. Now press the fucking button.'

With a heavy heart Jack clicked on the worst-case scenario.

'Good. Now click "none of the above" for "other diseases".'

'There's a load of them there – we should read through them.'

'No need. Aside from stage-four cancer, Rabbit Hayes is as healthy as a racehorse,' Molly said. Once again, Jack did as he was told. The next tab was more clinical. Molly scanned through it quickly and delivered answers to questions Jack found difficult to pronounce. 'Positive, negative, positive, bone, lung, liver and "no" to lymphoedema. Next.'

Jack nodded. 'All right, calm down. My fingers aren't as quick as your brain.'

The next tab was on the topic of Rabbit's treatments and, again, Molly didn't even have to look at the notes before she rattled off the answers to every question. The lists were endless and laborious but she knew every tedious detail.

'Are you sure she was on AC followed by Taxol? The next one down is AC followed by—'

Molly flicked open the file, which she had tabbed with coloured stickers months previously. 'See there.' She pointed.

'Fair enough.'

'Next tab,' she prompted.

They moved on to racial type and schooling, although Jack had a hard time wondering why that mattered. Then they reviewed the health summary and agreed it was correct. They looked at the button marked 'Finished/Find Trials' for the longest minute. Molly prayed silently. 'Just click it, Jack, before the bleedin' thing times out and we have to start again.'

He nodded slowly, gulped loudly, stretched his neck and clicked. It took less than two seconds to tell them that Rabbit was eligible for twenty-six trials.

'Twenty-six bloomin' trials, Molls.' Jack jumped to his feet.

'Twenty-six trials, Jack.' She stood up and hugged him.

'Twenty-six trials,' he repeated, and waltzed her around the kitchen.

'You see? All's not lost,' she said. 'It's going to be expensive but we'll sell the house.'

'We'll sell the lot. Hell, I'd even sell myself if I thought it would make the difference.'

'Twenty-six trials,' she whispered in his ear.

'It's going to be OK.' He kissed her cheek.

'Right, back to business.' She pulled away. 'You put on the kettle and I'll start studying the difference between hormone, targeted and bisphosphonate therapies. When we go to Dunne tomorrow I want to be armed.'

'Good girl. I'll throw in a few chocolate Wagon Wheels so you can keep up your strength,' Jack said, but she was gone, lost in research. He settled himself in an armchair and watched the tea go cold, the biscuits remain on the plate and his wife studying biology.

Davey

Davey was staring out of Rabbit's window, watching night fall and talking to Francie.

'I'll tell her,' he said, clicking off his phone. He turned to his sister, who was awake and propped up in bed. 'Francie can't make it. Some emergency needs attending to. He'll come tomorrow.' He sat beside her, picked up the TV remote and began whizzing through the channels, like a man possessed.

'It's nice of him to think about coming,' Rabbit said.

'Why wouldn't he?' Davey said, and settled on a channel.

'Do you think I'll ever leave here?' she asked.

He muted the sound. 'Absolutely.' He meant it. If anyone could, it was Rabbit.

'Have you ever heard of anyone leaving a place like this?'

'I haven't asked.' *No.*

'I feel better now than I did this morning.'

'Good.'

'I've heard of one case,' she said.

'You have?'

'There was a sixteen-year-old girl in Munich who was dying of end-stage leukaemia and one day, out of the blue, she got out of her bed and insisted on going for a walk. They couldn't believe it. She hadn't walked in weeks. But she did walk, Davey, she walked right out of the hospice and never went back. She's a teacher now in Hamburg. She has a blog.'

'How?'

'Just happened. No new drugs, no prayers, no voodoo or alternative therapies. She said it was mind over matter. She decided she was going to live so she lived.'

'Do you believe that's possible?' Davey asked.

'I'd like to. I want to. I wish.' A stray tear escaped her right eye and rolled towards her ear.

Davey pulled a tissue from the box on her locker and dabbed it away. 'Me too.' *So do it. Get better and live, live, live, Rabbit.*

'But no pressure.' He grinned and she smiled at him, took his hand and gently squeezed it.

'I missed you,' she said.

Marjorie bustled through the door, laden with shopping. She raised her arms high, allowing the bags to swing. Rabbit gave her a big, warm, welcoming smile. 'You're back, Marj.'

'And of course you missed me because life is very dull without me.' She dropped the bags and put her arms round her friend. 'I leave you for two bleedin' weeks and you end up here.' She was making a valiant effort to be upbeat and Davey silently appreciated it.

'I see you were shopping,' Rabbit said.

'Rome is underestimated as a shopping destination.' She picked up some bags and placed them carefully on the bed, well away from Rabbit's legs.

'You could find something to buy in an Afghan desert,' Rabbit said.

Marjorie grinned. 'Probably me own life, knowing those mental cases.'

'What would that be worth? About a fiver?' Rabbit said.

'LOL, baldy.'

Rabbit giggled.

Marjorie turned to Davey, who was happy watching Rabbit and her best friend banter. 'Am I going to get a hug or wha'?' she asked.

He stood up and obliged her. 'It's good to see you, Marjorie.'

They pulled apart and she brushed his jacket down. 'Still spending most of your time on a bus?'

'Yeah.'

'Looks like it.' She delved into the bags she had put on the bed. 'So, I found this little place that does the most incredible nightwear.' She took out a beautiful black silk nightdress and matching dressing-gown. 'Feel it,' she said.

Rabbit did so. 'It's gorgeous.'

'It's yours.'

'No,' Rabbit said. 'That's something you wear on a dirty weekend. It doesn't belong in a place like this.'

'Well, neither do you, but here you are. It's yours.'

'Thank you.'

'And look,' she said, her hands disappearing into another bag, 'for Juliet.' It was a pretty sundress with cool gold gladiator sandals.

'She'll love them,' Rabbit said.

'And I've got more for you.' She picked up a bag from the floor, but by the time she'd pulled out a woolly cardigan Rabbit was sound asleep. Marjorie slumped into the chair, all pretence gone. Her eyes filled and, without making a sound, she allowed fat tears to roll down both cheeks. She stared at her best friend and it was as though, Davey thought, she was looking at someone she didn't quite recognize. The woman in the bed wasn't her Rabbit. Rabbit had lost a lot of weight in the past two weeks, her skin was paler and dry, her shaved head clammy, and her knuckles dwarfed her fingers. She was an odd colour, somewhere between grey and blue. The last time they'd seen one another, Marjorie had been in town shopping for her trip and Rabbit had come from the newsroom to meet her for a coffee. She was wearing her blonde wig and makeup; her skin was clear, following an intense facial she'd had the day before.

'It was just two weeks ago,' Marjorie whispered.

Davey moved across the room to her, took Marjorie's hand and they walked outside together. The canteen was still open.

'Come on,' he said.

Over coffee, Marjorie filled Davey in on Rabbit's struggle during the past year. 'It's been hard. Every blow took that much more out of her.'

'She's still fighting,' he said.

'I know.' Marjorie's eyes filled. 'And it's only going to get worse from now.'

Davey didn't say anything. He knew she was right, but he

wasn't ready to accept it. He just stirred his coffee with one hand and rapped the table with the other. Neither had the will to make small-talk, or the stomach to engage in their usual flirty banter. They drank their coffee, lost in their own misery.

'I should go,' Marjorie said, and stood up.

'I'll walk you to your car,' Davey said.

'No need. You go back to Rabbit.'

They walked together along the hallway to Rabbit's door. They stopped and faced one another.

'I was really sorry to hear about the divorce.'

'Thank you.'

'I've never apologized for my part in it . . .'

She stopped him by placing her hand on his arm and shaking her head. 'No, honestly, it wasn't you, it was me. Neil is a lovely man and I did love him once, but then I didn't and I faced sleepwalking through the rest of my life or . . .'

'Cheating with me.'

'Being with you woke me up and I'm grateful.'

'How about Neil? Is he grateful?'

'He's seeing someone else and she's pregnant. I hear they're very happy.'

She looks sad. I should never have gone there. I'm a selfish arsehole. 'I should have kept in touch.'

'No. You shouldn't. I didn't want you to.'

'Rabbit was keeping me up to date with everything. She said you handled yourself so well despite everyone piling in to judge and criticize.' *Christ, I could at least have sent an email. What the hell is wrong with me?*

'Every marriage break-up needs a bad guy.'

'Is your mother talking to you yet?'

'No.'

'I'm sorry.'

'My mother is a cold bitch, Davey. She always has been. Why do you think I spent so much time at your place when we were kids? I would have killed to have a mother like yours.'

86

'I thought it was because of me,' he said, and they laughed a little.

'Goodnight, Davey.'

He watched her walk down the hallway before steeling himself to open the door to his sleeping sister. *I let everybody down. I can't do that any more. I have to get my act together. Be an adult, Davey. Fight the urge to run.*

Johnny

Molly had made flapjacks and mugs of tea for everyone. In the sitting room, Francie and Jay were on the sofa, Davey was on the floor, sitting between them even though there was plenty of room for three – the lads liked to stretch out. Grace was swaying on the rocking chair and holding her tea high: if it spilled, it would miss her. Jack was bent over the video recorder, shoving in a tape to see if it was good enough quality to record over. *Miami Vice* appeared on the screen and he paused the tape. 'Molls,' he shouted, 'have you seen *Miami Vice* or will I keep it?'

Molly appeared at the door with another plate of flapjacks. 'I don't give a shit about *Miami Vice*.'

'Ah, great,' Jack said, rewinding it. 'It's a fresh enough tape.'

'Time check?' Francie said, chowing down his third flapjack.

Molly looked at the clock above the mantelpiece. 'Five minutes to show time. I'll make more tea.'

Rabbit sat on the window ledge, watching for Johnny. 'He's going to miss it.'

'Nah,' Jay said. 'He'll be here.'

Marjorie appeared, holding a mug of tea. Francie and Jay bunched up so that she could sit with them. She was a tiny thing, half Rabbit's height, with wild curly blonde hair and baby-blue eyes. She looked younger than her twelve years. Wearing her best Sunday dress and little ankle socks with a pink frill under her favourite patent-leather buckled shoes, she sat up on the sofa, waiting for the show to start.

Rabbit was still glued to the window. *Where is he?*

Molly entered with a fresh pot of tea and the lads all offered her their cups for a refill. She made Grace get off the rocking chair to pass around the flapjacks. Jack refused tea: it would distract him from pressing Record on the remote at the exact second the show started.

'This will be the first, lads,' he said, finger hovering.

While Grace was serving flapjacks, Molly stole her place on the rocking chair.

'Ah, Ma!'

'Don't ah-Ma me, Grace Hayes. Now give me a flapjack, love.'

Rabbit stayed quiet: still no Johnny. *Where are you?* Just when she thought all was lost, he rounded the corner with his hair tied up and his black leather jacket open and flapping. It was a second before she registered the girl he was walking with, arm in arm.

The programme started and Jack went to press Record but in his excitement he knocked the remote off the chair. 'Oh, Lord, no!' he shouted, jumping to his feet.

'Da! Get out of the way,' Grace ordered, from her position on the floor next to Davey, who was hunched over and peering through his father's legs.

'Ah, for God's sake, Jack, will ya move yerself?' Molly said.

'Calm down,' Francie said. 'We're not on till halfway through.'

Jack stood up. 'Maybe I'll wait till you hit the stage. That way I save the tape.'

'No, Da, record now,' Grace said.

'Why?'

'Because I want to see meself in the audience.'

'Right.' He pressed Record just as Johnny entered the room with the mystery girl.

'There you are, son,' Molly said.

'Hiya, Mrs H. This is Alandra.'

Molly nodded and smiled, but everyone else looked at Alandra as if she was an alien.

'Marjorie, sit on the windowsill with Rabbit. Francie, Jay, bunch up for Johnny and Alandra,' Molly ordered. Everyone did as they were told as the two TV presenters talked about the bands that were about to hit the stage. When they mentioned Kitchen Sink, the lads roared and Jack clapped his hands together. Then the room fell quiet and everyone watched the first band intently. No one spoke. Everyone faced forward, except Johnny, who was staring at Alandra, and Rabbit, who was staring at Johnny staring at Alandra. She was tall, with long black silky hair and olive skin, rocking a simple black dress and big silver jewellery. She wasn't just the coolest person Rabbit had ever seen in real life, she was also the most beautiful. Johnny was mesmerized. Rabbit fixed her glasses on her face, holding them against her forehead, and focused on not crying.

When Kitchen Sink were finally introduced the room exploded. Even Davey, who was usually so reserved, raised his arms and hollered. On screen, Davey clicked his sticks together, 'One, two, three, four . . .' beat the drum and the band kicked off. Jack wiped away a tear and Molly rapped on the armrest in time with her son. Rabbit shifted her gaze from Johnny on the sofa to Johnny on stage. He sang so beautifully it made her want to cry even more.

'Are you all right?' Marjorie whispered.

'Fine,' Rabbit said. 'Why?'

''Cause you look like you're in pain.'

'How?'

'Your face is doing this.' She demonstrated.

'Oh.' Rabbit straightened it and glanced at Johnny, who wasn't focused on the TV but on the cool girl, who had intertwined her silver-ringed fingers with his. The sight made Rabbit's stomach knot.

Afterwards, when the band were done and the presenters had cited them the next best thing, Jack rewound the show and watched it ten times over while Molly cleared up and the band went into the garage to work on a new song. Marjorie wondered why Rabbit didn't want to watch them rehearse.

'It's boring,' she said.

'Seriously?' Marjorie didn't believe her friend for a second.

Instead they went outside to sit on the wall. It was a warm night and some lads were playing football on the green. After a while Marjorie joined them. Rabbit remained on the wall, determined to find something interesting in Marjorie and the boys chasing a ball. She heard the side door open and, without turning, she felt Johnny behind her. Alandra was stuck to his hip and they were still hand in hand when they stopped in front of her.

'So, what did you think, Rabbit?' he asked.

'Good.'

'Just good?'

'Great.'

'Good.' He turned to Alandra. 'Alandra, this is my good friend Rabbit.' He turned back to Rabbit. 'Rabbit, this is my girlfriend, Alandra.'

'It's so nice to meet you, Rabbit,' Alandra said, putting out her hand to shake Rabbit's.

My girlfriend? When? How? Why? Rabbit shook Alandra's hand.

'Well, we've got to get going,' Johnny said. 'See ya later, Rabbit.' He raised his hand in the air, and she watched them walking down the road together. *My girlfriend! Makes me wanna puke*, Rabbit thought.

It was dark when Francie and Jay left. Davey called Rabbit in from the wall and Marjorie off the green. 'Hey, short stuff, let's go,' he shouted. Marjorie grinned at him and ran over, happy to do as she was told.

'Hey, Davey, I thought yous were amazing,' she said, as they followed a very unhappy Rabbit inside.

'It's only going to get better from here on in,' he promised.

'When I'm old enough, will ya take me to one of yer shows?' she asked.

'Marjorie, when you're old enough, you and Rabbit will be at every show.'

Marjorie jumped and screeched a little. Rabbit made a face.

'What's with you?' Davey asked.

'I have a life, you know,' Rabbit said.

'News to me.' Davey closed the door.

Later, when Marjorie was clad in her Tinkerbell nightdress and jumping on the bed, singing a medley of Kitchen Sink's songs, Davey found Rabbit sitting on the stairs.

'What's going on?' He sat down beside her.

She looked behind her. 'Grace won't get out of the bathroom.'

'I'm not talking about that.'

'When do you think the Spanish girl is going home?'

'She's here for a year at least, maybe more.' Rabbit looked like she was about to cry. Davey put his arm over her shoulders. It was out of character for him to show affection to his sister, even if he felt it in spades, so the move was slightly awkward. Rabbit looked from his arm on her shoulders to his face.

'He's too old for you, Rabbit.'

'It's only four years. Me da is three years older than me ma,' Rabbit said.

'Four years is a lot when you're only twelve,' Davey said.

'I'll grow up, then.'

Davey laughed a little and nodded. 'OK.' He got up to bang on the bathroom door.

'And, Davey,' Rabbit said, 'when I do it's going to be great.'

Rabbit

Rabbit woke up in a foul mood. Jacinta came as soon as she was called.

'I need another stupid patch.'

'I just changed it an hour ago when you were sleeping.'

'Well, I'm in agony so it must be faulty.'

'Just relax for a minute.' Jacinta felt Rabbit's forehead.

Rabbit pulled away like a bold child. 'Leave it, leave me.'

Jacinta checked Rabbit's chart. 'I can give you a shot.'

'So just do it, then.'

Jacinta left to get the medication. Rabbit stared at the ceiling, counting to ten in her head. When Jacinta reappeared, Rabbit closed her eyes and waited. Once the shot was administered and she felt the liquid rip through her veins, she relaxed enough to respond to Jacinta's shock question.

'So, who's Alandra?'

Rabbit opened her eyes wide. 'What? Why?'

'You were shouting "Fuck Alandra" in your sleep,' Jacinta said, battling to curb her smile.

'I was?'

Jacinta nodded.

Rabbit sighed. 'She was a girl I used to know a long time ago.'

'A girl you didn't like?'

'She was lovely and always kind to me. I was just a jealous kid who wished really bad things would happen to her for the entire time she went out with the boy I loved.'

'Like what?' Jacinta asked, as she sat down.

'Like being hit by a car, run over by a train or brought down in a plane.'

'Remind me not to get on the wrong side of you.'

Rabbit gripped the bed, closed her eyes and her body stiffened. She moaned softly and tears trickled towards her already damp hairline.

'Count to ten.'

'Sick of counting to ten.'

'OK, I'll count down from ten. Ten, nine, eight . . .'

'Please, please, stop,' Rabbit begged.

'Tell me about Alandra.'

'It's not working.'

'Give it another minute.'

'Please, please, please.'

'Tell me about Alandra.'

Rabbit inhaled deeply and opened her eyes. *It's OK, you're OK, just keep talking, Rabbit, and the pain will fade away.*

'She was a stunner, and by the time she left she had a great Dublin accent,' Rabbit said, and smiled at the memory.

'Why did she leave?' Jacinta asked.

'Her father got sick.'

'Your boy must have been very sad to lose her.'

'He didn't seem to be. He was always so aloof and hard to work out.'

'Even for you.'

'Back then, especially for me. It took me a while to learn how to read him.'

'You've stopped gripping the rail.'

'It's passed.'

Jacinta fixed Rabbit's blankets. 'Want to go to the loo while I'm here? I can bring in a bedpan.'

'No.'

'Is there anything else I can do?'

Rabbit was in tears again. 'Just let me sleep.'

Jacinta nodded. 'Goodnight, Rabbit.' She closed the door and left Rabbit alone, blinking at the ceiling. The medication had slowly spread through her body, reaching the top of her head, making a dead weight of her brain, clearing her mind of cognitive thought. With numbness restored, her heavy lids closed and she disappeared into the welcoming darkness.

Rabbit Hayes's Blog

25 September 2009

One in the Hand . . .

Two days after the operation Marjorie began to refer to me as the 'One Tit Wonder'. She's been waiting a whole two weeks for my big reveal. The truth is, I was scared to look. I just couldn't seem to bring myself to stand in front of a mirror and strip off. It sounds vain and stupid – after all, it was only a breast, for God's sake, but it was *my* breast. My left one, specifically.

My mother pointed out last night that I was left-handed and right-breasted, which is a kind of symmetry in itself and, apparently, better than some piece of silicone shoved under my skin. I haven't decided. First, I have to beat cancer. Then I'll think about replacing parts.

So today came along and Marjorie visited with more food than Juliet and I could eat in a year, flowers, wine, two mastectomy bras, a prosthesis and a partridge in a pear tree! It was time to face the music. 'Get it out,' she said. So I stood in my bedroom, and just as I started to take off my top, she shouted, 'Stop!' and proceeded to whip off hers quicker than Matt the Flasher outside Nelly's Newsagent's. In seconds she was standing in front of me bare-chested with a stupid grin. I ripped off my pyjama top and there it was, my right breast, next to ugly, scarred flatland. I didn't want to cry, but I did. I couldn't help it. It wasn't me. Marjorie was quiet. We both just stood in front of the mirror, staring. She didn't try to comfort me or stop me reacting. Instead she handed me a hanky and there we stood until my eyes and nose stopped running.

By the time we replaced our tops my new physique didn't seem as horrifying. I'm not saying I've fully embraced it, but I feel better than I'd thought I would. And Marjorie? Well, she put her top back on and complained bitterly that, even though she still had two, my one was bigger, and you know what they say . . . 'One in the hand . . .'

I love my best friend.

DAY THREE

Chapter Five

Molly

MOLLY AND JACK SAT outside Mr Dunne's office, waiting to be called in. Molly held a large file, thick with details of the various trials for which Rabbit was considered eligible. She clasped it to her chest and rubbed the tips of her fingers on its edge, up and down, up and down, up and down. Jack hung on to a plastic bag, eyes glued to the black hand on the large white wall clock moving silently to mark each passing second. In the background, somewhere in the corridor, a radio was on and voices were debating whether or not the Americans should intervene in Syria. Jack's stomach grumbled. Molly shifted her hand from the file to her pocket and pulled out a bag of nuts and seeds for him. He took it without a word and ate the contents, all the while keeping his eye on the passing time.

The door opened and Mr Dunne beckoned them inside with a sweep of his hand and a merry hello. He shook their hands and they all sat down. He glanced from the file in Molly's hand to her face and back to the file. His sigh was audible. 'You've been on the net again, Molly.'

'I want to talk to you about some trials happening in Europe, specifically something called PDT.'

'Photodynamic therapy.'

'You've heard of it.'

'Yes, I have.'

'Well, then, you'll know that eighty-five per cent of applicants are deemed suitable, including people with deep-seated metastatic and late-stage cancers.'

'The effectiveness depends on many factors.'

'Doesn't everything?'

'Rabbit has a compromised immune system—'

'Which can reduce effectiveness, but many patients have still shown significant favourable responses with PDT in spite of prior heavy chemotherapy.'

'In Rabbit's case, the tumour has spread to critical structures.'

'I'm not saying it will cure her, but it could still prolong her life.'

'Molly, PDT is in its infancy. It's not covered by insurance and it's not available in this country.'

'So, so and so?'

'Rabbit is a late-stage palliative patient who is a very likely candidate to suffer from complications that can arise from rapid necrosis of tissue around the major arteries and some other areas of the body. That's if she would even be considered, which she wouldn't be because she's bed-ridden.'

'She is not bed-ridden,' Jack said, as if the very idea was an insult to his daughter.

'She is non-ambulatory, Jack.'

'What?'

'She can't walk independently.'

'Because she's got a broken fucking leg,' Molly said.

'She has a broken leg because her bones are compromised by cancer. It's too much.'

Molly and Jack shared a look of despair, then Molly shook it off. 'Fine,' she said.

Mr Dunne moved to stand.

'Ah, where are you going?'

'I thought we were finished.'

She snorted. 'We're only getting started. Jack, break out the sandwiches.'

Jack reached into the bag he was carrying. 'Chicken and stuffing, ham salad or tuna mayo?' he offered Mr Dunne.

'I'll take a ham salad,' Mr Dunne said, conceding defeat.

'Right. Bisphosphonate therapies, pros and cons,' Molly said.

Forty-five minutes later, Molly was on her feet shouting about advances in hormone therapy, and accusing the Irish medical system of being both backward and corrupt. Mr Dunne remained calm and even-toned. He repeated that he understood their anger and frustration, then explained again why the particular therapy Molly was pitching wouldn't work. Molly flopped back into her seat and flicked through her file until she realized she had exhausted every option.

'Twenty-six trials! Twenty-six! One of them will take her. I don't care how much it costs.'

'Maybe, but if they do, it will be experimental, not curative and not palliative. It's not what you want for her.'

The file fell onto the floor. She put her head into her hands and rubbed her temples, then met the doctor's eye. 'There has to be something we can do.'

'There is.'

'What?'

'You can prepare her.'

Molly shook her head. 'There has to be something else.'

Jack stood up slowly and took his wife's hand. 'Thank you, Doctor.'

Molly looked up at him, confused. 'No, Jack, wait.'

'It's all right, Molls. We'll keep looking.' He glanced towards the doctor. 'Sorry to take up your time.'

'It's fine, Jack. I understand.'

Molly hung her head and bit back her tears. 'I'm sorry for shouting, Mr Dunne.'

'It's nothing,' he said.

'We're grateful for everything you've done.'

'If you have any more questions you know where I am.'

Jack helped Molly from her chair and they walked out of the office, leaving the file on the floor.

They arrived at Rabbit's door in time to hear her agonized cries and Michelle's soothing words of comfort. 'Hang in there, Rabbit, any second now.'

'I can't, I can't – please help me.'

'Nearly there,' Michelle said, and Rabbit sobbed.

When Michelle emerged five minutes later, she walked into Molly and Jack, holding each other tightly. 'She's been suffering a little more breakthrough pain, but Mr Dunne's team have been notified and we will fix it.'

'I should go to her,' Molly said.

'She's sleeping. She'll be sleeping for a while. Why don't you both get out of here? It's a beautiful day and, God knows, we don't get many of them.'

Molly looked to Jack for guidance.

'I think that's a good idea, Michelle,' he said.

'I just want to see her before I go,' Molly said.

'Of course.'

Michelle opened the door to reveal tiny Rabbit, lost in blankets and shallow breathing.

'Her head looks bigger than her body,' Molly said, moving closer, picking up a tissue and wiping the sweat from Rabbit's brow.

'It's bloating,' Michelle said.

'It's terrifying,' Molly said sadly, then bent to kiss her daughter's face.

They left her to sleep and sat in the car for a minute or two before Jack attempted to put the key into the ignition.

'I think we should call in Michael Gallagher,' Molly said.

'Who?'

'The seventh-son faith-healer.'

'Oh, Molly.' Jack rubbed his tired eyes.

'I know what you're thinking, but he has an eighty-five per cent success rate.'

'He didn't cure Johnny.'

'He was in the fifteen per cent. Maybe we'll get lucky this time.'

Jack turned to face his wife. 'Johnny had faith. He believed God would cure him. Remember the hours spent queuing for a glimpse of Mother Teresa, the quest for Padre Pio's glove and every bloody saint's scapular from John of the Cross to St Bernadette? It's a wonder he didn't strangle himself with all he had hanging from his neck. It didn't work for him when he believed so fervently. How do you expect it to work for Rabbit when she doesn't believe in all that mumbo-jumbo?'

'It's not mumbo-jumbo. Michael saved that woman's sight. I met her. She was blind all her life and after he had laid hands on her she could see.'

He sighed. 'And there's no chance she was making up stories?'

'I'm not a fool, Jack.'

'I'm not saying you are.'

'There are so many things we don't understand.'

'Well, I know one thing,' he said.

'What's that?'

'If you bring some self-styled agent of God into Rabbit Hayes's room, it's him who'll need healing by the end of it.'

'So we'll do it when she's asleep.'

'You're joking.'

'I am not.'

Jack turned the engine on. 'I can see this going wrong,' he said, then drove off. 'Where to?' he asked.

'Home. I need to find the number.'

'We haven't given up on finding a treatment, though, have we, Molly?'

'I'm not giving up on anything, Jack.'

'Good woman.'

I'm not giving up, do you hear me, God? she screamed in her head. *Does anybody fucking hear me?*

Juliet

The lunch bell went and not a minute too soon. Miss Baker had been banging on about osmosis for the full fifty minutes. She had a propensity to overcomplicate the easiest of topics: seemingly enthralled by her own intelligence, she never realized her entire classroom was silent not because they were engaged but simply because they had collectively lost the will to live. Juliet shoved her books into her backpack and walked quickly towards the door. Kyle caught up with her in the corridor.

'How's yer ma?'

'Good, thanks.'

'Oh, yeah?' He seemed genuinely surprised.

'Yeah, why?' Juliet was shocked by his reaction.

'Oh, nothin'.' He went puce red.

Kyle was a nice kid, not a master of deceit. Juliet surveyed him and decided against pushing the matter. Instead she made the position clear. 'She'll be home next week, maybe the week after at the latest.'

'Oh, great, good, that's brilliant.' He was still puce red.

'Yeah, it is.' She walked away quickly, leaving him standing in the corridor among the passing throng. The encounter disturbed her. *What's his problem?* she wondered. She joined Della in the canteen. Della had already bought and paid for two baked potatoes, with tuna, and bottled water for them both. Juliet dropped her bag and sat. 'Thanks.'

'No problem.'

'Saw Kyle after class.'

'Yeah? Does he still love you?' Della asked, and made kissing sounds.

'He was acting weird,' Juliet said, choosing to ignore Della's stupid insinuation.

'That's because he is weird.'

'He's not weird, Della.'

'If you say so.'

Kyle was Juliet's neighbour and they had been friends since they were two years old. He was shy and didn't like to mix with the kids in school: he had enough pals on the motorcycle track where he spent at least three hours every evening. His dad, Charlie, was a dedicated motocross racer, and even though he'd pretty much broken every bone in his body, he'd introduced Kyle to the sport as soon as he'd turned five. Kyle was a natural and his dad was grooming him to be a champion. Kyle and his dad had come to Juliet's rescue when she'd found her mother lying on the kitchen floor with a gruesome open fracture. Rabbit had passed out but she was breathing loudly so Juliet knew she wasn't dead. Juliet had felt panic rising but she battled it. She knew what to do. She'd rung the ambulance, then run over to Charlie, who had been clipping the hedge when she'd passed him less than two minutes earlier. She'd screamed, 'Please help us. She's on the floor. It's bad. Please.' He had dropped the clippers and run for her house. Kyle had come from nowhere and followed him inside. Rabbit had been barely conscious but Charlie shouted for a pair of scissors and a clean tea-towel. Kyle grabbed the scissors from the counter and handed them to his dad, who had cut Rabbit's trouser leg off, exposing the bone jutting through the flesh and the extent of the bleeding.

Juliet's heart was beating so hard it felt like it would break through her skin. She had struggled to control her breathing. 'Oh, no, it's spurting – spurting is bad,' she'd said, and held her hand up to her mouth. Her legs felt weak and she thought she might be sick.

'It's not as bad as it looks,' Charlie said. 'I've seen a lot worse.'

'Me too,' Kyle said, riffling through drawers to find a clean tea-towel. He threw it to his dad, who put pressure on the wound. Rabbit moaned, sounding as if she might choke, but Charlie was on it.

'It's all right, Ma – do you hear me? Charlie knows what he's doing and the ambulance is on the way.' Juliet could hear tears in her voice. She put her hand to her cheek. It was wet.

Kyle disappeared and was back in seconds with a cushion on which his dad rested Rabbit's head. Juliet collected herself: just having them there calmed her enough to think clearly about what had to be done.

'I'll take care of everything, Ma. You don't worry about a thing,' she said, and while her mother was safe in the neighbours' care, Juliet ran around the kitchen grabbing her mother's medicines, her medicine chart and her file, then tore upstairs to get fresh nightclothes and a washbag. By the time the ambulance came, she had a full suitcase packed, including books and snacks for the inevitable long night ahead. Rabbit had passed out again but Juliet talked to her anyway. 'I've packed your favourite nightdress and perfume and that lip balm you like. Everything will be OK now.'

Kyle offered to go with her in the ambulance. It was really nice of him but she declined his offer, and she could tell Charlie was glad that she had: A&E on a Friday night was no place for the average twelve-year-old. He had waved at her as the ambulance doors closed. 'She'll be OK, Juliet,' he shouted. 'Don't worry about anything. We'll watch the house!' Kyle and Juliet hadn't hung out that much since she'd turned eight. She'd found some girls to go about with, and he'd disappeared into his motocross racing, but no matter how little time they had spent together in the past four years, he was always on her side.

Juliet was ruminating on Kyle's earlier reaction to the news of her mother's wellbeing when Della clicked her fingers in her face. 'Hello? Earth calling Juliet?'

'Sorry.'

'Are you going to finish your lunch?'

Juliet pushed it towards her. 'Have it.'

Della finished it off in three bites. 'I'm always hungrier on my period.' She turned towards the counter and surveyed the contents of the glass case. 'You feel like sharing a slice of carrot cake?'

Della was having her fifth period and Juliet hadn't started hers yet, so it pissed her off when Della talked about it. Deep down she knew she wasn't boasting, but it always felt like it.

'Not hungry.'

'Crap, don't want to eat the whole thing myself.'

'So just eat half.'

'You know if it's there I'll eat it.'

'So don't buy it, then.'

'Ah, screw it, I'll have it.' She got up and brought back the slice of cake with two forks. 'Just in case.'

Later, they sat on the grass watching the lads play football. Della was antsy and it wasn't just because she had her period. Juliet pretended not to notice. She was too tired for drama. Grace's sofa did not make for the most comfortable of beds, but even if it hadn't been hard and lumpy, she would have found it difficult to sleep. As soon as she lay down, her brain would take off in so many directions her head actually ached. She'd relive the days, hours, minutes and moments leading up to finding her mother on the floor. Over and over she'd pick apart what she should or could have done to prevent her mother's fall. She mentally checked the floor: it was clear she hadn't left anything lying around for Rabbit to trip over. The chairs had been pushed under the table; there was no spillage or damp spot. She had brushed the floor before she'd gone to school. She'd been brushing the floor twice a day every day, along with cleaning every surface with disinfectant, since her mother had been diagnosed. She hadn't forgotten.

She wondered if Rabbit had fainted. Sometimes she did after chemo, but she hadn't had chemo in a while, and usually Ma was pale and tired before she fainted but she had been perfectly fine that morning. She'd had a meeting with her editor about her cancer blog and she'd looked good in her wig and makeup. They had talked about Juliet's French test and Ma had made a joke about her transferring to German, seeing as Germany would own Ireland within the year. She was sick but she was fine. If she hadn't been, Juliet would have known. She would have noticed the change, no matter how subtle – she watched her ma like a hawk every minute she was with her. *So what happened? And why? And what if?* She'd lie awake, eyes streaming, heart racing and body shaking, wondering, *What if. . .*

During the day, she put on her game face, and the only thing she allowed herself to think about was when her mother would come home. Life would resume as normal, which, of course, wasn't really normal but it was normal enough, and that was OK. Juliet, much like her mother, was good at putting on a happy face and even better at fooling herself. Every new morning brought fresh hope. *It's going to be OK.*

Della coughed and shuffled as though she was trying to soften the ground with her bum cheeks. Juliet remained silent, pretending to watch the game. In the absence of an invitation to talk, Della came out with it: 'Me ma wants me to ask you if you want to stay at ours.'

'That's nice of her, but I'm fine at Grace's.'

'But you don't even have a room there. We have a spare.'

'It's only for a short time.'

'OK.' Della didn't sound convinced. 'Still, me ma said you're always welcome, like for as long as it takes . . . Even for ever.'

Juliet looked at her friend quizzically. Della sat on her hands. 'Not that you'll need to stay for ever. It's just that me ma really likes you. Sometimes I think she likes you better than me.' Della was nervous, Juliet thought. She spoke quickly, then trailed off. She couldn't meet Juliet's gaze. Instead she pretended to be fascinated by Alan Short's control of the ball. 'Jaysus, he's deadly, isn't he?'

Just as she said it Alan Short tripped and landed face down in the dirt. On another day they would have laughed loudly, but not then. Juliet got up.

'Where are you going?' Della asked, but Juliet didn't answer. Instead she just walked away.

Don't cry, Juliet. Don't overthink it. Everything is fine. Ma is coming home. All we have to do is get through the next few days. We'll be OK.

She started to run.

Grace

Grace had fallen in love with Lenny on the day she met him. He wasn't the handsomest man in the world, but he had a warm smile and sad, soulful eyes, and when he accidentally brushed against her in the office break room, her skin tingled and her stomach turned. 'I'm Lenny,' he'd said, and put out his hand. Her da had warned her of the dangers of a weak handshake so she shook it firmly, too firmly, in fact, so much so that he yelped and rubbed it with his other hand as soon as she let go.

'So sorry,' she'd said. 'Nervous, first day.'

'Don't be, we're all lovely here.' He offered her a mug from the shelf above the sink. She took it, smiled and held his gaze.

'Really?' she said hopefully.

'No, but I'll let you decide who to avoid.'

'Oh.'

He poured himself a coffee, then poured some into her waiting mug. 'So, what drew you to the wonderful world of banking?'

'Me da.'

'He works here?' Lenny said, a little alarmed.

'No, he's with the opposition.'

Lenny went to the fridge and sniffed the milk, then lifted it high in Grace's direction. She nodded and he poured. 'Sugar?'

'Sweet enough,' she responded, and he laughed. He was wearing a black suit and a crisp white shirt; his tie was sky blue and matched his eyes. He wore his top button open and the tie a little loose, as though he'd just tugged at it absentmindedly, but

Grace could tell even then that he had carefully orchestrated it to look nonchalant. It was Lenny's small rebellion. He looked really good in that suit, although, when he reached for the top shelf to retrieve the biscuit tin, she noticed he was wearing white socks with black loafers. *They'll have to go.* He offered her a biscuit and she politely declined, even though they were chocolate HobNobs, her absolute favourite.

'Right, I'd better get back to work,' he said, and she stepped out of his way.

'Me too.'

'It was nice meeting you.'

'Yes, you too.'

As he walked away, she couldn't help but notice he had a lovely arse. He turned as she was cocking her head to get a side view. 'You didn't tell me your name,' he said.

'Grace.'

'Nice to meet you, Grace.' He held out his hand again, remembered the pain and retracted it with a grin. 'Still tender.' He winked.

'Sorry.'

Five minutes later, sitting in her cubicle, she looked around nervously to see if anyone was watching. Those around her were typing, filing or talking business. Her immediate boss was in a meeting so she took a moment to call her ma.

'Ma?'

'How are you gettin' on?'

'I've just met the man I'm going to marry.'

'Ah, would you ever fuck off, Grace.' Ma hung up.

Watch this space, Ma.

Within a month they were going out, and a year later they were engaged. Two months before her wedding day, Grace discovered she was three months pregnant with Stephen. That had been twenty years ago, and Grace loved her husband more every day. It sounded cheesy, even to her, but it was true. She had been lucky. Sometimes she felt bad about it. When her best friend

Emily's marriage collapsed, because of her husband's constant philandering, and she was forced to move into a council flat with her two young sons, it was a cold reminder of how good Grace had it. When her neighbour Sheena's husband walked out on her to join a New Age cult in Dorset, it came out of nowhere. One day they were a happy couple, always up for a few drinks in the local on a Friday, the next he was a shaven-headed commune-dweller living off the land, and she was a single mother. Then there was her sister-in-law Serena's sister, Kate, who had caught her husband pulling himself off to gay porn while wearing her red silk knickers and bra. He'd said he was just experimenting. After a huge fight and a few weeks apart, she'd decided to believe him. Three kids down the line, they were still together and she appeared oblivious to the fact that her husband was a 'screaming' queen.

Grace was a lucky woman. Lenny was a one-woman atheist, who shuddered at the notion of sucking another man's cock. He was a good father, too. He loved his kids and would have done anything for them. When Stephen was five he loved Irish dancing, and Lenny, who would have preferred to shove his head in a gas oven, had gone to every competition, clapping and cheering his son on to many wins. Bernard had been a sick baby, and even though Lenny had had to work in the morning, he did his share of walking the floorboards, never avoided changing a nappy and, although he and Grace often almost killed each other from sheer exhaustion, he was always quick to apologize if he was in the wrong.

They'd known Ryan would be trouble as early as two. He just had something about him. He was cute as a button, stubborn as a mule and the craftiest little bugger. Ryan didn't do rules. They just didn't apply. So much so that Grace was hauled into the office of Tesco twice on suspicion of theft and only released with a caution when the tape revealed Ryan had been lifting items from the shelf at his eye-level and shoving them into his jacket whenever his mother wasn't looking. He was banned from two supermarket chains before he was four, and on the rare occasion she was forced to bring him shopping, she handcuffed him to the trolley until he was six. When it came to Ryan, Lenny was the calm one. Grace was too emotional and, with a temper like her mother's, it was a miracle, and thanks to his level-headed father, that the child wasn't buried under the patio.

Jeffrey was their video-game kid. He was a whiz on computers and even at nine he was the go-to person in the house for anything technical, but he was physically lazy and, of course, he ate far too much. Lenny had tried to get him interested in Bernard's various football, swimming and athletics teams, and even brought him to Stephen's old Irish-dancing hall, but he wouldn't have any of it. Yet the child was always *starving* and Grace didn't believe in saying no – at least, not until his medical revealed that he was obese. Lenny had shared his concerns about Jeffrey over the years and she had dismissed him. He was kind enough not to say, 'I told you so.'

Lenny Black was a very good man, so it really made no sense at all when Grace packed a bag and walked out of her house when he simply suggested that she had ruined a lentil roast.

The incident had started off amiably enough. Lenny had arrived home from a half-day's work and found Grace in the kitchen, poring over a cookbook. He'd kissed her cheek and turned on a radio show he'd been listening to in the car. He put on the kettle and automatically took two mugs off the shelf. The radio presenter was talking to a woman who was raffling her house. The tickets were a hundred euro and she was giving out a website address to anyone interested in buying one. She'd sold 150,000-euro-worth of tickets already and needed just another fifty thousand to pay off her mortgage and leave the country.

'What if you don't meet the mortgage?' the presenter asked.

'The bank can swing for the rest.'

'Do you think we should buy a ticket?' Lenny had asked, handing his wife a mug of coffee.

'Where's the house?'

'Mayo.'

'No.'

'Mayo's nice.' He sat at the counter opposite her. 'What's that smell?'

'It's the lentil roast.'

'No. Really? Jesus, if we had a dog I'd swear it had farted.'

And that was all it had taken for Grace Black to lose her mind. She grabbed an oven mitt, opened the oven, took out the lentil roast and threw it at the wall. Lenny jumped up. 'What the hell, Grace?'

'You do it then!' Grace screamed. 'You shop and chop and cook and listen to everyone whine and whinge and belly-fucking-ache. You take over, Lenny! You're so much better at everything than I am.'

'You need to calm down.' He really couldn't have said anything worse, because it was then that she briefly considered picking up a carving knife and ramming it through his head. She grabbed a cup inches from the knife and slammed it onto the tiled floor. It smashed.

'OK, OK! Whatever it is, we can talk about it.' He was waving his hands in front of him in a bid to hold her off.

'Whatever it is? Whatever it is?' she screamed. 'Ah, what could it be, Lenny? I wonder! Whatever could be wrong?' She grabbed a mug and was about to throw it.

'Stop! Stop this bullshit, Grace! You are not five years old, and tantrums are not acceptable.'

She didn't think. She just threw the mug and it hit him hard in the face. His nose was instantly bloody and his eye began to swell. The shock of seeing blood and watching him wobble on his feet sent Grace running from the room. *What have I done?* Instead of helping her husband or even apologizing, she had the terrible urge to leave. Upstairs in her bedroom she put some fresh underwear, jeans and a few tops into a case; she grabbed her washbag and, thankfully, her handbag was in the hallway. She could hear Lenny in the downstairs bathroom, washing the blood from his face as she opened the front door. She didn't know if she'd broken his nose, blackened his eye or both. She couldn't think about that, couldn't yet admit what she'd done. The shock had dissipated her rage but her head was still spinning. He called to her. He sounded more shocked and confused than angry. She couldn't face him, so she quietly closed the front door behind her and ran to her car with no destination in mind, only the desperate need to run and hide.

Davey

The school called the house just after two thirty. Juliet had a severe headache and Grace wasn't answering her phone. Molly and Jack had come home for just long enough to grab an old diary full of numbers, so Davey agreed to pick Juliet up as soon as he could. He called a taxi and made a sandwich while he waited for it to arrive. The cab was quicker than expected so he ate en route. The taxi man was a talker from Uganda; he ended each sentence with either a laugh or a snort. He liked to bang on the steering-wheel to emphasize a point.

'You know what I think about abortion?' he asked, out of nowhere. Davey didn't have a clue what he thought about abortion. 'Nothing,' said the taxi driver. 'I don't care about abortion. This legislation is a distraction from what's really going on.'

'What's that?' Davey asked.

'Robbery.' He slapped his steering-wheel. 'I didn't leave Uganda to come to Ireland to be robbed. They tax, tax, tax – everywhere I look, tax.'

Davey stayed quiet. He had nothing to add to the conversation.

'Ah, but the Irish women . . .' The driver chortled. 'They are nice.'

Davey didn't remember Irish women being nice. The last girlfriend he'd had before he left for the States had set her two brothers on him when he broke up with her. If it wasn't for Francie and Jay he would have been a dead man. He said nothing.

'You married?' the man asked.

'No.'

'Gay?'

'No.'

'Alone?'

'No.'

'Ha.' He snorted. 'You look alone.'

'Well, I'm not.' *Actually!*

'OK.'

'Define alone,' Davey asked.

'Not accountable.'

Davey thought about it for a few seconds. He had been off the grid for two days, and the only text he'd received was from Casey sending kisses and her wife Mabel asking what she could do. Not one of the women he slept with had called or even noticed he was missing. 'Yeah, OK, I'm alone.'

'You like being alone?'

'I don't think about it.' *I'm lying to a stranger.*

'A man needs a woman.'

'I think I'll survive.'

'Surviving is not living.'

Fine. I'm lonely. Are you happy? Davey was sorry he'd engaged. In his head he told the Ugandan to fuck off.

'You like music?'

'Yes.' He was grateful for the distraction.

The guy smiled and turned on his CD player. It was some high-energy, beat-driven Ugandan band. 'You like?' he said.

'No,' Davey answered.

The taxi driver shrugged. 'Too bad.'

The school grounds were quiet. Davey made his way to the main door and looked around for someone to assist him when he entered the dreary hallway. He hated schools and hadn't been in one since he was kicked out. He knocked on the door marked 'Office', but nobody answered. He walked towards the staff room and, before he knocked, he actually felt his stomach flutter. *I'm an adult, for Christ's sake*, he thought, but still he fixed his hair and straightened his T-shirt. A woman answered his second knock. She was in her twenties, pretty and armed with a bright smile.

'I'm looking for my niece, Juliet Hayes,' he said.

'Oh, OK, just give me a second.' She allowed the door to open, revealing that she was the only one in the room and halfway through a sandwich. 'Come in.'

'Sorry to interrupt.' He stared at the chipped paint, fold-down tables and plastic chairs. *So this is what a staff room looks like.* He wasn't impressed.

She wiped her hands on a towel and grabbed her coffee. 'It's no trouble. Follow me.'

They walked down the corridor together. 'I have Juliet for English and maths.'

'Oh.'

'She's a good student.'

'So was her ma,' he said. 'Brains to burn.'

'How is her mother?'

Davey felt uncomfortable. He didn't know how to answer. *Oh, God, she's dying. Rabbit's dying.* She must have noticed he was struggling because she didn't wait for an answer.

'Juliet has been through so much but she's very strong.'

'Yeah, she is.' *Whatever that means.*

She asked Davey to give her a minute, then disappeared into an unnamed room. She returned not long after with Juliet.

'Davey?' Juliet said, surprised and delighted to see him.

'Grace is MIA so you're stuck with me, Bunny.'

She nodded and smiled, dropped her schoolbag and flung her arms around him. 'I'm glad you're here, Davey. Thanks, Miss Hickey.' She pulled away from Davey and picked up her bag.

'You're welcome, Juliet. I hope you feel better.'

Outside it was unseasonably warm. Juliet took off her jacket and hung it on the straps of her backpack. Davey watched her face change. 'Why are you here, Davey?'

'The school called.'

'I mean why are you in Ireland, ya eejit?' she said playfully.

'Hey, my ma is the only one allowed to call me that.'

'Sorry, my bad, so why are you home?'

'I missed you.' *Please, please, don't push, Juliet. I don't know what to say. I can't be the one to tell you. It's not my place.*

She thought about what he had said and chose to accept it. 'I missed you too.'

Davey wanted to cry. 'Do you have a key for Grace's?' He changed the subject.

'No.'

'Wanna go to your nan's to lie down?'

'No.'

'I can take you to a doctor if you need one.'

'There's nothing wrong with me.'

'What about your headache?'

'I just said that.'

'Why?'

'I needed to get out of there,' Juliet said. She could always be honest with her uncle Davey.

Davey sighed. Nobody could understand that better than he did. 'OK, so what do you want to do?'

'I want to go to Stephen's Green.'

'Haven't been there for years.'

They got onto the bus, made their way up to the top deck and sat right at the front. Davey hadn't seen Dublin from that vantage-point in a long time. It was nice. They talked together about all the changes Dublin had undergone in the fifteen years he'd been living in America. Juliet pointed out the Luas tram system. He hadn't noticed it on previous trips. 'It looks really good.'

'And it actually works.'

'Wow! Public transport that works.'

Davey bought them takeaway coffee and apple Danishes before they headed into the park. 'Do you want me to buy breadcrumbs for the ducks?'

'I'm not five.'

The park was surprisingly busy for just after three o'clock on a weekday. Even though it couldn't have been more than eighteen degrees centigrade, various people had stripped off and were sunbathing on the grass. A young band played in the bandstand. They were good. The music was fun and the boys were pretty. They made Juliet smile.

'Let's stay here and listen,' she said, and Davey was happy to oblige her so they sat on the grass, drank their coffee and picked at their pastries.

'You still play guitar?' he asked.

'Sometimes.' Davey had bought Juliet her guitar and she had promised him she'd be the best guitar player ever.

'Bored?' he said.

'Oh, no, just busy.'

Davey understood. The kid spent most of her time caring for her mother. He should have done more to help them. *I'm a dick. I've let you down, kiddo.* 'You were good.'

'I was OK.'

'No, you had promise.'

'Thanks.'

They focused on the band for another song.

'Davey?'

'Yeah.'

'Maybe we'll visit you in Nashville some time.'

'I'd love to see you there.' He studiously avoided the 'we' in her sentence. If she noticed, she didn't challenge him.

'Ma's always talkin' about her time in America and how great it was. I bet she'd love to get back there.'

Davey wanted to change the subject. 'I visited her that first summer she lived in New York.'

'Yeah?' Juliet said.

Davey knew she loved hearing stories about her mother. 'She was living in this cramped little shoebox just off Broad Street.'

'With Marjorie?'

'Yeah.'

'Was that before or after you played leapfrog with Marjorie?' she asked. A cheeky grin spread across her face.

'Before.' He covered his face with his hands.

She reached over and pulled them away from his eyes. 'Keep talking.'

'It was July, and it was so hot that the girls used to keep their makeup in the fridge and that was pretty much all they had in it. We used to go to the bar just for the air-conditioning.'

'And lots of beer,' she said.

'That too but, seriously, I thought I was going to melt. I'd never felt heat like it. Couldn't wait to get out of the place, but yer ma, she loved it.'

'She said you left because you missed me nan too much.'

'Yeah, there was that.'

'But you went back.'

'Didn't feel I had a choice.'

'But you like it now?'

'Yeah.'

'Why did she leave if she liked it so much?'

'Johnny.'

'But he told her to go. He wanted her to stay in America.'

'I know, but it was hard for her to stay away.' He shuffled uncomfortably on the grass. He didn't like talking about Rabbit and Johnny's relationship. It was too painful.

'I used to wish he was my da,' Juliet said.

'Yeah? Why?' Davey was shocked. It seemed such an odd thing for young Juliet to wish for.

'Because of all the stories, because she loved him so much and he was so amazing and cool, whereas me da, well, there's really only one story.'

'What's that?'

'He ran after a thief when he snatched her handbag.'

'Really?'

'That's how they met. How come you don't know this?'

'I don't know. I suppose I missed out on a lot of stories over the years.' He wondered why he'd never asked his sister how she'd met the father of her child. *What the hell is wrong with me?* 'Well, that's romantic, isn't it?' he said.

'He didn't even catch the guy.'

'But he tried.'

'Suppose.' She paused. 'Me ma asked me if I wanted her to find him.'

'And?'

'I said no.'

'I understand that.'

'She said he was nice but she didn't really know him. Three weeks is no time. He could be a psycho-killer.'

'Or, worse, an accountant.'

She smiled at his joke. 'Besides, I don't need him. I have Ma.'

Juliet was testing him, whether consciously or not. Davey felt like crying again. *If the kid can hold it together it's the least you can do. Mental note: get Francie to punch me in the face. I fucking deserve it.* It was time to move on. He stood up. 'Come on.'

'Where are we going?'

'A trip down Memory Lane,' he said.

'OK.'

As they walked out of the park, she linked his arm. 'Thanks for this, Davey.'

Juliet and Davey were always so comfortable together. She had the easy relationship with him that her mother had always craved when she was a kid. He had been so busy telling Rabbit to piss off he had missed all the good stuff she'd shared with his best friend. Now Juliet was growing up and he was missing that too.

'I'm going to Skype you more,' he said.

'You always say that.' She laughed. 'Ma says you were born useless.'

'She's right.'

'I tell her you're just busy doing what you love. You're living your best life.'

'How did you work that out?'

'Ma's an *Oprah* addict. She says shite like that all the time.'

'I love you, Bunny,' he said, and he meant it with all he had in him. It might have been the first time he'd ever told anyone other than his ma that he loved them. It was a big moment.

Juliet went red and punched his arm. 'Shut up.'

'I do.'

'Seriously, shut up.' She was embarrassed but smiling.

'OK, I will, but only because I love you.'

'Big eejit,' Juliet said, under her breath.

They reached the narrow street a little before five o'clock.

'When you said Memory Lane, I didn't think you meant an actual lane.' Juliet was walking ahead of her uncle. 'Nice graffiti.'

'It's the U2 wall,' Davey said, scanning it from top to bottom.

'What are you looking for?'

'We left our mark here that last summer before it all fell apart.'

'What did you put?' Juliet asked, joining him in his search.

'"Johnny, Francie, Louis and Jay, Davey and little sis Rabbit here to stay",' he said, reading it. It was faded and barely legible, but as soon as he pointed to it, Juliet could see it.

'Wow, really profound.'

'Not our best work, I admit.'

'Does that say "Kitchen Sink"?' she asked.

'Yeah.'

'Shit band name, Uncle Davey.'

'Great band name.'

'You were never going anywhere with a name like that.'

Davey traced his finger on the wall. 'Back then we thought we were going all the way.'

'Yeah, well, you were thicks,' she said.

He laughed. 'Maybe, but we were happy thicks.'

'What was me ma like back then?' Juliet asked, following him down Windmill Lane.

'Annoying.'

'But you loved her.'

Davey chuckled. 'You couldn't help it.'

'What age was she when you wrote on the wall?'

'Fourteen.'

'People say I look like her.'

'You do.' He failed to mention that, aged twelve, Juliet, *sans* heavy spectacles and two bunches at either side of her head, looked a lot better than her ma had.

'Do you still have the music?'

'Probably on a tape in the attic.'

'Do you even have a tape player?'

'Maybe in the attic.'

'Will you play me the music some time?'

'Yeah. I'd like that.'

'Cool.'

They walked on towards Pearse Street.

'Davey.'

'Yeah.'

'Can we go and see me ma now?'

He nodded, put his arm around her shoulders and they headed towards the taxi rank. On the way Davey reflected on how proud he was of his niece and worried for her. *When are we going to talk about Juliet?*

Johnny

Uncle Terry opened the back doors of his old bread van to reveal the band and Rabbit sitting among their gear, half killed with the heat. 'Up and out,' he shouted to them.

Davey stood up, his hair stuck to his head with sweat. He wavered a bit, then steadied himself by placing a palm against the roof. Francie and Jay stayed sitting and panting. Johnny shook Rabbit gently. Even though her eyes were open, she seemed sleepy.

'Come on, ya big Marys.' Uncle Terry banged the side of the van. 'It's show time.'

Kitchen Sink's new manager had booked them into every small venue and festival he could find that summer. He was planning to get them a deal by October and it was going to be big. Already there was interest from the UK. They had the songs, just needed a toilet tour under their belt and to find their stage legs. Once they'd broken Ireland, they'd be ready for the world stage. Paddy Price was going to take Kitchen Sink all the way, and after two years of practice, writing and waiting, they were ready. It was a shoestring operation, with only enough money to pay Uncle Terry for his questionable transport. The lads would have to take care of their own gear. Initially Grace had signed on as roadie, but when she'd realized she'd have to lift dirty speakers and set up her brother's kit, she'd told them to fuck off.

Rabbit had been put forward as their sound engineer. She knew every song inside out and she'd shown a flair for the work, which was handy because she was learning on the job. After a few questionable gigs, she had found her groove and she was actually pretty good. At fourteen Rabbit Hayes was too young to be in most venues, but at five foot seven, having swapped her spectacles for lenses and finally let her long silky hair hang down to her waist, she looked the same age as her eighteen-year-old brother. Much to Davey's annoyance, when she wore makeup, she looked even older.

It was Rabbit's job to carry the bag of leads and Davey's kick drum. The lads managed the rest between them. Tonight's venue was dark and mercifully cool. Another band was on stage, sound-checking. Rabbit walked up to the guy on the desk, a real Johnny Rotten wannabe. He was probably twenty and had a safety pin in his nose. 'You'll be done in fifteen, yeah?' she said.

He looked her up and down. 'We'll be done when we're done.'

Johnny nudged Francie, alerting him to the altercation that was about to happen.

'You'll be finished in fifteen minutes.'

'Who says?'

'The call sheet and me.'

'Who the fuck are you?'

'It doesn't matter who I am. What matters is what I'm going to do. Can your band afford new gear?'

The would-be Johnny Rotten looked her up and down again but this time with caution. She stood still, allowing him to survey her. Finally he nodded. 'Fifteen minutes.'

'I told ya she'd be a natural,' Johnny said to Francie.

'You did.'

The gig was packed to the rafters. After initial feedback, which Rabbit easily sorted, the gig went brilliantly. Halfway through she spotted her school friend Chris waving to her. She waved back but kept working. Johnny had the crowd in the palm of his hand throughout; the lads didn't make a single mistake, just bounced around effortlessly. It was a good night, maybe even one of the best. Johnny's voice was crystal clear, the vocals sitting perfectly on top of the music, no more feedback issues and lovely reverb. By the time Johnny finished the last song, the crowd were going crazy, shouting, 'More, more, more!' Johnny quietened them with a hand gesture. 'How about I sing you something I wrote about a girl?'

The crowd screamed and clapped.

'OK, I haven't shared it with the band yet, so is it OK if I sing it a cappella?'

More screams, although it was entirely likely that most of the crowd weren't quite sure what a cappella was.

Davey rested his sticks, Louis picked up his beer and slugged it from behind his keyboard, Francie and Jay crossed their hands over their guitars and stood back – until they saw that Louis had a beer and made fierce gestures to their girlfriends to get them the same. Johnny took the mic off the stand, sat on the speaker and sang.

The room fell silent and everyone listened without moving, including Rabbit. Alandra had left for home two weeks before; Rabbit figured the song was about her. It had such a beautiful melody and he sang it from his soul. Rabbit had got over her jealousy of Alandra a long time ago. She'd felt sad when she left, especially because the poor girl's dad was so ill. When it was over, the crowd clapped and cheered and the band left the stage to renewed screams of 'More, more, more!'

Rabbit was about to leave the desk when the Johnny Rotten wannabe came over to shake her hand. 'Good gig.'

'Thanks.'

Chris was waiting for her. 'That was amazing! You are serious.'

'Glad you liked it.'

'I like you.'

'Fuck off, Chris.'

'Seriously. I'm stuck down here in poxy Wexford the whole bleedin' summer, but when I come home I want to go out with you.'

Rabbit grinned. Chris was cute: he had bullied her when she was twelve but ever since he had been her bodyguard and friend. 'I'll think about it.'

He nodded. 'Nice one. Now come and get chips with me.'

She laughed. 'I'm leaving in the van in an hour.'

'It only takes ten minutes to eat chips.'

'OK. I'll tell the lads.'

On the bus going home, the lads were drunk, laughing and talking until Uncle Terry turned up the heat to knock them out. Only Johnny and Rabbit remained awake.

'You like Chris?' he asked.

'He's nice.'

'What about the other kid?'

'Eugene?'

'Yeah.'

'Oh, he lives in Spain now with his ma.'

'How come?'

'His da is in prison.'

'Who's his da?'

'Billy the Bookie.'

Johnny nearly choked on his own tongue. 'You had us attack Billy the Bookie's kid?'

'Well, to be fair, I didn't ask you to attack him and I didn't know who Billy the Bookie was until the court case last year.'

'We could have been kneecapped.'

'Or worse.'

'Do me a favour.'

'Wha'?'

'Don't tell Francie or Jay.'

'OK.'

She reached into her bag and found a few packets of crisps. 'You hungry?'

'Starving.'

She threw him a packet. He tried to catch it, but missed. It landed right beside his leg, but instead of just picking it up, he felt around for it. It was dark, but his eyes had had long enough to adjust. It was weird. When he did find the packet, he couldn't seem to grip it. Rabbit leaned over and picked it up for him. She opened it and put it in his lap. 'Here.'

'Dunno what's wrong with me.'

'You're just tired.'

'Yeah, it must be that.'

He pushed the crisps away.

'Are you not going to eat them?'

'Nah, not hungry any more.' He leaned his head against the side of the van and closed his eyes.

Chapter Six

Rabbit

RABBIT TURNED TO FACE Juliet, who was lying on the bed
beside her. She put her fingers through her daughter's long
light-brown hair and twisted it around them. 'You look so
pretty today.'

'You look terrible, Ma,' Juliet said.

Rabbit laughed and touched her face. 'It's just a little bloating. It'll go down.'

'Do you want some water?'

'Nah, I'm OK.'

'You didn't eat your lunch.'

'Wasn't hungry. Did you eat?'

'A little.'

'You need to eat more. You're so skinny.'

'I'll eat more if you do,' Juliet said.

Her mother smiled. 'Deal.'

'I can get you something from the canteen?'

'How about I start tomorrow?' Rabbit said.

'OK.'

Davey walked in with two coffees and two sandwiches. He
handed a coffee and a chicken sandwich to Juliet.

'I'm fine, Davey.'

'Eat it.'

128

'Not hungry.'

'Eat it.'

'Seriously?'

'Seriously.'

Juliet thought about it for a few seconds, then opened the packet and took a bite. 'It's nice,' she said, sitting up. She propped up her pillow behind her and tucked in.

'I had her open it and add a little more mayo and black pepper.'

'Cool.'

Rabbit smiled at her brother and mouthed 'Thank you,' then returned to gazing at Juliet. Rain pelted against the window and the light died outside. Davey turned on the lamp, and when he noticed his sister shiver, he picked up her favourite lambskin blanket and wrapped her in it.

Francie arrived, soaked to the skin. 'It's the end of days out there.' He shook himself off, strode over to Rabbit and enveloped her without breaking her.

'It's good to see you, Francie,' she said.

'Of course it is.' He laid her down carefully. He stopped to ruffle Juliet's hair before he sat down. 'Sorry I didn't get here last night.'

'What was the big drama?'

'One of the lads at work cut his hand off.'

'You're joking!' Davey said.

'Clean off at the wrist.'

'How?' Rabbit asked.

'Fucking around with a samurai sword.'

'No!' Juliet said. It was enough to stop her eating the second half of her sandwich.

'What happened?'

'Ah, the gobshite who cut it off ran out cryin' and a few of us held the other thick down and tried to stop the bleedin' with one of the girls' belts. You remember Sheila B?'

'Yeah,' Davey said.

'Impossible to forget,' Rabbit added.

'Her daughter Sandra works with us. She picked up the hand, gave it a wash and put it in a bag of ice, so I had it with me when we got to the hospital. They attached it last night so hopefully he'll be all right. Sandra's already convinced him that it's turned into a claw.' He laughed.

'How is Sheila B?' Davey asked.

'Mental.'

'She was always mad,' Davey said, smiling.

'Well, now she's seriously mad,' Francie said. 'She's been an in-patient in the nut-house for months.'

'That's terrible,' Rabbit said. 'I really liked her.'

'She never threw you in a canal,' Francie replied. Rabbit and Davey laughed at the memory.

'She threw you in the canal? Why would she do that?' Juliet asked.

'Francie and Sheila B used to go out together. Sheila was the jealous type,' Rabbit explained.

'Small understatement,' Francie said.

'Believe it or not, Francie used to be a good-looking boy back in the day and the women loved him,' Davey said.

'Used to be? Bleedin' neck of you! I've still got it,' he said, flexing his muscles. 'The auld ones in the local supermarket go mad for me.'

'Every time a girl went near him, Sheila had to be practically held down,' Rabbit recalled.

'Remember the time she locked you in the Olympia dressing room when some fans wanted an autograph?' Davey said.

'Yeah,' Francie laughed, 'and she threatened to set the place on fire.'

'Wow!' Juliet said.

'She was good fun, though, and she was always kind to me,' Rabbit said.

Francie nodded. 'We could always count on Sheila B for a laugh.'

'And she could always find a lock-in,' Davey said.

'It was like a sixth sense,' Francie said.

'Did she ever marry?' Rabbit asked.

'Nah, I ruined her for other men. You can't follow this act.' Francie patted his beer belly.

'So her daughter Sandra's yours, then?' Davey said, in jest.

'Don't even fucking mess about that,' Francie replied. 'The first day Sandra joined, I asked her how old she was and had to count the months on me fingers. I was sweating like a paedo in a Barney suit, until I worked out the maths.'

'Sandra is Wet Carbery's daughter,' Rabbit told them.

'The short fella with the eye-patch?' Davey said, and Rabbit nodded.

'Why was he called Wet?' Juliet asked.

'He wore a nappy until first class,' Francie said.

'A few months after Francie broke it off with Sheila, Wet won a few quid on the bingo and took her away to Spain for two weeks. She came back pregnant.'

'No!' Davey said.

'Where's he now?' Francie asked.

'Last I heard he was a barman in Brooklyn,' Rabbit said.

'Does Sandra know her dad?' Juliet enquired.

'Nah,' Francie said. 'Sheila tried to stab him in his good eye with a cocktail umbrella on the second last night of the holiday. They didn't really speak after that.'

Juliet laughed. 'That's totally insane.'

Molly arrived, with Jack tagging behind. Francie stood up. 'Mrs H.' He hugged her.

'Ah, Francie, it's good to see ya.' She held him away from her so she could look at him. 'Still handsome,' she said, and he nodded towards the others triumphantly.

'Howya, Mr H?' Francie shook Jack's hand warmly.

'Better for seeing you, son.'

'Sit down there,' Francie told Molly, pointing to his chair as he moved to sit next to Davey. Jack sat on the sofa at the end of the bed.

'So, what's going on?' Molly asked.

'Sheila B's in the nut-house,' Rabbit said.

'Of course she is,' Molly said. 'God love her, she's a fucking lunatic.'

'She was a lovely little Irish dancer in her day, all the same,' Jack said. 'Good enough to be in *Riverdance*.'

'I forgot she was in *Riverdance*,' Francie said.

'That's because they kicked her out after five minutes,' Molly said.

'What happened?' Rabbit asked.

'Dunno, but the rumour was she sexually harassed some guy in tights.'

'Well, that would do it.' Jack sighed. 'It's an awful shame, she was such a lovely dancer.'

'Where's Grace?' Molly asked.

'Dunno, Nan,' Juliet said.

'Who picked you up?'

'I did,' Davey said.

'She hasn't answered her phone all day,' Molly said.

'She's probably just busy, Ma,' Rabbit said.

'Busy, me eye,' Molly replied, and just as she spoke, Lenny appeared, sporting a black eye.

Molly and Jack stood up. 'Christ on a bike, Lenny, what happened to ya?' Molly exclaimed.

'Some kid tried to mug me.'

'Did you sort him?' Francie asked.

'He ran away.'

'Did you know him?' Francie said.

'No.'

'Pity.'

'Why? Were you going to sort him out?' Davey asked, amused.

'No. I was going to ask the kid to join Freddie's new boxing club. He could do with a few scrappers.' Francie winked to signal he was joking.

'Where's Grace?' Molly asked Lenny, touching the bruise

around his eye. He moved his hands up to protect himself but she slapped them away. 'Did you wash that cut?'

'Yeah.'

'So?'

'So what?'

'So where's Grace?'

'I was hoping she'd be here,' he said.

'Her phone's been off all day,' Molly said.

'I know.'

'Well, should I be worried?'

'No.'

'Hmm.'

Everyone was quiet for a few seconds, so Juliet seized the moment. 'Can I stay at yours tonight, Nan?'

'All of your stuff is at Grace's,' Molly reminded her.

'No, it's not, and, anyway, I need to pick some stuff up at home tomorrow.'

'Well, your granda and I are busy tomorrow.'

'Where are you going?' Rabbit asked.

'None of your beeswax.'

'Must be something sexy, then,' Francie suggested.

'Don't you start, Francie Byrne,' Molly told him.

'So can I stay?'

'I'll take care of her,' Davey said, and Juliet grinned.

'Are you all right with that?' Molly asked Lenny, who nodded and sat beside Jack on the sofa.

'You're pale,' Rabbit said to Lenny.

'Haven't eaten.'

'You can have this chicken sandwich, if you'd like,' Juliet said, lifting it up in its paper packaging.

'Ah, great.' She passed it to Davey, who handed it to Francie, who gave it to Lenny. He took a bite. 'Lovely.'

'The trick is to ask them to open it and add more mayo and black pepper,' Juliet said. Davey nodded proudly.

Jacinta appeared with a plastic bowl of meds. 'I don't want

to be a party-pooper, but there's a lot of people in here.'

'Don't worry, I have to head out anyway,' Francie said. 'Promised I'd visit the Claw before it gets too late.'

Rabbit laughed. 'The Claw. That poor bastard has a nickname already.'

Francie leaned down to kiss her forehead. 'Get better soon, Rabbit,' he said, knowing full well that that wasn't possible.

'I will,' she lied, to him and to herself.

Juliet grinned at him and shook his hand when he offered it to her.

'Just like your ma.' For a second his face crumpled.

Davey jumped up. 'I'll walk you out.'

'Jay will be in on Sunday,' Francie said, and Rabbit nodded.

Rabbit focused on Jacinta. 'No pain meds for a while.'

'Are you sure? You've had a lot of breakthrough pain today.'

'I know, but I'm OK, and it makes me so tired.'

'All right. I'll be outside.'

She was gone when Molly turned to her daughter. 'What breakthrough pain?'

'It's nothing, Ma,' Rabbit said. 'Juliet, tell your nan about the Claw.'

Juliet laughed. 'Some eejit got his hand chopped off by a samurai sword at Francie's work.'

'That's like Gerry Foster,' Molly said.

'How is it like Gerry Foster?' Jack asked.

'He got skewered on a gate.'

'Which is totally different,' Rabbit said.

'He lost a fucking kidney, didn't he?' Molly said.

Jack grumbled to himself while Juliet and Rabbit shared a knowing smile.

'Lector Kenny bit off a piece of his own tongue and swallowed it,' Lenny said.

'Was his real name Lector?'

'Nah, it was Kenneth.'

'Kenneth Kenny?' Juliet said.

'His ma was deranged.'

'Speaking of which, did you hear about Sheila B?' Molly asked.

It had been such a good visit and Rabbit tried her best to stay awake, but sleep claimed her before Molly said any more.

Davey

Davey and Francie had a smoke outside the hospice.

'Thought you were off these,' Francie said.

'I was.'

'Fair enough.'

The rain was still pouring down and rattling the plastic sheeting they were standing under.

'She doesn't look good, DB.'

'No.'

'You've got to watch out for your parents.'

'I will.'

'This will kill them, Davey.'

'I know. I will.'

'And Juliet?'

'I don't know.'

'Well, yous had better start working it out.' Francie stubbed out his cigarette.

'Don't bury Rabbit before she's dead,' Davey said.

'Don't shove your head up your arse,' Francie riposted. 'Rabbit was the baby but she took care of her ma and da and she took care of you. She can't do it any more, so it's time to step up.' He put a hand on Davey's shoulder. 'I'm here for you, but if you let her down, I'll batter you.' He slapped Davey's face gently, and Davey nodded. His friend was right.

Francie passed Marjorie on the way to his car, waved at her and blew her a kiss. He pointed to the shelter where Davey was still smoking. She approached him with a face on her that would have curdled milk.

'What's wrong?' Davey asked.

She grabbed the cigarette out of his mouth and stamped it out. 'Your sister is dying of cancer. I see you with another one of these in your mouth and I'll slap you one.'

'Why does everyone want to hit me tonight?'

'You've a punchable face,' she said, and he laughed at her.

They walked inside together and met Molly, Jack and Juliet coming into Reception. Molly was fixing her coat and giving out to Juliet for not wearing something warmer. She pointed to an umbrella stand near the door.

'Mine's the one with polka dots,' said Juliet. She waved at Marjorie as she headed for the umbrella.

Molly hugged Marjorie. 'You look fantastic, love. How was your trip?'

'Super,' Marjorie said. 'I just wish . . .' She welled up.

'I know.' Molly patted her arm. She looked anxiously towards Juliet, who was battling with the umbrella.

'We should go. Oh, and, Davey, your da and I will be away most of the day tomorrow so I'm trusting you to take care of Juliet and Rabbit.'

'Where are you going?'

'Cavan.'

'Why?'

'We've an appointment with Michael Gallagher,' Molly said sheepishly.

'Michael Gallagher,' Davey repeated. 'Johnny's faith-healer. That Michael Gallagher?'

'Yeah.'

'Oh, no, Mrs H,' Marjorie said.

'She'll go mental, Ma,' Davey protested.

'We're not going to tell her.'

'So how does that work?' Marjorie asked.

'That's what we'll find out when we talk to him tomorrow.' Molly put a finger to her lips.

When they had gone Davey worried that his mother was

doing the wrong thing. Rabbit was an atheist, and introducing a man like Michael Gallagher was an insult to her strongly held belief in nothing. Davey could see it being a serious bone of contention. 'Your ma is just grabbing at straws, Davey,' Marjorie said, as they walked into Rabbit's room.

Lenny was sitting there, watching Rabbit sleep. He nodded at Marjorie, who nodded back. He stood up. 'The nurse came in and gave her the meds. She didn't wake.' He picked up his jacket. 'She's gone to the world.'

'Thanks for everything, Lenny,' Davey said.

'No thanks required. She's family.' He went to the door. 'And if you see or hear from my wife, tell her I love her.'

'Is everything all right?' Davey asked.

'No,' Lenny said, looking at Rabbit shallow-breathing in the bed. 'No, but then how could it be?' He left.

Davey and Marjorie sat on the sofa together. He told her about poor old Sheila B and about the poor sod whose hand had been cut off at work. She spoke about returning to work and the stresses associated with her first day back. Marjorie was a bank manager. During the boom she had been everyone's best friend, but since the recession had kicked in, stepping through the bank's door had been like stepping onto a battlefield. It was harrowing saying no to desperate people, fighting unwinnable cases with Head Office and pressuring customers to pay debilitating debts. 'I'm the bad guy.'

'You do the best you can.'

'Tell that to the seventy-year-old man in my office today who is losing his house because he put it up as collateral against a bloated mortgage for his son.'

'You didn't ask him to remortgage his house.'

'You weren't here when the TV advert told men like him to do exactly that.'

'You're just doing your job.'

'And I need to stop for the sake of my soul.'

'What would you like to do?'

'Honestly? I'd like to write a book, but I'm rubbish at writing so it probably won't work out.'

He smiled. 'Anything else?'

'I'd like to open a boutique.'

'So do it.'

She snorted. 'Do you know how many boutiques are closing down every week in this country?'

'No.'

'Loads.'

'Well, you'll do it differently.'

'Ridiculous upward-only rents, taxes, fees, and people like me saying no to the smallest line of credit.'

'So take up the accordion,' Davey said.

'You think there's a lot of work for an accordion player?'

'They'd love you in Nashville.'

She giggled. 'I'm sure.'

Rabbit moved in the bed. She groaned softly and made a weird choking sound. They remained still, fearful that they were witnessing something terrifying. The moment passed and she seemed to be breathing normally again. Marjorie sighed with relief. 'We're in hell, Davey.'

'Yes.'

The door opened and Grace poked her head around it. Her face was puffy, she was soaked through and she looked like crap. 'Hi.'

'Hi,' Davey said. Marjorie tilted her head and beckoned her with an index finger. Grace walked in, shoulders hunched. Davey and Marjorie parted on the sofa and Marjorie patted the space. Grace sat down between them and all three stared at Rabbit for a minute or two.

'What happened?' Davey asked.

'I freaked out.'

'Understandable,' Marjorie said.

'And?' Davey asked.

'I threw a mug at Lenny's face.'

'You gave him the black eye?'

'I really didn't mean it.'

'That's what you said after you punched me in the face when Rabbit took your bike and wrote it off.'

'I was sixteen and Rabbit ducked.'

'Juliet is staying with us tonight.'

'OK,' she said.

'And Lenny said to tell you he loves you.'

'OK.' She burst into tears. Marjorie put an arm around her. 'I can't do this,' Grace sobbed.

'I know how you feel.' Marjorie was staring at her best friend in the foetal position in the bed.

'We need to stop pretending,' Davey said. Grace raised her head and stared at him. 'We need to start making plans and we need to talk about Juliet.'

Grace nodded sadly. 'I know.'

'Ma and Da are in Cavan tomorrow, so we'll meet in Ma's on Sunday.'

'What are they doing in Cavan?'

'Michael Gallagher.'

'Oh, for fuck's sake.'

Rabbit twisted, turned and moaned a little more. They watched her until she settled.

Marjorie was the first to leave. Davey walked her outside and waved her off, then returned to Rabbit's room, where Grace had moved into the chair beside the bed. She was holding her sister's hand and praying quietly. When Davey appeared, she said, 'I know she doesn't believe, but I do.'

He sat in the chair opposite. He fixed the lambskin blanket, smoothing it down over Rabbit.

'Maybe Michael Gallagher will fix her,' Grace said.

'He won't, and when he doesn't, we need to be strong for Ma and Da.'

'I know.'

'And you need to stop throwing mugs at your husband.'

'I will.'

'We need to make sure Rabbit has a good . . .' he struggled a little '. . . death.'

'What's got into you?' She sounded impressed.

'I took me head out of me hole.'

'About time.'

She reached over and he took her hand. They held hands over Rabbit for just a moment or two, but that gesture bonded them. It was the first step in their relationship as sister and brother without her.

Johnny

The venue was stuffed to the rafters. It was the biggest that Kitchen Sink had ever played. The dressing room was huge, well lit and complete with a beer-and-crisps-filled rider. The noise of two thousand fans waiting for the band to hit the stage seeped through the walls. Davey was in the loo, shitting his brains out. Francie was smoking his brains out in the office while their manager, Paddy, was trying to remove a very drunk and belligerent Sheila B from backstage. Jay liked to sleep before a gig and was out cold on the floor under the dressing rail.

Rabbit met Louis hanging out with his best friend Dillon in the corridor and he directed her to the dressing room. Johnny was warming up his vocals when she entered the room. She had been talking to the house sound guy, swapping notes. He had been impressed by the fourteen-year-old when he'd encountered her at the sound check. Of course he didn't know she was fourteen. If he had, he wouldn't have spoken to her, but as it was, he respected her experience as Kitchen Sink's touring sound engineer. Johnny had fought for her to do the gig but the others, including Rabbit's brother, were adamant they wanted to use the guy who was actually qualified. Rabbit understood. She was happy to relinquish control. Sound engineering had never been her dream, and she knew that night would be the end of her short-lived career. Kitchen Sink had moved up a gear to better things, and Rabbit was relieved. She sat on the dressing-table leaning her back against the mirror Johnny was gazing into.

'I look wrecked,' he said.

'You look great.'

'I'm exhausted, Rabbit.'

'You're going to be great.'

'We're launching a single tonight.'

'I know.'

'Surreal.'

'Cool,' Rabbit said.

Jay was snoring and Johnny laughed. 'Who the hell sleeps before a gig?'

A young woman knocked on the door and opened it. 'The support band is going on. You have twenty minutes.'

'Thanks,' Johnny said. As he stood up, he faltered. He grabbed the counter and steadied himself. He looked shaken and vulnerable, but for only a second.

'Are you OK?' Rabbit asked, jumping off the counter and holding him up. He shook her off and pretended he was fine.

'I'm OK. I'm fine, just tired.'

Paddy got rid of Sheila B so the coast was clear for Francie to leave the safety of a locked office. He was indulging in his first beer when Davey emerged from the loo with nothing left in his system.

'Beer?' Francie said, offering one to him.

'Do you want me to explode?'

Louis appeared as Jay woke up. With five minutes to stage time, Rabbit left the band alone to get their heads together. She walked out into the audience and joined Grace, Marjorie, Grace's current boyfriend, Conor, and Jack. He was dressed head to toe in denim.

'What are you wearing, Da?' she asked.

'This is fashion.' He winked.

'Did you do this?' Rabbit asked Grace.

'He loves it.'

Before Rabbit had a chance to berate her sister the band was announced. Rabbit turned towards the stage and watched as Davey sat behind the drums, Francie and Jay strapped on their guitars, and Louis stood behind his keyboard. Davey clicked his sticks four times, the lads played, and she waited for Johnny to hit the stage. He missed his cue, the boys played on, the audience didn't notice. Even Grace and Da didn't notice.

Where is he?

He appeared and waved, the crowd cheered and he broke into song. Rabbit saw Francie visibly relax. After that, the gig went well. The crowd loved them, and when the lads played the single, they were mad for it. Grace, her boyfriend and Marjorie were bouncing and screaming. Rabbit's da was standing proud, tapping his toe. Rabbit watched Johnny, waiting for something bad to happen.

Just before the encore, she made her way backstage and waited in the dressing room. She knew Davey would be upset: the dressing room was for the band only just before and directly after a gig, but she needed to see Johnny close up so she could work out what was going on.

Johnny was the first into the dressing room and when he entered he didn't see her. He leaned against the wall.

'You're not just tired,' she said, and he glanced at her, then dragged himself to a chair. He sat down, all energy expended. He was sapped, empty and unable to function. He put his head into his hands.

'Why did you miss your cue?'

'I got stuck.'

'Stuck?'

'I couldn't move, Rabbit.'

'You were scared?'

'No. I just couldn't put one foot in front of the other.'

'You need to see someone.'

'I know.'

'I'll come with you.'

'No.' He was adamant. 'And, Rabbit, please don't say anything.'

'I promise.'

Just then the boys appeared, high on adrenalin and ready to party. They were so happy, they didn't even notice Rabbit at first.

'We're going to number one,' Francie said.

'And when we do, London record companies are going to kill one another for us,' Jay added.

'It was a good gig.' Johnny was trying his best to match their exuberance.

'What the fuck happened on the first song?' Louis asked.

'Sorry, needed a piss,' Johnny said. Francie and Jay laughed.

Davey nodded sympathetically. He looked at Rabbit. 'What are you doing in here?'

'I asked her to report on the sound,' Johnny said.

'Nice one! How was it?' Francie asked.

'Perfect.'

Francie grinned. '*Top of the Pops*, here we come.'

Rabbit slipped out while the boys were busy celebrating.

Later, when the venue was about to close, she found Johnny leaning against the corridor wall. She walked over to him and put her arm around his waist.

'The lads are going on to a club but I need to go home,' he said. She let him lean on her. 'I'm really tired, Rabbit.'

'So we'll go home,' she said, and they walked out through the front of house. Rabbit took off her backstage pass and Johnny handed his to her. She gave them to Grace and her boyfriend.

'Can you drop Johnny home, Da?' she asked.

'Of course I can,' he said. 'A little too much to drink, son? If there was ever a night to down a few too quickly, this would be the one.'

Marjorie bounced in front of him and told him how deadly he was. 'Deadly, deadly, deadly, the best ever, ever, ever.'

Johnny smiled and thanked her, and Rabbit helped him into the front seat of the car. He fell asleep instantly, and even though Marjorie talked excitedly throughout the entire journey home, and Jack played the radio, Johnny didn't wake once. Rabbit watched him with a knot tightening in her stomach. It had been the best possible night and at the same time it had been the worst.

DAY FOUR

Chapter Seven

Molly

MOLLY AND JACK WERE on the road by eight a.m. It was dull, and heavy grey clouds threatened rain. Jack was tired; they had both been up studying alternative therapies and clinical trials in America. Their search had been frustratingly fruitless. Molly had looked into everything from Biofeedback to Labyrinth Walking and concluded that the Americans were mad. 'How in the name of God and all that is holy does walking in a fucking circle cure cancer?'

Jack was listening to a Snow Patrol album while Molly continued to read the various trials they'd printed off the previous night. 'Any luck?' he said, as he pulled into a garage for petrol.

'These are mostly about studying patients as opposed to fixing them.'

'Mr Dunne did say . . .'

'Don't mind Mr Dunne. He's only one man.'

'He was the one man who gave our girl a chance. Remember the others.'

'Every last one, and that's why we need to go abroad. The Irish are backward, always were and always will be,' Molly said.

He got out of the car. She continued to read as he filled the tank. He leaned in. 'Do you want anything inside?'

'No.' He moved to walk away. 'Actually, hold on, I'll have a cup of tea.'

'Right.'

'And don't buy any chocolate.'

'I won't.'

'And pick up a lotto ticket.'

'Will do.'

'And the paper.'

She leaned out of the car and shouted the last order. Jack had his back to her but he raised a hand to acknowledge he'd heard it.

Molly was sitting in the car and minding her own business when a knock came at the window. She looked up and saw a man she recognized but wasn't sure from where.

'Mrs H?' he said.

'Yes?'

'It's me, Louis.'

'Louis! I can't believe it. How long has it been?'

'About twenty years.'

She put her hand to her mouth. 'Twenty years! Did you ever marry?'

'That's my wife there.' He pointed to the car parked across from her. A woman waved and she waved back. 'And there are my two as well.' A boy and a girl were sitting in the back seat.

'They're lovely. I'm delighted for you. So, Louis, did you stay with the music?'

'Nah. I went to college and studied IT.'

'Good for you, son.'

'How's everyone?'

'Davey's still in America, working with the country singer.'

'I've followed his career. He's done well, Mrs H.'

'He never married, no kids – at least, not that I know of.'

'Davey was always about the music.'

'A set of drums doesn't keep you warm at night.' She looked towards his car. 'Nothing beats family, Louis. Of course, I wouldn't say that to Davey – you know how bloody moody he gets if ya dare to have an opinion.'

Louis laughed. 'You haven't changed, Mrs H. How's Grace and Rabbit?'

'Great,' she lied. 'Grace is married with four boys and Rabbit has one girl.'

'I follow her work in the newspaper. I was sorry to read about her cancer.'

Molly often forgot that Rabbit had written about her battle. She blushed a little and wondered if he was aware he had caught her out in a lie. Rabbit hadn't written anything since her leg had snapped and her previous article had been hopeful: she had felt very well.

'She's a fighter, but you know that.'

'I can still see her intimidate sound guys who were twice her age and three times her size,' he said. 'She could have been a brilliant sound engineer if she'd wanted.'

'I always thought she'd make a lovely nurse,' Molly said.

'I'm glad she's doing well,' he said.

Molly remained silent. She couldn't bring herself to tell him the truth. She just couldn't face it. 'I'll tell her. She'll be delighted I saw you.'

He waved and walked into the garage. She returned to her reading material. It was another ten minutes before Jack appeared. The lotto ticket was in his mouth. He handed her the tea and the newspaper, then gave the ticket as he got into the car.

'You'll never guess who I bumped into inside the garage.'

'Louis.'

'He's piled on the weight. He'd want to watch that. I told him about Jeffrey. He said he's giving himself till September to knock himself into shape.'

'You didn't mention Rabbit, did you?' she said, as he took off onto the motorway.

'No. Why?'

'He asked about her and I said she was great.'

'She is great.' He smiled at his wife.

'Yeah,' she said. 'She's fucking fantastic.'

He laughed at her, then fell silent. She read on, but there was nothing appropriate in the documentation. He turned up the music. She looked out of the window at the fields of cows, sheep and fodder. He focused on the road, but they were both thinking about their daughter and how long they could keep up the pretence that everything would be all right.

Michael Gallagher looked frail and thin when he ushered them into his old broken-down bungalow. They followed him to the kitchen, which was inhabited by six cats, all, apparently, happy to sit anywhere but the floor.

'Christ on a bike,' Molly mumbled.

'Tea or coffee?' he asked.

'You're all right,' Molly said. There was no way she was drinking or eating anything in that house. He pointed to two chairs tucked into his kitchen table. They pulled them out and sat down. He sat opposite.

'What was so sensitive you couldn't talk about it over the phone?'

'It's not sensitive, not really. I just prefer to discuss business face to face,' Molly said. People found it much harder to say no to her in person.

'OK.' He rubbed his prominent nose with his forefinger and thumb.

'You probably don't remember my daughter Rabbit.'

'How could I forget her? She called me a charlatan and threatened to have me arrested for quackery and fraud.'

'Good memory,' Molly said. *Damn it*. But Molly would not be deterred. 'Well, anyway, she has cancer.'

'Don't we all,' he said.

'What?'

'Prostate.'

'Oh, I'm sorry.'

'I'm sorry too,' Jack added.

Michael shrugged.

'I didn't think a healer would get sick. Stupid, really,' Molly said.

'And you can't heal yourself?' Jack asked.

Of course you can't heal yourself, Molly thought. *Rabbit was right. You are a charlatan.*

'It doesn't work like that.'

'Can you still heal even though you're sick?' It sounded like a stupid question when asked out loud, but Molly didn't care.

'Under the right circumstances.'

'Will you visit Rabbit?'

'Does she want me to?'

'Well, no.'

'So you're thinking about surprising her?'

'We were thinking of saying nothing.'

'Nothing?'

'We were going to bring you in while she was asleep.'

'You do realize the patient has to want to be cured for healing to occur?'

'Well, she does want to be cured.'

'Just not by me.'

'It's nothing personal.'

'She doesn't believe in mumbo-jumbo,' Jack said.

'Not helpful, love,' Molly told him, and turned back to Michael. 'If you would lay your hands on her, we could have you in and out in a jiffy.'

'So you're planning on smuggling me into her home in the middle of the night?' he asked, one bushy silver eyebrow raised high.

'No, she sleeps a lot – it's the medication – and she's in a hospice,' Molly said. The words sounded strange coming out of her mouth.

Michael Gallagher took her hand. 'Stage four.'

'Yes.'

'I'm so sorry, Molly.'

'Don't be. Just help us.' She detected the panic in her voice.

'I can't.'

'Why?' she pleaded.

'She's dying, Molly.'

Jack's fist came down on the table and he covered his face and eyes with his other hand. 'But you helped that blind woman and the boy in Tralee with leukaemia and the rest.'

'It's too late for Rabbit, and even if it wasn't, she has to believe.'

'I believe. I'll believe enough for both of us.'

'I'm sorry.'

'Please.'

'I'm not going to take your money or waste your time, Molly. You need to go home and prepare yourself to say goodbye.'

Jack remained absolutely still. Molly looked from Michael Gallagher's sad face to her husband's. 'Is there nothing I can say?'

'No, Molly.'

She wiped away a stray tear roughly with the palm of her hand, then rested it on her husband's shoulder. He placed his on hers and patted it.

'We were just hoping . . .' Her voice broke, so she gave up talking.

'I know,' Michael said.

He apologized once more at his front door, as Molly and Jack walked down the narrow footpath arm in arm, Molly sobbing and Jack holding her head close to his chest.

Grace

Grace walked through the front door with her suitcase. Before she had her coat off, Lenny was halfway down the stairs. When she saw his face, she covered her eyes with her hands. 'I'm so sorry,' she said. 'I have no idea what happened.'

He held her close and kissed the top of her head. 'You lost it.'

'I hurt you.'

'It was an accident.'

'I threw a mug at your face on purpose.'

'I should have ducked quicker.'

'If this conversation was the other way around, you apologizing for hurting me and me making excuses for you, people would call it domestic violence.'

He laughed. 'Oh, for fuck's sake, Grace. We've been together for twenty years and this is the first mug-in-the-face incident we've had. I think I'm safe enough.'

'I'm so, so, so sorry.'

They walked together into the kitchen.

'I know,' he said. 'Now can we forget it?' He put on the kettle and she sat down on a stool facing him. 'Toast?'

'Yes, please. I'm starving.'

He popped two pieces of bread in the toaster.

'Where are the kids?' she asked.

'Stephen is in the library, Bernard's playing football, Ryan's still sleeping and Jeffrey is playing video games in Stuart's house. Did you sleep?'

'No, but Rabbit did.'

'She was in good form,' he said.

'Yeah, she was. I heard you were mugged.'

'Well, I was hardly going to say you were mental. Speaking of which, did you hear about Sheila B?'

'Yeah, poor cow.'

He poured them coffees and served his wife toast. She couldn't help but stare at the damage she'd done to his face. 'I'm a lunatic,' she said.

'Why? What did you do?' Stephen asked, appearing from nowhere in his ripped jeans and an old Blondie T-shirt.

'Nothing.'

'So where were you?' he quizzed, opening the fridge and grabbing the orange-juice carton.

'I stayed with Rabbit.'

'How is she?'

'She's in good form.'

He closed the fridge. 'I didn't ask how her form was. How is she?'

'Stephen . . .'

'Ma, will you stop treating us all like we're stupid?' Stephen poured a glass of orange juice and sat on the counter. 'So?'

'She's really sick.'

'No – really? I had no idea.' He was being sarcastic.

Grace briefly considered throwing a mug at him.

'Don't be cheeky to your mother,' Lenny said.

Stephen sighed and jumped down from the counter. 'You need to start telling the truth, especially to Juliet.' He downed the orange juice and walked out. They heard the front door slam.

Grace looked at Lenny. 'Davey's called a meeting in Ma's tomorrow to discuss just that.'

'We could build on an extension,' he said, out of nowhere.

'For what?'

'For Juliet.'

'We can't even get an overdraft on our current account, never mind extend the house.'

'We could tell Stephen to get out.'

She laughed. 'I don't believe this is happening. I know it *is* happening but I just don't believe it.'

'I know.'

'I'm really lucky to have you.'

'I know.'

'I'm really grateful.'

'So you should be.'

'I'm so sorry.'

'Stop.'

'You can throw a mug at me, if you'd like,' she said.

'No.'

'Please.'

'No.'

'What can I do to make it up to you?'

'You really have to ask?'

'You're so easy.'

He grinned and rubbed his hands together. 'I'm getting sex, Saturday-morning sex, living the dream, folks.' He danced around the kitchen, amusing his wife with his antics.

'What about Ryan?'

'I'll deal with it.'

He walked to the bottom of the stairs and shouted, 'Ryan.'

'Wha'?'

'Get the fuck out.'

'Wha'?'

'You heard.'

'But I'm grounded.'

'Not any more. OUT!'

'Nice one.'

Ryan was dressed and gone in less than five minutes. Lenny and Grace were undressed, intimate and spent fifteen minutes after their second youngest son had shouted, 'See ya later, losers,' and slammed the front door.

They lay together in the afterglow.

'He's probably robbing a bank.'

'Who?'

'Ryan.'

Lenny laughed. 'Nah, he's going to be fine.'

'We thought Rabbit would be fine.'

'Ryan is not Rabbit.'

'No, he's not.'

'He's just finding out who he is. He's not a bad kid.'

'Tell that to the kids whose iPhones he lifted.'

'He's not going to do it again.'

'I hope not.'

'Still can't believe he had a market stall in Dún Laoghaire we knew nothing about.'

'He's a smart kid.' It was true. Not only had Ryan run a stall selling items he had stolen from his classmates over three months, but he had put the money he'd earned into high-performing shares. He had lied to the police and said he'd spent it, but Grace had found the website on his open computer when she was snooping. She made him cash enough to compensate the kids, but he continued to invest and re-invest the profits from his ill-gotten gains. Initially Grace had had a real problem with this, but she'd given up after he'd agreed to pay the kids back and donate a hundred euro to a cancer charity.

'It's as good an offer as you're going to get, Ma,' he'd said. 'Take it or leave it.'

'I think he's bored.' Grace gazed at her poor husband's black eye.

'I know he is,' he replied. 'I just wish he was as into football as Bernard.'

'Maybe we should check out some advanced learning pro-grammes for him.'

'At what cost?' Lenny said.

'Doesn't matter. He can pay for it himself.'

Lenny laughed. 'Good luck.'

'Did Jeffrey stick to his diet yesterday?' she asked.

'Well, after the lentil roast had painted the wall and I'd re-covered from my mugging, I bought some steak and we all ate it with salad.'

'Thanks.'

'And I took him for a run before I visited Rabbit.'

'Did he run or did he just hold his side and complain?'

'There was a bit of that but he's getting better. You need to stop worrying about the kids. You've enough on your mind.'

'Honestly, it's sorting the problems with the kids that keeps me going. If I allowed myself to think about Rabbit every minute of every day, I swear to God I'd be joining Sheila B in the nut-house.'

They were both exhausted. Grace had spent an uncomfortable night on the sofa in Rabbit's room. She hadn't intended on staying but Rabbit had woken just as she was leaving and it was nice to have her sister to herself. They'd talked about Francie, how funny he was and how lovely it was to see him. They'd reminisced about his wedding and what a great time everyone had had, even poor Johnny, who'd been in a wheelchair by then. They'd talked about Rabbit's wigs and J.Lo's arse, where it had all gone wrong for Michael Jackson and why Pakistan held the rest of the world by the nuts. She'd fallen asleep again after about an hour of chat and by then it was easier for Grace to stay snuggled under the blanket Jacinta had provided. It was also nice to be there, listening to Rabbit breathe in and out.

Grace knew Lenny couldn't sleep properly without her in the bed. He'd known where she was: she had texted him, told him she loved him too, apologized and said she was staying, but he had tossed and turned all night, she was sure. Lenny was a fixer by nature. If Grace or his kids had a problem he would rack his brains to find a solution and wouldn't rest until he had made things better. He couldn't make this better and it was paralysing.

Eventually they fell asleep and were woken by Bernard's horrified scream. Lenny shot straight up in the bed and Grace automatically covered her exposed breasts.

'Ah, me eyes, me fucking eyes!' Bernard said.

'Don't say that word,' Grace said.

'Don't flash your tits, Ma, and I won't.'

'Don't come barrelling into our private room without knocking,' Lenny said.

'It's disgusting.' He was backing out. 'Shouldn't be allowed.' He closed the door behind him.

Grace and Lenny looked at one another and laughed.

Davey

Davey sat drinking coffee by the bay window, staring out onto the green. As a kid, he'd always loved Saturday. It was his absolute favourite day. Every other day he'd have to be dragged kicking and screaming from his bed, but on Saturday he'd been a morning person. He'd wake naturally at nine and, still in his pyjamas, he'd rush down the stairs to make his cereal. Just as he finished it, Rabbit would meet him in the sitting room. She'd curl up on the sofa and he'd sit on the floor in front of Da's armchair and they'd wait for the show to start. Neither ever had much to say to the other at that hour of the morning, but as the yellow BBC clock appeared and the announcer said, 'Now, at nine thirty, it's *Swap Shop*,' they had whooped and raised their hands in a tiny uncoordinated Mexican wave.

The show ran for two hours and forty-five minutes. By the time it ended, the whole house was up and noise leaked from everywhere. Grace would insist on vacuuming as soon as she was upright; Davey's ma would be talking to one friend or another on the phone in the kitchen while Da listened to the radio blaring and made a big Saturday fry-up for everyone. As the world outside invaded the sitting room, Davey and Rabbit would move as close as possible to the TV, both sitting cross-legged on the floor gazing upwards, until their ma entered with their fry-ups and screamed at them to get back into their chairs before their eyeballs exploded or their heads caught fire from the static.

Davey had loved those noisy, happy, exciting mornings, but he especially loved it when it was quiet and he and Rabbit waited, full of anticipation, for an almost always brilliant show.

Afterwards he'd get dressed and run out onto the green where some of the local lads would be starting a game of football. He wasn't a bad player, not as good as his da in his day but definitely better than most of the other kids on the road. His skills made him popular and he was often fought over by the teams, which made him feel really good.

'Hayes is on mine.'

'He is in his hole.'

'He was with you last week.'

'So?'

'So.'

Once in a while there would be a scrap and he'd have to intervene. After a particularly nasty altercation Bobby Nugent had gone home with a broken nose, and Davey's ma had decreed that, from there on in, all players would be picked out of a hat. The boys had grumbled, but not one of them dared challenge Davey's ma. After that Davey had felt less of a star but, to be fair, no one went home crying either so it was a decent enough trade-off. He had spent many happy Saturdays running around the green all day, only stopping when his ma made him eat a sandwich and drink a bottle of orange. Saturday was trash-food day in the Hayes household and the girls really appreciated an unhealthy alternative to their usual wholesome diet. At seven he was called in for his bath and by nine he was sitting in front of his favourite show of all time, *Starsky and Hutch*. Rabbit wasn't allowed to watch that, which made the experience all the sweeter. And even though he'd played on the green through spring, summer, autumn and winter, when he reminisced it was always sunny in his head.

'What are you looking at?' Juliet asked from the doorway, following his eyes to the empty green.

'The past.' He stood up.

'Me ma said you were a local legend.'

'For a very short time.'

'Aren't drummers in successful American country bands con-sidered local legends?'

'No.'

'Oh. Do you still know anyone around here?'

'Nah. Before I left the only people I hung with were the band.'

'Francie, Jay and Johnny,' she said, and he nodded. 'What about Louis?'

'He always had his own life.'

'What's that supposed to mean?'

'Just that. The four of us were tight, brothers, but Louis, he was in it to win it, and when it all went pear-shaped, he was the first to leave.'

Juliet sat down on the sofa and curled her feet under her, like her mother used to do. 'Was Ma a good sound engineer?'

'Who told you about that?'

'Francie.'

He smiled to himself.

'Well? Was she good?' she persisted.

'She was the best money could buy.'

'She worked for free.'

'Exactly.'

'Ah, Davey.' She threw a cushion at him.

He caught it and threw it back to her. 'I'm only joking. She was good at sound and she was even better at intimidating the other sound guys.'

'And that's an important skill?'

'You've no idea how important.'

Juliet nodded. 'Do you think I could intimidate some sound guys?'

'Juliet, you are a Hayes woman. You could intimidate Attila the Hun if you put your mind to it.'

Juliet seemed happy to hear that. She picked fluff off the sofa for a minute or two.

'Why?' he asked.

'Dunno.'

'What would you like to do when you grow up?'

'Plan A, cure cancer. Don't really have a plan B.'

'Do you like school?'

'Hate it.'

'Me too.'

'I was expecting you to bang on about how important it is.'

'I got thrown out when I was fourteen so I'm hardly going to preach to you.'

'Were you scared?'

'I was too stupid to be scared.'

'Did you always want to be a drummer?'

'Not always, but once I got my first set of drums, it was the only thing I ever wanted to do.'

'I hope that happens for me.'

'It will.'

'Thanks, Davey.' She got up. 'Is it OK if I go back to bed? I'm really tired.'

He nodded. 'I'll be here when you wake up.' When she left he returned his gaze to the empty green. *It would have been full by now and our third game in. Fucking internet.*

Jack

All the way home in the car, Jack thought about the gravity of their situation. *Now the charlatan's refused to take our money we're really screwed.* The time for hope, fight and pretence was nearing its conclusion. They had hit the wall. *What now?* It didn't compute. *A future without Rabbit, it's not possible.* But his brain couldn't conjure even one more possible solution.

'We could always drive the car into the sea,' Molly said, out of nowhere, as though she was reading his mind. 'It would be unfair on the kids but at least we'd get to go first, the way Nature fucking intended,' she added.

'I've always liked Dollymount Strand,' he said.

'Me too.'

'Howth is pretty at this time of year. And there are some lovely spots in Wicklow.'

'I won't survive this, Jack,' Molly said, allowing unbridled tears to flow. Jack pulled into the side of the motorway, turned on his hazard lights and faced his wife. He wanted to say something comforting but he couldn't think straight because his heart was beating so fast and his head was buzzing so loudly that, for a second, he imagined he was having a heart attack. *Oh, hell, no, don't do that to Molly.*

'Jack?'

'Molly.'

'Oh, God, Jack. What?'

And all of a sudden the dam inside him broke and he burst into tears. Molly clasped him and they held each other awkwardly, crying like babies on the side of the motorway and all the while the radio played Britney Spears's 'Born To Make You Happy'.

By the time they reached the hospice car park, Molly had recovered sufficiently to visit Rabbit. Jack was still so raw he asked her if it would be all right if he stayed in the garden for a bit.

'Of course.'

They kissed, and then he watched her walk away from him, admiring her steel. *I wish I was so strong.* Now that all hope had been snatched away, he was afraid he would distance himself again, but he knew he couldn't let that happen. He couldn't be the same guy everyone had worried about on the day Rabbit had entered the hospice; even Rabbit had worried for him, which was nonsense. He needed to pull himself together. He had to be there for his daughter during this, the worst of times, even though every fibre of his being was willing him to get into the car and drive it to Dollymount, Howth or one of those nice spots in Wicklow. *Come on, Jack, stop acting like a child.* He crossed the car park and entered the reception area. Fiona wasn't there. Instead he was greeted by a man, who introduced himself as Luke.

'Nice to meet you, Luke. I'm Jack Hayes, Rabbit's father. I was hoping to talk with Rita Brown, if she's available.'

'I'll just check for you now. Take a seat, Jack.'

Jack did as he was told. He was reading the newspaper when Rita appeared. She smiled and shook his hand. 'How are you, Jack?' she asked. He filled up. 'Follow me,' she said. They went down a long corridor to an office with her name on it. Once inside, she pointed him to a comfortable chair. 'How about a coffee?' she asked. 'Or tea if you'd rather?'

'I'm fine.'

She sat down in a chair opposite his. 'I don't think you're fine.'

'Rabbit is dying,' his voice was trembling, 'and there's nothing we can do to stop it.'

'That's right.'

'I can't watch her die.'

'It's going to be hard.'

'It's not hard. It's impossible.'

'Nothing is impossible.'

'OK. So if nothing is impossible it's still possible to save her.' His tone reflected his anger.

'Some things are impossible.'

'I can't do this.'

'You can.'

'I can't.'

'You have to.'

'Are you sure you're qualified?' he asked, and she chuckled a little.

'Rabbit told me you brought her into the world.'

Jack closed his eyes and told himself not to cry. 'I did.'

'You must have been terrified.'

'I was.'

'But you did it anyway.'

'I had no choice. It had to be done.' His lips trembled and his eyelids burned.

'I'm not going to labour the point.'

'I appreciate that.'

'You have a lovely family, Jack, so hang on to one another.'

He nodded and wiped away the last tears he'd allow himself that day. He stood up and shook her hand. 'Thank you.'

'I'm available whenever you need me.'

He walked from her room to the bathroom. He washed his face and straightened himself up. He ate a small salad in the canteen, then bought a chicken roll and a cup of tea for his wife.

Before he headed into his daughter's bedroom, he picked up a pretty beige floppy rabbit from the gift shop.

Juliet

The car pulled into the driveway and Juliet got out. Davey was listening to a soccer match on the radio so she went inside on her own. She hadn't been home since the accident. There was still some blood on the kitchen floor so she found a cloth and cleaned it, rubbing vigorously to get rid of the thick globules that had formed in the grouting.

Someone moved the mop behind her. She swung round, holding her heart. 'Christ, Kyle, you frightened the shite out of me.'

'Sorry.' He mopped where she'd been rubbing.

'What is it with you and sneaking up on people lately?'

'I don't manage to sneak up on anyone else.'

'What's that supposed to mean?'

'It means that maybe you're living in your head.'

'I am not.'

'I shouted "Hello" when I came through the door and I've been whistling the theme tune to *Dora the Explorer*.'

'Not loudly.'

'So why does everyone else tell me to shut up?'

'Habit,' she said.

'It's OK if you're stuck in your own head. I would be too.'

She stood up and brushed herself off. 'I really wish you'd stop feeling sorry for me. So me ma got sick and then broke her leg. It's not the end of the world.'

Kyle put away the mop. 'Lost me race this morning.'

'Sorry to hear it.'

'I've been losing a lot lately.'

'Why?'

'Don't know.'

'Do you care?'

164

'Big time.'

'Sorry.'

'Me da says I'm not focused.'

'What do you think?'

'I think I'm not good enough.'

'Why?'

'Because I'm killing meself on the track but there's always one guy who's better than me.'

'Who is he?'

'Simon Davis.'

'Well, he's only one guy,' she said, leaning on the counter.

'One's enough.'

'So you'll keep trying.'

'Yeah, suppose.'

'I have to get some fresh clothes.'

'OK.' He followed her up the stairs. She hadn't really meant him to join her, but he had spent a large amount of his time in her room when they were kids. Still, it had been a while since then.

'It's really different,' he said, walking in behind her.

'Believe it or not, I no longer believe I'm a princess.'

'I still have my Batman duvet cover.'

'Not cool.'

'Very cool,' he said, which made her smile.

He sat on her bed while she took some clothes out of her drawers and wardrobe.

'Where are you staying?' he asked.

'I was in Grace's but I'm going to me nan's now.'

'Are you coming back?'

'Of course! Why are you being so weird?' She turned to look him in the eye. She was willing him to tell her what she already suspected. It was time. She just needed someone to confirm her fears and her old friend Kyle was as good as anyone.

'I'm not acting weird.'

'Spit it out, Kyle.'

'Nothing.'

'What do you want to say?'

'I don't want to say anything. I want you to tell me something.'

'Tell you what?' She was shouting now.

'It doesn't matter.' He got up.

She stood in front of him, blocking the doorway. 'It does matter.'

'I'm really sorry.' He pushed past her, ran down the stairs and out of the front door past Davey, who didn't even notice him as he was lying back on the seat engrossed in the match. Juliet didn't shout after him. She didn't cry or moan or say a word. Instead she just curled up and waited for the intense pain in her heart to pass. She wasn't ready for the truth, after all. *It's going to be OK. Everything is fine. Kyle's just a kid. He doesn't know anything. Please be OK, Ma. Please, please, don't leave me. I'll be better. I'll make sure nothing bad ever happens to you again. I promise. I swear. Please, please, stay here.*

She stood up when the pain in her abdomen was more severe than the one in her heart. She was on her feet for only a few seconds before she doubled over. 'Oh, my God!' she whispered. 'What the . . .'

She sat down again and waited for it to pass. When a few minutes had gone by, she stood up and finished packing her clothes, but when she made it to the car she must have been about seven shades paler than when Davey had last seen her because he said, 'Are you OK?'

'Have you had your appendix out?' she asked.

'No. Why?' He looked worried.

'Did my ma?'

Davey turned down the radio and thought about it. 'It was Grace.'

'Can you ring her and ask her what it felt like?'

Davey put the car into gear and backed out of the driveway. 'We're going to A&E.'

'We don't need to go to A&E. I just need someone to tell me the symptoms and then I'll know.'

'We're going to A&E.'

'That's stupid.'

'It's not stupid.'

'Do you know how long they'll make us sit there? I'll be twenty-one by the time we get through.'

'Don't exaggerate.'

'Me ma has cancer and we've been stuck in chairs for eight hours at a time.'

'Oh, Christ. OK, call Grace.'

Juliet rang her aunt and put her on the speaker. 'Grace?'

'Hi, Bunny. I hear you've moved to your nan's. I'm sorry I wasn't there yesterday.'

'It's OK, and thanks for everything.'

'You're always welcome, you know that.'

'I do.'

'So what can I do for you?'

'When you had your appendix out, what did it feel like?' Davey shouted.

'What did he say?' Grace said.

'He asked what a dodgy appendix felt like,' Juliet said, grimacing as she spoke.

'Why?'

'I'm in agony, Grace,' she admitted.

'Left or right side?'

'Middle.'

'Are you sure?'

'Middle and low, like I'm going to give birth to a bowling ball.'

'Take me off speaker,' Grace said.

'What?' Davey said.

'It's not appendix, Davey. Now take me off speaker.'

Juliet did as she was told and she put the phone to her ear. 'Have you had your period before?' Grace asked.

'No.'

'Have you checked your pants?' Grace asked.

'Ah, no.' She blushed.

'I think you're getting one and the sooner you get to a chemist the better.'

'Oh.'

'It's going to be all right,' Grace assured her.

'Um . . .' Juliet said. 'I don't have any money.'

'Put me onto Davey.'

'Ah, no. I'm fine, please, Grace.'

'I'm not going to embarrass you, I'm just going to tell him to give you some money and let you off at a chemist. Then I need you to buy a box of regular tampons, a box of maxi pads, just in case you don't feel comfortable using the tampons, and some painkillers.'

'OK.'

'You'll be fine, Juliet.'

'OK.'

'I'm sorry I'm not there,' she said, and Juliet nearly cried because she wanted her mother. She handed the phone to Davey, who seemed more distressed than she was. She watched him as he spoke to Grace. He was nodding and saying OK a lot, like she had before him. He put down the phone.

'OK,' he said. 'No A&E. Excellent. We'll find a chemist and then everything will be great.' He was trying to act cool but he was sweating and couldn't look her in the eye.

He knows. I'm so embarrassed I could die.

They reached the chemist, where Davey took fifty euro out of his pocket and gave it to her with a nod and a thumbs-up. She got out of the car and felt the world falling into her pants. *Oh, no.* The jeans she was wearing were black and tight. She was afraid to look down at herself as she walked across the road but she hoped that the blood was not showing. She pulled at her T-shirt, trying to make it longer than it was. The pain no longer bothered her; it was the humiliation she was most concerned about.

When she made it to the door of the chemist she instantly noticed two men behind the counter. *No, no, no. This isn't happening. How can I be so unlucky? Crap, crap, crap.* She could feel Davey watching, waiting for her to open the door and go inside. She looked back at him and he gave her another thumbs-up. *Kill me, kill me now.* She walked inside and instantly one of the men asked what he could do for her. *I could be standing in a shop for an hour and an adult wouldn't ask me what I wanted but, oh, no, today I get the friendliest most helpful man in the world. I hate my life.*

'I'm just looking,' she said. *Why did I say that?* She felt another gush so she hid behind the foot-cream stand and crossed her legs. *What am I going to do?* It was then, when Juliet was reaching the stage of blind panic, that a young woman appeared at the makeup counter. She sighed with relief, straightened up and went to her. The girl was pretty, sporting a diamond nose-ring and a bar in her tongue.

'What can I do for you?' she asked.

Juliet leaned towards her and lowered her voice. 'I really need your help.'

'What's going on?'

'I've just got my period and I'm with my uncle,' Juliet whispered.

The girl gave her a knowing nod. 'First time?'

'Yeah.'

'How bad?' Her eyes moved from Juliet's face to her crotch, then back again.

'Bad.'

Another knowing nod. 'Pain?'

'I'm in bits.'

'OK.' She took Juliet's hand and led her past the two men, who were now happily engaged with other customers. Behind the shop there was a clean single toilet. The girl directed her inside. 'Wait there.'

Juliet locked the door behind her and sighed with relief. She took her pants down to reveal something akin to a murder scene. 'Oh, no.' She sat on the loo. She really wanted to call Della: first, to tell her that she'd got her period, and second, to apologize for always thinking she was bragging when she moaned about it. She now understood she was not bragging: this was nothing to brag about. She cleaned off as much of the blood as she could with tissue, nearly crying when she got some on her hand. She wiped it off and felt a little sick. A few minutes passed and she began to think that the girl had forgotten about her when a knock came at the door.

'It's only me,' the girl said. Juliet opened the door a crack and a packet of maxi pads, a box of tampons, baby wipes and a fresh pair of knickers were shoved through. 'Do the best you can with those.'

'Oh, thanks so much.'

'Have you ever practised using a tampon?'

'No.'

'It might be a big ask here in the shop. Maybe you should keep them for later.'

'Oh. OK. Um . . . where did you get the knickers?'

'They're mine.'

'Oh.'

'I'm going out straight after work and staying over, so you were lucky.'

'I really appreciate it,' Juliet said, making a start with the wipes.

'It's no problem. I got my first period on a fishing boat with my dad and two brothers,' the girl said.

'That sounds awful,' Juliet said, removing her jeans.

'I was wearing a skirt. My brother slipped on the mess.'

'Oh, no.' Juliet wrapped her soiled knickers and binned them.

'He thought it was fish guts so I got away with it.'

Juliet's stomach turned.

When she finally appeared from the toilet cubicle, the girl turned on a tap so Juliet could wash her hands. When she was done she was handed two pills and a glass of water. Juliet downed them.

'Two every six hours. No more,' the girl warned.

'I promise.'

'Good.' The girl smiled brightly. 'It's shit but you'll be OK.' She took the tampons, wipes, pills and maxi pads, put them into a large brown-paper bag and handed them to Juliet.

Suddenly Juliet welled up. 'Thanks.'

The girl hugged her quickly and they went back into the shop.

Juliet paid at the till, and when she was leaving the girl winked at her. If the two men knew what was going on, they had the decency not to show it.

Juliet walked across the road to where she could see her uncle preparing himself to talk to her. She sat in the car uncomfortably, hoping she wouldn't stain the seat. She handed him his change.

'Keep it.'

'It's the guts of thirty-five quid.'

'Buy yourself something nice.'

He was really trying his best to be cool, but he was so far from cool that Juliet felt a lot better about things, even a little bolder.

'I'd like some new knickers,' she said.

He paled a little. 'Great. No problem. Any place in particular?'

She burst out laughing. 'I'm only joking.'

'Ah, Jesus. I was thinking we'd go home and you can get changed and then we can see yer ma. How about that?'

'Could we stop for some food too? Suddenly I'm starving.'

'Absolutely.'

'It's on me,' she said, holding up the money.

*

When they arrived home, Juliet grabbed her case out of the boot and high-tailed it up the stairs to the waiting shower. She spent a long time standing under it before she took out the box of tampons. She read the instructions, then rang Della.

'Yo,' Della said.

'Yo, yourself. I need help.'

'I'm listening.'

'How do you put a tampon up without hurting yourself?'

'No!'

'Yes.'

'Agony?'

'Yes.'

'Hungry?'

'Starving.'

'I swear, Juliet, there isn't enough sugar in the world.' Della sighed deeply, conveying her distress.

'So, tampons?'

'OK,' Della said, 'but you're going to need to relax your hoo-hoo.'

'How do I do that?'

'I breathe into it.'

'How?'

'I dunno – I just do.'

Juliet spent another fifteen minutes trying to negotiate safe passage of a tampon into her hoo-hoo. By the time she was done she was running out of phone credit. 'I've got to go.'

'OK, call me later.'

'I will, and thanks.' She hung up. She changed her clothes. She felt clean and the pain was gone. She headed down the stairs with new pep in her step.

'Are you ready to eat?' she asked Davey.

'Anywhere you'd like.'

She mentioned her ma's favourite local restaurant. 'After all, it is a special occasion.' She grinned, and even though she was the one joking about it, she still blushed a little.

'Oh, for fu– sake.' He covered his eyes much like Granda did when he wanted to hide from something he couldn't face.

'You were brilliant,' she said.

'I was a dick. I didn't do anything.'

'Exactly.' She walked back to the car.

Johnny

The single from Kitchen Sink's EP was riding high in the Irish charts and the record-company executive was coming along to see them play and to talk about making an album. The queue lined the entire street. Girls were wearing T-shirts with pictures of the band on them; some had only Johnny's face. There were a few guys but it was mostly girls – loud girls. Rabbit passed them until she reached the front of the queue and knocked on the glass part of the door.

'Ah, who do ya think ya are?' a girl said.

'I'm with the band,' Rabbit said, waiting for one of the security guys to answer.

'No way.'

'Yeah.'

The girl looked at her friends and back to Rabbit. 'Can you get us in?'

'Don't think so.'

'Why not?' She put a hand on her hip. She was aggressive, and even though she wasn't as tall as Rabbit, she was a great deal wider, with fists the size of barrels.

'I'm sorry.' Rabbit rapped on the glass more urgently.

'Yer one doesn't think her shite smells.'

Rabbit thought about running away and calling the lads from a phone box, but just as the girl put her hand on Rabbit's shoulder, Johnny appeared and opened the door.

'It's him!' the girl gasped, as he grabbed Rabbit's hand and dragged her inside.

'Yip, it's me. See yis at the show, girls.' He waved and closed the door behind them. The girls screamed and word of his brief appearance spread through the queue, sending most of it into frenzy.

'I thought I was going to be punched,' Rabbit said.

'Good thing I was passing.'

'They're all mad.'

'Well, I'm pretty irresistible.'

'Don't be a dick.' She scrunched up her nose, then pushed up invisible spectacles. Johnny loved it when she did that: it reminded him of the little girl who used to follow him everywhere and hung on his every word until Alandra had come along and changed everything. Even though they had spent the summer touring together, Rabbit was no longer Johnny's little shadow and he missed her.

'What are you looking at?' she asked.

'You.'

'Why?'

'Because you've grown up so much.'

'Oh, don't say that! You sound like me da. He had two drinks and started crying about it at Uncle Gem's wedding anniversary. I was mortified.'

They walked up the stairs together, and halfway up, Johnny's knees gave way – he flailed for the rail but fell hard like a sack of potatoes. Rabbit rushed to his aid but he didn't want help. 'I'm fine, I'm fine.' He batted her away.

'So stand up.'

'What?'

'You heard.'

He grabbed the rail and pulled himself up. 'I'm just tired.'

'You're always tired.'

'Well, in case you haven't noticed, we're very busy.'

'There's something wrong,' she said.

'There's nothing wrong.' He tried to walk away from her but his body refused to help him.

'There's something wrong, Johnny,' she insisted, her eyes blazing.

'You say that again and you're outta here!' he shouted.

She stood silently, watching him prepare to take his next step. He walked slowly up the stairs and she remained where she was, observing him. He wasn't so much unsteady as unsure. She said no more, just waited until he was out of sight before she sat on the stairs and chewed her nails.

Ten minutes later Francie found her there. 'What's going on?'

'You're late for sound check.'

'So why aren't you there?'

'I'm surplus to requirements now. Haven't you heard?'

'You might not be our engineer any more, but we still need ya, Rabbit. Come on, get off your arse and let's go.'

Rabbit followed Francie onto the stage. Johnny was sitting on a speaker and directing Davey, Louis and Jay. He was displeased about the sound coming from the keyboard, and Davey kept making a mistake in the same part of the song.

'Are you just trying to annoy me?' he asked Davey.

'Yeah, everything I do is about you,' Davey said. He was frustrated with himself and Johnny wasn't helping matters. Francie walked onto the stage.

'Where were you?'

'Sheila was having a meltdown.'

'So bin the mentaller.'

'Listen, man, I love ya, but if ya call me girlfriend a mentaller again I'll punch you in the face.' Francie put on his guitar.

'Sheila is off her nut and you're off your nut to be with her,' Johnny said.

'You're crying out for a hiding.' Francie took off his guitar.

'Ah, clam down, Francie, will ya? We all know she's fuckin' nuts,' Jay said.

'Shut it, Jay,' Francie snapped.

'Or wha'?'

Davey stood up behind the drums. 'What the hell is going on?'

'Francie's too busy running after a fucking loon to take care of band business,' Johnny said. Johnny never cursed; he and Rabbit's dad were two of the few people Rabbit knew who didn't treat the word 'fuck' as a verb, noun and/or adjective. It was so strange and jarring to hear the word fall out of his mouth, even more alarming because of its aggressive delivery. Francie moved forward to hit him. Jay grabbed Francie by the arms. Francie swung around and punched his brother on the nose. Louis ran out from behind his keyboards with his arms outstretched.

'All right, all right, enough of this.'

Jay tripped Louis, who fell on both his outstretched hands. 'Oh, shite! Me finger.'

Jay stepped over him, then punched Francie back, catching him in the eye, and Francie reciprocated with a kick to his twin's balls. Jay head-butted Francie. They fell to their knees at the same time, bloody-nosed and black-eyed.

'What the fuck, Johnny?' Davey said, pointing to the twins.

Johnny walked off the stage, leaving the boys and Rabbit to stare after him.

Davey helped the two boys to their feet. Rabbit gave Jay a tissue and he held it to his nose. Davey examined Francie's eye. Louis lay on the floor, screaming blue murder about his finger.

'Well, this is brilliant. You couldn't let it lie, Francie,' Davey said.

'He shouldn't have got involved,' Francie retorted, pointing at Jay.

''Cause you decking Wet Boy would have worked out well? He'd be fucking dead,' Jay said.

Francie nodded. Jay had a point: Johnny was a lover, not a fighter.

'Rabbit, go down to the dressing room and find out what in the name of fucking fucksy is going on with him,' Davey said.

'He doesn't want to hear from me.'

'You're the only one he'll listen to,' Jay said.

'Not tonight.'

'Just do it, Rabbit – seriously. Our lives are on the line here.'

'Why don't you do it, Davey? It's your band.' She was too frustrated to admit she was scared.

'She has a point,' Francie said.

'So you do it,' Davey told him.

'If I go in there, I'll lay the fucker out.' Francie held his hands in the air. 'I am what I am.'

Davey sighed. 'Biggest night of our careers and I'm surrounded by arseholes.'

He walked off the stage, leaving Francie, Jay, Louis and Rabbit. Jay cleaned the blood from his nose and pocketed the stained tissue. Louis straightened his finger and walked behind his keyboard. 'It might need splinting but if someone gets me a drink I think I'll be OK.'

'Wanna jam?' Jay asked Francie.

'Fuck it.' Francie picked up his guitar. Rabbit made her way towards the dressing room and arrived in time to witness Davey being thrown out.

'He's lost it,' Davey said. 'He's totally fucking lost it.'

He walked onto the stage, leaving Rabbit to stare at the door for a minute or two before she knocked. Johnny didn't answer. She knocked again.

'Go away.'

'I'm really sorry,' she said.

'Please go away.'

'Just talk to me.'

'Can't.'

'Why not?'

Johnny opened the door. 'Because I'm screwed.'

Rabbit walked inside and closed the door. 'What's happening, Johnny?'

'I can't seem to hold meself up, Rabbit. When I close me right eye, I can't see a thing. The fans are wearing their laces open on

their biker boots like me because they think it's a fashion statement. It's not. Me stupid feet are swollen to twice their size.'

'So we'll go to the doctor. Maybe it's a virus. Me ma's friend
Pauline picked up a virus in Jersey and she lost some hair and
was on her back for weeks.'

'It's not a virus.'

'Are you a doctor?'

'No.'

'Well, then . . .'

'I don't think I can do this gig.'

'Yes, you can.'

'You don't get it. I'm going to fall on me face.'

'So sit down.'

'It's hardly rock and roll.'

'It is if you've just been in a tour-bus crash.'

He cocked an eye. He was listening, so she went on: 'Francie's
nose is smashed, Jay has a black eye, Louis's finger is probably
broken. We'll splint your leg and one of the lads can do something to Davey. You say you crashed on the way here but you're
still going on because you love your fans and that's how hard-
core you are. We can sell it to the lads because they're in bits
anyway.'

'That might work.'

'It will work. You'll get a magazine cover out of this.'

'Rabbit, you're my saviour.'

'So we'll go to the doctor tomorrow.'

'You don't have to come.'

'I'm coming.'

Johnny apologized to the lads and convinced them that a bus
crash was a good idea. Back in the dressing room, Davey needed
extra convincing because Francie was flexing his fist, ready and
waiting to give him an injury.

'What if we say I travelled in a separate car?' Davey pleaded.

'Not rock and roll,' Rabbit said.

'Ah, come on.'

'Don't be a bleedin' baby. I'll just give you a tap,' Francie said.

'Your version of a tap is brain damage.'

'It'll be over before you know it,' Johnny said.

'How come you can fake it?' Davey complained to Johnny, who was having his leg fake-splinted by Rabbit.

'We can't splint your arms because you couldn't play and we can't see your legs, so it has to be the face,' Jay said, and Francie nodded.

'Now, do you want to go down in the Rock and Roll Hall of Fame or not?' Francie asked.

'I do,' Davey said.

'Nice one.' Francie punched him in the mouth.

That night Kitchen Sink played to a packed house. Johnny sat in a chair with his splinted leg up, backed by his banged-up band. He sang his heart out to a grateful and fawning crowd. Afterwards he gave an exclusive about Kitchen Sink's near-death experience to a rock journalist, and when he was so tired he needed Rabbit's help to walk to the bar, Peter Moore, the record-company man, was waiting with a pint. 'You just went up a gear tonight, guys,' he said, and the lads smiled at one another.

'Keep this up and our sister company in the UK will get on board. You are going to be huge.' He raised his glass and the other lads raised theirs. Johnny looked at his, picked it up slowly and clinked it before putting it down. He didn't take a sip. Johnny wasn't a big drinker. 'Remember this night,' Peter said.

'Oh, I will,' Johnny replied. 'It's going to be hard to forget.'

Chapter Eight

Rabbit

WHEN RABBIT WOKE UP, she was surrounded by family. Her ma and da, Grace, Davey and Juliet, who was asleep, her head resting on her nan's lap.

'What time is it?'

'Just after seven,' Molly said.

'I missed the whole day?' Rabbit asked.

'You must have needed the rest,' Grace said.

'Maybe I'll ask for a vitamin.' She tried to pull herself into a sitting position. Grace rushed to help.

'I can do it,' Rabbit argued.

'Yeah, well, I can do it better,' Grace said. She raised her sister and fixed her pillows behind her.

'How long has Juliet been asleep?' Rabbit asked.

'I'm awake now.' Juliet scratched her head and sat up slowly.

Rabbit grinned at her. 'Hello there, Bunny.'

Juliet went to her mother and hugged her. 'Hello yourself.'

Rabbit surveyed her. 'You're pale.'

'I'm fine.'

'Have you eaten?'

'Davey took me to Fiddlers.'

'Oh, fancy.'

Juliet looked towards her uncle, seated by the window, and smiled at him. 'Yeah, it was really nice.'

'My pleasure,' he said.

'Are Stephen and Bernard still here?' Juliet asked, and Grace said that they were.

'Do you want to see them, Ma?' Juliet asked.

'Of course.'

'OK, I'll get them, but we can't all stay here,' Juliet said.

'I could do with stretching my legs,' Jack said, getting up. He picked up the beige bunny from the floor and handed it to his daughter, then kissed her forehead. 'A rabbit for my Rabbit.'

She laughed. 'I love it, Da.'

'I love you.' For a split second everything stopped in the room. 'Right, come on, Juliet. Let's put the boys out of their misery.'

When they'd left, Rabbit looked at her ma and then Grace. 'What's wrong with Juliet?'

'Nothing,' Davey said, and not because he felt Rabbit needed protecting from the news of her daughter's menstruation, but because he couldn't face talking about it.

'Grace?'

'She got her period today.'

Davey covered his face.

'Oh,' Rabbit said. 'Is she OK?'

'She's fine. Davey sorted it.'

'Davey?'

'I gave her money. She went to the chemist. The end. Now can we move on?'

Grace laughed. 'I really wish I could have been there to see his face.'

Rabbit was entertained by the idea of her easily embarrassed brother having to deal with a young girl's period, but part of her felt like crying.

Molly piped up, 'I got mine when I was riding a horse. I got off Duke and Ricky Horgan shouted that I'd jam on me arse. It wasn't jam at all.'

Rabbit and Grace laughed. Davey went puce. 'Jaysus, Ma.'

'I was on a camping trip with the Girl Guides. I filled me knickers with dock leaves, said nothing and no one was any the wiser,' Grace said.

'There you go, Grace, a green sanitary-towel option. You could package that,' Molly said, over Davey's groans.

'I've no story,' Rabbit said.

'Good,' Davey said.

'Everyone has a story,' Grace said.

'Shut up, Grace,' Davey pleaded.

'Shut up yerself.'

'Ma, seriously, tell Grace to shut up.'

'Are you twelve, Davey Hayes?' Molly asked.

'Go on, Rabbit,' Grace said.

'I was just on the loo, saw blood and called me ma.'

'Right, that's it, I'm going to the canteen,' Davey said, and was gone.

Molly chuckled. 'I remember, you were only ten. You screamed, "Ma, Ma, I think I'm dying . . ."' Rabbit's eyes instantly filled with tears and there was silence in the room. 'I didn't mean to say that,' Molly stuttered. 'I shouldn't have said it.'

The room fell into total silence. The three women cast their eyes downwards and that was when Rabbit accepted the truth.

'Ma,' she said, her voice trembling. 'Ma, look at me. Ma, please, look at me.'

Molly took a deep breath, then met her younger daughter's eyes.

'I think I'm really dying, Ma.'

In a second, and despite two titanium hips, Molly was up and out of the sofa, holding Rabbit and wiping away her tears. 'I know ya are, love. I know.'

'I'm sorry, Ma,' Rabbit said, and Grace gulped as hot fat tears rolled down her face.

'*Noooo*, don't be sorry, love. We love you so much.' Molly stroked her head.

At that very moment Stephen and Bernard strolled in.

'Hiya, Auntie Rabbit,' Bernard said.

'Fuck off!' Grace shouted. The two lads assessed the situation and backed out without another word.

Rabbit cried in her mother's arms for a few more minutes, then wiped her eyes and promised no more tears.

'You cry all you want to,' Grace said.

'I'm done,' Rabbit said, then asked the question that was on everyone's mind. 'Juliet?'

'We need to tell her, Rabbit,' Molly said.

'Davey's organized a meeting tomorrow at Ma's to talk about who's going to take her and, don't you worry, everyone wants her,' Grace said.

Rabbit nodded and bit her lip. 'Davey did that?'

'He was very assertive,' Grace said.

'Good for him.' Rabbit addressed her mother: 'Can we wait just another day before telling her?'

'Of course.'

'If I get worse . . .'

'I know, love,' Molly said.

'OK.'

They fell into silence again. '"Ma, Ma, I think I'm dying,"' Grace repeated, with a big grin. 'Jaysus, Ma, another classic.'

Molly looked at Rabbit for a signal. Rabbit's grin was enough. 'The other day I told her the bath was big enough to drown in,' Molly said sheepishly.

Rabbit and Grace were laughing when Juliet popped her head around the door. 'Where are the boys?'

'They've been in and gone,' Grace said.

'Oh,' she said, coming in and taking a seat by her mother. 'Quick.'

'But memorable,' Rabbit said, and Grace laughed.

'All right, yous are all acting strange but that's OK. It's been a strange day,' Juliet said.

'I heard,' Rabbit said, and squeezed her daughter's hand. 'I bet it's a good story.'

'Oh, it's a story,' Juliet agreed, much to her mother's enjoyment.

When everyone had gone home, Rabbit lay in bed attempting to make peace with her imminent demise. She wasn't angry or even that frustrated. She wasn't scared or worried. She wasn't bitter or vengeful. She was just sad to leave the people she loved most, especially her daughter. She had fought for so long, but finally she knew that she couldn't go on. It was hard to have to say goodbye to life, with its ups and downs and all the things that made it beautiful. Marjorie was on her mind. She wished her friend was in a happier place and in a relationship. Rabbit's death wouldn't hit so hard if she had someone's shoulder to cry on. She briefly daydreamed about bringing Davey and Marjorie together; it would be a fairy-tale ending of sorts. Rabbit pops her clogs and Davey pops the question; they'd adopt Juliet and live happily ever after. She laughed to herself as she remembered Sister Francine's stark warning to her when she was sixteen and had dared to admit her scepticism in religion class: 'It's easy to turn your back on the Lord when the going is good, but wait till you're on your deathbed, my girl. Then you'll go looking for Him and I hope it won't be too late.' The way Sister Francine had said 'I hope it won't be too late' implied not only that she hoped it *would* be too late but that she'd be disappointed if it wasn't. Sister Francine had been pushing eighty back then, so she was long dead. *Pity. I'd love to give her a call and tell her I'm dying and still not looking for the Lord, so screw you, penguin. We can all be bitchy, Sister F.*

When she looked back on her life, she had no regrets. Well, maybe a few, but overall she had done her best, and she wouldn't change anything, except maybe leaving for America when Johnny had told her to go. Maybe if she had stayed, things would have worked out differently, although, either way, by the time she got on the flight to JFK she had lost him anyway. The things she regretted were in the future she'd never have. She regretted not being around for Juliet, never finding another love and not finishing the book based on her blog. She regretted not putting more money away for Juliet's education and basic needs, and leaving the burden of that on her family. She wondered why she wasn't angry. It was all so unfair. Maybe it was because she was so tired.

'Have you any pain?' Jacinta asked, changing her patch.

'I didn't hear you come in.'

'You're coming in and out.'

'I was mean to you last night. I'm sorry,' Rabbit said.

'No, you weren't.'

'I was rude.'

'You were in agony. I've had to deal with way worse than you,' Jacinta said.

'How long do I have left, Jacinta?'

'It's hard to say.'

'Not long, though.'

'Probably not.'

'But it's hard to say.'

'Exactly.'

'I have no pain,' Rabbit said.

'Good,' Jacinta said. 'Sleep well, Rabbit.' But Rabbit was already gone.

Rabbit Hayes's Blog

4 December 2009

S Is for Shitting Yourself

I haven't been writing for a while. Chemo has a way of making death seem like a holiday. So here's a list of my side effects in alphabetical order: abdominal pain, acid reflux, bruising, chest pain and chills, dry mouth and diarrhoea. Nothing in the Es, so moving on to F: flu-like syndrome and fatigue; nothing I through L, but under M, memory loss, mouth sores, then numbness, skip O, pain under P, rash under R, skip to V for vomiting and finishing off with W for weight loss. X, Y and Z are letting the side down. Other than that, chemo is a breeze.

Juliet's being great. She's reading about cancer foods on the net and insisting that we juice. We produced a green concoction that made her throw up through her nose last week, and when she stopped gagging and crying, she said, 'Ma, at least you're not vomiting alone.' The thing is as bad as it gets – and, trust me, with constant heartburn, bad breath, vomiting, shitting yourself and forgetting where the clean pants are kept, it gets bad – but I've never felt alone. My mother is on the phone morning, noon and night, and when she's not on the phone, she's in my house, cleaning, cooking and giving out about deaf Annie next door.

'Who in the hell watches daytime TV at that level? There's fucking discos that are quieter than that auld one's sitting room.'

She's banged on the wall a few times and threatened Armageddon, but if deaf Annie heard her she doesn't let on, she just waves and smiles and shouts about the weather every time they pass each other on the street. Grace is always here, and when my mother isn't cleaning she is. She tries to cook and it's appreciated (mostly by next-door's Husky and deaf Annie's three cats). My dad has learned to text just so that we can talk even when my buzzing head aches too much to speak. Davey Skypes and sends care packages from various spas around the world. The last one was from India and smelt of rotten eggs. It's in the garden shed only because it's too expensive to throw out but definitely not expensive enough to try.

Marjorie is my light relief: she flits in and out, never outstays her welcome and always knows what to say and do, even if it means her saying, 'I don't know what to say or do.' Sometimes she sings me a little song she's made up on the journey over. She's funny, funnier than she knows. I wish she'd find someone. Juliet is my constant.

I may be sick to my stomach, exhausted and absolutely terrified, but I am definitely not alone.

DAY FIVE

Chapter Nine

Molly

MOLLY LIKED TO WALK when she couldn't sleep, while Jack favoured lying there, eyes wide open, staring. He could have been mistaken for a dead man if he hadn't been a sniffer. Jack sniffed a lot. It was a tic and/or a habit he'd had since he was a child. The amount of sniffing was directly linked to how much pressure he was under. If there was a world record in sniffing, Jack Hayes would probably break it overnight. Molly put on a coat and walked around the green in front of her house, around and around, until darkness faded into light and Pauline Burke came out of her house in her dressing-gown and slippers, holding two mugs of hot tea.

'You're freezing.'

'I'm fine.'

'Your slippers are soaked in dew and you've either got snot or an icicle at the end of your nose.'

Molly rubbed it off and stared at the offending item. 'I think it's just dry skin.'

'Come inside. I've got a fry on,' Pauline said, taking her old friend's arm and dragging her in. After thirty years, Molly knew that Pauline wasn't taking no for an answer.

Once inside Molly realized how cold she was. She started to

shiver so violently that Pauline covered her with a blanket and insisted on bathing her feet in hot water.

Molly sat quietly, cradling her mug in her hands, while Pauline got on with the business of making a fry-up. She turned the radio on to an early-morning light-hearted breakfast show. Daylight streamed through the kitchen window and Pauline's dog, Minnie, ran around in circles, then jumped up and down at the back door. Pauline opened it and the dog bounced outside, barking at the birds and the world. When she placed the cooked breakfast in front of Molly it came with a warning: 'I want to see at least half the plate cleared.'

Molly sighed deeply, but she didn't argue. She was hungry even if she felt suddenly so tired that raising the fork to her mouth would be a mammoth task.

'I'm glad you managed time to get your hair done,' Pauline said.

Molly put her hand to it and patted it down. 'They did it in the hospice.'

'That was good of them.'

'It's a nice place.'

'So I've heard. Now eat your sausage.'

Molly ate her sausage.

'I think we'll go away in September. I'm thinking about France because it's so handy to get to and the weather will still be warm but not too hot. You know I hate the heat,' Pauline said.

'I can't,' Molly said.

'Of course you can.'

'I'll have Juliet to consider,' Molly said.

'So you're taking Juliet?' Pauline asked, sounding surprised.

'Of course I am. Who else will?' Molly said.

'Jesus, Molly, it's a lot to take on at your age.'

'Davey's holding a meeting about it later today. I don't know why he's bothering, but I suppose it's his way of doing something.'

'How long?' Pauline asked, in a voice just a little above a whisper.

'Not long,' Molly said, without a trace of a tear.

'What can I do?' Pauline asked.

Molly looked from her half-eaten breakfast to her feet soaking in warm water. 'You've just done it, old pal.'

Pauline stood up and cleared away the plates. As she was passing her friend, she paused to kiss her lightly, then went to the sink. 'We're going to France, old woman,' she mumbled to herself, loud enough for Molly to hear her.

The first time Molly laid eyes on Pauline she was standing on the Hayes doorstep with a bloody face, and a small crying terrified boy under each arm. It was a winter's night in 1980 and Molly and her family had just moved into the area. Pauline was hysterical. 'Please, please, let us in! He's going to kill us all!'

It was then Molly realized that the man who was threatening Pauline was coming across the green, waving something that looked like an old man's walking cane. Jack wasn't home and the man was huge, strong, aggressive and possibly insane. She didn't think twice. She ushered Pauline inside and shut the door before he reached the gate. She bolted it top and bottom and stood right back when his balled fists banged against the wood with such force she was afraid the whole front of the house would fall in on them. The kids started to scream, and Pauline tried to shush them, but she was so frightened and so injured that they only roared louder.

Between the screaming and the banging it wasn't long before Grace and Davey were marching down the stairs in their pyjamas, rubbing their eyes and wondering what was going on. When they saw the bloodied woman and the screaming kids in their hallway, Grace sat on the stairs and cried, and Davey ran to his mother. The man was shouting blue murder.

'What's his name?' Molly asked Pauline.

'Gary.'

Molly sat her son beside his sister on the stairs, then walked to the door and banged on it as aggressively as he was doing. 'We can both beat the door, Gary,' she said.

That stopped Gary in his tracks. Aside from the crying children, it was quiet enough for everyone to work out their next move.

Gary spoke first. 'I want my wife and kids.'

'Well, you can't have them.'

'You open this door or you'll be sorry.'

'The guards are on their way, Gary,' she lied.

'I am the guards.' He sounded smug and proud of himself.

'Oh,' she said, 'so that's why you think you can get away with beating a woman and terrifying little children. You're the big I am.'

'You don't speak to me like that!'

'Or what?'

'Or I'll come in through your fucking front window.'

She could hear him walking away from the door and towards her sitting-room window. Without thinking, she unbolted and opened her front door and slammed it behind her. He turned in time to see her pick up the stick he had dropped, which he had used to bang on the door. He walked towards her slowly – he was probably as shocked as she was that she had locked herself outside with him, but those windows would have cost a fortune to replace, never mind the impact a lunatic coming through the front room would have on her kids. She could hear them screaming inside.

'What are you planning to do with that?' he asked her, looking at the stick.

She daydreamed about shoving it through his mouth. 'I'm going to lean on it while I tell you to fuck off.'

'Really?' He seemed almost amused. He wasn't shouting now: he was intrigued.

She leaned on the stick. 'Go home, Gary.'

'And what if I don't?'

'When your friends roll up, I'll tell them what you've done to your wife, and even if they cover for you at least some of them will judge you as you should be judged. When you're all gone I'll put in a call to my uncle, the Garda commissioner, and I'll make sure he knows just what kind of a man you are.' She was lying but he didn't know that. He left without a word or his big stick.

Pauline and the kids stayed over that night. It was the first of three similar incidents before Pauline finally had the strength to boot him out. When she did, their local priest at the time, Father Lennon, called to the house to talk her into allowing her husband home. Maybe he would have been successful in his guilt trip if Molly had not come to the door as he was pointing out how Pauline had 'made her bed'. Molly had no time for Father Lennon. He had proved himself unworthy of her respect when she had witnessed him taking money from a sober, contrite Gary's pub stash to pray for his tortured soul after he had beaten Pauline so badly she was in hospital for two weeks. The money Father Lennon took was the equivalent of a week's wages, and at the time it was clear that the man didn't provide for his own family. Pauline and her boys were half starved, and if it wasn't for her ability to sew, they would have been in rags. The priest had shoved it into his pocket and told Gary he'd pray that they'd be reunited in harmony or some such rubbish. Jack had had to hold Molly back in the corridor at the hospital where Pauline lay battered and broken.

'You're a disgrace, do you hear me, Lennon?' she shouted.

On the day Molly entered Pauline's kitchen while Father Lennon was advocating for Gary, he paled at the sight of her.

'What shite are you spreading?' she asked him.

'There's no need for that.'

'What's he saying?' she asked Pauline.

'That my vows mean something and my soul is at risk,' Pauline said.

'And do you believe him?'

'Honestly, I don't care if it is. Since Gary left, my kids are happier, more content, I'm not scared, and I've even got myself a part-time job.'

'Time for you to go,' Molly said to the priest.

'Just a second.' He raised a finger to Molly.

He really shouldn't have done that. He was a very small, slight man. She looked down on him. 'You either get the fuck out of this house on your own two feet or you'll be lifted out, but either way it's going to happen.'

Pauline giggled, not just because Father Lennon's face was a picture but because it was something she did when she was nervous.

'Never darken the inside of my church again, either of you,' he said as he was leaving.

'Our pleasure,' Molly replied, and slammed the door.

After that Molly, Jack and the kids went to the airport church, with Pauline and her kids; they'd all enjoy lunch at the airport afterwards. It was there that Molly first encountered Father Frank. They had their share of disagreements, but he was a good, decent man and when he met someone who needed a little guidance and help, he knew he could always rely on Molly. They had a lot of respect for one another and a friendship of sorts. She'd been thinking about him over recent days. As she walked from Pauline's house to her own, she made a mental note to phone him as soon as Davey's meeting was over.

When Father Frank rang her doorbell, it was as if he had read her mind and, even though she hadn't been to mass in months and the last time they'd spoken they had argued, it was good to see him. Jack and Juliet were in the hospice with Rabbit. He knew about Rabbit: her illness was the reason for his visit. He was hospice chaplain and, although she wasn't listed for spiritual guidance, he'd seen her name and there was only one Rabbit Hayes.

'What can I do for you, Molly?'

Molly appreciated him cutting to the chase. 'You can bless her.'

'You know she doesn't want me to.'

'But I want you to, and please don't say no to me because I can't take another no.'

He considered it for a moment. 'I can wait till she's asleep.'

Molly winked at him. 'Great minds think alike.'

'It's not ideal, Molly.'

'But it's better than nothing and, right now, it's the only thing keeping me going.'

'I'll do my part.'

'And that's all I can ask.'

'Do the others know what you've got planned?'

'They don't and it's none of their business.'

'Be careful, Molly. The last thing you need is in-fighting.'

'I'll handle it. Now, you'll stay for dinner.'

It wasn't a request and Father Frank knew better than to argue.

Grace

Stephen joined his mother in the garden. Until that point she had been enjoying a coffee alone. It was cold, but with a jacket on she was perfectly comfortable. He sat down beside her. She said, 'I'm sorry you have to take some time away from study to help distract Juliet.'

'It's no big deal. I'll make up for it.'

'Fingers crossed.' She was still annoyed that he hadn't applied himself all year.

'What do you want us to say to her?' he asked.

'Just tell her you want to hang out.'

'Because that won't raise questions.'

'Just tell her . . .'

'The truth?'

'Not yet.'

'Jaysus, Ma, what are ya waiting on?'

'Rabbit wants one more day.'

Bernard came out with a Manchester United scarf on and matching gloves. He sat down beside them. 'What are we talking about?'

'What we should say to Juliet when we take her out later.'

'Nothing,' Bernard said.

'She'll ask questions,' Stephen said.

'No, she won't.'

'She's just going to get in the car and say nothing?'

'She might ask where we're going.'

'Bollocks.'

'Stephen, mind your language.'

'Sorry, Ma, but she's going to ask and I don't want it to get out on my watch.'

'She won't ask because she already knows,' Bernard told him.

'No, she doesn't,' Stephen said. 'She thinks she's going home.'

'She might not want to know, but she knows,' Bernard replied.

'Speaking of . . . Is she coming to live here?' Stephen asked, as Lenny joined the table with a pot of coffee and some fresh cups.

'Of course we're taking her,' Lenny said, shook the cushion and sat down.

'I suppose I could share with Bernard until I find a room somewhere and Ryan and Fat Boy could go in together.'

'Don't call your brother "Fat Boy",' Grace snapped.

'He's not fat anyway. He's obese,' Bernard said.

'Not funny, Bernard. Besides, those two rooms are too small to share.'

'I was only saying.'

'We could sell Ryan to the tinkers,' Stephen suggested.

Bernard laughed. 'Yeah, but they'd send him back after two weeks.'

'Ha-ha,' Ryan said, coming out of the kitchen. He pulled over a chair and joined them. 'Talking about Juliet?'

'Yeah,' Lenny said.

'I saw a caravan on sale online for a hundred and fifty euro

– lovely little thing. Park it up outside and I'll move into it,' he offered.

'Finally Ryan would be where he belongs, Juliet could have my room, I move in with Bernard and Fat Boy stays in the box room,' Stephen said.

'We're not shoving your brother into a caravan.'

'I don't mind,' Ryan insisted.

'Of course you don't. I can't even imagine what you'd get up to in there,' Lenny said.

Ryan grinned to himself. 'Cool stuff.'

'Here, Da, did the Unabomber live in a caravan?' Bernard wondered.

'I think it was a tent.'

'Yous can all laugh, but I don't see anyone else come up with a solution,' Ryan said, and he was right.

It was going to be really tight, no matter what they did, but Grace was heartened by her boys embracing Juliet. She was proud. Then she remembered her baby. 'Where's Jeffrey?'

Ryan leaned back and looked in through the glass window at his brother, whose nose was stuck in the fridge. 'Where do you think?'

'Jeffrey, get your head out of the fucking fridge!' Grace screamed. The three other lads laughed.

Jeffrey appeared, hurt and appalled. 'I was only looking, Ma.'

She grabbed him for a hug before he had a chance to get out of her reach.

'Ma, let me go.'

'I love you, kids,' she said, and suddenly she was crying.

Ryan got up. 'I'm outta here.'

Stephen slunk off without a word, and Jeffrey struggled free, then went into the house. Bernard gave his ma a kiss and left his parents alone.

'Well, I've got to hand it to ya, ya know how to clear a room,' Lenny said.

'And that's why I wanted a girl.'

He poured her another coffee, then stood up. 'Looks like you're going to have one, after all.' He walked inside, leaving Grace to contemplate her new reality.

When Rabbit was a baby, Grace used to put her in her red dolls' pram and wheel her around the green. Rabbit was a fat, squirmy little thing, who didn't appreciate the confines of a doll-sized pram, so much so that she burst through its undercarriage. Grace wasn't sure how her baby sister had managed to wreck her pram, but she was sure it had been a deliberate act. Rabbit lay screaming on the grass, fists balled and legs kicking. Grace left her there because she couldn't carry her broken pram and her baby sister at the same time. No one was going to rob a screaming baby, but even though the pram was broken, it was still beautiful. When she returned to collect her sister, with her irate mother in tow, Rabbit had calmed. She was gurgling happily, kicking towards the sky. Molly didn't pick her up right away because she looked so content that it seemed a shame to disturb her. Instead she and Grace just watched her have a wordless and invigorating conversation with the blue sky above her.

'My friend Alice's sister has to go to a special school,' Grace said.

'So?' Molly asked.

'Just saying.' Grace eyed her sister.

When Rabbit was five, she fell down a drain. The Hayes family were on a day out and Rabbit found the only uncovered drain on a thirty-acre farm. She fell far enough that she couldn't be reached but could still be seen. Grace was standing close to her when it happened. They were looking at cows in the field and Rabbit was intrigued. Grace was bored and hungry. She preferred the zoo: at least there was ice-cream there. She looked away from her little sister for one minute and, during that time, Rabbit had climbed over the fence into the field and disappeared.

'Ma, Da!' Grace roared. Her parents and the farmer came running. Grace was the first to reach Rabbit. She looked down the drain and saw her sister, who was stuck but remarkably calm.

'Are you all right?'

'I think I've broken my shoe.'

The farmer reassured Rabbit that she'd be OK. It was only then that it occurred to her that anything else was a possibility, so she burst into tears and repeated that she thought she'd broken her shoe.

'Don't mind your shoe, love.'

'They're my favourites.' She sobbed. 'And I'm stuck, Ma.'

'We'll get you out,' Molly said. The farmer went to call the fire brigade; Jack paced up and down, mumbling to himself; Grace sat on the grass and made daisy chains, and Molly told stories to her daughters about a girl who fell down a well. Grace listened as she threaded flowers. Molly said that the girl who fell down the well was brave and didn't cry one bit. She was patient because she knew it took time for the men to come and save her. She was funny because even though she was down a well she could tell a story that had everyone above her laughing.

'What was the funny story, Ma?' Rabbit asked.

'You tell me, love,' Molly said.

Rabbit thought for a minute or two. 'There was a girl called Rabbit, she had a really bad habit, she forgot to look and fucked her foot and now she's in trouble for cursing.'

Grace had never heard her baby sister say 'fuck' before, and as much as her ma liked to say that word, it was not a children's word. She stopped threading daisies, expecting Ma to lose it, but she didn't. Instead she burst out laughing. 'You see, love, everything is going to be OK,' Molly said, and Rabbit believed her.

It was another hour before the fire brigade managed to get her out. Davey missed the whole thing because he didn't do farms and had insisted on staying in the car, reading comics and listening to the radio. He missed Rabbit telling her story and being winched out of a hole, smiling and waving even though her ankle was broken and she'd lost her shoe. The car park was far enough away that he didn't see the paramedics treat her and the ambulance take her away. She was wearing the daisy chain Grace had made for her and Ma was by her side. She had been strong even back then.

Grace sat in her garden, thinking about the sister who used to follow her around long before she'd fallen in love with Davey's band. She regretted the many times she'd shouted at her to leave her alone, to get out of her room or to just go away. *I'm so sorry, Rabbit.*

In the years between childhood and adulthood they had become friends. After Johnny had died and Davey left for America, Grace and Rabbit had grown close, and even more so when Rabbit found herself pregnant by a man she hardly knew. She had considered abortion for about five minutes, then conceded it wasn't something she could bring herself to do. Life would be so much easier if she could just board the plane and get the situation sorted. Grace was by her side from the start. She didn't judge, she didn't preach, and she knew Rabbit was facing hardship as a single mother. She also knew it would be the greatest thing she'd ever do.

'It doesn't matter who the father is,' she'd said, when Rabbit cited that as another reason to consider abortion.

'I don't even know what part of Australia he's from. I mean, he mentioned it once but it's some country town somewhere in the middle of nowhere. I've no idea.'

She'd felt terrible about bringing a child into the world without a father.

'When I think about who I am, I see my ma and my da,' Rabbit said. 'I see you and Davey, too, but I see them first, you know?'

'I know,' Grace said.

'My kid will just see me. A part will be missing.'

'Your kid will see herself reflected in you, Ma, Da, Davey, me, Lenny, the kids. We are all her family. We are part of who she will become and we're not so bad, right?'

'Good enough for me,' Rabbit said.

'There you go.'

'I'm having a baby, Grace,' she'd said.

'Yes, you are.'

'Will you tell me ma?'

'We'll tell her together.'

'Can I stand behind you?'

'For the sake of the baby, yes, you can.'

Grace was there for her sister right through the pregnancy, but it was her ma who held her hand during labour, not because Grace wasn't welcome but because, four days before Rabbit's due date, Ryan had come down with measles so she wasn't allowed near the maternity ward. Instead she paced her garden, waiting for the phone to ring. It was one minute past seven when the call came.

'Grace, we finally have a girl,' Molly said.

Grace had burst out crying. 'How's Rabbit?'

Before her ma could answer, Rabbit had grabbed the phone. 'She's beautiful! Wait until you see her, Grace! She looks like you. Doesn't she, Ma? She has your eyes. I'm so thrilled she has your eyes.' She was breathless, excited, euphoric.

'How are you?' Grace said.

'Blown away.'

'I'm talking about your fanny.'

'Ma says it's a car crash down there.'

'Don't worry, it does get better.'

'Honestly, Grace, I don't care. I'm a mother.'

'I'm so happy for you, Rabbit.'

'I know it sounds corny, but I've never felt love like it,' Rabbit said. 'Gotta go and try to feed Juliet.'

'Juliet? You were thinking of Rose.'

'The second I saw her . . . She's a Juliet.'

'Beautiful.'

'Wait till you see her, Grace! She has your eyes.'

'You said.' Grace chuckled.

'Grace.'

'Yeah.'

Rabbit whispered, 'I didn't think I'd ever be really happy again.'

'I know.'

'I just wish Johnny could have seen her.'

'Maybe he's looking down.'

'Ah, Grace, you know I don't believe that shite.'

'I thought maybe the miracle of birth might have changed your mind.'

'I always believed in Nature.'

'All right, all right.'

'Now, seriously, I have to go and be a mother.' Rabbit giggled. 'I'm a mother, Grace.'

Molly had been annoyed when Rabbit had revealed she wouldn't be christening Juliet. Even though her daughter had expressed her atheism since she was a child, it had never occurred to her mother that she would pass it on. Grace was forced to intervene when the subject came up over a Sunday roast in her house a month after Juliet's birth. It was Lenny who initially put his foot in it.

'Seeing as it's summer and we have the big garden, you're more than welcome to have the christening party here.'

Rabbit laughed. 'Right, thanks.'

She was being sarcastic, but Molly chose not to hear that. 'That'll be lovely,' she said.

'Ma, are you on drugs?' Rabbit asked.

'Lipitor, Atenolol, aspirin and lactulose. Why?' Molly matched her daughter's sarcasm.

'Juliet is not being christened.'

'Don't be ridiculous.'

Grace gave Lenny a filthy look and he mumbled 'Shite' under

his breath. Jack kept eating as though it wasn't all about to kick off. Stephen and Bernard were quiet, watching and waiting. Ryan was only two at the time – he was sitting in his high chair, clapping and laughing as though he knew what was happening and was really happy about it.

'Ridiculous is indoctrinating my child in a bogus belief system.'

'That's blasphemy, Rabbit.'

'Ah, blow it out your arse, Ma.'

'Oh, no,' Grace said, while Ryan bounced up and down on his high chair.

'Rabbit, don't speak to your mother like that,' Jack said, then asked Lenny to pass him the roast spuds.

Molly stood up. 'Let me make this very clear, Rabbit Hayes. You may not believe in God but I do, with every fibre of my being, and if you think my grandchild is not getting christened, you are very wrong.'

Rabbit laughed. 'Ma, if you want to take her down the road so that Father Frank can splash a bit of water on her head, go for it, but don't expect me to put on a dress, throw a party or even acknowledge it, because it means nothing to me. No matter what you say or do, Juliet will not be brought up a Catholic.'

'Fine,' Molly said. 'I will then.'

'Good. Have a nice time,' Rabbit said.

'I will,' Molly replied. 'And I will tell her the Good News.'

'The Good News? Seriously, Ma, you've been reading too many posters.'

'Maybe, but make no mistake, your daughter may not accept God in her life but she will be introduced to Him,' Molly said.

Grace silently prayed that Rabbit wouldn't retaliate, because their ma meant business and nobody, not even her own kids, messed with Ma when she meant business. Rabbit remained silent, even though the anger was clearly written on her face. Jack asked for more carrots. When Lenny managed to catch Grace's eye he mouthed, 'I'm sorry.'

Everyone ate quietly for a few minutes until six-year-old Bernard piped up, 'My friend Aamir doesn't believe in the Baby Jesus. He's a vegetarian.'

Everyone at the table burst out laughing, breaking the tension. That would be the first of many arguments Rabbit and her mother had about Juliet's right to a religious education. It was the only thing that Grace ever remembered her mother and sister butting heads about. Rabbit was adamant that if Juliet needed God in her life she could go off and find Him when she was old enough to make a decision about her own spiritual needs. Molly believed that Juliet had a right to learn about God, and then, if she chose to reject Him as her mother had, at least she would have been given the opportunity to know Him.

Now Juliet was not a Catholic but her nan pretended she was. Unlike her sister and, she suspected, her father, Grace did believe. She didn't know why and she didn't like to examine it. She went to mass once in a while, the kids were brought up as Catholics and Grace prayed when the going got bad. She wondered how she could bring her own kids up as Catholics and Juliet as an atheist under the same roof. *Dear God, give me the strength to raise an atheist.*

Lenny appeared from the kitchen. 'It's time to go, love.'

Grace picked up her mug and went into the house.

'Are you ready?' he said.

'No.'

'It'll be fine. We'll work it out.' Then he called out to the boys, 'Stephen, Bernard, let's go. Ryan, Jeffrey, don't burn the place down.' He grabbed his keys.

Grace and her boys followed him to the car.

Juliet

When Juliet was five she became obsessed with having a dad. All her school friends had dads. Some of them lived in other places but they visited and took their kids to McDonald's. In all the books she read and cartoons she saw, the characters had dads. Juliet's cousins had a dad, her neighbours had dads – even the dog next door had a dad, who lived three houses down from him; they used to walk around the cul-de-sac together, first thing in the morning and last thing in the evening. Juliet's mother explained to her that her dad didn't visit because he lived just too far away. It was around that time that Juliet Hayes started to tell anybody who would listen that her dad was an alien.

'He lives in a galaxy far, far away,' she told Kyle, while they were sitting on her front wall eating crisps.

'Makes sense,' Kyle said. 'That's why you can bend your thumb back so far.'

'And I can do this.' Juliet got off the wall. She stood in front of him and joined her hands behind her back before raising them to her head without letting go. Kyle dropped his crisps on the wall and stood beside her. He copied her, joining his hands behind his back. He couldn't raise them beyond his shoulder blades.

'Wow.' He picked up his crisps and got back onto the wall. 'I wonder where your dad's from.'

'Mars,' Juliet said, with great authority.

'How do you know?'

'I just feel it.'

'Do you think he has powers?'

'Dunno.'

'Do you have any powers?'

'Maybe.'

'We should find out.'

'OK.'

That was the day Juliet jumped off the garage roof and broke her wrist. Even though it was really sore and she was crying, they both waited for a really long time before telling Juliet's ma in the hope that her self-healing powers might kick in. When they didn't, and Juliet had to have it set in a cast, it didn't deter either of them. Instead they decided she'd probably have to wait until she was older for her powers to work.

When she was eight, she gave up on the notion that she was part alien. She accepted her father was Australian and not Martian, but it was a blow. She asked a lot of tough questions, but Rabbit was determined to be as honest as she could be.

'Did you love him?'

'He was really lovely.'

'How come you don't have a picture of him?'

'Because I didn't have a camera on my phone back then.'

'Why didn't you go to Australia with him?'

'Because I belong here.'

'Does he miss me?'

'He doesn't know you're here.'

'In Ireland?'

'I mean he left before you were born.'

Juliet had to think about that for a few minutes. She walked away and sat on the stairs. After a few minutes, Rabbit joined her.

'Why can't we find him?'

'Australia's a really big place.'

'So?'

'He has a really common name.'

'What do you mean?'

'I mean Adam Smith over there is like Paddy Murphy over here. There are lots of them.'

'How many?'

'Millions.'

'Why don't you know where he's from?'

'I'm really sorry, sweetheart.'

'Me, too.' Juliet climbed the stairs and took to her bed. She fell asleep without dinner that night, and the next morning, when she woke up, her mother was asleep beside her. She didn't bring up her dad after that. She let him go.

It was only a few months after their talk that they were forced to have another. This time Juliet's nan and her auntie Grace were there. Kyle's ma had seen her to the gate, and when she dropped her schoolbag in the hall, she could hear them talking. She rushed in to hug her nan, but as soon as she entered the kitchen, she sensed something was wrong. 'Have you been crying, Ma?' she asked.

'No,' Rabbit said.

'Your eyes are all red.'

'Allergies.'

'Oh.'

'Sit up there,' her nan said, pointing to the counter. 'I made you your favourite apple crumble.'

Juliet did as she was told. Grace was busy cleaning the kitchen.

'Why are you cleaning our kitchen, Grace?'

'I just want to help your mammy out,' Grace said.

'Do you have allergies too?'

'They're going around.'

'Oh.'

Juliet was halfway through her apple crumble and a glass of milk when her ma explained that she would be going into the hospital for an operation.

'What kind of operation?'

'I have to have a lump removed.'

'What kind of lump?'

'It's going to be fine.'

'Your mammy might just be a little tired for a while,' Molly told her.

'How tired?'

'I don't know yet, sweetheart,' Rabbit said.

Juliet finished her apple crumble. 'I have homework to do.' Before she left the kitchen, she hugged her mother. 'I'll mind ya, Ma,' she said, and she'd been minding her ma ever since.

Juliet and Rabbit had their routines: they changed according to whether Rabbit was undergoing chemo or radiation, surgery or simply medication. Juliet had charts for everything and she was not just an expert on her ma's meds: she was also good at wiping up vomit, changing beds, cleaning toilets, and she'd even changed a few adult diapers when things had got very bad. She kept the house spotless, and knew good cancer foods from bad cancer foods. When her mother was feeling better, she'd teach her how to cook and Juliet turned out to be a quick student; she often took care of dinner so as to give her mother a rest. She was the first up every morning and often the last to bed. She didn't stay up too late, but her ma was tired a lot of the time. Sometimes she'd hear her ma crying in her bedroom, but she'd never go in. When Juliet cried, she preferred to be left alone, so she guessed her ma felt the same. Once, when the crying went on for a really long time, she shouted, 'I love ya, Ma,' through the wall.

Her mother stopped sobbing and shouted, 'I love ya back, Bunny.' She didn't cry after that, or if she did she was quieter.

Juliet knew every one of Rabbit's doctors and nurses, and they all knew her. She insisted on taking notes when something new was happening, and the staff were always patient, answering any question she had, no matter how silly it might have seemed. In hospital and after surgeries she watched the nurses clean her ma's wounds so that she could help if need be. At home she was the door police. She insisted on answering to all who knocked, and no one got through without first cleansing their hands with the antibacterial gel she kept on the hall table. And when Rabbit was at her most uncomfortable, Juliet was the only one who knew where to place that extra pillow or how to fix her temperature or when to insist that she eat or drink and when to walk away.

The last four years of Juliet's life had been sometimes hard and sometimes sad, but mostly they were great, because Juliet's mammy needed her just as much as she needed her mammy. They were best buddies in the trenches together, fighting for one another. They shared an empathy and closeness that, even at twelve years of age, Juliet Hayes recognized as special. They also laughed a lot – Juliet's ma was funny. She didn't tell a lot of jokes, although when she did, they were always the best ones. Her humour came from her reaction to the world. She was positive and buoyant; she smiled a lot more than she frowned, and even when things were really difficult she had a way of finding something to laugh about. But Juliet's favourite thing was the way she and her ma talked to one another and the things they talked about.

After a bout of chemo they'd often lie together in bed and talk about school and boys and Kyle's latest motocross accident, or the article her ma was working on, her cancer blog and whether or not she would go for breast reconstruction.

'I think you should go big.'

'Your auntie Grace big or Pamela Anderson big?'

'I was thinking Kim Kardashian big.'

'I thought it was her rear that was big.'

'Up top, too.'

'So she's well balanced. I might fall over.'

'Beyoncé has big booby-doos.'

'Susan Sarandon's would be my ideal.'

'Who's she?'

'She's an actress.'

'Has she done any cartoons?'

'I don't know.'

'What was she in?'

'Oh, lots of things. *Thelma & Louise* was one of my favourites.'

'Did you see her booby-doos in that one?'

'Don't think so. *Bull Durham* was great, and I really liked *White Palace*, even though I missed the end.'

'Why?'

'I'll tell you when you're older.'

'Gross.'

'And then there was *Dead Man Walking.*'

'Did you see them in that?'

'She played a nun, so it's doubtful.'

'Oh. So when did you see them?'

'Can't remember exactly, but I did think, Wow.'

'If you could remember the film, we could look them up online.'

'Doesn't matter, Bunny. Even if I do reconstruct they'll never look like Susan's.'

'Even if you don't do it you'll still be pretty.'

'And we can share T-shirts, at least until yours grow.'

'They're growing already.'

'That reminds me. We need to get you measured for a bra.'

'Won't that make you sad?'

'Nah, I bloody hate bras.'

'And you could do with another wig.'

'You don't like my wig?'

'I do, but it's nice to have options.'

'Wouldn't even know what else to go for.'

'What colour hair has Susan Sarandon?'

'Red.'

'You'd look lovely with red hair, Ma.'

'So if I can't have her booby-doos I can still have her hair?'

'Yeah.'

'I like it.'

That night they watched the DVD of *Thelma & Louise* together, and they'd watched it many times since. They quoted lines to each other when things got rough.

When they did get around to shopping for training bras and wigs, they discovered Juliet was already a 28B. 'Oh, Juliet's going to have big Grace-type booby-doos.'

'I am not.'

'Are so. You're going to need to wear bras the size of small children's tents.'

Juliet laughed. 'Will not.'

But then her ma became serious. 'It doesn't matter what size they are. You're perfect.'

'So are you, Ma.'

'That's right.'

It turned out that blonde wigs suited better than red ones, but Juliet and her ma had a great time re-enacting their own version of the last scene of *Thelma & Louise* in the shop, much to the assistants' entertainment. Juliet, wearing a brown wig, turned to her mother really seriously: 'Ma, let's keep goin'.'

Her ma fixed her red wig. 'What do ya mean, Juliet?'

Juliet looked forward and nodded. 'I mean go, Ma.'

Her ma pretended to rev the invisible car they were supposed to be sitting in. 'Now are you sure?'

'Yeah, Ma, let's do it.'

Her ma pretended to push the gas, they clasped hands, ran forward and fell onto their knees. 'The End,' Juliet said to the ladies, who were clapping enthusiastically.

'Those two girls really knew how to turn suicide into a happy ending,' the larger lady said. Juliet and her ma took a bow, then Ma exchanged the red wig for the blonde.

That evening they dined in their favourite restaurant, Juliet in her brand-new bra and Ma in her blonde wig.

'That man is staring at you, Ma.' A waiter's eyes were trained on her.

'Still got it, Bunny.' Her ma had winked.

It had been a great day, one of Juliet's best. She told herself that there would be plenty more days like it, but she was scared that she was wrong. Each day her ma spent in that hospice she felt a little more distant from her. *When are you coming back to me, Ma? I don't work without you.*

Juliet was back from the hospice and reading in her nan's spare room when she heard the front doorbell ring and Stephen's voice saying 'Hi' to Nan.

'Juliet, your cousins are here for you,' Molly shouted.

Juliet went to the top of the stairs. 'What?'

'Stephen and Bernard are going to some flower show in the park near them.'

'I just want to read.'

'It's a lovely day and they've come for you, so here's your jacket. You're going.'

Juliet looked from her nan to Grace, who was standing beside her, grinning widely.

'There's a carnival – well, a few swings and a waltzer.'

Outside, Bernard beeped the horn. Juliet walked down the stairs. Her nan handed her the jacket and she walked out of the door in silence. The lads were waiting in the car. She got into the back seat and Stephen took off down the road.

'I thought you were studying,' Juliet said.

'Needed a break.'

'So you chose to go to a flower show with me and Bernard?' Juliet said, and her tone reflected her doubt.

'Hey, I'm good company,' Bernard said, feigning hurt feelings.

'And so are you,' Stephen added.

'Hmm.'

Stephen switched on the CD and turned it up really loud. Bernard sang along and played air guitar.

When they arrived at the park the boys were starving.

'Let's eat first,' Stephen said. They found a food tent they liked the look of and Juliet followed them inside. It was a fiver a head for all you could eat, so the two boys were in seventh heaven, sitting at a wooden table with mounds of food in front of them. Juliet picked at a burger.

Bernard pointed to the toffee fudge on a table behind Juliet. 'When I'm done with this, I'm going for a boatload of that fudge.'

Juliet looked over her shoulder. 'Ma loves fudge.'

'Grab her a bag,' he said.

'I will.'

'You can get her a plant, if you like,' Stephen suggested.

'They don't like plants in hospitals, but I suppose I could get it for when she comes home.'

'That's a brilliant idea,' Bernard said, a little too enthusiastically.

Stephen kicked him under the table. Juliet pretended not to notice.

'Stephen, what are you going to do when your exams are finished?'

'Well, I was thinking of going to Germany with some friends to work, but I can't really go anywhere until . . .' He stopped.

'Until what?' Juliet said.

'Until I sort out me passport,' he said, and Bernard raised his eyes to Heaven.

'What's wrong with your passport?'

'Have you ever thought of working as an interrogator?' Stephen asked.

'No,' Juliet said.

'Well, you should. You'd be very good.'

'Don't think so. I haven't got one straight answer out of you yet.'

'Let's go on the waltzer,' Bernard suggested.

'What do you think?' Stephen asked her.

Juliet nodded. 'OK.'

'But we'll get the fudge first,' Bernard said. 'Don't want to risk missing out.'

After they'd got their fudge and a plant for Juliet's ma, she excused herself to go to the toilet before they ventured on the waltzer.

Bernard and Stephen waited by the ticket office. 'You nearly landed us right in it earlier.'

'Oh, really, Mr Over-enthusiastic? "Yeah, amazing, brilliant, what a fantastic idea!" You really know how to keep your cool.'

'Well, at least I didn't almost say that I couldn't make travel plans until Rabbit died.'

'What?'

They turned to see their younger cousin's huge eyes full to the brim and overflowing. Their hearts sank.

'N-nothing,' Stephen stammered.

'We were just messing around.'

'No, you weren't.' She dropped the plant and ran away from them as fast as she could. She darted in and out of the crowd, managing to disappear without a trace in a matter of seconds. When it became clear that they had lost her, the boys split up and searched the park high and low. Eventually they had to concede that they had really messed up.

Marjorie

Marjorie had always hated Sundays. In the eighties, very few children had escaped mass and she hadn't been among them. Every week she was made to wear a stupid striped dress and blue patent shoes, and was dragged kicking and screaming to church. The service seemed to last for ever, the smell of incense turned her stomach, and when her mother insisted on singing every hymn louder than the one before, it annoyed her to the point of murder. If God really had the power to delve into Marjorie's head, and if He was as vindictive as advertised, He would have struck her down where she stood.

Sunday dinner was another endurance test. Marjorie hated meat, particularly beef, but a meatless diet was not tolerated in 1980s Ireland. She was force-fed a big slab of beef, roast potatoes drowned in gravy, then sent out to the garden to play, rain or shine, because TV was only for adults on a Sunday. All the shops were closed so she sat on the wall and read a book until her saviour, Rabbit, cycled along, put her on the back of her bike and pedalled her to freedom.

Marjorie was an only child to two very conservative parents. She grew up in a picture-perfect little house that gleamed inside and out. She wore the very best clothes and was always pristine.

Marjorie looked like a little doll because, to her mother, that was what she was: something pretty to dress up and show off. But dolls don't have personalities, they don't rebel or ask questions, they don't have opinions or, God forbid, come home dirty. If her mother wasn't cleaning, she was reading or praying, and her father worked on the ships, so he was rarely at home. When he was in the house, Marjorie was told he needed his rest so she had to keep quiet and stay out of his way. She didn't know her father very well then, and she didn't know him now. Rabbit had once joked that he was the kind of man who probably had a family in every port. Marjorie had laughed, but it had made her wonder.

Marjorie was very well cared for but there was no warmth in her house. Rabbit's world was so much brighter, grubbier and real. In Rabbit's house, nobody had to take an aspirin and go to bed if Rabbit spilled something on her dress. In Rabbit's house there were hugs and laughter, and it didn't matter what you wore, what you did or what state you turned up in: nothing was a problem, everything was solvable.

Rabbit had a very glamorous life, as far as young Marjorie was concerned. She had a cool older sister and brother, and the fact that Davey was in a band with other cool boys was a bonus. For three birthdays in a row, when Marjorie blew out her candles, she wished to be a member of the Hayes family.

Some Sundays the band would rehearse, and she'd sit behind the curtain with Rabbit and listen to them. They were the best Sundays. Even though she was still half choked on a lump of beef, she felt lucky and honoured – better than that, she felt in-cluded. Mrs Hayes let her change into one of Rabbit's tracksuits so she didn't have to worry about dirtying her Sunday best.

Then there were those terrible Sundays when Marjorie was forced to stay at home because some relation she didn't know or care about would visit for the afternoon. She'd be forced to Irish-dance for them, then take out her medals and plaques. She'd sit quietly while the adults talked, and only spoke when spoken to, which rarely happened. Those were some of the longest days of Marjorie Shaw's life.

When Marjorie left home, she stopped going to mass. She became a vegetarian and spent a lot of Sundays shopping, lunching, going to movies, matches, anything to fill the void, but still she couldn't shake that awful Sunday feeling.

It was after ten a.m. when the doorbell rang. She answered it, fully expecting to see Simone from the apartment next door looking to borrow something, but it was her ex-husband, Neil. Marjorie's heart leaped in her chest.

'I rang the wrong bell. Simone let me in downstairs.' *Of course she did, stupid Simone. That's the last teabag you borrow from me, Simone Duffy.*

'I was going to phone you,' he said, 'but I didn't think you'd pick up.'

She hesitated. *Should I slam the door in his face or not? Yes or no? To slam or not to slam? Jesus, he looks great.*

'Come in.' No need to be childish. *The separation is done with, the divorce is just a formality. There's nothing left to fight about . . . so why is he here?*

She led him into the kitchen. He hadn't been here before. He looked around and took it in. 'Nice place,' he said.

'Tiny place,' she said. 'Would you like some coffee?' *Of course you wouldn't. Just stab me, rob me or send me on another guilt trip and go home.*

'I'd love one.'

Balls. Marjorie turned on the kettle. He sat down. She spooned coffee into two mugs. 'I'm afraid instant will have to do.' *Because the sooner you drink this, the sooner you leave.*

'Instant is fine. You're probably wondering what I'm doing here.'

Ya think? Marjorie didn't respond.

'I came because I heard about Rabbit.'

'Oh.' Neil had taken the wind from her sails. He was always fond of Rabbit, even during the split. In fact, Rabbit saw more redeeming features in Neil than Marjorie did and was always quick to defend him. He knew that and appreciated it.

'I just wanted to say that I'm so very sorry.'

'Oh.' *Don't cry, don't cry, please, don't cry.*

The kettle boiled. Marjorie pulled herself together and poured the water into the mugs. 'Do you still take it black?'

'Yes,' he said.

'Me too.' *Why did I say that?* They sat down at the counter and she passed him his mug.

'How is she?'

'Bad.' *Do not cry.*

'Does she have long?'

She shook her head.

'Are you OK?'

'No.'

'Of course not,' he said. 'So far Rabbit Hayes is the love of your life.'

'Yeah, she is,' Marjorie admitted, because it was true. Marjorie did love her best friend more than anyone or anything else in this world.

'I used to envy her,' he said.

'Not any more.'

'Look, Marjorie, I know there's a lot of water under the bridge and we've both said and done a lot of hurtful things.'

'I've done them, you've said them.'

'Well, yes, but I just wanted to say that I really hope you'll be OK.'

'Thank you, Neil.'

He put down the mug and stood up. 'I should go. Elaine is waiting in the car.'

'It was nice of her to let you come here.'

'She has nothing to fear.'

His comment should have hurt, but it didn't.

'I'm really happy for you.'

She followed him out to the door. Just as he was leaving he turned to hug her, taking her by surprise.

'Tell Rabbit I send my love.' His voice was laced with tears.

'I will,' she stumbled.

'I hope you find someone, Marjorie.' He kissed her cheek, and when he was gone she wasn't sure what to think or what to do, so she sat on the hall floor and banged her head gently against the wall.

When Marjorie had moved into her apartment she'd got rid of her car. She didn't need one and Rabbit had introduced her to the benefits of cycling around the city. She really enjoyed it, even in winter, but it made life awkward on rare occasions like today, when she needed to be at Rabbit's parents' house. It was too far to cycle and there was no direct bus route. She had intended to get a taxi there and back, but Davey had said he'd pick her up – after all, he'd insisted she was there in the first place.

Now she stood up, showered, dressed and waited for him. Briefly she considered what would have happened if her ex-husband had bumped into the man she had cheated with in the narrow corridor outside her apartment. *A fist fight? Maybe not.* Neil was happy, probably much happier than he'd been with the woman who hadn't appreciated him. *He wouldn't punch Davey: he'd probably thank him.* Her doorbell rang. She answered on the intercom.

'It's Davey.'

'I'll be down in a minute.'

She sat in the car and he took off. 'You look great,' he said.

'Neil knocked on my door this morning.'

'I thought you two weren't on speaking terms.'

'He'd heard about Rabbit.'

'And what?'

'And he came to say he was sorry and hoped I was OK.'

'That was good of him.'

'Yeah, it was.'

'Are you OK?'

'No, I'm totally fucked up, Davey. Aren't you?'

'To be fair, I've always been fucked up.'

'True . . . Are you sure it's appropriate for me to be at this meeting?'

'Rabbit would want you there.'

'I wish I could take Juliet, Davey. If I hadn't left Neil we could have.'

'If "If" was a donkey we'd all have a ride.'

'We *were* donkeys. We did have a ride. That's why I live in a one-bed apartment.'

'You couldn't let it slide.' He was amused.

'You were wide open.'

He pulled up to his parents' house. Grace's car was already there. He parked and turned to Marjorie. 'You are Rabbit's advocate, OK?'

She nodded.

'So if you have something to say, say it.'

'I will.'

They got out of the car. Molly met them at the door. 'Come in, come in. I've a roast on.'

Marjorie walked into the kitchen, where Grace, Lenny, Jack and Father Frank were all seated. The table was laid for a meal. Everyone except Father Frank and Molly seemed a little awkward.

'Father Frank, I didn't know you were coming,' Davey said, glaring at his mother.

'Oh, I just popped in for a visit and your mother invited me for dinner. I couldn't say no to that. I love a roast.'

'Right.' Davey was still giving his mother dagger looks over the priest's head. Molly cast him a glance. *Shut your face, Davey.*

'You sit in there beside Father Frank, Marjorie. I hope you like a roast.'

Fucking Sundays.

221

Johnny

The hospital corridor was pretty empty except for Johnny, Rabbit, Davey, Francie and Jay. Rabbit was sixteen, and Davey had turned twenty that week, the last of the lads to do so. Johnny was staring straight ahead and humming a melody just loud enough for Rabbit to hear and for it to stick in her head. She had grown up a lot in two years, but then they all had since Johnny's diagnosis.

The first time he had said the words 'multiple sclerosis' nobody had known what he was talking about. It was during a band meeting in the Hayes kitchen. Molly and Jack had been invited. Everyone sat nervously, wondering what the hell was going on. Rabbit was the only one who knew Johnny had been having tests. What she didn't know was that multiple sclerosis was incurable, that his was the worst kind and that it would steal him away from them. Johnny was strong and full of hope. He was going to fight it and imagined he would go into remission soon.

'What does that mean?' Francie had asked.

'I stop falling, me eyesight gets a bit better or at least no worse . . . I don't know, just things will stop falling apart, I suppose.'

'Are you falling apart?' Jay had wondered.

'I'll be OK.'

'What's it like?' Francie said.

'It's like being under water.'

'What about the record deal?' Louis asked.

'It's not going to affect that,' Johnny had promised. The four Hayes family members said nothing and Johnny noticed. 'What do you say, Mrs H? I'm going to be OK, right?'

Molly was stunned. 'Of course you are,' she said, stammering a little.

'Mr H?'

'We'll deal with it. We're all in this together,' Molly said.

'She's right. Nothing's insurmountable,' Jack added. Johnny,

Rabbit and the lads visibly had relaxed and the mood lifted. *If Ma and Da Hayes say it'll be OK then it will be.*

Of course, nobody knew how bad Johnny's case was, but despite every medical intervention, he never really had a chance. He couldn't perform as often or as well as he used to; the band were forced to cancel one out of every three shows, and when rumour spread in the local industry they soon lost their small Irish record deal. The next day Louis announced he was leaving Kitchen Sink. After a week in bed, and when he was strong enough, Johnny returned to the garage to announce they would become a new band called the Sound. They got another guitarist instead of a replacement keyboard player, and Kev fitted in well with the lads. Everyone knew it was going to be an uphill battle, but their new music reflected a more mature songwriter, and his pain, anguish, hope and desperation seeped into every haunting lyric he wrote. They couldn't play as many gigs, and they were right back down at the bottom of the pile, but the lads didn't care: they were together, family, doing what they loved, and they were still determined to make it work. In the two years since the demise of Kitchen Sink and the birth of the Sound, Kev had become another brother and, after a slow start, in part due to Johnny's health, they were beginning to gain a fan base. It was a new era.

Now Kev appeared beside them, holding his motorcycle helmet. 'Traffic's a nightmare,' he said, sitting down beside Francie. 'Did yous eat?'

'Had some sandwiches from the canteen,' Jay said.

'Have they worked out why he's pissing himself yet?' Kev asked.

Johnny threw a magazine at him. Kev ducked.

'Nah, although he's been drinking shite and filling bottles all day,' Francie said.

'Do you think we'll make the gig?'

'If we have to leave before they're done with me, we'll just go,' Johnny said.

'We will not,' Rabbit contradicted him.

'We will,' Johnny said. 'Conversation over.'

'This is bullshit,' Rabbit said.

'It's an important gig for us,' Davey reminded her.

'His health is even more important, Davey Hayes, and well you know it.'

'He'll get done and we'll make the gig, so, everyone, chill the fuck out,' Jay said.

'And Rabbit's right. We're not leaving till whatever they're shoving in comes out,' Francie said.

'Stop talking about me like I'm not here,' Johnny said.

'Well, stop acting like a thick,' Francie replied.

'This is my band, my life and my say.' Johnny got up and moved slowly away, hand on the wall to steady himself as he walked.

'Nice one, Davey.' Rabbit was clearly pissed off.

'What did I do?' Davey said.

Kev stretched his legs and shouted after Johnny, 'Get us a Twix, will ya?'

Rabbit found Johnny at the vending machine. 'They're ready for you.'

'Don't want to be here.'

'Me neither.'

'I'm so sick of this.' He leaned his back against the wall.

'It's shit.'

'I just feel worse. Shouldn't I feel better by now?'

'With the amount of stuff they have you on, I would have thought so, but sometimes things take time.'

'My voice isn't going, is it?' he asked.

She saw the fear in his eyes. 'No way. Your voice has never sounded better.'

'Promise?'

'I promise.'

'If I can't do it any more, you'll tell me, won't you?'

'If you can't do it any more, you'll know. Now, come on, you've a date with a tube.'

He transferred his weight from the wall to her shoulder. When they returned to the waiting area, Francie and Kev were flirting with a pretty nurse, Jay seemed to be asleep with the magazine over his face, and Davey appeared from the toilet, ashen-faced.

'What's wrong with you?' Johnny asked.

'Me guts are at me.'

'Your guts are always at you – it's his arse you should be shoving a pipe into,' Francie told the nurse.

'It's just this place, the bleedin' smell of it. No offence,' Davey said.

'We need to go in now,' the nurse said to Johnny.

Johnny let go of Rabbit and walked slowly behind the woman. When he had disappeared, Rabbit turned to the band. 'If he's not out in an hour we're cancelling.'

'Since when have you become the boss of all things Johnny?' Davey asked.

'Since I told her she was,' Francie said.

'No, you didn't.'

'Rabbit, will you be the boss of all things Johnny?'

'Yeah.'

'There. Done.'

'Are yous listening to this?' Davey said to Kev and Jay.

'I'm trying to snooze over here, man,' Jay grunted.

'She's the only one he listens to,' Kev said to Davey.

'For fuck's sake, she's sixteen years old. Next you'll be telling me she's taking over as manager.' He walked off in a huff.

They got to the gig just in time to sound check. Since he'd become ill, Johnny had spent more time playing piano than guitar. He could sit at the piano and it suited their new sound. He had slept on the table during the test at the hospital and in the van on the way to the venue. After sound check he slept for another hour in the dressing room. By stage time, he had recovered sufficiently to walk onto the stage unaided, and when he sang, he lifted the roof off the place. The venue was small but packed to the rafters. Grace and Lenny were at the front waving. Jack was by the bar and Rabbit sat by the sound desk. The house guy was working it, but he had no problem with her input: it made his life easier and she was nice to look at.

The gig ended and the crowd cried out for more. The lads put down their instruments and the crowd booed.

'Come on, lads, just one more,' Johnny said, from his seat at the piano. The lads pretended to concede, then put their instruments back on, and Davey sat behind his kit. The audience roared. Johnny began the song with just his voice and the piano. Everyone hushed. Rabbit looked over to the bar and shared a smile with her da. The band kicked in on the chorus and they bounced up and down to the beat. Rabbit left the desk before the song ended. She went back to the dressing room to sort out water and a few beers for the lads. After that she went to the toilet and queued for ten minutes in the main venue because Davey had blocked the backstage ones with his dodgy guts. When she got out she found the band celebrating at the bar.

'I have beers backstage,' she said.

'We wanted to be out here,' Francie said.

'What about Johnny?'

'What about him?' Jay asked.

'Where is he?'

Jay asked Davey, but he was surrounded by girls and not in the frame of mind to engage. He raised his hands in the air.

Kev was kissing the face off a tall blonde. Rabbit grabbed his shoulder. 'Kev, where's Johnny?' As she spoke, the crowd parted and she saw him still sitting behind his piano on stage. She looked from Kev to Francie. 'You left him on stage?'

'Oh, fuck.'

Rabbit walked onto the stage. She could see Johnny was in a temper. 'I couldn't walk off by meself – there's too many dangerous wires. Davey's effing gaffer-taped them everywhere. And it's so dark I can't see.'

'They just were high, full of adrenalin,' Rabbit said.

'They left me.'

'They just forgot.'

'I've been sitting here like a spare prick with drunk dickheads coming up to me.'

'We'll go.'

'I need your shoulder, Rabbit.'

'I've got you.' She helped him stand. He was exhausted now and his hands were shaking. He leaned on her and she negotiated their way back to the dressing room. She left him there and found her da sitting in the front bar with Grace and Lenny.

'Da, we need to go.'

'OK, kiddo. I'll bring the car around.' He finished his glass of orange. 'I'll leave yous to it. Don't wake your mammy when you stumble in, Grace.'

'I was thinking of staying at Lenny's,' she said coyly.

'Over my dead body.' He stood up to leave. 'Don't get on the wrong side of my wife, Lenny. She'll hunt you down.'

'I won't, sir.'

Johnny didn't want to see the lads. He was too annoyed. Instead he left by the side door, Rabbit holding him tightly. He fell asleep as soon as he got into the car.

Jack was worried. 'How long can this go on?'

'He could still go into remission, Da. I've been reading about it and it could still happen.'

'Of course it could. He's only a young fella.'

Rabbit helped Johnny out of the car and up to his front door. Johnny's ma called his da, who took him inside and upstairs. Johnny's ma thanked Rabbit and waved at Jack in the car, then closed the door. Rabbit got into the front seat of the car.

'If he doesn't go into remission, how long has he got?' Jack said to his youngest child.

'Not much longer, Da.'

They drove away.

Chapter Ten

Davey

B Y THE TIME Father Frank had left, it was well after six when the meeting finally kicked off. The dishes were washed and everyone had the obligatory cup of tea. Molly was anxious that it was wrapped up quickly so that she could visit Rabbit. She'd been keeping tabs on her over the phone. Jay had spent an hour with her but she'd slept the rest of the afternoon away. Molly wanted to be there when she woke up and, with that in mind, she felt it unnecessary to beat about the bush. She sat down at the table and looked at everyone sitting around it.

'Obviously Jack and I will be taking Juliet,' Molly said.

'There's nothing obvious about it, Ma,' Davey replied.

'We'd like to take her,' Grace said, raising her finger.

'Don't be ridiculous, Grace. You haven't got the room for her,' Molly said dismissively.

'We'll make room.'

'You did. It was called your sofa, and we already have a room,' Molly said.

'It's not just about a room, Ma,' Grace said.

'Then what's it about?' Molly asked.

'It's about what's best for Juliet,' Davey said.

Molly stood up and placed her hands on the table. 'And we're not? We raised you, didn't we?'

'Exactly. You've done your raising,' Davey told her.

'What's that supposed to mean?' Molly said, straightening herself.

'It means you're seventy-two, and Da is seventy-seven,' Davey said.

'And we're fit as fleas.'

'You're not being realistic, Ma,' Grace said.

'I bloody am.'

'She can't have another parent die on her,' Davey said.

His statement had sounded harsh and he hadn't meant it to. He could see that it had taken his mother by surprise. Of course she knew what age she was and of course she had worried about it, but still it hurt. She sat down heavily and looked at her husband. 'Jack?'

'He's right, and deep down, you know it,' he said.

'Grace can't fit another soul into that house,' Molly protested.

'Maybe I could sell and either buy or rent a two-bed apartment,' Marjorie suggested.

'That's kind, but you have your own problems, Marjorie, and Juliet is ours,' Grace said.

'She's not a problem, Grace.'

'I didn't mean it like that, Ma.'

'My problems are not that big, so I'd like to be considered,' Marjorie said.

'She's coming to us,' Grace insisted.

'That has not been decided,' Davey reminded them.

'Really, Davey? Well, what do you think?'

'I think she should come and live with me.' The words just fell from his mouth. There had been no thought or consideration. He just heard himself say it. Everyone stared at him, as if they were waiting for him to burst out laughing and yell, 'Joke!'

'Oh,' Marjorie said. 'That's why you wanted me here – you thought I'd vouch for you.' She sounded annoyed.

Davey was still surprised by what he'd just said, but he didn't want to take it back. 'No. I thought you'd speak for Rabbit.'

'OK,' she said. 'It's a bullshit idea. Whatever about your ma and da's ages, Grace's lack of space and me not being family, you're a bachelor who lives between two American states and a bus, you've never been in a relationship that's lasted longer than six months, and you haven't even taken care of a pet, never mind a child.'

'Couldn't have put it better myself,' Grace said.

'I appreciate your candour and you're right. I do have homes in New York and Nashville, and I do spend months on a bus. I've never been in a relationship that's lasted more than four months, not six, and I'm not really an animal person. What I am is Juliet's uncle. I have the money and I can make the time to take care of her.'

'So you want to take her away from her grandparents, her aunt, uncle, cousins and everything she knows in the wake of her mother's death?' Marjorie asked.

'Yes.'

'You can't do that,' Grace said.

'I plan on living a long time and I have the room, not just in my house but in my life. I can do this.' It was as though someone else had possessed him and was speaking through him, because Davey couldn't believe what he was saying, yet it felt right. *What the hell is going on? What am I saying? Could I really take care of a twelve-year-old girl?*

Everyone was silent for a few moments, mostly due to shock: certainly no one appeared to be considering his pitch.

Jack stood up. 'Juliet belongs here. Grace, if you can work out a way to fit Juliet into your household, you'll take her. Until then her nan and I will keep her here. It's not ideal and it's not what I want for her, but, right now, it's all we can do.'

He walked out of the room. The meeting was adjourned. Molly followed her husband.

Grace sighed heavily. 'Well, Da told us.'

Davey stood up. 'I should take you home,' he said to Marjorie.

'I can find my own way.'

'I brought you here, I'm bringing you home.'

'OK.'

She said goodbye to Grace and Lenny, who were still sitting at the table, drinking tea.

In the car Marjorie was quick to apologize to Davey. 'I'm sorry I didn't support you.'

'You did what you felt was right for Rabbit.'

'I did.'

'And so did I.'

'At least we can both sleep easy tonight.'

They didn't speak again until he parked the car outside her apartment.

She hesitated before she got out. 'You're a good man.'

'Honestly, Marjorie, you don't have to explain.'

'I wasn't judging you. Rabbit says I can be a bit judgey, which is ironic because I'm a cheat so who am I to judge?'

'You are perfectly entitled.'

'It just seemed to come from nowhere.'

'It did.'

'What do you mean?'

'I hadn't considered it for one moment until suddenly you were all arguing over who was best to care for her and I thought, Why not me?'

'Just like that,' Marjorie said.

'Just like that.'

'She's not a toy. You can't return her.'

'I know that.'

'Do you, Davey?'

'I want her, Marjorie.'

'You don't know what you want. You never have.'

'Please don't make this about us.'

'It's not about us. It's about you taking a young girl who's lost her mother away from the people who love her most.'

'I know what you're saying and I hear you, I do, but I can do this and, more importantly, I really want to.'

'As of five minutes ago.'

'My da can decree all he wants, but I'll fight for her.'

'Oh, I know,' Marjorie said, 'but you'd better talk to Rabbit about it.'

'And if she supports it, will you?'

'If she supports it, it won't matter what I think.'

'It'll matter to me,' he said.

'It's been a long day, Davey.' She got out of the car.

He rolled down the window. 'So sleep on it,' he said. He waited until she was safely inside her flat before driving off. *Am I insane?* he asked himself on the drive home, but despite the weight of responsibility in raising a teenage girl, Davey Hayes felt lighter than he had in years.

Jay had a pint waiting for him in the pub. The place was quiet, not like back in the day when Sundays were busy. Jay finished his meal. 'The missus has the kids at her mother's.'

Davey supped his pint and nodded.

'Visited Rabbit today,' Jay went on.

'Ma said.'

'I knew she was bad but . . .' He was shaking his head.

Francie appeared behind Davey and ruffled his hair. 'Hey, DB, what's going on?'

Jay got the attention of the girl behind the counter. 'Can we get another one of these, love, over here?' He pointed to his pint and then to his brother.

Francie pushed in beside Davey. 'How's Rabbit?' he asked.

'Shocking,' Jay said.

'She's in good enough form, though,' Francie said.

'She was quiet today,' Jay mused.

'What was she saying?' Davey asked.

'Just talking about the past mostly.'

'Johnny?'

'Yeah.'

'Wonder if he's waiting for her,' Francie said, as much to himself as anyone else.

'Well, if he is he won't have long to hang about. I'm sorry, DB,' Jay said, and Davey nodded.

'She told me you were discussing what to do with Juliet today,' Jay added.

'Yeah, we did,' Davey said.

'And?'

'And I want her.'

'You want her?' Francie said. He didn't disguise the shock in his voice.

'Fuck off.' Jay started to laugh. 'Seriously?'

Francie sat back in his chair. He let Jay do the talking and Davey do the answering.

'I'm serious.'

'Here's the thing, DB. Just because you screw teenage girls doesn't mean you can raise one,' Jay said.

'Georgia is twenty-five.'

'Is this because you're lonely?' Jay asked.

'No.'

'Because this is not about you.'

'It's not that.'

Francie picked up the pint the waitress had placed on the table during Jay's interrogation.

'You have no idea how hard it is to raise kids. You've never had anyone relying on you,' Jay said.

'I know, I know. I've never even had a dog . . .'

'A dog! You've never even had a plant. No, strike that. You had a plant, we smoked it and Louis got the shits.'

Kev walked through the door, spotted the lads and made a beeline for Davey. He picked him up from behind and shook him. 'Howya doin', DB?'

'He's losing his fucking mind, that's how he's doing,' Jay said.

Francie was still unusually quiet.

'What's new?' Kev said. He nodded at the girl behind the bar and pointed to the pints the lads were drinking. She nodded. He gave her the thumbs-up and sat down beside Jay. 'So what's he done now?'

'He wants to take Juliet,' Jay said.

'Sorry about Rabbit,' Kev responded.

'Thanks.'

'Now, don't be a fucking eejit. You can't even take care of yourself,' Kev said.

Francie sipped his pint.

Davey was beginning to get the impression the people in his life didn't think as highly of him as he'd hoped. 'I'm really trying hard not to be insulted, lads.'

'Well, you shouldn't be. You're a single man who travels most of the year. I work from home and my wife is there most of the time and I swear to God sometimes I just want to kill them, or myself, or all of us.' Kev sighed. 'I never would but, Christ, it's tempting.'

'Your kids are under the age of five. Juliet's twelve,' Davey reminded him.

'Because tweens and teenagers are such a dream to handle. My Adele is fifteen and her mother found condoms in her room. Fucking condoms!' Jay's face reddened. 'She says she's minding them for a friend – like we just came down in the last shower – and you know what her mother said to me? "We need to think about putting her on the pill." She's *fifteen*!'

'I didn't get a feel of a tit over a jumper until I was fifteen,' Kev said.

Francie laughed.

'It's not funny,' Jay said. 'Teenage boys are one thing, but a teenage girl . . . She'll break you, DB.'

Davey had time for only one pint. He left Kev and Jay consoling each other over their kid troubles. Francie walked him to his car.

'I noticed you were very quiet,' Davey said.

234

'Jay was doing enough talking for both of us.'

'So you agree I'm being a selfish arsehole.'

'I think you're losing your sister, you're grieving, you're lonely and everything he said in there is right. You haven't a clue how hard it is. But I also think you and that kid fit. You caring for Rabbit's young one seems right to me.'

'Really?' Davey hoped his friend wasn't being sarcastic.

'Really.' Francie slapped Davey's back. 'Of course you'll probably fuck it up, but that's life.'

'What about my lifestyle?'

'You'll change it.'

'Yeah, I will.'

'Go on, visit your sister and make your case,' Francie said.

'Cheers, Francie.'

It was just after eight thirty and Davey was halfway to the hospice when his phone rang. It was Grace and she was hysterical. 'The boys have lost Juliet.'

Rabbit

Rabbit was screaming when Molly entered the room. The doctor was trying to calm her, but he was fighting a losing battle.

'Who the fuck are you?' she shouted.

'I'm Enda.'

'Jacinta!' Rabbit shouted into the poor man's face. 'Jacinta!'

'Jacinta's off, but I'm the doctor on call. I'll be taking care of you tonight.'

'Get out.'

'Rabbit.'

'My name is Mia, I am Mia Hayes. Rabbit's a stupid fucking name.'

'I'm sorry. It says "Rabbit" on your chart.'

He was so engaged with the screaming lunatic in the bed he didn't see Molly step into the room. If Rabbit noticed her mother she didn't let on. Her IV-fluid drip had slipped from her vein and the fluid had built up in the tissue, causing swelling in her arm. 'I just want to remove the IV,' he said, but she wouldn't let him touch her.

'What's all this?' Molly said, alerting the beleaguered doctor to her presence.

'I'm sorry . . .' he said.

'No need, son. It appears that my daughter is the one acting the arse.'

'Go away, Ma,' Rabbit ordered.

'I'm Enda,' he said to her mother.

'Molly.'

'It's nice to meet you, Enda.'

'You too, Molly.' He leaned over the bed to shake Molly's outstretched hand.

'Can the two of you just fuck off?' Rabbit said emphatically.

'No, we can't. Now what's going on?' Molly replied.

'Oh, nothing, Ma. Everything is amazing. I am unbelievably grateful. Top of the fucking world.'

'You need to calm down, missy.'

'Don't talk to me like I'm a fucking child.'

'Then don't act like a fucking child.'

Clearly there was a little too much 'fucking' going on for Enda because he said, 'I'll give you a minute.'

'Thanks, son.' Molly smiled at him as he passed her. When he was gone she sat on the side of the bed. 'If you don't let him fix that he can't deliver your meds and you'll be in screaming agony in no time at all.'

'I'm already in screaming agony,' Rabbit said, through gritted teeth.

'So your defiance makes even less sense.'

Rabbit turned slowly to face the wall. 'Did you decide who is taking my daughter?'

'So that's what this is about,' Molly said.

'Just answer the question.'

'Your da and I are taking her for now.'

A tear slid from Rabbit's eye onto the sheet below her. 'Wow, that's great,' she said. Her sarcasm and bitterness were impossible to ignore.

'Say what you have to say, Rabbit.'

'I'm thrilled she gets to watch me die, then you and me da before she's shoved off to who knows where.'

'Grace will take her when she has the room.'

'Well, that's everything a dying mother could wish for.'

'Don't be so fucking dramatic, Rabbit.'

Rabbit turned to face her mother. '"Don't be so fucking dramatic." I'm fucking dying, Ma. If I can't be dramatic now, then when?'

'You have a point.' Molly laughed, and after a moment Rabbit laughed too. It wasn't funny, but they laughed until their bellies ached and then they cried, laughed some more and cried again. When it had taken everything out of Rabbit and they had finally stopped, Molly apologized about Juliet's short-term future. 'We're doing the best we can, love.'

'I know, Ma. I'm sorry. Yesterday I thought I was OK with leaving her, but today I just want to . . .'

'Punch a baby?'

'No.'

'Kick a pensioner?'

'No.'

'Harass some poor doctor?'

'Yeah.'

'It's OK to be angry, Rabbit.'

'No, it's not. I don't have time.'

Her words cut Molly deeply, but she recovered well and lifted the mood. 'Speaking of angry, Grace hit Lenny in the face with a mug.'

'She told me.'

'Of course she did,' Molly said.

'Serious black eye all the same.'

'She did some damage all right.'

'Poor Lenny. I'll bet he didn't see that coming.'

'It's OK to be angry, love,' Molly said again, gently. 'We're all angry.'

'Thanks, Ma.' Rabbit was crying. 'Can you ask Enda to come back in? I really need my meds now.'

'Of course.'

Rabbit lay in the bed building bricks in her head to block out the pain and at the same time she practised her speech to her daughter. *'Juliet, it's the end of the road for me.'* No, too country song. *'Juliet, I'm dying.'* Too *direct.* *'Juliet, I have to leave . . .'* Sounds like I'm walking out on her. *'Juliet, I tried my best . . .'* No, too self-pitying. *'Juliet, I love you. I'm sorry.'* Too sad. Christ, what am I going to say? I can't mess this up.

If Rabbit had believed in God and eternal life, she could have comforted her daughter. She could have promised she would watch over her and protect her from above, or possibly from below, depending on how strict God was on the matter of sex before marriage, contraception and theft. Rabbit had once stolen a bag of guitar leads from a band of dickheads called the Funky Punks; it was her one and only dabble with crime and she couldn't quite bring herself to regret it. If she'd been a believer she could have told her daughter that they would see one another again and it wasn't the end, but as much as Rabbit wished she could offer her daughter some comfort, she couldn't lie, and if she did, Juliet would know. It would be cruel.

Enda arrived back on his own.

'I'm really sorry,' Rabbit said.

'No need.' He took her arm in his hand.

'I was an ass.'

'I've met worse. A man of seventy tried to kick me in the face last week,' he said, examining her arm and hand for a vein. 'Your veins are shot.'

'Why did he do that?' she asked. 'This one is still good.' She showed him a vein in her other arm.

'He took issue with me inserting a catheter.'

'I haven't left this bed in ages. Do I have one of those?'

'Yes.' He inserted the needle.

'Huh, I don't remember getting it.'

Enda fixed the cannula. 'There. All done.' He injected the meds. 'I'm going to change your patch too.'

'Enda?'

'Yeah?'

'Where's my ma?'

'She's on the phone.'

'Is it late?'

He looked at his watch. 'Just after nine.'

'My daughter said she'd come back tonight. It's too late now. She has school in the morning.'

'There's always tomorrow.'

'If I'm still here.'

'Oh, you'll still be here, with that kind of fight in you, trust me.'

'Promise?'

'Goodnight, Mia.' Enda didn't have to make any promises because Rabbit was already drifting into sleep.

'Rabbit,' she said, as he closed the door to her room. 'My name is Rabbit.'

Johnny

It wasn't often a living saint came to town. At least, that was what Johnny said to Rabbit when he tried to convince her to bring him to see Mother Teresa. Rabbit was not convinced, insisting to Johnny that her da would take him.

'But I've only got two tickets and I want you there.'

'Why?'

'Because I know it'll annoy you.'

'I'm not going.'

'Please! I'm really sick and she might help me.'

'If she could really help you, that kip she runs in India would be called the living rooms not the dying rooms – and stop playing the sick card.'

They were lying side by side on the sitting-room floor, listening to music and staring at the ceiling.

'It's getting worse, Rabbit.'

She turned on her elbow and gazed at him. He was still so handsome, but he always looked tired now and older than his twenty years. She sighed heavily. 'OK, fine. I'll do it.'

He smiled at her. 'Maybe she'll change your mind.'

'Doubt it.'

'If she fixes me.'

'If she fixes you, I'll definitely change my mind.'

'This is a big deal, Rabbit. These tickets are gold dust. We're really lucky.'

That made her sad, because she was staring at a beautiful boy, with so much talent and so much love to give and life to live, and he was struggling to sit up. He wasn't lucky at all.

The next day Rabbit's mother insisted she wear her best dress, and when Davey picked Johnny up he was wearing a suit. Molly took a photo of them by the window. Johnny sat on the edge of the sill and put his arm around Rabbit so that he could lean on her. If you didn't know he was sick in that photo, they looked like a happy young couple about to go out on a date, not a disabled man with his best friend and part-time carer. Davey drove them to the church. Now Johnny had to use a stick, but he insisted on walking up the church steps himself, so it took a while and Mother Teresa was speaking by the time they made it through the door.

Although they were late, Johnny walked with his stick right up to the front and Rabbit followed obediently. He pushed in beside a woman with a large growth on the side of her head. She smelt of antiseptic. The church was packed and it was a hot day. The smell of incense, mixed with antiseptic, cheap perfume, sweat and desperation, turned Rabbit's stomach, and when black dots floated in front of her eyes, she put her head into her hands and hoped she wouldn't faint. Johnny didn't notice: he was mesmerized, but all Rabbit could see was a tiny woman dressed in blue and white tea-towels. She spoke in a low and sometimes inaudible voice. He leaned forward: he didn't want to miss even one word that fell from her mouth. Rabbit was too busy telling herself not to fall down or puke to engage in what the woman had to say.

At the end the sick lined up for a blessing. Johnny got up more quickly than he had in a long while and, despite heavy competition, he managed to be one of the first in her receiving line. Rabbit stood behind him ready to catch him if he fell and hoping no one would have to catch her. She could see his legs shake a little, but she wasn't sure if it was the disease or his nerves. The old woman stood in front of him and blessed him, then moved on. She wasn't in front of him for longer than four seconds and she mumbled a prayer rather than engaging with him. When Mother Teresa was ten people ahead, Rabbit whispered into his ear, 'Can we go now?'

'Are you joking?' he whispered back.

'How many Irishmen does it take to screw in a light-bulb? One to hold the light-bulb and twenty to drink until the room spins. That's a joke. "Can we go?" is a request.'

He gave her a filthy look, which told her they were going nowhere any time soon. It was another two hours before they got to leave. Davey was asleep in the car, but he woke up to their heated argument when Rabbit opened the passenger door.

'No, I'll do it myself,' Johnny shouted, and pulled away from Rabbit when she tried to help him into the car.

'Fine. Take another half an hour to get into the fucking car. After all, we're young and we have time.' She climbed into the back seat and slammed the door.

'It went well, then?' Davey asked, starting the engine.

'Your sister is the most disrespectful person I've ever known,' Johnny said. It was clear he was both hurt and angry.

'You've only copped that now?' Davey asked, trying to lighten the mood, but it was a losing battle: his sister was as angry as his friend.

'I sat in there for three hours listening to a talking walnut tell us that suffering is a fucking gift,' Rabbit said.

'You see?' Johnny said. 'She's unbelievable. That's a saint you're talking about.'

Rabbit gave Johnny the finger.

Davey shook his head. 'Jaysus, Rabbit, ya can't be calling Mother Teresa a talking walnut – it's fucking blasphemy.'

'Oh, don't you start too, Davey. It's all bullshit, smoke-and-mirrors shite talk. Why can't you see that, Johnny?'

'I should never have taken you there.' His disappointment was almost palpable.

'You're right.'

'You've just taken a deeply special once-in-a-lifetime ex-perience and totally ruined it.' His knee started jerking. He slammed his hand on it hard to try to stop it but the spasm continued.

'Just stop!' he roared, and hit his leg again, scaring Rabbit. He did it once more, and his leg kicked out, his knee hitting the dashboard. Davey and Rabbit looked at one another in the mirror. They were both savvy enough not to say anything to Johnny, who had covered his face with his hands and was softly crying. Rabbit felt terrible. She had done her best to support him, but she felt awkward in churches and he knew that none of it made sense to her, and when the old woman had talked about the abomination of abortion, it had really rankled. She shouldn't have muttered that the nun should mind her own busi-ness, especially as she had spoken loudly enough to be heard by the monk in the wheelchair and the woman with one leg sitting next to him. They weren't impressed. The monk had whispered to her that if she felt like that she should leave. The woman had tutted and glared at her.

Johnny was incandescent with rage. He didn't speak for the

rest of the trip home. He would allow only Davey to escort him into his house. It was the one real fight Rabbit and Johnny had ever had and they didn't speak for two whole weeks. Finally Rabbit broke. She threw stones at his bedroom window and threatened to climb the tree in the twins' garden and burst through it if she had to. At sixteen, she was still too young to understand that Johnny's outburst in the car had had little to do with her lack of respect and everything to do with his disappointment at entering and leaving that church as a cripple. She apologized profusely for being a total dick and promised faithfully never to enter another church with him. He was lying on his bed; his guitar was beside him. His eyes were closed. He didn't speak and she worried that her apologies and promises weren't enough.

'And I will never, ever call Mother Teresa anything other than Mother Teresa. It's great that she cares for the sick, and she can say whatever she likes about anything. We're all entitled to our opinion.'

'That's big of you.' His eyes were still closed, but the smile on his face encouraged her to go on.

'And I should never have threatened to kick that nice one-legged lady.'

'Probably not.'

'Even though she deliberately jammed her crutch on my foot.'

He opened his eyes. 'I'm sorry too. I shouldn't have asked you to come. It was unfair.'

'More painful than unfair.' She sat down in the armchair his mother had placed by his bed.

'I've written loads of new songs.'

'Let me hear them.'

He sat up slowly and she placed his pillows behind his back just the way he liked them. He picked up the guitar. He sang and played her the songs.

She closed her eyes and listened. When he was done, she stood up and kissed him on the lips. 'Let's never fight again.'

'OK.' He seemed a little shocked at her boldness.

'Got to go,' she said, standing at the end of his bed and putting on her jacket.

'Where to?'

'I'm going to break up with my boyfriend.'

'Why?'

'Because I'm in love with you.'

'Rabbit, I'm too old and too sick for you.'

'I don't care.'

'We're just friends,' he shouted to her, as she went down the stairs.

'I can wait,' she yelled back.

Juliet

When Ryan and Juliet were smaller they had played together all the time. They were the closest cousins in age, so it made sense that they always gravitated towards one another. If the photos their mothers pulled out at least once a year were indicative of how they truly felt, they were completely obsessed with each other. In every single photo, and there were too many to count, the cousins were either holding hands, hugging or kissing. They were less than five at the time but still it caused huge embarrassment every time their parents took a trip down Memory Lane.

In recent years they hadn't hung out as much. They went to different schools; they were interested in different things. Ryan was always so sure of himself and what he wanted out of life and, aside from wanting to cure cancer, Juliet had no idea who she was or what she wanted. Ryan was popular with girls and always the centre of attention. Juliet preferred life on the sidelines. She'd been asked out a few times but the thought of a boy shoving his tongue down her throat was too much to take. Besides, she was busy with her mother. She had far too many things to think about and do to waste any time running after some boy. Ryan had had girlfriends since the age of nine. He was experienced. Juliet's only experience had occurred when she was ten and Timmy Sullivan had licked her face for a bet. It was wet and disgusting and left traces of cheese and onion crisps on her cheek. He was gone before she could kick him, and she was so shocked she started to cry. She had not touched cheese and onion crisps in the two years that had passed since the incident.

Before Ryan had turned nine and discovered girls they had spent most of their time in her wooden playhouse at the end of her garden. It was their getaway, a place where they could hide out from the rest of the world. They'd have picnics, talk about cartoons and play Ludo, Connect 4 and Ryan's favourite, Buckaroo. Juliet hadn't ventured into her playhouse since Ryan had virtually disappeared from her life. Kyle hated enclosed spaces and Della thought it smelt like old socks. She hadn't really noticed it before today, but Della was right: it did smell of old socks.

It was dark, too. She found a torch on the shelf beside the games, switched it on and looked out of the window towards her house, which was also in darkness. Earlier she had thought about going inside but had known that if she did they would find her, and she'd been right: twice that evening Grace and Lenny had been through the house from top to bottom, screaming her name, and Davey had waited for her for a few hours. She had watched him pace around the kitchen. He had left an hour ago but he would come back.

She wasn't sure what she was doing. She just wanted to be left alone. Her heart was aching so badly she wanted to reach inside her chest and rip it out. She hadn't eaten and the tips of her fingers were white and numb. She was tired. She checked her watch. It was ten p.m. She opened the press and pulled out the old blanket she and Ryan used to picnic on. She wrapped herself up in it and fell asleep.

She woke with a start to the light of her own torch being

shoved into her face. She shielded her eyes. 'Who's there?' she asked, in a squeaky, terrified voice.

'The local paedophile,' Ryan said, shining the light on his face. 'Wha-ha-ha.'

'Please go away.' She covered her face with the blanket. She heard him sit down.

'This place is smaller and smellier than I remember,' he said.

She didn't answer. Ryan had let her down when he hadn't wanted to hang out with her any more, but he'd really hurt her when she had gone to stay in his house. He was the only cousin who hadn't made an effort to talk to her or welcome her. Even pre-diabetic, half-starved and traumatized Jeffrey had tried. Ryan had just walked out of every room she entered and it killed her. She had wondered what she had done wrong, but she hadn't asked him – he hadn't been near her long enough for her to be able to. He poked her with the torchlight.

'Leave me alone,' she said.

'Can't.'

'Really? You've been doing a good job of it up to now.'

'Sorry.'

She lowered her blanket. 'Why?'

'Because everyone was lying to you and I didn't want to.'

She sat up and rested her back against the playhouse wall. He was sitting opposite. 'How long has everyone known?' she asked.

'Pretty much since your ma broke her leg. They just didn't want to believe it, that's all.'

'Does she know?' Juliet asked.

'Yeah.'

'Why didn't she tell me?'

'She wants to. She will. I suppose it's hard.'

'How long?'

'Not long.'

'Well, what's not long?' Juliet said, her eyes filling and her voice trembling with panic.

'I don't know, Juliet. Nobody tells me anything. I have to work out what I can from earwigging.'

'Maybe they're wrong.'

'They're not wrong. Stephen and Bernard said she looked mental last night.'

'She's not mental!' Juliet shouted angrily at him.

'I didn't mean that, and you know it. She looks like she's dying because she is.'

Juliet's tears ran down her face. 'But she can't. I don't want her to.'

'It doesn't matter what you want.'

'Easy for you to say – you have two parents. I hate you.' She stood up. 'I really hate you.' She moved to run outside but he got up quickly and blocked the door. 'Get out of my way.'

'No.'

'Ryan, I'm serious.'

'No.'

'I'll kick you.'

'So kick me.'

'I really will.'

'So do it.'

She kicked him in the shin so hard he crumpled to the floor. 'Holy shit, Juliet, what the hell?'

'I told you I'd do it.'

'I think you've broken it.' He was clutching his leg and wearing a pained expression.

Juliet was concerned. She couldn't leave him lying there, especially if she'd broken a bone. 'Show me.'

He stretched it out slowly and made whimpering noises when she pulled up the leg of his jeans. She took the torch from him and examined it closely. It was really red and there would be a shocking bruise, but it wasn't broken.

'You'll live,' she said, and burst out into loud and messy crying. Ryan sat beside her in silence while she cried her eyes out.

'It's going to be OK,' he said.

'No, it's not.'

'I know it will. You'll have to trust me.'

The light went on in the kitchen. He crossed to the window and peered out. 'It's Davey,' he said, sitting down beside her. 'Me ma is losing her mind, Stephen and Bernard are going mental, and everyone's really worried about you.'

'They shouldn't have lied.'

'You lied too.'

'I did not.'

'Don't play games with me, Juliet Hayes. You knew.'

Juliet nodded and the last tear she had left inside her slid down her face. 'I just wanted it to go away.'

'Well, it won't.'

'I think we should go inside now,' she said, and Ryan followed her out of the damp wooden playhouse.

When Davey saw them walk into the kitchen, his face lit up. Without a word, he came over to them and took them both in his arms. Ryan pushed him off. 'Seriously, Davey.'

But Juliet stayed in his embrace and they held each other tight. He kissed her head. 'You're home now,' he said.

Ryan had snuck out and was long gone when they broke free. 'I'm sorry for worrying everyone,' Juliet said.

She was freezing so Davey ran her a bath and she could hear him talking to Grace on the phone from the hallway. When he discovered there was nothing edible in the cupboards, he shouted up the stairs that he was going to the shops. Juliet lay there surrounded by bubbles, warm and exhausted. She didn't fall asleep but she did disappear into herself. When she heard the door open, she dragged herself out and dressed in her own bedroom. It was the same room as it always had been, but she felt like a stranger in her own home. Nothing seemed real or hers. Davey called her. She arrived in the kitchen in her pyjamas and dressing-gown. He had made her an omelette.

'Just eat as much as you can,' he said, but Juliet was hungry so she finished most of it.

'You're a good cook,' she said.

'If you like eggs, pasta and shepherd's pie, I'm your man.'

'What's going to happen to me, Davey?'

'I don't know yet, Juliet, but I promise that, whatever happens, you'll have your say.'

'I just want me ma.'

'I know you do, kiddo.'

'That's what me granda calls her.'

Juliet lay in her bed that night, her uncle Davey in the spare room. She tossed and turned and watched the night become morning, knowing it was probably the last night she'd ever spend in her own home. Just before dawn she walked out of her room and into her mother's. She slipped into her bed and smelt her perfume on the duvet and sheets. She hugged the pillows and it was there that she finally fell asleep.

DAY SIX

Chapter Eleven

Davey

IT HAD BEEN A long time since Davey had had trouble with a nervous gut, but when he opened Juliet's bedroom door and discovered she wasn't there he very nearly shat himself. He recovered quickly when he found her sleeping soundly in the middle of her mother's double bed. He took the breakfast he'd made back to the kitchen and scraped the food into the bin to allow her to sleep on. He put the kettle on and spoke to Grace on the phone while he drank his coffee. She was still very upset that her two sons had lost her dying sister's only child, and even though it appeared that Ryan had saved the day, he had imparted very little about Juliet's state of mind. 'He said, "Her ma's dying, what do you think?" Then he went to bed,' Grace said.

'She's asleep in her mother's bed,' Davey said.

'Ah, God, that's so sad.'

'I was thinking maybe the two of us could stay here until Rabbit passes.'

Grace fell silent at the other end of the line.

'Juliet's whole world is crumbling around her and this is her home.'

'You're not going to give up on taking her, are you?'

'No.'

'Ma and Da won't have it, Davey.'

'I think they will.'

'You're dreaming.'

'Maybe.'

Davey heard the front door open while Grace was still on the phone. Molly entered the kitchen. She was haggard. 'Ma's here,' he said.

Grace moaned. 'She's going to kill me.'

'No, she's not – you're not going to kill Grace, are ya, Ma?' Davey said.

'No. I'm going to kill her kids,' Molly said, putting on the kettle.

Davey put down the phone and took over making coffee for his mother. She removed her coat and sat at the kitchen table.

'Juliet?'

'She's still sleeping. Have you eaten?'

'I had some toast. It's still stuck in me throat.' She wrung her hands, then ran them through her hair. 'We need to bring her to the hospice. Rabbit missed her last night.'

'I know, Ma. Just another half-hour.'

Molly nodded. Davey handed her a coffee and sat down beside her. 'Did you have her blessed last night?' Davey asked.

'She was a little too agitated. I thought if she woke up in the middle of it we'd be going to two funerals.'

'You should leave it, Ma.'

'Can't.'

'Speaking of—'

'No, Davey, you're not taking Juliet to America.'

'What if I stayed here?'

Molly laid a hand on his cheek. 'You were always so kind, Davey, but your life is over there, son.'

'My life is wherever I choose it to be. We could keep this house.'

'Rabbit is a freelance journalist and a single mother. She rents it.'

'So I'll buy it.'

Neither Davey nor Molly heard Juliet's footsteps on the stairs or hallway. She was standing next to them before they knew it.

'Juliet! You nearly scared me half to death,' Molly said.

'You must be hungry?' Davey asked her.

'Nan.'

'Yes, love.'

'I want to live with Davey.'

'Davey can't stay here, love.'

'I know. I want to leave with him.'

Molly looked as if she was either about to cry or box Davey in the face, he wasn't quite sure. He pulled back in his chair slightly, unsure what to do or say.

'We'll talk about this another time,' Molly said, in the voice she employed when she would not tolerate argument or discussion. Juliet sat down opposite them. Davey got up, the kettle went on again and two slices of bread went into the toaster. After a moment or two of silence, Molly asked her granddaughter if she had any questions for her.

'No,' Juliet said.

'Are you sure, love?' Molly asked.

Juliet stood up before the kettle was boiled or the toast had popped and made for the door.

'What about your breakfast?' Davey said.

'I'm not hungry.' She left the room.

Davey's mother turned to him. 'What have you just done?'

Molly left soon after. Davey showered and changed in the main bathroom; Juliet used her mother's en-suite. They met downstairs, fresh and ready to see Rabbit.

'Davey?' Juliet said, on the way to the car.

'Yes?'

'Can I go in alone?'

'Of course.'

They sat in the car.

'Davey?'

'Yeah?'

'Do you really want me?' Juliet asked. Her voice cracked slightly, betraying her fear.

'Juliet, everybody wants you.'

'What does me ma want?'

Davey could have said something trite, like 'She wants you to be happy,' but instead he admitted the truth: 'I don't know.'

He pulled out of the driveway and Juliet turned on the radio. There was an old Dolly Parton song playing. She turned it up a little and pulled her seat back.

'You like country music?' Davey asked.

'Not really.' She closed her eyes.

She was asleep when they reached the hospice. Davey parked the car and sat there for at least five minutes before he attempted to wake her. He watched people come and go and mused on the events of the past five days. He looked down at his sleeping niece and felt a terrible unease. *What the hell have I done?*

Juliet woke up and focused on her uncle staring out of the car window, lost in his thoughts.

'What do I say to her, Davey?' Juliet asked, when their eyes met.

'Whatever you want.'

'I want to run.'

'Me too.'

They got out of the car and walked up to the hospice doors, hand in hand. Once inside she let go and he watched her walk to her mother's room alone.

'I'll be here when you come out,' he said, before she opened the door. It wasn't until it closed behind her that he spotted Mabel sitting on the chairs. She had a book in her hand and a wide grin on her face.

'Mabel?'

'In the flesh.'

'What are you doing here?'

'Now, you know if Casey can't be here she'll send second best.'

She stood up and they embraced. He melted into her warmth. 'You could never be second best and you have no idea how good it is to see you,' he said.

'I'm so sorry, honey,' she said.

'Where are you staying? Where are the kids?'

'On the road with a minder and their other mother.'

'How's the tour going?'

'Forget the tour.'

'How long are you here for?'

'As long as it takes.'

Davey hugged her again.

'What's that for?' she said.

'This is the first time since I've been back that I've really felt at home.'

They returned to the chairs, where Davey explained the events of the last five days and how Juliet and her mother were only just coming to terms with her death.

'It's so sad,' Mabel said.

'Casey's worried I'm not coming back, isn't she?'

'Every time you get on a plane to Ireland she worries about that.'

'This time she might be right.'

She nudged him with her shoulder. 'Let's just take one day at a time.'

The first time Davey had met Mabel her tongue had been down his best friend's throat. They were backstage at a festival in Washington. Casey had just come off and Mabel had been waiting in the wings, a tall, broad, bald, striking African-American, who lived in leather pants and skull T-shirts and passed for a rock star everywhere she went.

Mabel had caught Davey staring at them kissing. 'Why is he staring at us?' she'd asked, when they had pulled out of their embrace and he continued to stare.

'He's judging you,' Casey said.

'And?'

'Nice form,' Davey said, and Casey laughed.

'I like him,' Mabel said.

'He's a keeper,' Casey agreed.

'So are you.' Mabel leaned in for another kiss and that was it: Casey was hooked. Mabel was acting tour manager for a band sharing the bill. Within a week she had left the other tour and was living on their bus. Within a month she had replaced their old tour manager, a stoner named Job, without him ever realizing it. He stayed until the end of the tour but after that Mabel was Casey's official tour manager for two years until she became her wife. Mabel was a fair-minded, hard-working ball-buster. She had a devilish sense of humour, she liked a drink, and from the start Davey had a friend in her. Since they'd had the kids, Mabel had spent less time on the road but she still managed to organize every aspect of the tour, Casey's life and sometimes even Davey's from home.

Davey waited outside his sister's door. Mabel went into the canteen and returned with teas and wraps. 'I got them to take out the cucumber.'

'Thanks.'

'Have any of these people ever seen a black person before?' she asked, when the third person double-took as they passed her.

'It's your bald head. The visitors think you have cancer and they pity you, and the dying think you have cancer and wonder how the fuck you manage to look so good.'

She laughed a little.

'You don't have to stay here, you know,' he said.

'I didn't fly all this way to sit in a hotel.' Her phone rang. She looked at it and handed it to Davey. 'It's for you.'

He took it and answered: 'Hey, Casey.'

'It's good to hear your voice.'

'Yours too.'

'How are you?'

'Better for seeing Mabel.'

'If I could cancel, you know I would.'

'I do.'

'I miss you. We all do.' There was a whoop and a cheer from the busload of men and women she was travelling with.

'Tell them I miss them too.'

He passed the phone back to Mabel, who walked off and spoke in a hushed tone. He sat alone outside his sister's room, wondering what was going on behind the closed door, and daydreamed of the many days and nights he'd spent with road moving under his feet, a set direction and destination, and no real worries of his own. *Nothing will ever be the same again, Rabbit. How could it be when you're gone?*

Juliet

Rabbit was alone and sleeping. Juliet crept in towards her mother, slowly and carefully, afraid to wake her but more afraid of what would happen when she did. She settled on the chair by the bed, and for the first time since Rabbit had entered the hospice, Juliet allowed herself not just to look at her mother but to really see her. She examined her poor ma's bloated face, the discolouring around her dry, chapped lips, her battered and bruised arms and hands, and she heard the loud, laboured breathing that emerged in spurts from her open, dry mouth. She didn't look anything like her old self. Her hair and cheekbones were gone, and when she was awake the colour seemed washed out of her swollen eyes. Lying mostly in the foetal position, her once long, lean body seemed shorter and puffier. Even her fingers were fluid-filled, knotted and unrecognizable. She looked like a broken someone else from one of those hard-to-watch films that the boys loved. There was blood around the fresh cannula in her arm. The swelling in her hand had gone down but the tiniest droplets of fluid still leaked from the puncture hole.

The breakfast tray was untouched. On her locker there were

swab lemon and glycerine lollipops. She was holding the cuddly rabbit close to her chest. She looked like a lost little girl, and in that moment, Juliet experienced such overwhelming warmth, love and tenderness she felt as though she was the mother in the room. She touched Rabbit's arm lightly; her skin was still soft. She unwrapped a swab lollipop and gently rubbed it on her mother's cracked lips. She went to the bathroom, dampened a cloth and ever-so-tenderly cleaned away the caked blood from around her cannula.

'I love you, Ma,' she whispered.

Her mother's eyes opened slightly. 'Juliet?'

'If I could have chosen anyone in the world to be my ma, I would have chosen you. You've been amazing. You are amazing.'

Tears slid down mother and child's faces.

'You are the best thing that ever happened to me, Juliet Hayes.' Rabbit was trying to open her eyes wide so that she could really see her little girl.

'I know, Ma,' Juliet said, wiping away her mother's tears with a tissue.

'I'm so tired, Juliet,' Rabbit said.

'So sleep.'

'Jump up, baby.' Rabbit attempted to pat the bed.

'OK.' Juliet walked around to the other side, got in and spooned her ma, who cuddled her rabbit. Within ten minutes they were both sound asleep.

Jack

Jack spotted Mabel sitting with his son before she noticed him. He was immediately struck by her kindness. *She came all this way for Davey.* It was easy to forget that although Davey didn't have a traditional family in the States he wasn't alone. Now he saw his parents approach and stood up.

'Ma, this is my friend Mabel.'

'Howya, love,' Molly said, and shook her hand. 'Jack's always banging on about how great you are.'

'He's great himself,' Mabel said, and embraced Jack. 'It's good to see you, old man.'

'Hah, that's what I call him,' Molly said.

'It's lovely that you came,' Jack told Mabel.

'Wouldn't be anywhere else.'

Over the years Jack had travelled to see Davey play with Casey numerous times. Sometimes he joined Francie, Jay and Kev – they made a boys' weekend of it; other times he was with Grace and Rabbit, Rabbit and Juliet, or Grace, Lenny and the kids. Molly was a more reserved traveller: she liked Blackpool and Wales and everywhere else could fuck off. The first time Davey had broached the subject of her spending time in Nashville she had laughed in his face. 'As if,' she'd said, chuckling away to herself, 'and why don't I fly to the moon while I'm at it? I hear the atmosphere is out of this world.'

Whenever Jack went, and sometimes he went alone, Casey and Mabel made such a fuss of him that he felt teary going home. He'd even travelled on the tour bus, which was exciting for about a day and a half, then a little tiresome, but worth it. He loved driving from city to city, watching the never-ending road meet the blue, red, orange and black skylines, then land in massive venues. He'd watch the band sound-check in empty arenas and he was welcomed on those incredible stages. He'd kept every backstage pass he'd ever worn, from Kitchen Sink to the Sound to Casey, and every one of them held a memory he'd cherish for ever. Seeing Mabel made him want to cry. It reminded him of the time he and Rabbit had taken Juliet to join the tour when it hit Las Vegas for ten shows. Juliet had been only five, so it was during her 'I'm an alien' period. They had spent an incredibly happy five days together, Mabel and Casey fussing over and spoiling Juliet as if she were their own. Rabbit had been healthy then, well able to run around after the alien, but the girls had insisted on taking her to the top shows and the best pools, the coolest kids' restaurants. They'd bought her clothes, shoes and dolls until Rabbit had to put her foot down because the extra luggage would cost a fortune. With the girls taking care of Juliet, Rabbit got to hang around with her da and Davey a lot over those five days. It was like when she had been Davey's sound engineer and her da was head of the band's fan club.

Johnny's death had pulled Rabbit and Davey apart; it had destroyed the closeness they had built without even knowing it. They had disappeared into their own grief and guilt. Those hot days and nights spent pottering in the shops, hanging out by the pool and talking in bars till late at night had rebuilt their broken bridge. At the venue, Davey had shown Rabbit off to the band and crew, his baby sister, sound engineer *extraordinaire*. She had stood behind the big desk and marvelled. When Eddie, the head sound guy, asked her if she wanted to have a go, she told him she wouldn't even know how to turn it on. Jack had felt her brother's pride when he said, 'But if you gave her an hour she'd take your job.' Mabel and Casey knew the story of Davey, Rabbit and Johnny; they knew that brother and sister were both still grieving and they had played their part in the healing. Jack would always be grateful to them for that.

Molly, Jack, Davey and Mabel sat on the chairs in a straight line, watching the door. It was imperative that they gave Juliet and Rabbit all the time they needed, but door-watching is hard, especially under such circumstances. Molly reached into her bag and pulled out a bag of lemon bonbons. She passed them to Jack, who passed them to Davey, who passed them to Mabel.

'Lemon and toffee. Very nice, but you need strong fillings,' Molly said to Mabel, who took one and passed them back up the line.

'I don't think we have these in America.'

'Shame,' Molly said.

Jack asked after Casey and the kids, and Mabel talked about how fantastic they all were, except for six-year-old Emmet's insistence on licking his twin brother Hopper's face. 'It's like he can't help himself, every damn day. Hopper loses it and lashes out. Then the crying begins, followed by one or both of them having a tantrum. Oh, God, it's insane.'

'Vaseline,' Molly said.

'Excuse me?'

'Rub a little on Hopper's face. When Emmet licks him, it will coat his tongue. He won't do it again.'

'The shrink said he'd grow out of it.'

'He'll grow out of it a lot quicker if his brother's face tastes like shite.'

Mabel thought about it and nodded. 'That shrink cost nearly five hundred dollars an hour.'

'Next time call me. I'll charge half for an actual solution,' Molly said.

Mabel agreed she would. 'She's just as incredible as you de-scribed, Jack.'

'Oh she's incredible, all right,' he agreed proudly.

Jack Hayes loved his wife more than he loved his life. During the worst of times she had sat on that chair with her head held high, comforting everyone by being herself. *If there is a God I'd thank Him for you, Molly Hayes. Of course, I'd give Him a kick in the hole for everything else.*

Time moves very slowly when you're sitting in a hospital corridor. Jack needed to stretch his legs and Mabel offered to go with him. He took her to the garden and they walked around it slowly, arm in arm. Light rain fell on them – Jack didn't notice at first, and Mabel enjoyed it.

'It's not Ireland unless it's raining,' she said.

'I suppose not.'

'Did I ever tell you about my mother?'

'No.'

'She died when I was twenty-one. She was a single mother too.'

'I'm really sorry.'

'She was hit by a car, some speed freak asshole. She died at the scene. There were no goodbyes.'

'I suppose we're lucky because we get to say goodbye,' he said.

'Hell, no, it's not saying goodbye that I miss, it's her.'

'How did you deal with it?'

'At first really badly. I was alone and young, and I was scared about who and what I was. It was dark and I made a lot of mistakes, but then I cleaned up my act, started working, got focused, became driven. Slowly I became comfortable in my own skin, and it was still hard but life went on.'

'I'm really glad Davey has you, Casey and the kids.'

'He's family to us, you know that.'

'I'd forgotten. I won't forget again.'

Davey appeared, running towards them. 'Da, come quick! Something's wrong with Ma.' He was already racing back, Jack and Mabel chasing after him from the gardens into the reception area and from there to a treatment room. Molly was lying on a trolley and Mr Dunne was attending to her.

'Molly,' Jack said, terror in his voice.

'I'm all right! I'm fine, do you hear me? I'm perfectly fine.' She had spoken without raising her head.

Mr Dunne pushed Jack and Davey out of the room, then closed the door behind him. Mabel hung back, not wanting to intrude.

'What's going on?' Jack gasped.

'She dropped her bonbons, grabbed her chest and nearly fell off the chair,' Davey said.

Mr Dunne reappeared. 'Does Molly suffer with angina?' he asked.

'No.'

'Well, she's stable and we need to get her an ECG.'

'Here?' Jack said.

'Afraid not.'

'She won't leave,' Jack said.

'She has no choice. The ambulance is on its way.'

'Oh, my God,' Jack murmured.

Mr Dunne insisted he sat down. 'Jack, this was a mild event. She will be diagnosed and treated and she will be fine.'

'I can't lose her too.' He buried his head in his hands.

'You won't.'

Mr Dunne went back to Molly. Davey, Jack and Mabel heard her complain bitterly about leaving. Two ambulance men passed them and walked into the room.

When Jack raised his head, Davey was pacing and talking on the phone to his elder sister. 'Grace, are you on the way? Well, turn around and head for the hospital. It's Ma – they think she's had a heart attack.'

Molly appeared in the hallway, strapped to a trolley, covered with a navy-blue blanket. 'It wasn't a heart attack. Don't exaggerate to your sister.' She insisted on stopping to talk to her husband. She told him to find her hand so he moved the blanket and held it.

'I'm fine. It's nothing. I'd know if it was. I always know, and you know I know.'

'I do.'

'I'll get this stupid ECG and I'll be back.'

'I'm coming.'

'No. Stay with Rabbit.'

'Davey, stay with Rabbit and Juliet. Grace and I will be with your mammy.'

'OK,' Davey said.

'Mabel, take care of him.'

'I will.'

'I'm not leaving you, Molly,' Jack said. She didn't argue because it was clear that he meant it.

Jack sat in the ambulance beside his wife, and although it didn't occur to him to pray, he focused on repeating one mantra. *This time it's going to be OK.* Rabbit was dying and the terrible truth was that her father would survive her. Guilt-ridden, Jack would grieve for the rest of his days, but he was wise enough to accept that he would live on, he would smile and laugh again. He would endure because he had Molly. She was his right side and bright side. Molly made him tick. Jack Hayes adored his children and would willingly have sacrificed himself to save each and every one of them, but he couldn't live without his wife.

Grace

Grace nearly crashed the car, narrowly avoiding driving into the back of a truck. Lenny yelled, 'Christ almighty!' She braked hard and Jeffrey smashed his nose on the back of his father's headrest. He shrieked.

Lenny turned to see blood pouring from his youngest son's nose. 'Oh, for fu—'

Grace looked in the rear-view mirror. 'Where the hell is your seatbelt?'

'Sorry, Ma.'

'You could have gone straight through the fucking windscreen. Does everybody in this family have some kind of death wish?'

'The belt's uncomfortable.'

'That's because of your size, Jeffrey.'

'Not cool, Grace,' Lenny muttered.

'You're right, Lenny, it's not cool. The pre-diabetic nearly dived through a car windscreen.'

Jeffrey did up his belt with one hand and held his bleeding nose with the other.

'You're all right, son, we'll be at the hospital in five minutes.' Lenny turned to his wife. 'You are the one who nearly drove into the back of a truck, Grace. You need to calm down.'

Grace took a deep breath. 'I'm sorry, love,' she said to Jeffrey.

'Me nan'll be OK, Ma. And I'm not going to get diabetes. I'm going to lose weight and I'll wear me seatbelt from here on in.'

'Thanks.'

'Sorry, Ma.'

'Sorry, son.'

As soon as they got out of the car Lenny examined Jeffrey's nose. Although his face and T-shirt were a mess, the blood had stopped flowing. 'There's nothing broken here.'

'Feels OK,' Jeffrey agreed.

'You sure?' Grace asked, grabbing a bag from the boot.

'Yeah.'

'Let's go.' She walked to A&E so quickly that Lenny and Jeffrey had to run to keep up.

Grace knew the inside of that hospital's A&E department like the back of her hand. She didn't stop to ask anyone for attention. She'd learned long ago that if you walked in with purpose and confidence no one bothered you. The medics were too busy, and even security was fooled by her air of authority. Lenny and Jeffrey headed for the waiting area. She found her parents quickly, mainly because she could hear her mother arguing with a doctor from behind the curtain. She pulled it aside to reveal Molly sitting up in bed with wires attached to her chest, her father standing beside her, and a harassed young doctor attending to her. A drunken girl two cubicles away was yelling 'Vodka stat,' over and over again.

'What's going on?' Grace asked.

'I'm just explaining that I'm fine now and surely I can re-schedule tests for a more convenient time.'

'And the doctor disagrees. He says your mother should be admitted for investigation.'

'Ma, you're going to have to stay.'

'I'm not staying.'

'Doctor, can I talk to you for a minute outside?'

The young man followed Grace and closed the curtain behind him; they walked a few paces away and kept their voices low.

'Is it possible to medicate to avoid further complications until my mother can reschedule tests?'

'I wouldn't advise it.'

'But is that because she's in very real danger or you have to cover your arse?' Her direct approach made him bristle. She didn't care. She didn't have time to be polite.

'Your mother is a seventy-two-year-old woman who presented with chest pain and shortness of breath. Her symptoms were resolved when Mr Dunne administered nitroglycerin. She needs an ECG to determine whether she is suffering from angina and, if confirmed, she'll need further tests to establish which type.'

'You haven't answered my question.'

'Just because she's not in immediate danger doesn't mean she won't be if she leaves this hospital. That is why I'm covering our collective arses.'

'How long will these investigations take?'

'Depends.'

'On what?'

'How many people are in the line and the severity of each individual case.'

'Are special circumstances taken into consideration?'

'Everybody has special circumstances of their own.'

'Does everybody have their forty-year-old daughter dying in a hospice?'

The young doctor's expression froze. Almost instantly his attitude and body language changed. 'I'm very sorry. Let me see what I can do.'

'We'd really appreciate it.'

Molly was lying down and Jack was holding her hand when Grace reappeared.

'It's going to be all right, Ma. They'll do the tests as quick as they can. You'll be out of here in no time.'

'I need to be out of here now.' Molly's eyes were welling. 'We don't have time for this.'

'Just hang on. I'll get it sorted, I promise.'

'Good girl, Grace.' Jack turned back to his wife. 'She's a fighter, like her ma.'

Lenny and Jeffrey weren't in the waiting area. She rang Lenny, who confirmed they were in a coffee shop across the road. Jeffrey had the morning off school to see a paediatrician. It had been an early appointment but they had woken late and missed breakfast. It was lunchtime, and when Grace entered, smelling coffee and toast, her stomach growled and she felt a little faint. After ordering, she joined Lenny and Jeffrey at the table.

'I'm eating a salad, Ma.' Jeffrey pointed to his plate.

'Good boy.'

'How's me nan?'

'Pissed off.'

'That's a good sign,' Lenny said.

Grace agreed. 'She just needs to get out of there.'

She ate her sandwich and drank her coffee. When they were paying, her phone rang. It was her father. 'They've taken her upstairs.'

It was good news. She would have her tests and, all going well, she'd be out sooner rather than later. Grace told Lenny to drop Jeffrey at school and go to work; it wasn't necessary for the pair of them to hang around. Lenny didn't want to leave her there alone. 'I have me da,' she said, and insisted they go.

Grace stopped off at the Spar to buy snacks for her parents, but when she returned her father was sound asleep on a chair and her mother was locked behind a closed door. Grace rifled through the bag, found a cereal bar and ate it. Then she pulled out a bag of sweets and ate them; after that she decided that, as she'd already broken her strict regime, she might as well go the whole hog and eat the little chocolate egg. Then she felt sick and berated herself for eating so much rubbish. She spotted a magazine on the chairs opposite. She'd read it from cover to cover the week before in the hairdresser's, but she read it again – anything to keep her mind off what was going on. It was all too much.

Her da was snoring. Normally the sound annoyed the heart and soul out of her but today it was comforting. Every now and then she worried about Rabbit and what was going on. Jeffrey had wanted to visit his aunt after he'd seen the paediatrician but he'd missed his opportunity. Bernard and Stephen hadn't had a chance to speak to her when they'd gone in. The only one of her boys who hadn't pushed to see Rabbit was Ryan. She wondered why, but of the four, Ryan was the one who mystified her most. There was a large black clock on the wall with white numbers and hands. She wondered if her boys would get a chance to say goodbye to their aunt, if she was missing her own chance, and how long Rabbit would last if she knew her beloved mother was struggling. *Don't worry, Rabbit, Ma's going to be all right, you know that, right? Nothing's going to kill Ma. If anyone could live for ever it's her, so hang on, and wait for us. Don't go yet. Please, Rabbit.*

She spent the rest of the afternoon talking to doctors, taking care of her father and texting Davey after he had messaged her:

> How's me ma?

> They think it's angina. How's Rabbit?

> What the fuck is angina? She wants to go to the garden but it's still raining.

> Some doctor came out to us and said not to worry it's most likely the good kind, whatever that means. DO NOT let Rabbit out into the garden when it's raining.

> Is Ma coming out this evening? If Rabbit is intent on doing something she does it, not to mention Juliet and Mabel fighting her corner. I'm trying me best.

> Don't know yet. Just put your foot down Davey.

> Keep me posted. She's just gone asleep, crisis averted.

The doctors decided to keep her mother in for observation but would probably allow her to leave the next morning. Once settled, Molly insisted Grace take her father home and that she be left alone. 'I'm tired. I just want to sleep. Please, Grace, go to your sister.'

'OK, Ma.' Grace was relieved. Her anxiety levels dipped slightly. *Wait for us, Rabbit.* Jack wanted to see his daughter but even he was too tired to object when Grace parked the car outside the house.

'What if she goes on us?'

'She won't, Da.'

'You don't know that.'

'I do. She'll wait.'

He leaned over and kissed Grace's cheek. 'Tell her that her mammy and daddy love her and we'll see her tomorrow.'

'I will.'

He got out of the car and she watched him open the gate and walk up the path to the door. He tried to put the key in but his hand was shaking. Eventually the door opened. He waved at her, then went inside, closing it behind him. It was just after five o'clock. Grace decided to go home, shower, change, feed her kids and bring them all to see their aunt. Grace was sure Rabbit would wait for her parents, but she knew time was running out.

Johnny

In the two years that had passed since Rabbit had declared her love for Johnny, a lot and nothing had changed. The band had gone through another two managers; Johnny's health was continuing to deteriorate. He walked with a cane, he was slower, weaker. Once in a while his body refused to co-operate, but oddly never on stage. He could still sing. His voice and his talent were intact, but it was hard to sell a band with a disabled lead singer, no matter how good the tunes and how solid the act. The lads forged ahead. They had long ago agreed they wouldn't give up until Johnny said the word, but Francie took a part-time job in a local pharmaceutical factory, Jay started a sound-engineering course and Kev deputized for the guitar player in a wedding band. Davey still believed: he invested himself completely in the band. He took over management in the absence of representation.

'If Stevie Wonder can do it, we can,' he said, and repeated it over and over, much to the lads' enjoyment and Johnny's frustration. They still gigged when they could; they kept it local most of the time, but if there was a good-paying gig somewhere, they could still rely on the twins and Uncle Terry, who would take them in the bread van, only now they created a makeshift bed in the back so that Johnny could sleep on the journey there and back. It was a tight squeeze but they put up with it, and even though the great hope they'd once shared was gone, it was still a lot of fun.

Davey sent a tape of songs to a new record label in London and within a week had received a call from an excited A&R man called Billy Wilde. He loved the songs. He asked for a photo. Davey sent one that was four years old. The guy flipped for the handsome lead singer, not to mention the rest of the band. They looked good together, like rock stars: he couldn't imagine why they hadn't been picked up before. Davey said nothing. The guy wanted to see them play. They didn't have a gig coming up so Davey suggested they play for him in the garage. The guy was happy with that and the sooner he saw them the better.

Rabbit turned eighteen and even though she and Johnny were still not romantically linked, they were closer than ever. When they were gigging she was his right-hand woman. Nothing came to Johnny that didn't pass through Rabbit. She made sure he had everything he needed, before, during and after his performance. She brought him on stage and took him off. Before it became apparent that he couldn't really function without her, the lads were a little resentful of her constant presence, but that phase faded quickly. When they went out drinking and trawling for women on a Friday and Saturday night, Johnny and Rabbit stayed in with a curry and a video. Francie and Jay treated them like a couple, and neither ever complained. Kev often wondered why they just didn't get on with it, but only when Davey was out of the room: he reacted badly to the notion of anyone, even one of his best friends, having any kind of relationship with his baby sister.

The afternoon Billy Wilde flew into Dublin was hot and sticky. Johnny couldn't stand the heat – it made him feel even more exhausted than usual. He was shaky and he'd been experiencing painful muscle spasms all morning. He needed to sleep, and they had an hour before Billy was due to arrive. The lads had a sound check without him. Rabbit dragged him upstairs, practically carrying him on her back. No one batted an eyelid because they were used to it. She helped him into her bed, closed the curtains and tucked him in.

'I'll come and get you when he arrives,' she said.

'I'll feel better after a sleep.'

While he slept, the lads sat outside in the garden enjoying the sun. Davey was anxious: everyone else seemed a little too relaxed. They were talking about everything and anything but the guy coming to see them, who would perhaps offer them a record deal. Davey was perplexed and Rabbit knew it, but he didn't bring it up, just paced up and down the garden, then disappeared to the loo. The absence of excitement told Rabbit everything she needed to know, but still she hoped. *Maybe.*

Molly answered the door to Billy. He was a stocky red-head with whiskers and there wasn't one centimetre of earlobe without a piercing stuck through it. He was hyped. When she brought him out into the garden to meet the band, he shook their hands and assured them he was there to do business. He swung his briefcase and tapped it to ensure they knew there were contracts inside. Rabbit went to get Johnny and her ma insisted that Billy come inside for something to eat and drink.

When she woke Johnny, the spasms had worn off but his

feet were numb and his balance was off. She helped him fix his beautiful hair; he put on his vintage velvet jacket. 'How do I look?'

'Handsome.'

'Let's do it,' he said, but even as he said it she knew he was upset: he was having a bad day. If he had been lucky enough to experience a good one, the guy might have signed them, but as Rabbit carried him down the stairs, they knew it was over.

The guy was sitting at the table with his briefcase open and the contracts visible. The lads were with him and Molly was pouring tea. He looked up at Johnny, and it was instantly obvious that the singer in the photo was not the same as the ravaged man walking with a cane, his arm around the young woman holding him up. Billy's smile faded.

'I'm Johnny.'

Johnny took his arm from around Rabbit's waist and the two men shook hands.

'It's not going to happen, is it, Billy?' he said.

Billy shook his head, his exuberance replaced by sadness.

'Would you listen to us anyway, Billy?' Johnny asked.

'It would be an honour,' Billy said.

They all went into the garage, Molly included, to watch Johnny and the Sound play their last ever gig. Only one person in the room didn't cry that day and it was the man hunched on a chair, singing passionately from the darkest corners of his soul.

Chapter Twelve

Rabbit

JULIET HAD FIXED RABBIT'S pillows so that she was sitting up straight when Grace, Lenny and their four boys piled into the room. Davey and Mabel decided it was best to leave to give them some room. Juliet was desperate to stay, so Grace agreed to drop her home later. Rabbit called to Mabel on her way out, 'Don't forget to bring photos of the kids tomorrow.'

'I won't.'

'And tomorrow I'm going out to that garden,' she told Davey.

'If it stops raining.'

'The sun will shine tomorrow,' Rabbit said.

'You've got ESP now?'

'Or I just watched a weather report.' She pointed to the TV set.

Everyone laughed, probably more than the comment deserved, but it was good to see her so on top of things. 'What's ESP?' Jeffrey whispered to his mother, but she just smiled. It didn't matter and Rabbit had the floor.

'Thanks for today,' she said. It had been a good one, even though she had slept through a lot of it. When she'd been awake, she'd watched Mabel and Davey teach Juliet to play poker. She was cleaning Davey out after only a few games. Mabel was impressed and Juliet was charmed. She remembered Mabel from their time in Las Vegas but only vaguely. Mabel, Davey and Rabbit regaled Juliet with their memories of her as a child and the adventures they'd shared.

'You danced a jig on stage in Caesars Palace,' Rabbit said.

'During Casey's sound check and to one of her songs,' Mabel added.

'Which song?' Juliet asked.

'"Keep On Keeping",' Davey told her.

'I love that one,' Juliet said.

'Me too,' Rabbit murmured.

'I remember the chips in the place with the puppets. They were amazing,' Juliet added.

Mabel despaired. 'That's what you remember? We took you to meet the real Barney and you remember fries?'

Rabbit was reminded of better times and how good their lives had been.

When Davey and Mabel were gone, Juliet talked excitedly about beating Davey at poker, with her proud mother looking on. Ryan challenged her to a game but Mabel had taken the cards. 'Another time,' Grace said.

Rabbit asked Jeffrey about his diet.

'It's OK.'

'It'll get easier.'

'Yeah.'

She remembered that Stephen had exams coming up and enquired as to how he was getting on.

'Not sure.'

'Hang in there.'

She asked Bernard how his football team were doing.

'Shite.'

'Don't curse,' Grace said.

'Sorry. We keep losing.'

'Why?'

'Because we're a sh— crap team.'

'Sorry,' Rabbit said.

He shrugged. 'I've started playing hurley.'

'How's that going?'

'Crap.'

'What about you, Ryan?'

'Dee O'Reilly let me drop the hand the other night.'

Lenny gulped. Grace looked from her husband to her son, her mouth literally hanging open. Juliet was clearly stunned. Rabbit burst out laughing and when she laughed the entire room laughed so much that Linda, the nurse who'd replaced Jacinta on night duty, popped her head in to see what was happening.

'I'm sorry, Linda,' Rabbit said.

The nurse beamed at her. 'Never be sorry for laughing. We can always do with a bit of that around here.' Then she was gone.

Every time Rabbit looked at Ryan he winked at her and she chuckled.

Jeffrey was a little lost. First he didn't know what ESP was, then he was confused about how Ryan could have dropped his hand and why it was so funny.

All that laughter had exhausted Rabbit.

Grace told Lenny, Juliet and the boys to wait for her in the car. The boys lined up to say goodbye to their aunt, each one painfully aware it might be the last time. They tried their best not to cry, but it was hard, and they were experiencing varying degrees of success. When each boy leaned in for a kiss, Rabbit held her head high and made sure she was smiling. Juliet insisted on fixing her pillows so that she was comfortable. 'I'll see you tomorrow, Ma.'

'What about school?' Rabbit asked.

'It can wait,' Juliet said, and Rabbit nodded.

Juliet left Grace alone with her sister.

'I can stay over, if you like?' Grace said.

'Nah, you go home.'

'Night night, Rabbit.'

'Night night, Grace.'

Grace picked up her handbag, and Rabbit asked one last question. 'Where's me ma?'

'I thought Davey told you,' Grace said.

'He said she was tired.'

'Exhausted.'

'Look at me.'

Grace met her eye.

'Where is she?'

Grace put her bag down. 'She's fine. She's in the hospital for observation. She'll be out in the morning.'

'What happened?'

'A very, very mild heart attack.'

'Jesus Christ,' Rabbit said.

'It's fine, Rabbit.'

'Promise?'

'I promise.'

'She's out tomorrow?'

'First thing, if she has her way.' Grace picked up her bag again. She went to her sister and kissed her cheek. 'It's Ma.' She didn't need to say any more: it was understood that Ma was invincible.

'Goodnight, Rabbit.'

Grace left, but Rabbit wasn't alone for long: Linda appeared with her meds. 'Still awake?' she said.

'Wide awake.'

'How about breakthrough pain?'

'I feel fine.'

'Fine is good.'

'Fine is better than good.'

Rabbit watched Linda fill a syringe. 'Not yet. A few more minutes.' Its contents would send her to sleep. She liked being back in time with Johnny but it was also nice to enjoy the present while she could. Linda put the hypodermic into a plastic bowl and sat down.

'Michelle is the trouper, Jacinta is the singer. What's your story?'

'You heard about Michelle's boyfriend, then?'

'Really harsh.'

'I met him at a few Christmas parties. She'll do a lot better, but still living in the same house is a nightmare.'

'I'd change the locks,' Rabbit said.

'Me too,' Linda agreed. She seemed almost relieved that someone else felt the same. 'Why doesn't she do it?'

'She plays by the rules.'

'What about you, Rabbit? Do you play by the rules?'

'Sometimes,' Rabbit said, and smiled, 'and others, you've just got to make them up as you go along.'

'Amen,' Linda said.

She was a medium-built woman with a dyed red bob and kept herself well, but Rabbit guessed she was in her early fifties. 'Do you have kids, Linda?'

'Two girls. One is an accountant and the other is training to become a vet.'

'Do they have boyfriends?'

'If they do, I don't know about them. What about you? Any of those laughing hyenas yours?'

'The girl. She's twelve. Her name is Juliet.'

'Beautiful name for a beautiful girl,' Linda said.

'She's perfect,' Rabbit said. 'God, I hope this doesn't destroy her.'

'It won't.'

'You don't know that. She's already had a lot to deal with. What if my death is the thing that turns a beautiful, charming, intelligent girl into a wreck? What if it makes her sad, bitter and angry? What if it sends her on a path to a lifetime of misery?'

'It looks to me like she has good people around her,' Linda said.

'She does, but she won't have me.'

'You trust her to get through it and you trust the people around her to help her through it.'

'I have no choice, do I?' Rabbit said.

'No. All you can do is the best you can for her now.'

'You're right,' Rabbit said. 'Thank you, Linda. I'm ready for my injection now.'

Linda injected Rabbit and said goodnight. Rabbit waited for the liquid to surge through her veins to her head and eyes. She surrendered quickly to the darkness because she knew her old friend would be waiting.

Rabbit Hayes's Blog

12 March 2010

Cancer 0 – Rabbit 1

I win! I win! I win! The cancer is gone. I received the all-clear this morning and I've been floating on air since. Juliet keeps jumping up and down and singing 'YMCA' for some reason. My mother cried, then blamed it on the menopause. (The woman is seventy.) My dad is so happy he whistled all the way home in the car, and when a man in a black Honda beeped him on the roundabout, he happily gave him the fingers. If you knew my father, you'd appreciate how out of character that is. He giggled as he did it. Life is good. Grace keeps squeezing me and Lenny keeps squeezing her. Marjorie is away on business but she hasn't been off the phone.

We went out for a celebratory family lunch. My nephews lined up so sweetly to congratulate me, except Jeffrey, who was busy at the buffet counter. Ryan told me it was great news and not to worry: his mate's ma had had cancer and it only took her a year to get her looks back, so that was lovely. That kid always makes me smile. I love all my nephews, of course, but watch this space for Ryan . . .

I can't wait to talk to Davey tonight. I can't wait to tell him that finally it's over.

I have to go – I'm putting on my best wig, dress and ballet pumps (note to self: buy some decent shoes) and I'm going to the pub with my mother and my sister to have a proper drink. Roll on the rest of my life.

Rabbit Hayes. Over and out. X

DAY SEVEN

Chapter Thirteen

Davey

DAVEY WOKE UP TO the radio playing downstairs. He showered and dressed, and by the time he hit the kitchen, Juliet had made scrambled eggs and toast. She ordered him to sit down. He did as he was told while arguing that he should be the one taking care of her.

'Don't be silly. I make breakfast for me ma all the time,' she said, pouring him orange juice.

He sampled the eggs. 'Delicious.' He meant it.

'The secret is cooking them in a little butter.'

'Good to know.'

She sat down opposite him and sipped her tea.

'Are you not eating?' he asked.

'Never hungry in the mornings. I can sew too,' she said. 'I mean, I'm not Dolce or Gabbana, but I've made a blouse and three skirts.'

'Good for you.'

She smiled. 'I can take care of you, Davey.'

He stopped eating and put down his fork. 'Oh, Juliet, you don't have to take care of me. I mean, I know I look like a dope and maybe I sometimes act like one, but I'm the adult, the one who looks after you, OK?'

'I just want you to know that I'll play my part.'

'Just being a kid is playing your part and, Juliet, we have to talk to your ma. What she says goes, and I don't know if she'll want this for you.'

Juliet became quiet and reflective. Davey tried to engage her in other subjects, like cinema and music, and he even talked about clothes, but she didn't bite. To someone who was unaware of what she was going through, it might have seemed that she was sulking, but Davey knew better: she was sad, confused, guilty and terrified. She didn't have to talk if she didn't want to. She excused herself and went to her room. He took the opportunity to ring Grace and ask after his mother. Juliet had not been made privy to Molly's scare: she already had enough to worry about. Grace was on her way to pick her mother up from the hospital. She would take her home for a shower, then drop both parents to the hospice.

'When are you leaving?' Grace asked Davey.

'Within the hour,' Davey said.

'OK. Ma isn't supposed to drive for a few days and Da's eyes have been too affected by the diabetes, so if I drop them, will you take them home?'

'No problem.'

'Great.'

He was about to hang up, but she added, 'And, Davey, don't get comfortable with having Juliet.'

She hung up before he could respond.

Davey answered the door to a boy. 'You're the uncle,' the boy said.

'You're Kyle, the weird kid from across the road,' Davey remembered.

'I'm not weird.'

'When you were four I caught you eating a worm.'

'No, you didn't.'

'You said yum-yum.'

'No way.'

'Juliet, you have a visitor,' Davey shouted up the stairs. His phone rang so he answered it and walked away, leaving Kyle standing in the doorway. He didn't recognize the number but when he answered he immediately knew the voice. It was his young girlfriend, Georgia.

'Wanna hook up?'

'No.'

'You away?'

'Yeah.'

'How long?'

'Not sure.'

'Damn, I'm bored.'

'Oh, well.'

'Wanna talk dirty?'

'Not really.'

'What is up with you?'

'My sister is dying.'

He heard a gulp followed by dead air. She stuttered a little. 'Did you know her well?'

'She's my sister,' he said slowly, as though he was talking to a two-year-old.

'Yeah, sorry, brain fart.'

Another silence followed.

'I should go,' she said.

'Yeah, you should.' Davey hung up. He knew that that had been the last time he would speak to Georgia and it didn't cost him a second thought. *Grace is right. I don't know what a real relationship is.*

He was sitting at the dining table, halfway through his coffee and the newspaper, when Juliet appeared with Kyle.

'There's coffee in the pot. Wait – are you two old enough for coffee?'

'Is he retarded?' Kyle asked Juliet, who giggled a little.

'I'm not the one who ate worms,' Davey said, without looking up from his newspaper.

287

'Me neither.' Kyle pulled out the counter chair and sat up on it.

'Clearly you don't remember, but I do, yum-yum,' Davey said.

'He's just joking. He told me once that I had to have a sixth finger removed from each hand when I was a baby,' Juliet said.

'I remember – it was around the time you thought you were an alien,' Kyle said.

Davey chuckled. 'She asked us all to call her Juliet Tron.'

'I have a really good memory. I'd remember eating worms,' Kyle said.

'And you used to run around the garden with your Willy Wonka hanging out,' Davey said.

'No, I didn't!'

'I remember that!' Juliet said, and Davey pointed at Kyle.

'Nice work, by the way.'

Kyle huffed. 'And he calls me weird.'

Juliet was amused, and even though Kyle wasn't entirely happy with the content of the conversation, she'd seemed to forget about all the bad stuff. *He knows what I'm doing and he's playing along*, Davey thought. Kyle had always been a good kid.

Juliet climbed into the car. Davey called Kyle as he reached the other side of the road, walked over to him and handed him a twenty-euro note. 'Buy yourself something.'

'It's OK.'

'You're a good friend.' Davey folded the money into his hand.

'Are you really going to take her and look after her?' Kyle asked.

'There's a lot to work out,' Davey replied.

'She's counting on you,' Kyle said. He thanked Davey for the money and walked away.

Davey got in behind the steering-wheel. 'What was that about?' Juliet asked.

'Nothing,' Davey said, but he was freaking out. *What if*

Rabbit says no? What if Ma throws a fit and has another heart attack? What if I can't do this?

She's counting on you and *Don't get too comfortable with her* were rushing around his head for the entire drive to the hospital. *I shouldn't have opened me big mouth. Jay was right, I'm not a parent. I'm the guy who makes promises that I'm not sure I can keep.*

'What are you thinking about, Davey?' Juliet asked.

'Nothing. You?'

'Kyle running around the garden with his mickey out.'

Davey chuckled for Juliet's sake, but his mind was elsewhere. *Juliet is counting on you. Don't get too comfortable with Juliet. Me ma is going to kill me.*

Molly

Molly left the hospital with a prescription, a diet sheet and an appointment to see a specialist six weeks later. Grace wasn't thrilled that her mother would be forced to wait so long, but Molly could reassure her that she was in no immediate danger and, other than a short argument about what was and wasn't appropriate resting, the matter was resolved quickly. 'I'm planning on sitting in an armchair in a hospice, not heading down a Chilean mine.'

Jack was waiting by the front door. He was ageing by the day, Molly thought. He hadn't slept – he never did when he was in their bed without her – but insisted on making toast and tea while she showered. He'd even walked to the local shop and bought her favourite custard Danish.

Molly heard Grace and Jack whispering as she walked down the stairs. Their conversation ended abruptly when she entered the room. Her new diet plan was already fixed to the fridge. She sat in front of her unwanted toast and Danish and sipped her tea while Grace told them about the *craic* they'd had with Rabbit the previous night. 'She's much brighter, Ma.'

Molly was thrilled but also sad she'd missed out. Jack kept repeating that things were looking up, happy in the moment, mentally parking the fact that, although she was brighter, Rabbit was still dying, and that his wife might or might not have to undergo heart surgery. Molly loved Jack for that: she was a worrier, but once he had been given the smallest bit of positive news he ran with it. If anyone was Mr Brightside it was Jack. It was the reason she'd caved in and gone out with him in the first place.

When they had met, Molly's heart had been set on another man. He was dating a friend of hers who was totally wrong for him, so it was only a matter of time before the relationship ended. Molly wasn't known for her patience, but she was willing to wait. She was at the weekly dance, sitting with a friend, when Jack had approached to ask her onto the floor. She politely declined, saying she'd stubbed her toe. The following week came around quickly and this time Jack waited until she was sitting alone before he asked her onto the floor. Once again she politely declined: 'If only it wasn't for me bloody toe.'

'Don't worry,' he said, and had a word with his best friend, Raymond. The first time Molly ever saw Raymond he was pushing a wheelchair towards her.

'You're not serious,' she said, when Jack suggested he take her for a spin.

'Just ten minutes on the floor.'

Even though she felt like an eejit, she sat in the chair, and in the ten minutes he spun her around, she forgot about the other fellow and finished the night dancing in Jack's arms. When she asked him, weeks into their courtship, why he had persisted when he knew she was faking the injury, he told her that she was the type of woman who wouldn't have bothered to lie if she hadn't felt something. He was right. She asked how he knew.

'You told my friend Joseph to eff off when he wouldn't take no for an answer a month ago.' It was clear he understood her. And he wasn't intimidated by strength in women: he was attracted to it. Not to mention that he could find hope in a lie. Jack Hayes had revealed himself as one of a rare breed the day Molly had fallen in love with him.

Rabbit was clearly relieved to see her walk through the door. 'You scared the shite out of me, Ma.'

'Now you know how I feel,' her ma said. Jack and Grace grinned.

Molly sat in the armchair and Grace and Jack took to the sofa.

'I don't want you staying long today, Ma,' Rabbit said.

'I'll do what *I* want.'

'I'll have you thrown out.'

'You wouldn't.'

'I would.'

'Jesus, you're harsh,' Molly said.

'She didn't lick it off the stones,' Jack observed.

'Maybe I'll go home for a sleep in the afternoon.'

Rabbit asked after her health but Molly didn't want to talk about it. She kept saying it was nothing and not to worry. The girls pushed it, but Jack, of course, knew better. It was no time before she blurted out, 'Oh, for God's sake, I'll bury the lot of you!' Then she said 'Fuck' quietly to herself, through gritted teeth. 'I'm so sorry, love,' she said. 'It's the auld one with the prosthetic arm all over again.'

Rabbit, Grace, Jack and, finally, Molly laughed.

Minutes later, Davey and Juliet arrived just in time to see Rabbit wipe away a tear of laughter.

That afternoon Molly lay in bed in her husband's arms. They were both so terribly tired. He was the first to fall asleep. She watched the wall for a while and thought about all the things that needed to be done. Father Frank was waiting for her call. She was still determined that he bless Rabbit, with or without her consent, and now that she was in brighter form it was probably the best time to do it. She also needed to talk to him about a funeral. It was difficult to think about it but it had to be done. She needed to talk to Rabbit too. *Does she want to be buried or cremated?* Molly didn't know. *What kind of funeral would she like? Low key, probably, but Rabbit has many friends, and although it's not appropriate for them to visit the hospice, they'd want to attend the funeral. What will she wear? She has so many beautiful clothes, but will they fit? Would she like to wear her wig, presuming she'd have an open casket – but then again would she want an open casket? She'd never really liked the spotlight. What kind of music? Do corpses wear shoes? I can't remember what we did with Mammy but she was never a shoe person. Rabbit has lovely shoes . . .*

Molly fell asleep.

Juliet

It was unseasonably warm when Juliet pushed her mother's wheelchair through the garden. It had taken a lot to get her into the chair and the sight of her disabled body being pulled and lifted, the near-empty catheter with tiny droplets of urine on the inside of the see-through tube and the still raw, stitched, swollen and bruised leg, turned Juliet's stomach. The memory of the injury was still too vivid. She pretended she was OK with everything and that it was all perfectly normal when her mother cried out in pain and bit her lip so hard it left a red mark. She backed away when Rabbit's nightdress rode up, exposing her bare red backside, disappearing into the shadows to allow the nurse to manage her, momentarily pretending she wasn't there. Davey had made no bones about where he stood. As soon as the nurse had pulled Rabbit's blankets down, he had run out of the room as fast as his legs could carry him. Juliet didn't want her ma to feel abandoned, so she'd stuck it out but wished she was with Davey, messing around and being normal. She battled with that guilt as she made her way to the bench in a pretty little spot among trees and fresh daffodils. She parked the chair and Rabbit inhaled the air, gazing up to the cloudless blue sky. 'Feels like summer.'

Juliet fixed her ma's blanket, which was a soft, warm wool mix that had cost Marjorie a fortune. Rabbit pushed it down but Juliet insisted on tucking it in around her waist. 'It's not that warm, Ma.' She wasn't sure if she was trying to hide from her mother's deterioration or if she was actually concerned that Rabbit would catch cold. Another wave of guilt followed. Davey sat on the bench with a coffee in hand.

'Remember all those years we went to Blackpool, Davey?' Rabbit asked.

'Hard to forget.'

'We had a ball.'

'Yes, we did.'

'I should have taken you to Blackpool, Juliet.'

'It's OK. I loved France and Spain, Vegas and New York.'

'Still . . .' Rabbit said.

'What was the name of the old donkey that used to walk up and down the pier?'

'Desmond,' Rabbit said.

'Desmond the Donkey?' Juliet said.

'Desmond was no ordinary donkey,' Rabbit said. 'He could count to ten with his hoof and fart on command.'

'"Blow hard," the guy would say – what was his name?' Davey wondered.

'I just remember he smelt of tobacco and Old Spice,' Rabbit said. 'But he said "Blow hard" and Desmond blew hard.'

'Every kid on holiday visited the farting donkey. I tell you, if you want to really make money, invest in a farting anything. Kids are helpless when it comes to farts.'

'It's true. The year we went and he'd died, I cried for hours,' Rabbit recalled.

'I remember that,' Davey said, in a high-pitched voice that suggested he'd only just remembered it and was enjoying the recollection. 'We had to have a mock funeral for Desmond in the hotel car park.'

'But you didn't bury the actual donkey,' Juliet said.

'No, we buried a Desmond the Donkey key-ring me ma had bought for Pauline across the road,' Rabbit explained.

'Under some wildflowers. Da dug the ground with a dessert spoon and Ma said the eulogy,' Davey added.

'RIP, Desmond the Donkey. You brought joy, you brought pain . . .' Rabbit said.

'And the likes of your arse will never be seen again,' Davey concluded.

Rabbit smiled. 'Make Ma say something at mine. She won't want to, but make her, OK, Davey?'

'I will.'

Juliet changed the subject. 'Would you like something to eat, Ma?'

'No thanks, love.'

'You haven't eaten anything again today.'

'Not hungry.'

'Even a snack? The canteen has almond fingers.'

'I'm fine,' Rabbit said. 'How are you and Juliet getting on at the house, Davey?'

'Great,' Juliet said, before he could answer.

'Juliet's a lovely cook. She made me scrambled eggs this morning.'

'You should try her scones.'

'You make scones? What age are you – ninety?'

'I've had a breadmaker for two years plus,' Juliet told him.

'Oh, excuse me,' Davey said, and Juliet grinned.

Juliet and Davey had always had a way with each other, and even though she saw him less than the rest of the family, they always reconnected easily.

'Why are you squeezing your temples? Have you got a head-ache?' Rabbit asked.

'No, just thinking.'

'What about?' Rabbit asked.

'I'm sleeping in your bed. Is that OK?'

'It's great. Are you sure you want to stay at my place, Davey?' Rabbit asked.

'He's sure,' Juliet said.

Davey nodded. 'She's happier at home, and with Ma just out of hospital, we're better off giving her space. If we stay with her and Da, she'll just take care of us.'

'I'm really happy with Davey, Ma,' Juliet said.

'I can see that,' Rabbit said, and before anyone could say any more, Derek Salley, Rabbit's favourite editor, was coming towards them.

She held out her hand and he took it. 'Who knew you'd be better-looking without the wig?'

'Charmer.'

'We miss you.'

'This is my brother, Davey, and you know Juliet.'

Juliet said, 'Hi.'

'Davey, why don't you take Juliet for a snack?' Rabbit suggested.

'I'm not hungry,' she said.

'Yes, you are,' Davey insisted, getting up and dragging his niece by her collar. She feigned distress, then fell into step, waving back at her mother.

In the canteen, over Davey's fifth coffee of the morning and Juliet's second cupcake, he asked her about the editor.

'She's been writing a blog for the newspaper, but she's done extra for a book,' Juliet told him.

'What kind of book?'

'About being sick and other stuff.'

'What stuff?'

'Grown-up stuff.'

'I didn't know that,' he said.

'Nobody does.'

'Good for her.'

'Davey, she's having a really good day, isn't she?'

'The best yet.'

'That's a good sign, isn't it?'

'Yeah, kiddo, it's good.'

Derek stayed for fifteen minutes. As soon as he'd left, Rabbit needed to be taken back to her bed: she was suffering break-through pain. It was bone-crunching and more than enough to end a pleasant afternoon in the garden. It was obvious to Juliet that her ma was doing her best to be strong and brave, but even though she kept her mouth firmly closed, her cries still escaped. Once inside, the nurse called one of the doctors. He asked Davey and Juliet to give him a moment with the patient. He was in there for fifteen minutes.

Davey and Juliet sat outside on the plastic chairs.

'What do you think is taking so long?' Juliet asked.

'I don't want to know,' Davey said.

'She'll be OK,' Juliet told herself. 'I've seen this before lots of times. She'll sleep now and then she'll wake up and everything will be OK. She's having her best day.'

'I'm going to get a coffee.'

'You've already had too many,' Juliet said.

'Oh, sorry, Ma.' He stuck his tongue out at her.

'Hold on, wait for me.' Juliet didn't want to sit outside that door on her own.

By the time they returned, Rabbit was asleep and the doctor was gone. Davey made some stupid excuse to leave the room. Juliet knew he was going to find the doctor. She sat with her mother and watched her closely, listening to her breathing through her mouth. *Just sleep, Ma. It will be better when you wake up.*

Grace

Lenny had gone to work early. Grace found it hard to drag herself out of bed. She wanted to stay there, cocooned and in stasis. She heard the kids get up, argue over the bathroom, tramp downstairs and bang around in the kitchen. Jeffrey called her a few times but didn't dare enter her room, which had been a dedicated child-free zone since he had stopped peeing in his bed at the age of three.

Ryan knocked once. 'Ma, is it OK if I go out with the lads later?'

He was still grounded, but ever since he had broken his curfew to find Juliet, she had felt bad about imposing it. She wanted to answer, but whether to stick to her guns and say no or relent and let him off with her blessing was a dilemma too far, so she stayed silent.

'I'll take that as a yes,' he said, and she was glad he had made the decision for both of them.

She heard the front door slam once, then twice. She couldn't remember if Stephen had left for the library with his dad or not. It was likely that she was alone. Grace rarely lay on in bed. Usually she was the first downstairs, making breakfast, shouting at the kids to hurry up and planning her day. She left the house at the same time as they did to join her friends for a canal walk or to shop; there was always something. She needed to get up: she had a million things to do before she visited Rabbit but still she couldn't get out of bed. She was tired, she was awake – perhaps too awake. She could hear the birds singing loudly, she could feel the breeze from the open window tickle the fine hair on her arms, and she could smell Breda-next-door's honeysuckle. A magpie sat on her windowsill with its back to her, surveying the area and minding his own business. *One for sorrow.* He hung around just long enough to make Grace deeply uncomfortable. *What's next? A crow?* She didn't realize she was crying and she certainly didn't realize she was crying so loudly that her eldest son could hear her from his bedroom down the landing. A knock startled her.

'Ma?'

She wanted to tell Stephen to go away but she couldn't catch her breath properly to speak.

'I'm coming in,' he warned, more for his sake than hers. He'd heard about Bernard's scarring encounter with his ma's breasts. He opened the door gingerly and sat on the floor beside her. He said nothing while she did her best to control herself. When her emotions were finally in check, he offered her some of her own duvet to wipe her face; instead she used the flat of her hands.

'What are you doing here?' she asked.

'Studying in my room.'

'What about the library?'

'Too crowded.'

'You mean too many distractions?'

'Susan started seeing Peter.'

'I'm sorry.'

'Ah, he's a nice guy. I'm not for her. So, what are you going to do?' He hunched his shoulders.

'I can't seem to get out of bed,' Grace said.

'I'll help you.' He stood up and stretched out his hand. She clasped it. He hauled her up and kept hold of her until she was standing.

'Do your thing. I'll make you something to eat,' he said.

'No, don't. Go back to your study.'

'Ma, if I fail, I'll repeat in August.'

'What about your trip?'

'There will be others.'

All the anger she'd felt at his failure to knuckle down during the year dissipated, and suddenly she was overwhelmed with pride. *He's becoming an adult.*

He had coffee, a boiled egg and toast waiting for her when she finally came down the stairs. He also had laid out the advert about the caravan that Ryan had spotted. He sat beside her at the counter.

'Nan can't take Juliet, can she?'

'She probably doesn't know it yet, but definitely not.'

'So, we get the caravan, but instead of Ryan sleeping in it, I will.'

'Stephen . . .'

'It's a short-term solution. I'll pass these exams, if not next week then next month, and I'll buckle down next year. I'll study, get a part-time job and move out.'

'I'm not pushing you out of your own home.'

'I'm big and bold enough, Ma.'

Out of nowhere Grace was bawling again.

'I didn't mean to upset you,' he said, as she rocked and sobbed and snotted into her hands.

'I know you didn't. I'm so proud. I'm sorry.'

She moved to hug him but he pulled back. 'I'll get you a tissue.'

'OK, son,' she managed, then burst into a third wave of tears. He phoned the caravan seller while she pulled herself together. It was still up for sale and not too far away, so she agreed there was no time like the present to go and see it.

Stephen drove and they got lost once, but he quickly worked out an alternative route and they got to the guy's house in less than half an hour. The caravan was parked in the front garden. It was up on bricks and looked like it might once have been white, but over the years it had turned a weird yellow and grey. It was small.

'The word is bijou, Ma,' Stephen said.

They were surveying its shell when the guy came out of his house. He was a small man, bald with a long beard. Immediately Grace thought it odd that such a short person would wear such a long beard. *You look like a wizard or an elf, or an elfin wizard.* He was tanned and had big biceps that emphasized his tiny hands. He wore a fitted biker jacket, even though it was warm and he'd been indoors. Stephen was the first to say hello and shake his hand. His name was Ron and he was friendly, a talker. Once the greetings were dispensed with, Grace remained tight-lipped, letting her son do the business. He took Stephen around the outside of the caravan, pointing out how solid and strong it was. It didn't seem rusty, at least not to the unprofessional eye, and Ron swore that, aside from slight discoloration, it was as good as the day he had bought it. He opened the door and went inside. Stephen followed, then Grace wedged herself in – it was a real squeeze. Ron stood in one spot, pointing to the dining area-cum-bedroom, the kitchenette, which comprised a cooker, tiny sink and counter, and a shelf with a toaster on it. They shuffled in a line to the bathroom, which was so small that Stephen had to duck and turn sideways to get into it. He was closest to the door so he was first out, followed by Grace, then Ron.

'She's a beauty, isn't she?' Ron said, without the slightest hint of irony.

'I like it,' Stephen said, looking from Ron to his mother, who remained completely unmoved.

'I mean, a hundred and fifty euro is practically giving her away.'

'There is the issue of it being up on bricks,' Stephen said.

'I have wheels in the garage. They're pretty threadbare because me and Rhonda here travelled the length and breadth of New Zealand together for four years.' *Ron and Rhonda, Jesus Christ.* 'They'll hold to get you home, but if you want to take her travelling you'll have to buy new ones.'

'Will you throw in the tyres and the bricks for the hundred and fifty?' Stephen asked.

'Absolutely.'

'What about the contents?'

'It's all yours.'

'All around New Zealand, huh?' Stephen said.

'Yeah. Worked as an extra on *Lord of the Rings*, parts one and two.'

'That makes sense,' Grace said.

The two men glanced her way; she stared back at them blankly until Stephen re-engaged him. 'Yeah, serious bit of wear and tear doing that, I'd say.'

'She's built for it.'

'Take fifty off and you have a deal.'

'No way.'

'I bet the underside of that van is as bollixed as the tyres.'

The guy looked Stephen up and down. 'You're a chancer.'

'I'll bet there's two of us in it.'

'I'll take a hundred and twenty-five and it's a deal.'

'Done.'

They both seemed very pleased with themselves when they turned to Grace, who was silently crying again.

'You get into the car, Ma.' Stephen handed her the keys. She did as she was told and watched Stephen head into the garage with the elfin wizard.

Her phone rang. It was Davey. He'd witnessed Rabbit's break-through pain and it had freaked him out. She tried to calm him down but he was hyper. 'Is she asleep now?' she asked.

'Yeah, they knocked her out. I spoke to the doctor. He says we'd better make preparations.'

Grace was crying again. Her face burned; her jaw and ears ached.

'I don't understand. She was having such a good day,' Davey said.

'Where's Juliet?'

'She's with her now.'

'What about Ma and Da?'

'Rabbit sent them home. Pauline collected them. Where are you, Grace?'

'Buying a caravan.'

'Excuse me?'

'Stephen's going to sleep in the caravan to make room for Juliet.'

'Keep your money, Grace.'

'Don't start again, Davey.'

'Stop treating me like I'm an idiot. I have just as much right to her as you do.'

'Grow up, Davey, for fuck's sake. This is not about you. How many times?'

'Fuck you, Grace. You think you're better than me, but she wants to be with me.'

'Oh, so you told her. Of course you did, why wouldn't you? Christ, Davey, she needs an adult in her life, not a child.'

She hung up as Stephen crossed the road. He got into the car, clearly chuffed with himself. He didn't notice his mother's anger at first but then she mumbled some random curse words under her breath.

'What?'

'Fucking Davey.'

'What about him?'

'Nothing. Did you do the deal?'

'He's going to put the wheels on and I'll come back and hitch it up with Da later.'

'You didn't pay him, did you?'

'I may be failing but I'm not slow.' He took off down the road. 'Where to next?'

'I want to be with Rabbit.'

'So that's where we'll go.'

Before Rabbit had got sick, Grace had used the excuse that she hated hospitals to avoid going to see anyone she knew, no matter how deep the friendship or the connection. It was a fear, she told them, a genuine honest-to-God phobia, even. The truth was that it wasn't the hospital that freaked her out, it was the sick people in it. She hated the smells, the wasted bodies and the cries for help. She despised the vulnerability and the indignity. Grace had never been sick in her life and, much like her mother, she had been made for childbirth so she never spent more than two days in a maternity unit. She'd always gone private, the only real luxury she'd ever insisted upon. She'd wanted to have her baby in her own room with an en-suite and a fridge for her celebratory vodka. Grace didn't believe in breastfeeding. She had been reared on the bottle and it had been good enough for her – besides, she wasn't the kind of woman to lob out a tit in Tesco. Rabbit had breastfed Juliet. She'd read the books and gone to the classes. She'd even joined a breastfeeding group, which, of course, Grace and Davey had made fun of, but she didn't care. Rabbit had always forged her own path and to hell with everyone else. It was one of Grace's favourite things about her sister.

The first time Rabbit had got sick, Grace hadn't been to see her. She'd made that terrible excuse and Rabbit was kind enough to accept it, but Marjorie had been there for her the whole time and Rabbit didn't really need anyone else when Marjorie was around. It was only when the cancer had spread that Grace had become scared. Breast cancer is curable and everything was going to be fine. It was no big deal until it wasn't curable and it was a big deal, and by then Grace had felt so guilty *she* had wanted to die. Since then she'd been doing everything she could to make it up to Rabbit. She'd sat with her during her chemotherapy, waited for her during radiation. She'd been the last to see her before she went under anaesthetic and the first there when she woke. She had sat by so many beds during the past few years she couldn't count them, and sick people didn't frighten her any more. The only thing that frightened Grace Black was death.

Rabbit

Mabel was playing solitaire on the bed when Rabbit woke up.

'Wow, you're lazy,' Mabel said, without taking her eyes off the cards.

'What time is it?' Rabbit asked.

'A little after four fifteen p.m.'

'Where's Juliet?'

Mabel put down her cards, grabbed a swab lollipop and wiped it over Rabbit's cracked lips. 'Davey took her to get something to eat. The poor thing has been just sitting there staring at you for hours.'

Rabbit sucked the lemon and glycerine lolly as Mabel talked. 'Can you take her later?' she asked.

'Juliet? Sure.'

'I need you to tell Davey to make sure all the family, including Marjorie, are here tonight.' Rabbit was speaking in a rush: getting through the sentence was a matter of urgency.

'OK.'

'They have to wake me or wait for me.'

'I'll tell them.'

'I'm really tired, Mabel.'

'Go back to sleep.'

'You'll make sure?'

'I promise they'll be here.'

'Thank you,' Rabbit said, and relaxed. She took a moment to focus on Mabel's Gothic-rock inspired T-shirt. 'Nice T-shirt.'

'Picked it up in a vintage store in . . .'

Rabbit was already asleep.

Johnny

Back in the day, before Johnny was sick, whenever the boys toured the routine was always the same. Uncle Terry would pick them up at Davey's and they'd pile the gear from the garage into the van. Johnny was always the first in to secure the best possible spot, Francie and Jay next, then Louis or Kev, depending on whether it was a Kitchen Sink or Sound gig. Davey was always last because he was shitting his brains out or fucking around in his house – he had always forgotten something. It was driving the lads mad. To teach Davey a lesson and to encourage him not to waste their time, they came up with a simple solution. Uncle

Terry's van was partitioned: once he was up front he couldn't see or hear the lads, so he relied on one of them tapping the inside of the van to signal they were all on board and ready for him to drive away. The lads always waited until Davey was just about to step on board before one or all of them hit the side of the van and Uncle Terry took off, leaving Davey on the road shouting, running and risking his life to jump into a speeding van with its back doors flapping. He wasn't the quickest learner in the world, but after five or six near-death experiences, he copped on and was never last into the van again.

When Rabbit first joined them as their sound engineer she dared to keep them waiting once and, as a rite of passage, they waited until she was just ready to step in and hit the sides of the van. Uncle Terry took off but instead of running, shouting and risking her life, Rabbit stood in the middle of the road with her hands on her hips, watching the van with its flapping doors drive further and further down the long street. After a minute or two, Uncle Terry stopped and got out to see what all the fuss was about: once the lads had realized that Rabbit wasn't playing ball, they had clattered on the walls to get his attention. He was not pleased when he looked from the lads to Rabbit, who was still standing in the middle of the road. He slammed the doors and reversed back down for her. She jumped in and knocked on the side of the van. Uncle Terry took off. She sat down beside Johnny.

'Eejits,' she said.

'Jaysus, Rabbit, you really know how to suck the magic out of a thing,' Francie grumbled.

'Magic, Francie? Magic is making the Golden Gate Bridge disappear. That was acting the bollocks.'

Johnny laughed.

'It was your fucking idea,' Jay said to him.

'Yeah, but if yous had done it to me I'd have done the same thing. It's only that thick who would actually risk his life to get into a moving van that wasn't going anywhere without him.'

The lads laughed. 'Yeah.' They nodded to themselves. 'DB, you're a dozy prick,' Francie said, and everyone, including Rabbit, laughed again. Davey said nothing: he let his middle fingers do the talking.

When the band was finished and the lads had begun to move on with their lives, Johnny often talked about Davey running after the van. It was one of those nothing memories that stayed with him and entertained him long after he'd begun to lose his battle with MS.

It was six months after the band had played their last gig, and Johnny was having a good week. Francie was working and Jay was studying. Davey was drinking himself into a stupor and sleeping with any girl who had a pulse. Two weeks previously, Kev had followed a French girl to Paris, declaring it was true love and asking, 'How hard is it to learn French anyway?' Johnny and Rabbit were sick of watching films and eating curry every Friday night.

'Let's just get in my car and go somewhere,' Johnny said.

'Where?' she asked.

'Anywhere.'

'You'll get tired.'

'And when I do you can take over.'

'I can't drive.'

'It's easy. I'll teach you.'

'Da would kill me.'

'Come on, please, let's just go.'

It was the urgency in his voice, not the prospect of a trip, that made Rabbit relent. It was as if he knew this might be his last spell of good health. 'OK.'

Rabbit's da was still at work and her ma was out shopping so Rabbit left a note: 'On holiday. Wait for postcard. Love Rabbit and Johnny.' They got a taxi to Johnny's house, picked up some of his clothes and put them into the car he hadn't driven in a year. He sat behind the wheel, Rabbit beside him.

'Are you sure?' she asked, and he answered her by taking off.

They decided to go camping in Wicklow. The band had gigged there; it had a beach, it was a young, fun place, and it was away from home but not too far. It was about an hour into the trip when Johnny's legs gave out. He could still walk and he had very little difficulty moving around to the passenger side of the car, but he couldn't drive.

'Shit,' Rabbit complained. 'I knew this would happen.'

'Driving is easy. I'll be right next to you and we've not far to go.'

'Oh, that's comforting,' she said, getting into the driver's seat.

They spent half an hour by the side of the road, Johnny instructing her on how to use her mirrors, how to signal and which pedal did what. Halfway through a lecture on changing gear she got bored, started the engine and set off. After a little stopping, starting, chugging, and one incident in which Rabbit stopped just short of driving into the back of a bus, she felt she had everything under control – apart from Johnny, who kept shouting, 'Look left, mind your mirrors and indicate, indicate, indicate!' It was a pleasant trip. They stopped for lunch in a little café in Wicklow Town and, although Johnny was walking with a cane, they looked like an ordinary couple, even though technically they were still not a couple. Rabbit had given up thinking about it and hoping. She still didn't fancy anyone else, she still loved Johnny, and she knew he loved her. If he hadn't been so beaten up by his illness she might have wondered if he was gay, but he was ill and scared, so she had learned to give up all expectation and just enjoy their precious moments together.

It was dark when they reached the B&B that the lady in the café had recommended to them. They had booked a twin room from a phone box a couple of hours ago. Rabbit double-parked and they walked into Reception together. The owner brought them to the room and, to their surprise, it had a double bed. There was nothing else available, so they took it. Johnny seemed a little more perturbed by the happenstance than Rabbit. He sat on the bed and rapped his cane on the floor. 'We could try somewhere else.'

'Are you serious?'

'There's loads of B&Bs in Wicklow.'

'I don't have lice, you know.'

'Don't be ridiculous, Rabbit.'

'I'm not the adult in the room crying about having to share a bed.'

Rabbit was so pissed off that she grabbed her washbag and slammed the door when she left for the bathroom in the next corridor. She took an age to return, and when she did she found Johnny bare-chested in bed. Her heart skipped a beat.

'I sleep in boxers. I didn't bring any T-shirts.'

'It's fine,' Rabbit said, but it wasn't really. Her stomach had started to do the rumba. She placed her washbag on the dresser, turned out the light, walked over to the bed and, before she got into it, she heard herself saying the only prayer she ever said: *Dear God, don't let me faint.* They were both tall and the bed was not the largest double ever made. It was hard not to touch each other but they tried really hard. Rabbit was usually not spatially aware, but that night she could tell the distance between them to the millimetre.

'Are you OK?' he said.

'Grand. You?'

'Fine.'

'Great. Goodnight.'

He let out a deep long sigh and, knowing him as well as she did, Rabbit identified it as frustration. *Huh. Johnny's lying beside me and he's frustrated.*

'Goodnight,' he said.

'Goodnight,' she said once more, for good measure. 'Oh, and if you need help to the loo . . .'

'I won't need help,' he said, his early frustration turning to annoyance.

'Just saying.'

They lay in darkness, eyes wide open, side by side and tantalizingly close, both afraid to move a muscle. Rabbit worried about Johnny going into spasm, but she didn't say anything because she didn't want to incur his wrath. Time passed and it might have been a mere second or an entire hour before he spoke.

'Are you comfortable?'

'Very.' *Would you ever please just kiss me?*

'Good.'

'Are you comfortable?' she asked.

'Not really.'

'Oh, for God's sake, will you just get over yourself?' She turned over to face him – and as she did so he pulled her in for a deep kiss.

'Oh,' she said, and her voice quivered in line with her entire body.

'Oh? OK?'

'Oh, yes.'

That night Johnny Faye didn't spasm, tingle, tire or ache, and Rabbit Hayes lost her virginity.

Chapter Fourteen

Rabbit

Rabbit woke up to Grace, Davey, Lenny and Marjorie's muted faces. Even in her drugged haze, she sensed the tension. She buzzed Linda to come and help her sit up. She arrived quickly, and when she was happy that Rabbit didn't need anything else, she left the room, but not before giving Rabbit the eye and mouthing, 'What's with the Cold War?' Rabbit shrugged. 'Keep me posted,' Linda said, as she walked out of the door.

Another tray of uneaten food lay at the end of Rabbit's bed. Marjorie lifted the cover. 'It's still warm if you'd like to try some,' she said.

'Not hungry. What's going on with you two?' Rabbit asked Davey and Grace.

'Nothing,' Grace said, slightly too aggressively and shooting her shut-your-face look at Davey.

'Davey?' Rabbit said.

'It's just Grace being Grace.'

'Bossy?' Rabbit wondered.

'And arrogant,' Davey said.

'And Davey's being childish . . .' Grace retaliated.

'And stubborn,' Rabbit said.

'And blind,' Grace added.

'Says the know-it-all,' Davey said.

'So what's this all about?' Rabbit asked.

Both siblings said 'Nothing' at the same time.

'Oh,' Rabbit said. 'Marjorie?'

'I'm pleading the Fifth.'

'We're not Americans,' Rabbit said.

'I don't care,' Marjorie replied.

'Lenny?'

Lenny put his hands into the air.

Rabbit might have pressed them if their parents hadn't arrived. Molly was still pale but she appeared rested. Jack leaned in and kissed his daughter.

'Pauline got stopped by a copper for speeding – she was only a bit over the limit. I'd swear to God that fucker she married is still haunting her.'

Grace threw dagger looks at Davey. 'You could have gone to get them.'

'And you could have picked them up,' Davey retorted.

'How long have they been like this?' Molly asked Rabbit.

'Since I woke up.' She smiled at her ma.

'And you're loving it,' Molly said.

'There's nothing on TV,' Rabbit said.

When Jack and Molly settled themselves, everyone focused on Rabbit, waiting to hear what she wanted to say. She felt stronger than she had during the day but she needed to get to the point. 'I want to talk about Juliet.'

'It's already sorted, love,' Molly said.

'No, it's not, Ma.'

'We're taking her until—'

'Ma, please, you can't take her, not now.'

'She's right,' Jack said, and Molly gave him a dig in the ribs.

'We're taking her,' Grace said, and Lenny nodded his agreement.

'You don't have the room,' Rabbit said.

'Exactly. They don't have the room,' Davey agreed.

'And you do?' Rabbit asked.

'You know I do.'

'You're not seriously thinking about giving her to Davey?' Grace said.

'I'm not giving her to anyone,' Rabbit replied.

'I didn't mean it like that.'

'I can take care of her. I know it doesn't seem like I have it together, and sometimes I don't, but I'll sort myself out and I'll look after her according to your wishes,' Davey said.

'Da, tell him,' Grace said.

'I think Grace should consider it,' Jack said.

Grace and Molly turned on him.

'You've changed your tune, Da,' Grace said, in a high-pitched voice.

'You're not serious, Jack.' Molly turned to Davey. 'No offence, son.'

'Davey has room for Juliet and not just in his house,' Jack said.

Davey smiled smugly. 'Thank you, Da.'

'Are you saying we don't have room in our hearts for her? Because, seriously, Da—'

'That's not what he's saying.' Rabbit redirected their attention to herself. 'He's saying they need each other.'

'Something like that,' Jack agreed.

'Ah, this is just stupid. Juliet is not going to America,' Molly said.

'That's my decision, Ma,' Rabbit told her. 'Marjorie?'

'What?'

'What do you think?'

'I don't know.'

'It's OK, Marjorie, tell her how you feel,' Davey said.

'I think she needs stability and that will be really hard for Davey to provide, no matter how much he wants to. I'm sorry, it's just how I feel.'

'I disagree. We forget Davey has a strong support system over there. I think if he really wants to care for Juliet he'll do a good job of it,' Jack said.

'We're here. We can fit her in and we know how to parent,' Grace said.

'Davey, do you really think you can do this?' Rabbit asked.

'I don't fucking believe it!' Grace said.

'I'm shitless, and every second minute I think about backing out, but I want her. I'll get help, I'll make changes and, if you allow me to care for her, I'll make it work, I promise.'

Molly looked ready to burst into tears. Rabbit looked at Grace. 'You're a brilliant mother and I know you'd do your best for her and I love you for that . . .'

'But?' Grace said.

'But you have four of your own children to care for . . .'

'And?'

'And Davey doesn't.'

'That's what's selling him to you? That he's not a parent?'

'Yeah,' Rabbit admitted.

'Ma?' Grace said, looking for assistance, but her mother just covered her face.

'Juliet picked Davey. She's a lot of things, but she's not subtle,' Rabbit said.

Marjorie sighed loudly.

'What?' Rabbit asked.

'I'm sorry, but she's twelve years old. She shouldn't have a say,' her friend stated.

'I disagree,' Rabbit said. 'It's the only tiny piece of control she has in the midst of this whole mess. I trust her and I trust Davey.'

Davey started crying, drawing everyone's attention to him. 'I'm sorry.' He waved them all away.

'Grace, you know I love you and I'm grateful,' Rabbit said.

'I do.' Grace wanted to tell her sister she thought she was making a big mistake, but it would be cruel and it wouldn't change anything. Rabbit had made up her mind.

'Ma?' Rabbit said.

Molly looked at Davey. 'Are you taking her back with you?'

'Mabel and Casey have offered to help with schools and we're going to stay in Nashville full-time,' Davey said.

Without a word, Molly stood up and walked out of the room. Grace got up to follow her.

'Stay where you are, Grace,' Jack said. She sat down. 'She just needs a minute.'

'Marjorie?' Rabbit said.

'You know better than I do,' Marjorie replied, then to Davey, 'That sounded bad.'

He laughed. 'It's fine.'

'There's something else I want to talk about,' Rabbit said, 'and I need me ma in here to do it.'

Jack stood up. 'I'll get her, kiddo.'

Lenny kissed Grace. He whispered something in her ear and she smiled at him. He put his arm around her and the disappointment cleared from her face. Jack returned with Molly in tow. Her eyes were red-rimmed but she wasn't crying.

'Are you OK, Ma?' Rabbit asked.

'I'm fine, love,' Molly said.

'You're not going to lose Juliet.'

'I know.' Molly's eyes welled again. 'What else do you want to talk about?'

'My funeral.'

Jack had been very strong up to that point, but suddenly he was overwhelmed. He buried his face in his hands. 'Ah, Rabbit.'

'I'm sorry, Da,' she said.

'Go ahead, Rabbit,' Grace said, and Rabbit was glad her sister was coming around.

'No church. Do you hear me, Ma?'

'So what, then?' Molly asked.

'There are plenty of funeral homes that cater for the non-religious. Grace, pick a nice one with a big room.' Grace nodded. 'It doesn't have to be a big funeral. All I ask is that you speak honestly, you laugh, tell stories and remember me well.'

She was emotional but not as emotional as her poor father, who burst into loud sobs, causing Molly to shout, 'Would you ever stop fucking cryin' in her face, Jack!'

Grace, Davey, Lenny and Marjorie laughed, but Rabbit was past that. She needed to keep going: the pain was resurfacing and soon she'd need her meds; every dose was getting stronger and she felt herself growing weaker.

'I'll be back in a minute,' Jack said, and left the room.

'Go on, Rabbit,' Grace said.

'No priests, no prayers. Do you hear me, Ma?'

Molly mumbled something under her breath.

'Grace, you'll make sure, won't you?'

'Yes.'

'I don't want an open coffin – they freak me out – and I want to be cremated and, honestly, I don't care what you do with the ash.'

'What do you want to wear?' Grace asked.

'You pick, Ma.'

'Oh, great! I get to pick the outfit you'll wear in a closed coffin before being burned.'

The others chuckled, but Rabbit held her gaze. 'Forgive me, Ma. I'm sorry I don't believe what you believe.'

'Of course I forgive you, ya big eejit,' Molly said.

'No egg sandwiches at the reception.'

'Why no eggs?' Marjorie was trying to hide the fact that she was crying more than poor old Jack.

'Me ma hates eggs.'

'Fucking smell of them.' Molly was trying to keep it together.

'Davey, you'll pick the music. You know what I like.'

Davey nodded. He couldn't speak.

'That's it,' she said.

'OK.' Grace passed Lenny a tissue in a bid to stop him sniffling and wiping his running nose with his hand.

'Any questions?' Rabbit asked.

'Just one,' Grace said. 'Do you know anyone who wants to buy a caravan?'

Rabbit smiled. Grace had forgiven her for picking Davey over her and she was grateful. 'Thank you.'

Grace stood up and hugged her sister. 'Love you, Rabbit.'

'Love you, Grace.'

When Jack returned, everyone in the room got their turn to hug her and tell her how much they cared. Marjorie was the first and Molly was the last. Rabbit couldn't fight off the pain any more. She pressed her buzzer to call in Linda. As her family were leaving she called Davey back. The others gave them their moment alone.

'Davey,' Rabbit said, finally breaking down, 'you're going to make mistakes and I don't care about any of that as long as you make her feel loved. That's all anyone needs.'

'I'll love her more than anyone else alive.'

Rabbit and her brother cried together in each other's arms until Linda interrupted with her meds. 'I can come back.'

'No,' Rabbit said. 'It's time.'

As Rabbit's family left the hospice with heavy hearts, Rabbit waited for sleep to come.

Johnny

Rabbit woke up in Johnny's arms for the second day in a row. They spent most of their time in Wicklow making love, talking, laughing, kissing, caressing. It was almost normal except for when Johnny's dodgy bladder didn't allow him enough time to make it to the bathroom so he was forced to pee out of the second-floor window.

'It's hardly romantic,' he said, when she pushed him to do it.

'Just make sure you don't hit anyone on the head – and who cares about romance?'

'I love you, Rabbit,' he said, while taking a piss.

Before he could turn around she was jumping up and down on

the bed. 'Whoo-hoo – at last!' Rabbit could always make Johnny smile, even when he was harbouring the darkest thoughts.

They lay entwined for a while.

'You're mulling,' she said.

'Not.'

'Are.'

'Not.'

'Are.'

'All right, I'm mulling.'

'Don't ruin this, OK?' she warned.

'I won't. Not today at least.'

She knew he was already working out how to pull away. She'd deal with it again. She kissed him, he kissed her back, they made love one last time, then were forced to pack up and go.

He was tired in the car. Rabbit was happy to drive: she was on cloud nine and felt she could do anything. They listened to the radio and talked until he fell asleep. She wasn't sure what she was doing, but she read the signs and was making good headway until she took a wrong turn and ended up on the mountain.

It was pitch black and it took her a while to work out how to work the lights, but she found the switch eventually. They were alone on a dark, narrow road and she wasn't sure if that was a good or bad thing. They should have left earlier but, even driving in darkness, she was glad they hadn't. She heard the tyre burst before she felt it. She braked hard and drove onto the grass verge before coming to a stop.

Johnny woke with a start. 'What happened?'

'Something wrong with a wheel.'

'Where the hell are we?'

'Ah . . .'

He was weak: the weekend's activities had taken it out of him. He leaned heavily on his cane and examined the wheel as best he could in the dark, with his bad eyesight. 'We'll need to change it,' he said, but they both knew that by 'we' he meant

317

Rabbit, because his legs were shaking and a minute later he was lying on the grass in spasm, trying to direct her from there. She didn't know what she was looking for and, anyway, she couldn't see past her own nose.

'Are you crying?' he asked, from the ground.

'Nope,' she lied. Of course she was crying: Johnny was paralysed, she was clueless and they were both going to freeze to death. He tried to get up but he was as helpless as an upturned turtle. The spasm was severe and she knew it could be a long time before it passed. Even then he'd be so weak she'd have to lift him into the car. If someone didn't stop soon, they were in trouble, and Rabbit hadn't seen anyone on the road in at least an hour. She heard him praying. *Oh, for fuck's sake.*

Her face was buried in the boot, looking for a part that seemed to be missing from the car jack. There was still no one else on the road and Rabbit panicked until she felt Johnny behind her.

'I can do it,' he said. 'I feel better.' All of a sudden he was steady and strong. He was his old self. The spasm was over and the residual twitches were gone. He located the missing part from the car jack and changed the wheel in a jiffy with ridiculous ease. She pinched herself as he worked. *It's not possible.* She stared at him in the dark, drinking him in. All the strength that had drained out of him over months and years had returned in an unexpected surge. *It doesn't make sense.* When he was done and the jack had been returned to the boot, they got back into the car.

'Great job,' Rabbit said.

'Thanks.'

'You couldn't move ten minutes ago.'

'I know.'

'And then suddenly you were perfect like there was nothing wrong.' *Absolutely perfect. No MS. It was gone.*

'Mad.' His hands were starting to shake again. He crossed his arms and hugged himself. It was back. *Damn it.*

Rabbit turned on the engine and they drove for a while in silence.

'You know what just happened there, don't you?' Johnny said.

'Don't start,' Rabbit told him.

'It was a minor miracle.'

'I told you not to start.'

'Well, how else do you explain it?'

'I don't know. Sometimes you're better than others. Maybe it was spontaneous remission.'

'I was really strong, stronger than I've ever been. I could have lifted the car without the jack. That was a miracle.'

'Whatever.'

'God is good.'

That pissed her off. 'Really, Johnny! If God's so good why does He fix you for five minutes and not for life?'

Johnny said nothing, even after she mumbled an apology. Just as they passed back through the Dublin border he turned to her. 'I believe in eternal love, Rabbit. I believe we'll see each other again when I'm well and when this can be right.'

'It's right now.'

'Don't you even hope for that?' He was asking her to throw him a bone and she wished she could just say yes, but she wasn't going to lie to him. Anyway, he knew her better than that.

'No.'

'Why not?' He sounded so sad. It was not the conversation she wanted to end the weekend on. It meant too much to him and too little to her. She tried to change the subject but he refused to comply.

'Answer me.'

'I don't want to.'

'Please.'

'You can't make me believe in a fairyland in the sky just because you do. It doesn't work that way.'

'So I walk with God and you walk alone, is that what you're saying?'

319

'And what's the real difference between us? We're still here on the same street. Does it matter?'

'I experienced a miracle tonight. That's the difference.'

Rabbit's heart felt heavy in her chest. She knew deep down this conversation was more than just talk. Johnny was silent. She wasn't sure if he was crying – it was dark and her tired eyes were on the never-ending road – but it was possible.

'I look forward to moving on, and you happily accept the end. I believe in life and love eternal, and you believe that this is it.' He hit his legs with his hands, partly out of frustration and partly to make his point. 'I don't want to spend eternity waiting for the girl who never shows up.'

'Oh, I'll show up, if you're right and I'm wrong.'

'It doesn't work like that.'

'How the fuck do you know?'

'Heaven is for believers.'

'Oh, right, Peter at the gates.'

'Exactly.'

'And has there ever been a doorman I couldn't get by?'

She heard him chuckle. 'No.'

'That's right.'

'So in my head we'll live in a fairyland happily ever after.' His sarcasm was evident, but so were his lifted spirits. 'And in your head these moments right here and now will last for ever.'

'Couldn't have put it better myself but, then, you're the poet.'

'I suppose I can live with that, but I'll tell you something. Francie was right: you do suck the magic out of everything.'

Even in the dark she sensed he was grinning. He had forgiven her and she was grateful.

DAY EIGHT

Chapter Fifteen

Marjorie

No one ever accepted who and what Marjorie was quite like Rabbit did. After too many glasses of wine, Rabbit had once predicted Marjorie would have an affair. Of course, even Rabbit couldn't have predicted that it would be with Davey. She didn't relish the drama and gossip potential in it, she didn't wish it for her, but in her heart she knew it was the only way that Marjorie could leave an empty marriage. Marjorie wanted to argue but she didn't, and it wasn't because she was planning to be unfaithful or had even dreamed of it: it was because Rabbit knew her better than she knew herself. 'Maybe Neil will do it first,' she said, and they changed the subject.

He didn't do it first, or if he did, he didn't get caught. Four years after Rabbit had made that comment, Marjorie's husband found an explicit note from Davey while rooting through her bag for the spare car keys. He waited for her to come downstairs, and five minutes into the conversation that followed, their marriage was over.

Terminating a bad marriage should be a relief, but when Marjorie's whole world was crashing down, it felt like the end of the world. She was under massive, unrelenting pressure at work: the bank was in a crisis of its own that dwarfed her petty marital woes. Neil acted as his friends and family had suggested:

he packed her bags, left them on the lawn and changed the locks. Her solicitor was adamant he had behaved illegally and she had a case to be allowed back home, but he had moved his friend Tom, a casualty of the property game, into their spare room.

Her husband had nothing but contempt for her and Tom had a great reason to make her life a living hell. She was out-manoeuvred and outnumbered, so she let it go. She was also suffering from scarlet-woman fever. Friends and family were quick to judge, and why wouldn't they? Neil was a great guy and didn't deserve to be cheated on. They were right. Her mother seemed to like Neil better than she had ever liked her daughter. She was particularly vicious. 'His mother said to me on the day of your wedding that he was too good for you, and I'm sorry to say she was right. You'd want to get on your knees and pray for the Lord's forgiveness because if you don't you'll burn in Hell for this.' Marjorie left her mother's house in tears for neither the first nor the last time. Her mother could be hateful and spiteful, and Marjorie could never work out if it was because she was unhappy or she was born that way.

Whenever things got really bad in adulthood, Marjorie turned up on Molly's doorstep, as she had in childhood. That day, when Marjorie was at her lowest, Molly made tea and pulled out a cake. She sat her down at the kitchen table and listened to Marjorie's trauma with compassion and empathy, then offered her a suggestion for decisive action.

'We all make mistakes, love, and he was always wrong for you, but I'm sorry it ended the way it did,' she said gently. 'I'll batter Davey when I see him.' Suddenly she was angry: 'I mean, who the fuck writes notes, these days?'

Marjorie laughed. Molly could always make her laugh; sometimes Marjorie wondered if she feigned her over-the-top, theatrical fury just to make people smile, but whether she did or not, she was grateful.

'Look, Marjorie, you will get over this, and I assure you that one day he'll thank you for it, might not be in so many words but he'll feel grateful, trust me, and your ma, well, she's an arsehole, nothing you can do about that, but you warn her that the next time she hurts you like that, Molly Hayes will want a word.'

'Oh, there's no need for that, Mrs H.'

'There bloody is. You know who needs to get on her knees and pray for forgiveness? That auld one – but Hell wouldn't have her. I remember how she was with you as a child. No wonder you ran out of that place and into that marriage. Stupid bitch. And I'll tell you something else I've kept bottled up since God knows when. She's a cheat. There, I said it. There isn't a game of bridge in twenty years that that bitch has won fair and square.'

Marjorie burst out laughing.

'It's true,' Molly said, and she laughed as well.

'You always make me feel better, Mrs H,' Marjorie said.

'And I always will, love. Now, here's what I want you to do. I want you to stop beating yourself up, go to your solicitor and get what's yours. No more bullshit. The marriage is over. Split the spoils and move on. Do you hear me?'

Marjorie did, and that was exactly what she did. As soon as Marjorie let go of her guilt and put her work hat on, Neil was no match for her. The separation went through smoothly. The house afforded them an apartment each and a brand-new start. She found it difficult to be alone, but Rabbit and Juliet made it easier. Whenever she felt lonely, she'd just pack a bag and move into their spare room for a week, then a few days, until she found her feet and it was just a night here and there.

It was good to know she had people. Her work colleagues disappeared when the going got tough, her husband was gone, her mother was a cold-hearted bitch, but she always had the Hayes family. Now, though, the Hayes family was disappearing right in front of her eyes, and for the first time in her life Marjorie faced being truly, absolutely alone.

She couldn't think about that. If she did, she'd open the window and jump out of her third-floor apartment. Knowing her luck the fall wouldn't be enough to kill her and she'd be left paralysed from the neck down. Her ma would call it justice. *Stay away from the window, Marjorie.*

Marjorie had always loved her expensive clothes, her fancy car and her luxury accommodation, but when she used to look across the café table at her friend, who still lived on love, wearing her tight jeans and V-neck T-shirts, she'd often wished she could swap lives for just one day. Rabbit's life was simple. She knew exactly who she was and what she wanted. She might not have been the most pragmatic of people – Marjorie recalled the many times she'd brought up the subject of a college fund for Juliet and the need to invest in a pension – but Rabbit didn't care: she'd think about that next year. As it turned out, she didn't need to think about it at all. Rabbit's diagnosis became a kind of catalyst in Marjorie's life: the banking system was already in freefall, but after Rabbit had got sick Marjorie's world-view began to shift. She lived alone, was often lonely, and the job she had loved had changed into something terrible. Each new day wore her down, but if she could have had one wish, she wouldn't have asked to change any of that: instead, she'd want to talk to the old Rabbit, the fit, happy, healthy Rabbit, just one last time.

Early in the morning she received the news from Davey that Rabbit had taken a turn for the worse overnight. It wasn't entirely unexpected but it was still shocking. For a moment or two she wondered what she'd bring her friend. Then reality sank in. *Rabbit doesn't need anything any more.* She cried a little over breakfast and considered stopping at the local shop and buying a packet of cigarettes so that she could indulge in one to calm her nerves. She hadn't smoked in ten years. *Don't do it, Marjorie.*

When she arrived at the hospice, Molly, Jack, Grace, Lenny and the boys were already there. There were too many people to fit into the room. Molly and Jack were with their daughter so she joined Grace in the canteen.

'Where's Juliet?' she asked.

'Davey's letting her sleep in. It could be a long day,' Grace said.

'Didn't think I'd have to miss her too,' Marjorie said, meaning Juliet's emigration.

'Me neither.'

Marjorie had had no time for Juliet until she was four, when she had displayed a personality that was a mix of her mother and her nan. Then Marjorie had fallen for her, hook, line and sinker. She didn't want kids of her own, but now she felt like a mother towards Juliet who, in a small way, she'd helped to rear for all these years. But the plan she'd made to be the best 'aunt' in the world had come crashing down. America had changed everything.

Jack appeared, saying he needed a break. 'Where are the boys?'

'In the garden,' Grace said.

'I need some air,' he said, and walked out of the room, heading in the wrong direction. Grace didn't correct him: it didn't matter where he went – he just needed to move.

'Do you want to go in?' Grace asked.

'Do you mind?'

'Go.'

The room was silent, except for Rabbit's breathing. Molly was holding her daughter's hand. She looked up as Marjorie came in. They didn't speak. Instead Marjorie sat on the sofa and watched her old friend die. She wanted to say something important and memorable, but Rabbit was the wordsmith, not her. She silently reminisced about the day Rabbit had got into her journalism course – she'd been so happy. Everyone was shocked because she'd never mentioned journalism as something she was interested in. She was always so secretive. No one ever knew what was up until Rabbit wanted them to. She'd come up with the idea on a whim, based on her love of music and a documentary about a music journalist who travelled with a band; she had set her heart on music journalism. That had changed when Johnny died: she'd needed to stay away from all things music for a long time because it was too painful. If things had been different, Marjorie could have seen Johnny the rock star and Rabbit the music journalist turning into one of those celebrated golden couples. Unfortunately they were equipped for greatness but destined to lose. In the years since Johnny had died, Rabbit had rarely talked about him. She pretended she'd let go, but Marjorie knew better and, yes, Rabbit was happy being single, but it was only because nobody else came anywhere close to him in her eyes.

Molly stood up. 'I'm just going to the loo. Mind her, Marjorie.' She walked out of the room. Marjorie took her place close to Rabbit.

'Hey, Rabbit, it's Marjorie. I just wanted you to know that I'm here, OK? We're all here.'

Rabbit's eyes fluttered and her hand jerked.

Marjorie gently placed her hand over her friend's. 'I know you hate all the afterlife stuff but I really hope I see you again, because my life without you, pal, well, I don't know.'

Rabbit's eyes opened and her breathing changed slightly. *You'll be OK, Marjorie. Me ma will mind you and you'll mind her too.*

Marjorie gazed at her intently, waiting for just one word, but she closed her eyes again. 'Rabbit, if there's any chance of you surviving, please do it, OK? Please don't go. I know it's selfish but I'm an ass, you know that. It's all about Marjorie . . . so please, please, come back to me. I can do without everything else but I can't be doing without you,' she whispered urgently, but if Rabbit heard her she'd never know.

Molly returned and they swapped places.

'Anything?' Molly asked.

'No,' Marjorie said.

'She needs her sleep, don't you, Mammy's girl?'

'Excuse me, Mrs H,' Marjorie said, and left the room.

Grace

Grace was worried about her parents. She was worried about Juliet and Davey, and how her own kids were going to handle Rabbit's passing. She worried where she was going to ditch that fucking caravan and she worried that when the time came she'd be drinking coffee in the canteen, not in her sister's room. She'd let Marjorie go in because there was still time: she could feel it in her bones.

The boys had insisted on being there. Even Jeffrey had forgotten to complain about having to eat green food since he'd visited Rabbit. Stephen had grown up on her all of a sudden. Bernard was just his usual sweet self, and she wouldn't have it any other way. Ryan was the one she worried most about. He was the kid that disappeared into his own head. He acted like he was doing OK. When he bothered to speak he said all the right things. He was the cleverest of the bunch and maybe even the wisest, but he was also the one whom, when it cut, it cut deepest.

When she couldn't stand to drink one more coffee she left the canteen to check on Lenny and the boys. Lenny was on the phone to work. Bernard was kicking a ball around and making Jeffrey run after it. Stephen was studying on the bench. Ryan was nowhere to be seen. She panicked a little. She knew he wasn't four years old and that he could take care of himself, but where was he? She called his name a little hysterically. She didn't have to call twice because he jumped down from the tree in front of her, landing on both feet, like a cat. They walked on together.

'You OK, Ma?' he asked.

'Yeah.'

'You don't look it.'

'Are you OK, Ryan?'

He thought about it for a minute. 'The last thing I said to my aunt was "I dropped the hand." It was a shit thing to say.'

'You made her laugh, and that's not shit – that's not shit at all. Even though I'd appreciate it if you had a little more respect for the girl you're seeing.'

'We're not seeing each other.'

'Oh, my God. Please don't get anyone pregnant.'

'Ma, I'm fourteen.'

'Going on a thousand. Please, Ryan, just tell me if you want to take the next step.'

'As if,' he said.

Grace made a mental note to talk to Lenny about talking to Ryan. She'd also ring a helpline and talk to her local GP about when it was appropriate to hand her boy condoms. Stephen had been way more secretive when he was exploring his sexuality, or maybe they'd been more naïve back then, and Bernard, well, Bernard lived on a pitch or in his bedroom playing video games. He still kissed his mammy goodnight and hugged her in front of friends when he scored a goal, going so far as jumping into the air and screaming 'I love you, Ma' after he'd scored three in a row. The team still lost because he was right when he complained, bitterly, that he had been the only player on the field. Regardless, that moment had been a highlight for both of them, albeit for different reasons, and it proved, if proof was necessary, that the only girl Bernard was interested in was his ma.

Ryan and Grace walked on. She wondered what was going through his head and then, out of nowhere and for the first time in ages, he offered her some insight.

'Stephen and Bernard were crying the other night and so was Jeffrey, but Jeffrey's always crying.'

'Well, it's a really sad time.'

'Why can't I cry?'

'Not everyone is a crier.'

'Everyone *is* a crier – you, Da, Nan, Granda, Davey, Marjorie,

Rabbit, Juliet, even Mabel. Everyone is crying. I'm the only one who isn't. Am I really cold-hearted? Is that why you all think I'll end up in prison some day?'

'Ah, no, no, no, Ryan. We think you're too clever for your own good, that's all. You are not cold. When Juliet ran away you found her and you comforted her. When we needed a solution to keep her at the house you put yourself in a caravan. When Rabbit needed just that tiny chink of light, you made her laugh. You are not cold and if you end up in prison, which you won't, it will be white-collar crime all the way.'

'Thanks, Ma.'

They walked around the edge of the grounds in a circle.

'I think I'll invest in that smart kids' development course.'

'Yeah?'

'Why not?'

'No reason. I love you, son.'

When they got back to the others, Lenny was off the phone, Stephen had abandoned his book, and they were playing football with Bernard and Jeffrey.

'I got a goal, Ma!' Jeffrey shouted.

'Good for you, Jeff.'

'You all right, Ma?' Bernard asked.

'Hanging in there, love.'

Ryan joined the others, allowing Lenny to step out of the game. They sat together on the bench, watching the boys play football.

'Remember when Jeffrey was born and Ryan tried to sell him to the Noonans?'

'When they said how cute Jeff was he pointed to the baby, said the immortal words "You want him?" then held out his open hand. "Five euro,"' Lenny said.

'Five euro,' she repeated, and they grinned at the memory.

'The first pair of football boots Bernard ever got, he slept in them for two weeks. We used to creep into the room just to look at them poke out from under the duvet,' she said.

'And the first girl Stephen ever fell for . . .' Lenny said.

'He was twelve, she was sixteen,' Grace said. 'She gave him a kiss on the cheek and told him she'd wait for him.'

'And the way Jeffrey used to kick his arms and legs in his sleep when we put music on? It looked like he was drunk-dancing,' Lenny said, grinning. 'And that time we put a St Paddy's Day red beard and hat on Jeff and took a photo. Pity we didn't YouTube it. It would've been a classic.'

'We're really lucky, Lenny.'

'I know.'

'Sometimes I forget. I bitch and I moan but, honestly, these boys and you . . . I wouldn't have it any other way.'

'I know that too.'

Davey called to her from the back door.

'I should go. One last thing, tell the boys no one refers to Ryan as a criminal again or they're dead,' Grace said.

'You do it all the time,' Lenny argued.

'Just deliver the message.'

'You're a mental case,' he said, and waved her off, 'but you're my mental case.'

Inside the room, Davey and Grace sat with their sister.

'Did Ma say if she'd woken at all?' Grace asked.

'A second or two, but not really. The doctors are in and out all the time.'

'Where's Juliet?'

'She wanted to buy flowers. She's with Mabel.'

'Her new best friend.'

'Say what you have to say, Grace.'

'I'm being bitchy. You're right. Rabbit made her choice. More importantly, you made your choice and I accept that.'

'You do?'

'It's going to be hard on Ma and Da, but you'll come home more often.' It was an order as opposed to a request. 'And I'll make sure Ma gets on a plane to the States, even if it kills her.'

Davey chuckled. 'Just tell her she's going to Wales.'

'We'll come over when we can and it'll all work out.'

'Thanks, Grace.'

'Don't thank me because I swear to God, Davey, if anything happens to her, I'll come after you with a hammer.' Grace was most definitely her mother's daughter.

'Or a mug.'

'Who told you?'

'Rabbit and Ma.'

'I'm mortified.'

Rabbit's eyes fluttered. Her breathing became slightly louder and she moaned in her sleep. She seemed agitated, which indicated pain. Grace pressed the buzzer. A nurse they hadn't seen before came in and looked at her chart. 'I'll just be a minute.' She administered the necessary medication to get ahead of the pain.

'Where's Michelle this week?' Grace asked.

'She's in the South of France with some friends.'

'That's nice.'

'Yeah, it's a wedding.'

She left as soon as Rabbit was settled.

'She was supposed to get married.'

'Who?'

'Michelle, the nurse. Her ex is now shacking up with some young one in the house they bought together and she's in the spare room.'

'Hate that,' he said.

The conversation ended naturally. Neither was really interested in gossiping about the nurse and her tragic love life. Instead they focused on poor Rabbit's bloated, distorted, odd-coloured face, and her loud breathing through her cracked lips.

'She was so beautiful,' Grace said.

'She always wanted to look like you, Grace.'

'That ended the day Johnny Faye told her she would be the most beautiful girl in the world.'

333

He smiled. 'They were something, weren't they?'

'The odd couple,' she said.

'Yeah, they were definitely that.'

'She's been seeing him in her sleep,' Grace said.

'I know.'

'Going back in time, she says.'

'It's the drugs.'

'Maybe.'

'Come on, Grace.'

'I'm not like you pair. I believe.'

'In what? Going back in time?'

'Don't be a dick.'

'And, besides, I believe too. I'm just not sure what I believe in.'

'Hedging your bets,' Grace said.

'Exactly.'

'You're so like me da.'

Rabbit stirred, reached for her cuddly rabbit and held it close. 'Da,' she said.

Davey stood up and ran out of the room. He found Jack by himself in the prayer room. 'She called out for you, Da,' he said.

Jack blessed himself and turned to his son. 'If I'm not going to pray today then I never will again, son,' he said, as if explanation was needed.

Davey didn't follow his da to Rabbit. Instead he stayed in the prayer room. It was cool and less suffocating than Rabbit's room or the canteen. He sat there for at least half an hour, and if anybody had bothered to ask him what he thought about during that time, he would not have been able to answer them.

Juliet

Juliet arrived at Reception with a bunch of flowers big enough to cover her upper body. Fiona wasn't sure if it was OK to bring them into her mother's room but, having spoken with a nurse, she said to go ahead. Mabel walked behind the child, who insisted on carrying the heavy arrangement. She burst into the room flowers first.

'Ma, these are for you,' she said, peeping through them at her mother. Rabbit looked so unlike herself that she very nearly dropped them. Jack took them from her and placed them on the floor – the display was too big to fit anywhere else. 'They're beautiful, Juliet,' he said, but she hardly heard him: she was focused on her mother's shallow, fast-paced, open-mouth breaths. There was an urgency that hadn't existed before. Her body seemed smaller, skeletal, with the light blanket clinging to and emphasizing her bones; her face seemed puffier, darker, almost black in places. Her bed was like an island, no longer connected to life-saving fluids or machines.

Mabel put a hand on Juliet's shoulder in an attempt to steady the trembling child, but it wasn't enough to calm her. She flew into a fit of hysteria.

'She's thirsty! You can see she's thirsty – why aren't they giving her water? And when's the last time she ate?'

'We can use the lollipops, if you like,' Jack said, in a calm voice.

'She needs water. She needs food. She's dying because they're not doing anything. They're starving her in here. Ma – Ma?' She was grabbing at her mother's arm but Rabbit lay still even as Juliet shook her. 'Ma, please wake up.'

'Juliet, it's OK,' Mabel said.

'It's not OK, Mabel, it's not – they're killing her.'

'Juliet . . .' Jack couldn't say any more: he was crying again.

Juliet ran out of the room before Mabel could stop her. She raced down the corridor, shouting 'Nurse!' over and over again. Davey heard her and came running from the prayer room; Molly, Marjorie and Grace rushed out of the canteen, and Mabel had followed her out of the room, leaving Jack alone with Rabbit.

They converged on her, but Davey was the first to reach her.

'She's not dying! They're killing her!' Juliet screamed at him.

'Come here,' Davey said, and he opened his arms.

'No.' Juliet's eyes were so full they bulged.

'Come here, Juliet,' Davey said.

'They're killing her, Davey.'

'They're not, kiddo. It's just her time.'

'Not yet, Davey,' Juliet cried, and he walked up to her and took her in his arms. She didn't resist. Instead she hugged him tight and cried on his shirt. 'She can't go yet.' She couldn't catch her breath.

'Shush,' he said. 'Shush, Bunny.'

Slowly they started to turn, him guiding her in a tight circle, around and around, and gradually she calmed. He whispered something into her ear and she gulped. Her tears dried, her breathing steadied. The others stepped back and walked away, leaving Juliet to be comforted by her uncle.

Molly

Molly knocked on Rita Brown's office door. Even though she had sought her out, she was slightly relieved when Rita failed to answer. She turned to walk away but immediately spotted Rita coming down the corridor, file in hand and wearing what appeared at first glance to be an orange jumpsuit. *Christ on a bike.* Her bird's nest hairdo was still a sight to be seen, but her smiling face offered immediate if small comfort to a woman on the very edge of reason.

'Come in,' she said, and Molly followed. She didn't need to be asked to sit down.

'I was hoping to catch up with you. I heard about the incident. How are you feeling?'

'Oh, I'm fine. Have to have a few tests but I'll be fine.'

'I'm glad. How are you all doing?'

'Good, bad, fine, terrible, depends on the second of the day, really,' Molly said.

'Well, that's how it's supposed to be.'

'Rabbit's daughter Juliet and my son Davey are in with her now. Couldn't stick seeing my granddaughter watch her mother die – it's not right, but, then, how do you tell her to leave?'

'You don't.'

'What if it scars her for life?'

'This will scar her for life, no matter what you decide to do. You've just got to try your best to minimize the damage.'

'By making her suffer through every heart- and gut-wrenching moment of this?' Molly said.

'If that's what she wants.'

'It's not right,' Molly said again. She was so used to being sure about everything and now she was lost. For the first time in Molly's life, she didn't know what was best. She didn't know what to do. The loss of control was terrifying.

'Juliet will remember her mother dying. She will never wonder about it, she'll never regret not being there, she won't have questions, and she'll know that her mother had a good death,' Rita said.

'She'll remember her mother dying,' Molly repeated. The rest of the sentence momentarily lost meaning. 'That's what she'll remember.'

'It's not all,' Rita said.

'I was trying to think what I remember before I was Juliet's age and you know what I came up with?'

'What?'

'Fuck all.'

'It's different for Juliet. She'll hold on to those twelve years and you'll all help her,' Rita said.

'I'm impressed you know what age she is,' Molly said.

'It's my job.'

'Well, you're not bad at it.'

'Thank you.'

'You could do with hiring a stylist, if you don't mind me saying, but you have a way with people.'

Rita grinned and chuckled a little. 'Well, now, Molly, that's not the first time I've heard that but, honestly, I am what I am and I like what I like . . .'

'And I bet you've got more than one cat.'

'Four.'

'Good for you, love,' Molly said.

Molly felt marginally better when she left Rita's office. She had texted Father Frank earlier and he had responded to tell her he was in the car park. She climbed into his car.

'Well?'

'We're nearing the end.'

'Are you sure you still want me to do this?'

'She won't let me have a proper funeral for her but she mentioned nothing about last rites.'

'What about the rest of the family?' he asked.

'Leave them to me.'

'OK. I have a few visits to do.'

'Right. I'll text you when the coast is clear.'

Molly looked left and right before getting out of the car. She knew it was against everything her dying daughter wanted, but what she didn't know wouldn't hurt her.

She met Grace in the corridor. 'We were starting to worry.'

'I'm fine.'

'Where were you?'

'None of your beeswax.'

'Ma?'

'Wha'?' Molly said innocently.

'I know you. Spit it out.'

'Father Frank is going to give Rabbit the last rites.' Molly waited for her daughter to argue, but no protest came.

'Well, what harm could it do?' Grace said.

'Exactly.' Molly was relieved to have someone on her side. She knew Jack would go mad if he found out.

'Don't tell Davey,' Grace said.

'Agreed.'

'And we'll have to get me da out of the place.'

'So we'll send him off with Juliet, Davey and Mabel. Marjorie will be on our team.'

'Send them off to do what, though?'

'Get food?'

'There's a canteen here. They won't leave for food, not now.'

'I could always sound the fire alarm?'

'Jaysus, Ma, that's a bit extreme.'

'Well, then, we'll need to run interference. Marjorie can distract Davey – she knows how. You can distract your da and Mabel, and Lenny and the kids can do something with Juliet. He only needs five minutes,' Molly said.

'Right. You'll say you want some alone time with Rabbit.'

'I'll turf Davey and Juliet out.'

'And I'll talk to Marjorie and Lenny,' Grace said.

They parted ways at Rabbit's door.

'We're doing the right thing,' Molly said.

'What she doesn't know won't harm her.'

'Exactly.'

Grace moved to walk away, but her mother grasped her elder daughter's arm. 'I love you, Grace.'

'I love you too, Ma.'

Molly successfully managed to kick her son and grand-daughter out of the room on condition that she didn't spend too much time alone with Rabbit. Then she texted Father Frank.

The coast is clear.

Give me five minutes.

We don't have five minutes. Come now!

She would have added the angry-face emoticon if she'd known how to find it on her phone.

On the way.

He arrived two minutes later. She closed the door and ushered him over to Rabbit, who was slowly dying.

'Oh, Rabbit,' he said, and placed his hand on her forehead. 'I'm so sorry.'

'Yeah, yeah, enough of that, just do the job.'

He gave Molly a withering look.

'Don't look at me like that. We're on the clock.' She was watching the door.

He took out his sanctified oils and anointed Rabbit's forehead. She moved slightly under his touch. He waited a second before sprinkling holy water. She stirred again, her eyelids moved. He backed away.

'You know this has very little relevance if she—'

'You said. I know. Please.'

'I'm doing this for you, Molly.'

'I know, and I'm grateful.'

Rabbit settled and he stood over her. 'Purify me with hyssop, Lord, and I shall be clean of sin. Wash me, and I shall be whiter than snow. Have mercy on me, God, in your great kindness. Glory be to the Father, and to the Son, and to the Holy Spirit.'

He laid his hand on her forehead once more. Rabbit opened her eyes and, as loudly as she could, she whispered, 'Boo.'

Father Frank came close to wetting himself.

Molly shouted, 'Sweet Jesus.'

Rabbit smiled. 'You couldn't help yourself, Ma.'

'I'm so sorry, love.' She was sorry to have been caught but delighted to see her little girl again.

'Go on, Father. Skip to the good bit, for me ma's sake.'

'I will, Rabbit. May the almighty and merciful Lord grant you pardon, absolution and remission for your sins.'

'Amen,' Molly said. 'Tell Juliet and the others she's awake,' she said to him. He said he would and was gone.

Juliet arrived with Jack, Mabel, Grace, Lenny and Stephen.

'Ma?'

'Hi, Bunny.'

'It's all right, Ma.'

'Love you, Bunny.'

'Love you, Ma.'

The others didn't get a chance to speak because her eyes closed and she was asleep once more.

Molly wouldn't leave Rabbit's side for one moment after that. Time was precious and she was determined to spend every second of it with her daughter.

Davey

Davey missed Rabbit's short revival. Marjorie had suggested a walk and, with Juliet safe in Mabel's care, he took her up on the offer. They wandered around the well-worn garden path.

'I wanted to say I think you'll be great for Juliet,' Marjorie said.

'You don't have to lie.'

'I'm telling the truth, Davey. Part of me thought you were unsuitable and I've realized that another part of me didn't want to lose Juliet too.'

'I understand.'

'It was selfish and I'm sorry.'

'You were doing your best for Rabbit.'

'But she knew better than me. She always did.'

'Not about everything, Marjorie,' he said, putting an arm around her shoulders. She slipped hers around his waist and they walked on comfortably.

Davey and Marjorie were never destined to be a couple – they weren't even the very best of friends – but their lives had been embroidered together through the important moments they had shared in life. Davey owed Marjorie a lot. She had been the one to pull him out of the depression that had set in after the band had broken up. He had felt abandoned and directionless.

Johnny was battling for his life and the only person he'd have near him in the early days was Rabbit.

Francie had managed to dump Sheila B, and after one incident, in which she'd tried to run him down in a supermarket car park, she'd finally let him go. She'd disappeared into her own madness, and he had met Sarah, who turned out to be the love of his life. The band splitting up had made an adult of Francie: he loved music but he loved life more and he was content to let the past go. Within a month of the split, the factory sent him on a management course. Between that and moving into Sarah's flat in town, he hadn't really been around.

Jay had met a girl too. She was a singer in a band that had supported Kitchen Sink a few times. As soon as he'd broken the news that the band was gone, she'd fired her guitar player and he was installed. It wasn't his idea and he wasn't too sure, but the sex was good, they had their own bus and he could live the rock-and-roll lifestyle – if only for a year. Then their relationship had imploded and, coincidentally, she'd tried to run him over in a Navan car park.

Kev dumped the French girlfriend but stayed in Paris to study sculpture; much to everyone's surprise, he had a gift for it.

Davey was suddenly and catastrophically alone so he drank on his own down in the local. It was there that he bumped into Marjorie. She'd just turned eighteen and offered to buy him a drink now that she could do legally. He'd already had a few in him. He'd agreed and she'd sat down next to him at the bar.

'Where's Rabbit?' he'd asked.

'Johnny needed her.'

'When did my friend become my little sister's friend?'

'When he robbed her from me.'

She bought shots. They clinked their glasses and drank.

He bought shots. They clinked their glasses and drank.

She bought shots. They clinked their glasses and drank.

And so it went on, until they needed to hold onto one another to walk out of the pub. Halfway down the street Marjorie stopped.

'Do you want to puke?' he asked her.

'No. You?'

'No.'

'Why are we stopping, then?'

'I want to ask you something.'

'Do it.'

'What are you going to do now?'

That was when Davey Hayes burst into tears in the middle of the street. A few lads across the road jeered at him but he didn't notice.

'I miss him, Marjorie. I miss the lads, I miss the music, I miss fucking hoping.'

Marjorie had held him and told him that everything would work out.

'For who? Not for Johnny, that's for sure,' he said. 'It's just so fucked up.'

She didn't argue, because it was. Davey's tears sobered them both enough to get chips. After they'd eaten them and were halfway home, they passed the park. The gate was mysteriously open. Davey couldn't remember which of them suggested going inside, but he remembered what had happened next very well. They kissed and pulled at one another's clothes and he kept asking her if it was all right and she kept slapping him and telling him to stop asking. She lay on the grass and he lay on top of her and it was all so quick. Her jeans were around her ankles, his were around his knees, and at one point she screamed and pinched him.

'Ow! What's that for?'

'It hurt.'

'Shall I stop?'

'No, don't.'

'Are you sure?'

She hit him again.

'Stop hitting.'

'Well, stop stopping.'

When they had finished, and their trousers were back around

their waists, he realized she had been a virgin and was contrite. 'I'm so sorry.'

She was beaming, thrilled to have joined the ranks of the sexually active. 'What for? That was great.'

'Really?'

'Of course. Couldn't be happier.'

'It wasn't very memorable.'

'Oh, trust me, it was memorable.' She had walked home in a pair of white jeans stained with blood and grass, and he thought it remarkable that she didn't seem to give a shit.

After that they had been together a few more times, but theirs turned out to be an easy friendship rather than a great love story. It was Marjorie who had encouraged him to go to America two years later, after Johnny had died. She'd set him up with her uncle, who ran a music bar in New York, and changed the course of Davey's life. When he had returned home for three weeks, two years ago, they had engaged in a short-lived but passionate affair and he had changed the course of hers. They were both grown-up, he was lonely and she was unhappy. It was highly charged, exciting, but the passion that had burned in darkness was extinguished as soon as it was brought to light.

Davey had always cared for Marjorie, possibly more than she knew. They were on their second circuit of the grounds when he broached the subject of their past. 'Do you think if things were different we'd have ended up together?' he asked.

'No.' She said it in a good-humoured way but it was still a very definite no.

'Ah, come on, at least pretend to think about it.'

'No.' She chuckled at such a silly notion.

'We had some good times all the same.'

'We did.'

'We're always going to be in one another's lives, you know.'

'Are we, Davey?' she asked, and that was when she cracked.

They stopped walking. He faced her and pulled her to him. 'Yes, of course.'

'I feel like I'm losing you all,' she said.

He drew back to look her in the eye. 'You will not lose us. You are family, Marjorie, just like Francie, Jay and even Kev. It's just the way it is.'

'Thank you,' she said, and he kissed her. She kissed him back – and before he knew it they were leaning against a tree and going at it like two teenagers. It was getting a little hot, heavy and unseemly for two grown adults, even if the grounds were empty.

Marjorie pulled away. 'What are we doing, Davey?'

He sighed. 'Being stupid.'

They moved slightly apart. He took her hand and kissed it. 'We should go back inside.'

There, they learned that Rabbit had woken for a minute or two. Marjorie was gutted. 'I missed her.'

'You'll be here the next time,' he said but, looking at his sister, he wasn't sure that she would wake up again. *Come on, Rabbit, let us see you, please, one last time.*

Johnny

'Rabbit, I'm so sorry, but he doesn't want to see you.' Mrs Faye was holding her front door close to her chest, her full weight against it. Rabbit couldn't have got past her even if she'd made a run at it.

'Wha'? Why?'

'He's not well enough.'

'But I help him.'

'Not any more, love. He wants you to get on with your life.'

'No. He wouldn't do that to me, not like this.'

'He thinks it's the only way. You know he's not cruel, you know it's hard on him, but he's right. He's getting sicker, love, and you have your whole life ahead of you.'

'No, not acceptable,' Rabbit said, and she tried to push through, but Mrs Faye held firm. 'I'm sorry, love,' she said, and closed the door.

The next day Rabbit returned. Mrs Faye opened the door enough to talk to her through a small slit.

'Please.'

'I'm sorry.'

'Just five minutes.'

'No.'

'OK, two minutes.'

'I can't.'

'You can't be serious,' Rabbit said.

'Go home, Rabbit.'

On the third day, when Rabbit knocked, Mrs Faye didn't open the door. Instead she pulled the curtain away from the glass and shook her head.

'I'm not going away,' Rabbit said. She stood back in the garden and shouted to the upstairs bedroom window. 'Do you hear me, Johnny? You can't do this. It's not fair. I'm not going away.'

The fourth day she knocked but Mrs Faye didn't answer. Her car was there and Johnny's district nurse's car was outside, which meant he was there.

'I'm here. I'm sitting on your wall,' she shouted up to the window.

Maura Wallace, the Fayes' next-door neighbour on the right, stepped out of her house. 'Still no joy, love?'

'No.'

'Men are bastards.'

'It's not like that.'

'It looks like that to me.'

'Yeah, well, you're wrong.'

'He's sick, I get it, but he's still no right to treat you like this.'

'Mrs Wallace, you don't know me.'

'Of course I do. You're the slip of a thing who's been follow-ing Johnny Faye around since you were in bunches.'

'I just want to talk to him. Why won't he talk to me?'

Mrs Wallace sat on the wall beside Rabbit. 'Because he's afraid.'

'Afraid of what?'

'Not being able to say no and dragging you down that dark path with him.'

'Did he ask you to call him a bastard?'

'Yeah, but I knew it wouldn't work.'

'Jesus. Do you think I'm that stupid, Johnny Faye?' she shouted.

'He's doing his best for you, love. Why can't you accept it?'

'Because it's not just his choice.'

'It is.' She placed a hand on Rabbit's shoulder. 'Sometimes you've got to know when to let go.'

She left Rabbit alone on the wall. 'I'm not letting go, Johnny. I am not letting go,' she yelled up at the window, then walked away.

On the fifth day she knocked and, to her surprise, Mrs Faye answered. She opened the door wide and asked Rabbit in. Rabbit ran straight up the stairs and into Johnny's room. It was empty. The kettle was on when she reached the kitchen.

'Where is he?'

'He's gone, Rabbit.'

'Gone where?'

'A respite place, somewhere they can help him.'

'Where?'

'You know I can't tell you that.'

'So I'll wait. He won't be there for ever.'

Mrs Faye took an envelope out of her handbag and handed it to her.

'What's this?'

'Tickets for America.'

'You're messing,' Rabbit said, opening it.

'And there's a note too.'

'America?'

'Johnny had some money put away. Davey mentioned your friend Marjorie was going for the summer. He knows you got that J1 visa.'

'Marjorie applied with me ma. I didn't even know about it,' Rabbit said.

'So go.'

'No way.'

'He wants you to go, Rabbit.'

Rabbit looked at the plane ticket to America, then slumped into a chair and cried. 'It's over, isn't it?' she said.

'Yes, love, I'm afraid it is,' Mrs Faye said.

'Will he let me write to him?'

'I'm sure he'd love that.'

Rabbit walked home with the ticket and the note in her pocket. When she got to her wall she sat on it and opened the letter.

Dear Rabbit,

My stupid hands are starting to give up on me. Ma is writing this letter so forgive her handwriting and forgive me if I don't sound like myself. I wanted to tell you that life is a series of phases, at least that's how it appears to me. I remember you with your thick glasses and your bunches, the gawky girl who always said it like it was and then second-guessed herself. I remember you following me around and looking at me as if I was some kind of god. That kid was so sweet and kind and cool. Then came phase two and all of a sudden you were a teenager, strident like your ma, decisive under pressure, like your da, and with Davey's ear for music. You were the heart of Kitchen Sink back then. You didn't know it, of course. You've always underestimated yourself. Phase three, you grew up and I got sick, and there was this brief shining moment where you were old enough and I was still well enough to love you. I know you well enough to know that you'll never let go. I don't want you to, but let me go now and hold me in your mind's eye like you said you would that night in the car. I'll wait for you to get past the doorman, and in the meantime, go to America, Rabbit.

My love always,
Johnny X

Molly joined her on the wall. 'Mrs Faye was just on the phone.'

Rabbit handed her the letter and the ticket.

'I think it's for the best, Rabbit,' Molly said.

'It looks like I don't have a choice, Ma.'

'Nobody does when it really matters. It's all an illusion, love.' Molly put her arm around her daughter's waist and squeezed it. 'We just do the best we can, and that's all Johnny's doing.'

'What if I can't let go, Ma?'

'When the time is right, Rabbit Hayes, you'll let go, and in the meantime, we're all here for you, my love.'

Rabbit's ma kissed her daughter's cheek. 'Now, come inside before I burn the shite out of your da's steak.'

Chapter Sixteen

Rabbit

THE ROOM WAS SOMETIMES silent, sometimes alive with familiar voices, which came and went. Rabbit could hear the people coming and going.

Francie and Jay visited, and the usual chaos and fun ensued.

'Jaysus, Mrs H, talk about stealing a girl's thunder.'

'What shite are you talking now, Francie?'

'You and your dodgy ticker! Oh, you couldn't give Rabbit the spotlight for five minutes,' Jay said.

Ha-ha-ha.

'I'll burst the pair of you,' Molly said, and Rabbit could hear the others laughing.

They talked about the old days and relived the good memories. 'She was able for some amount of booze back then,' Francie said.

'I once won a tenner from some country gobshite. I bet him she could drink two Red Witches to his one,' Jay said.

'Excuse me, she was under age back then,' Molly said.

'Big mouth.' That was Grace.

'I'd forgotten that.' Davey.

'What's a Red Witch?' Juliet asked.

'It's the thing they had before Coca-Cola,' Jay told her.

'She was in drinking competitions with you?' Molly asked.

'Only once in a blue moon, and it's not like you're going to kill her for it now,' Francie said.

'I can still kill the pair of you,' Molly said.

Rabbit heard everyone laughing again.

'Francie and Jay knew your ma when she was your age, Juliet,' Davey said.

'What was she like back then?' Juliet asked.

'A Rabbit,' Francie said.

Rabbit liked listening to the banter. She'd heard everyone chat but her da.

Is he gone? Da? Where are you?

Francie moved on to joking around with Mabel. 'You know, you and Casey are the only two lesbians I've ever known? I'm not going to lie to you, but before I met yous, I thought lesbians were just ugly, mean girls making do.'

'But the pair of yous are really lovely . . .' Jay said.

'Don't be a perv,' Francie said.

'I'm not being a perv. I'm being honest and complimentary.'

'Sounded fucking pervy to me. It's the way you say it.'

Mabel enjoyed the guys. They had come to Nashville many times over the years and even slept on the tour bus. Jay loved it. Francie couldn't believe grown adults lived like that.

'When are you coming back on tour with us, guys?' Mabel asked.

'Tomorrow,' Jay said.

'In that moving fucking coffin? No offence, Rabbit,' *none taken*, 'but I'm too old for that shite.'

When the lads were going, they said goodbye to Rabbit.

'If this isn't the end, say hi to Johnny for me,' Francie said.

If it's not the end I'll do more than say hi, Francie.

'It's been a pleasure, Rabbit,' Jay said, and she felt him take her hand. 'We'll miss ya.' His voice cracked.

I'll miss you too, lads.

Her ma was ever present. Her da was in and out; sometimes when he was on his own he'd talk to her.

'Did I ever tell you that the day you were born was the best day of my life?' he asked. *A million times, Da.* 'You landed into this world with a bang. Your mammy wouldn't admit it, but you nearly scared her half to death. But I had you. Nothing was going to go wrong because your daddy had you.' *Thank you, Da. I love you, Da.*

Davey was never too far away from Juliet. She could hear him console her and talk her through what was going on. 'You can touch her, if you like, Bunny. Just tell her how you feel and she'll hear you.'

'How do you know?'

'Rabbit has never missed a trick.'

That's right, Davey Hayes.

'Ma . . .' *Yes, Bunny.* 'When I grow up, I hope I'm just like you.' *Me, too. I rock.* 'And, Ma, don't be scared.'

I won't if you won't.

Davey told her that he wouldn't let her down and promised that Juliet would never forget her. *Thank you, Davey. I love you, Davey.*

Marjorie admitted that she'd just nearly screwed Davey against a tree. 'What the hell is wrong with me? And I missed you saying "Boo" to the priest.' *Ha-ha-ha-ha-ha-ha-ha-ha! You could always make me laugh, Marjorie.*

Grace admitted how lost she'd be without her. 'I know I gave you a hard time about your lifestyle and I always thought you should be more like Marjorie.' *Bankers stick together.* 'I was wrong. I think you did everything right, except for dying. I could fucking murder you for that.' *I love you too, Grace.*

Mabel gave her a kiss on the cheek. 'Don't tell Grace, but you're my favourite sibling, and don't worry about Juliet. We've got this.' *Thanks, Mabel. I wish we'd spent more time together.*

'See ya, Auntie Rabbit.'

See ya, Stephen.

'Love you, Auntie Rabbit.'

Love you, Bernard.

Ryan whispered, 'She's going to be brilliant, Auntie Rabbit. She's going to have the best life.'

Thank you, Ryan.

'Jeffrey, don't be shy, say goodbye,' Grace said.

'I'm scared, Ma.'

'It's OK, it's OK, son. She knew you loved her.'

Bye, Jeffrey.

Lenny leaned in and kissed her cheek. 'Don't mind kissing but I hate tha'. Sorry, stupid joke.' *Ha-ha-ha-ha.* 'I have to take the kids home, but Grace is staying and your Ma, Da, Davey, Juliet and Mabel. Thanks for being good to me when I first sniffed around your sister. Thanks for letting me into the family. 'Bye, Rabbit.'

Thanks for loving my sister. Bye, Lenny.

When they were gone, everyone grew quieter. Juliet was asleep. They discussed what to do with her overnight: should she stay or go? They settled on Mabel bringing her home. *Bye-bye, baby.*

Davey brought her to the car. Grace went out to phone Lenny and Molly went to the loo.

'It's just you and me, Rabbit.' *Ah, there you are, Da.*

'You just take your time, love. No rush. You just do your own thing. You always did.'

Yeah, that's 'cause I had you to show me how it's done.

Johnny

Three months in America turned into two years. There was an opportunity to transfer into a journalism course in an American university and so, with her parents' support and because Johnny refused to respond to her letters, she went for it. She thought it would be easier to move on in another country, and she was almost right. She finished her degree and it was time to come home.

Johnny was living in hospital full time by then. His bowels

were tied; he was blind, paralysed from the waist down and capable of uttering only the odd word here and there. He had wanted her never to see him like that but she couldn't stay away. She stood in the doorway, petrified: he was in a worse state than she could have imagined. Jay was sitting by his bedside, reading a music magazine. 'Stones or Beatles for best band ever?'

Johnny stuttered, 'Bea-Bea-Bea . . .'

'Fuck the Beatles. Stones every time.'

'Bea . . .'

'Don't Bea . . . me, man.'

Francie had driven her there; Davey was living in America and working in Marjorie's uncle's bar. 'Are you sure about this?' he whispered.

She walked into the room and sat down. 'Hi, Johnny,' she said.

'Rabb-Rabb-Rabbit – is it?'

'Yeah, it's me.'

Tears streamed down his face.

'Good or bad tears?' she asked.

'G-good.'

'For me too.'

'Done . . . well.'

'Yeah, really well.'

'Proud.'

'Thanks.'

'Love . . . you.'

'Love you too.'

'Saps,' Francie said, breaking the serious mood.

'Fu-uck off,' Johnny replied.

'He says "fuck" now,' Jay said to Rabbit.

'It only took blindness, paralysis, a bowel bag and a fucking stutter, but we got him there,' Francie added.

Johnny laughed a little, then choked a little, then laughed again.

She wasn't there the day he died. She received a phone call from her ma. 'He's gone, love.'

'Oh,' she said.

'I'm on the way over,' Molly told her gently, 'if your father will ever get his finger out of his arse.' She'd shouted for his benefit. Rabbit heard her da mumble something in the background about missing keys and an impatient woman.

Davey flew back from the States on the first flight he could get, and that night Kev, Jay, Francie, Louis, Davey, Rabbit and Marjorie drank down the local pub. They told the old stories, made fun of each other, laughed, cried and toasted Johnny Faye.

The day they buried him, her ma asked her if she had let go.

'Not yet,' she said.

'In your own time, Rabbit, in your own time, love.'

Rabbit Hayes's Blog

13 May 2011

The Things I Know

It was too good to be true. I felt so good and then I had my check-up and now I'm back where I started. I'm losing righty after all but, really, saying goodbye to my right breast is the least of my worries. What if it's spread? I didn't even consider that the first time around. How stupid am I? It just didn't seem possible, and now everything and anything is possible. I just have to hope and batten down the hatches.

I'm dreading telling my mother, Grace, my da and Davey, and I honestly can't bear to tell Juliet. She was so brave the last time around but that tremble in her lip when she's trying her best to smile through pain is like a knife in me. And, oh, Marjorie, you made me promise to live for ever, or at the very least to go quietly in my eighties when you're too old to give a fuck and a funeral is a lovely day out. I'm gutted. I've let you all down.

My operation is booked in for two days' time so I'll tell them tomorrow. I have one more day of normality with my family before all hell breaks loose again. I'm heartbroken. It's hard to stomach the pain I'm about to cause. I'm so sorry. I did my best. I had it licked. It was done – and now it's back and I'm numb. I know what's ahead. This time I go in with eyes wide open. I'm not scared any more, I'm just angry.

But you know what? A pissed-off Hayes is not someone to fight with, so, ding-dong, round two . . . If I'm going, I'm doing it my way.

Maybe I won't be able to do all the things I said I'd do. I won't be the mother of the bride, and there will be no growing old and bouncing grandchildren on my knee. Maybe that wasn't going to happen anyway, but it doesn't matter now because I have a new plan. I'm just going to live. I'm going to be a daughter, a sister, a friend and, most importantly, a mother. I'm going to work and pay my rent. I'm going to take holidays and write postcards. I'm going to cook and read and spend time with the people I love. I'm going to allow myself alone time and to get bored. Every tree is not going to inspire a sonnet and every downpour won't encourage me to run, skip or jump into puddles. No, I'm going to bitch about the weather, like everyone else, because I'm Irish and that's what we do. I'm going to enjoy my mother because she's something special and it's been a privilege to be a part of her life. I'm going to throw my arms around my da more because I'm his Rabbit and he's my daddy. I'm going to spend time with my nephews and remind them that there is more to this world than leaving school and joining the bank. (Actually, the recession has probably done that – and who knows? Maybe by the time I eventually die banks will be just a bad memory. That would be nice.) I'm going to tell Grace and Davey that I love them, and I'll hug them as often as I can, even though it embarrasses them and they tell me to fuck off.

No matter what happens I'm going to live like I'm not dying because today I'm not. Today I'm here and floors need vacuuming, clothes need sorting and my little girl's homework needs looking at. Today I'm alive and here, and now it's my job to fill my daughter's world with love, happiness and security. She doesn't need Disney Land, she just needs me, and I'll do my best so that when I'm gone she'll have a head full of memories and a heart full of love.

I will be finished but, with the help of my often chaotic, sometimes infuriating and always adoring family, I know my daughter will grow, laugh, love and live on.

DAY NINE

Chapter Seventeen

Rabbit

OUTSIDE, THE BIRDS WERE singing, and Rabbit could feel the warmth of the light streaming through the window moving from her thighs to her stomach and face. Her da was snoring and she could hear Davey and Grace breathing steadily in their sleep. Her ma was the only one awake and holding her hand. She could feel her heart slow down. She was coming to a full stop. *Doing it me own way, Da.* As Rabbit's body slowly shut, she focused on the road ahead. It was her old road, the one she'd grown up on, and a young, fit, healthy Rabbit was sitting on her wall outside her house. She looked for Johnny and found him stepping into the back of Uncle Terry's van; he was perfect, grinning, singing softly to himself. She watched him disappear into it. Then he reappeared: 'Well, are you coming or wha'?'

'Don't bang the side panel,' she warned him, as she slowly approached the van.

He grinned. 'You'd better hurry up, then.'

'I'm not running after you.'

'Can't come back this time around, Rabbit.'

'So don't bang the side panel.'

He banged the side panel.

'Ya bollocks.'

The van took off slowly. She walked behind it. It started to

361

move faster and she broke into a little run. The doors started flapping and Johnny reached out his hand.

'It's now or never, Rabbit.'

In the room, Rabbit's hand gripped her ma's, making her start.

'Rabbit?' Ma whispered.

'Have to catch the van, Ma.'

'Safe trip, Rabbit,' Molly said.

Johnny leaned forward, with his arm outstretched, and Rabbit ran faster, reaching out as far as she could. He pulled her into the darkness and, in the midst of her final dying moments, she held on tight to the man she'd never let go.

Acknowledgements

Thank you to Dr Ruth Fenton for taking time to talk me through hospice medicine and care. Thanks to my pal Dr Enda Barron, who is always on the end of the line to talk medicine, whether it's for *Rabbit* or *Holby City*, and for lending me a computer when mine exploded. I'll be forever indebted. Thank you to all my friends for your patience and support. Thanks to my family, especially the O'Sheas for taking me in when I needed the most care and the Floods for watching over Mom and being my home away from home. Thank you to my agents Sheila Crowley and Jessica Cooper at Curtis Brown – you've opened up a whole new world and I'm so grateful. Thank you to Harriet Bourton and everyone at Transworld for your enthusiasm for Rabbit and your tireless work to give her the best chance of life. (See what I did there.) Finally, for your stories, relentless optimism and witty repartee, thanks to my husband, Donal McPartlin, his mother and father, Terry and Don, his sisters, Ruth, Felicity and Rebecca, his brothers-in-law, Mick Lambert, Mick Creedon and Aidan Cornally, his best and oldest friends, Charlie and Jerry Bennett, and of course not forgetting Ken Brown.

Jimmy Tague, RIP.

Questions for the Reader

Anna McPartlin says she finds humour and humanity in even the darkest situations – do you agree that human kindness and joy will always shine through even the bleakest moments?

Rabbit is well cared for, and her family and the hospice strive to give her a 'good death', but even so she endures pain and indignity. What do you think this novel tells us about the treatment of the dying? Does everybody have the right to a 'good death'?

Johnny does not want Rabbit to see him in his lowest moments, and she wasn't there when he passed away. Was Rabbit ever able to let him go?

How did you think the structure of the novel affected your reading of it? Did you know that Johnny was going to die, or did this come as a shock?

For a long time, Juliet refuses to acknowledge that her mother is dying, and denial is something many of the characters experience. How do they each come to accept Rabbit's death?

Molly puts her foot in it many times, but always makes Rabbit laugh. Is laughter the best medicine?

Juliet is with her mother until the end, and helps care for her when she is sick. What effect do you think being with a parent at such a harrowing time can have? Was it better for Juliet to be with Rabbit at the end?

Knowing she is going to die changes Rabbit's outlook on life. What do you think she learns?

All the characters have different attitudes towards religion and the Catholic Church. Many people turn to religion in their darkest moments, but not Rabbit. Why do you think this is?

Do you think the family made the right decision in letting Davey look after Juliet?

How does Anna McPartlin represent the different time periods in this novel? Did you get a real sense of past and present?

Ma is a powerful figure in the novel. What other representations of motherhood are there?

Who do you think is the strongest character in this novel? Fierce, outspoken Molly, who has fought for her children all her life or quiet, kind Jack, who refuses to give up on the daughter he helped deliver?

Anna McPartlin is a novelist and scriptwriter. *The Last Days of Rabbit Hayes* is Anna's sixth novel. Her previous incarnation as a stand-up comedian left an indelible mark. She describes herself as a slave to the joke and finds humour and humanity in even the darkest situations. Anna lives in Wicklow with her husband and animals.